THE SILENT AND THE DAMNED

THE SILENT AND THE DAMNED

Robert Wilson

HarperCollins*Publishers*

HarperCollins*Publishers*
77–85 Fulham Palace Road
Hammersmith, London W6 8JB

www.harpercollins.co.uk

Published by HarperCollins*Publishers* 2004

1 3 5 7 9 8 6 4 2

Copyright © Robert Wilson 2004

Robert Wilson asserts the moral right to
be identified as the author of this work

A catalogue record for this book
is available from the British Library

ISBN 0 00 711784 1

Typeset in Janson Text by
Palimpsest Book Production Limited, Polmont, Stirlingshire

Printed in Great Britain by
Clays Ltd, St Ives plc

For Jane
and
José and Mick

Ha, ha! what a fool Honesty is! and Trust his
sworn brother, a very simple gentleman!

SHAKESPEARE, *The Winter's Tale*

Fear is the foundation of most governments.

JOHN ADAMS, second President of the United States

RAFAEL
[blinking in the dark]

I am frightened? I have no physical reason for fear lying here in bed, next to Lucía, with my little Mario yipping in his sleep next door. But I am scared. My dreams have scared me, except they are not dreams any more. They are more alive than that. The dreams are of faces, just faces. I don't think I know them and yet I have strange moments when I'm on the brink of recognizing them but it's as if they don't want that right now. That's when I wake up because . . . I am not being accurate again. They are not exactly faces. They are not flesh. They are more ghostly than real but they do have features. They have colour, but it is not solid. They just miss being human. That's it. They just miss being human. Is that a clue?

If I am frightened by these faces I should be reluctant to go to bed, but sometimes I look forward to sleep and I realize it's because I want to know the answer. There's a key somewhere in my mind, which will unlock the door and tell me: why *these* faces? Why not any others? What is it about them that my mind has marked out? I have begun to see them quite clearly now, during the day, when my conscious mind is adrift in some way. My subconscious moulds these faces on to living people, so I see the phantom faces animated for a moment, until the real people reassert themselves. They leave me feeling foolish and shaken, like an old man with names on the tip of my tongue but unable to articulate.

I am shivering. That's what my mind can do to me. I'm cracking up. I've been sleepwalking. Lucía told me when I was in the shower. She said I went down to my study at three in the morning. Later that day I found a blank pad on the desk. I saw the indent of some handwriting. I couldn't find the original. I took it to the window and saw that it was something I had written: 'the thin air . . .'?

1

Wednesday, 24th July 2002

'I want my mummy. I want my mummy.'

Consuelo Jiménez opened her eyes to a child's face only centimetres from her own, which lay half buried in the pillow. Her eyelashes scratched the cotton slip. The child's fingers grabbed at the flesh of her upper arm.

'I want my mummy.'

'All right, Mario. Let's go and find Mummy,' she said, thinking this is too early for anybody. 'You know she's only just across the street, don't you? You can stay here with Matías, have some breakfast, play a little . . .'

'I want my mummy.'

The child's fingers dug into her arm with some urgency and she stroked his hair and kissed him on the forehead.

She didn't want to cross the street in her nightclothes, like some working-class woman needing something from the shops, but the child was tugging at her, wheedling. She slipped on a white silk dressing gown over her cotton pyjamas and fitted her feet into some gold sandals. She ran her hands through her hair while Mario sheafed her dressing gown and started hauling her away like some stevedore down at the docks.

Taking his hand she led him down the stairs one at a time. They left the chill of the air-conditioned house and the heat, even this early in the morning, was solid and unwavering with not even a lick of freshness from the dawn after another oppressive night. She crossed the empty street. Palm trees hung limp and frazzled as if sleep had not come easily to this neighbourhood. The only sound out on the tarmac came from the air conditioner's fans blowing more hot, unwanted air into the suffocating atmosphere of the exclusive neighbourhood of Santa Clara on the outskirts of Seville.

Water dripped from a split unit on a high balcony of the Vegas' house as she half dragged Mario, who'd become suddenly cumbersome and difficult as if he'd changed his mind about his mummy. The drips clattered on the leaves of the abundant vegetation, the sound thick as blood in the hideous heat. Sweat beaded on Consuelo's forehead. She felt nauseous at the thought of the rest of the day, the heat building on weeks of torrid weather. She keyed in the code number on the pad by the outer gate and stepped into the driveway. Mario ran to the house and pushed against the front door bumping his head against the woodwork. She rang the doorbell, whose electronic chime sounded like a distant cathedral bell in the silent, double-glazed house. No answer. A trickle of sweat found its way between her breasts. Mario pounded the door with his small fist, which made the sound of a dull ache, persistent as chronic grief.

It was just after eight in the morning. She licked at the sweat forming on her top lip.

The maid arrived at the gate. She had no keys. Sra Vega was normally awake early, she said. They heard the gardener, an Ukrainian called Sergei, digging at the side of the house. They startled him and he gripped his mattock like a weapon until he saw the two women. Sweat careened down his pectorals and the ridges of muscle on his naked torso to his shorts. He had been working since 6 a.m. and had heard nothing. As far as he knew the car was still in the garage.

Consuelo left Mario with the maid and took Sergei to the back of the house. He climbed up on to the verandah outside the sitting room and peered through the sliding doors and blinds. The doors were locked. He climbed over the railing of the verandah and leaned across to look in the kitchen window, which was raised above the garden. His head started back with shock.

'What is it?' asked Consuelo.

'I don't know,' he said. 'Sr Vega lying on the floor. He not moving.'

Consuelo took the maid and Mario back across the street to her house. The child knew that things were not right and started to cry. The maid could not console him and he fought his way out of her arms. Consuelo made the call. Zero–Nine–One. She lit a cigarette and tried to concentrate while she looked at the helpless maid hovering over the child, who'd thrown a tantrum and was now a writhing, thrashing animal on the floor, howling himself to silence.

4

Consuelo reported the incident to the telephone centre at the Jefatura, gave her name, address and contact number. She slammed the phone down and went to the child, took his kicks and thumps and pulled him to her, held him against her and whispered his name over and over in his ear until he went limp.

She put him in her bed upstairs, got dressed and called the maid to come and keep an eye on him. Mario slept. Consuelo looked at him intently as she brushed her hair. The maid sat on the corner of the bed, unhappy at being caught up in somebody else's tragedy, knowing that it would infect her own life.

A patrol car pulled up in the street outside the Vegas' house. Consuelo went out to meet the policeman and took him to the back of the house where he climbed up on to the verandah. He asked her where the gardener had gone. She walked down the lawn to a small building at the bottom where Sergei had his quarters. He wasn't there. She went back to the house. The policeman hammered on the kitchen window and then radioed information back to the Jefatura. He climbed down from the verandah.

'Do you know where Sra Vega is?' he asked.

'She should be in there. That's where she was last night when I called her to tell her that her son would stay the night with my boys,' said Consuelo. 'Why were you knocking on the window?'

'No sense in smashing the door down if he's just drunk and fallen asleep on the floor.'

'Drunk?'

'There's a bottle on the floor next to his body.'

'I've known him for years and I've never seen him incapable . . . never.'

'Maybe he's different when he's on his own.'

'So what have you done about it?' said Consuelo, the testy Madrileña trying to keep her shrillness down in front of the more relaxed style of the local policeman.

'An ambulance was dispatched as soon as you made your call and now the Inspector Jefe del Grupo de Homicidios has been notified.'

'One moment he's drunk and the next he's been murdered.'

'There's a body lying on the floor,' said the patrolman, annoyed with her now. 'He's not moving and he's not responding to noise. I have –'

'Don't you think you should try and get in there and see if he's still alive? He's not moving or responding but he might still be breathing.'

Indecision flitted across the patrolman's face. He was saved by the arrival of the ambulance. Between them the paramedics and the patrolman found that the house was completely sealed back and front. More cars arrived outside the front of the house.

Inspector Jefe Javier Falcón had finished his breakfast and was sitting in his study in the centre of his enormous, inherited eighteenth-century house in Seville's old city. He was finishing his coffee and looking at the manual to a digital camera he'd bought a week ago. The glass door of the study opened on to the patio. The thick walls and traditional design of the house meant that air conditioning was rarely needed. Water trickled in the marble fountain without distracting him. His powers of concentration had come back to him after a turbulent year in his personal life. His mobile vibrated on the desk. He sighed as he answered it. This was the time for dead bodies to be discovered. He walked out into the cloister around the patio and leant against one the pillars supporting the gallery above. He listened to the blunt facts stripped of any tragedy and went back into his study. He wrote down an address – Santa Clara – it didn't sound like a place where anything bad could happen.

He put the mobile in the pocket of his chinos, picked up his car keys and went to open up the colossal wooden doors to his house. He drove his Seat out between the orange trees flanking the entrance and went back to close the doors.

The air conditioning blasted into his chest. He set off down the narrow cobbled streets and broke out into the Plaza del Museo de Bellas Artes with its high trees surrounded by white and ochre façades and the terracotta brick of the museum. He came out of the old city heading for the river and cut right on to Avenida del Torneo. The vague outlines of Calatrava's 'Harp' bridge were visible in the distance through the morning's haze. He swung away from it and into the new city, grinding through the streets and buildings around the Santa Justa station. He headed out past the endless high-rise blocks of the Avenida de Kansas City thinking about the exclusive barrio where he was heading.

The Garden City of Santa Clara had been planned by the Americans to quarter their officers after the Strategic Air Command base was established near Seville, following Franco's signing of the Defense Pact of 1953. Some of the bungalows retained their 1950s aspect, others had been Hispanicized and a few, owned by the wealthy, had been torn down and rebuilt from scratch into palatial mansions. As far as Falcón remembered none of these changes had quite managed to rid the area of a pervasive unreality. It was to do with the houses being on their individual plots of land, together but isolated, which was not a Spanish phenomenon but rather like a suburban American estate. It was also, unlike the rest of Seville, almost eerily quiet.

Falcón parked in the shade of some overhanging greenery outside the modern house on Calle Frey Francisco de Pareja. Despite the terracotta brick façade and some ornate touches, it had the solidity of a fortress. He forced his foot not to falter at the first man he saw as he walked through the gate: Juez de Guardia Esteban Calderón, the duty judge. He hadn't worked with Calderón for over a year but that history was still fresh. They shook hands, clapped each other on the shoulder. He was astonished to find that the woman standing next to the judge was Consuelo Jiménez, who was a part of that same history. She was different from the middle-class woman he'd met the year before when he'd investigated her husband's murder. Her hair was now loose and with a more modern cut and she wore less make-up and jewellery. He couldn't understand what she doing was here.

The paramedics went back to their ambulance and pulled out a stretcher on a trolley. Falcón shook hands with the Médico Forense and the judge's secretary while Calderón asked the patrolman if there was any evidence of breaking and entering. The patrolman gave his report.

Consuelo Jiménez was fascinated by the new Javier Falcón. The Inspector Jefe was not wearing his trademark suit. He wore chinos and a white shirt with the sleeves rolled up to just below the elbows. He looked younger with his grey hair cut very short, a uniform length all over. Perhaps it was his seasonal style but she didn't think so. Falcón was feeling the weight of her interest. He disguised his unease by introducing another of his officers, Sub-Inspector Pérez. There was a moment of nervous confusion in which Pérez moved off.

'You're wondering what I'm doing here,' she said. 'I live across the street. I discovered the . . . I was with the gardener when he discovered Sr Vega lying on the kitchen floor.'

'But I thought you bought a house in Heliopolis?'

'Well, technically, it was Raúl who bought the house in Heliopolis . . . before he died,' she said. 'He wanted to be near his beloved Bétis stadium and I have no interest in football.'

'And how long have you been living here?'

'Nearly a year.'

'And you discovered the body.'

'The gardener did, and we don't know that he's dead yet.'

'Does anybody keep a spare set of keys?'

'I doubt it,' she said.

'I'd better take a look at the body,' said Falcón.

Sr Vega was lying on his back. His dressing gown and pyjamas had come off his shoulders and were constricting his arms. His chest was bare and there seemed to be abrasions on the pectorals and abdomen. He had scratch marks at his throat. The man's face was pale and looked hard, the lips were grey and yellowish.

Falcón went back to Juez Calderón and the Médico Forense.

'He looks dead to me, but perhaps you'd like to take a look before we break down one of the doors,' he said. 'Do we know where his wife is?'

Consuelo explained the situation again.

'I think we have to go in,' said Falcón.

'You might have a job on your hands,' said Sra Jiménez. 'Lucía had new windows put in before last winter. They're double glazed with bulletproof glass. And that front door, if it's properly locked, you'd be better off going through solid wall.'

'You know this house?'

A woman appeared in the driveway. She was difficult to miss because she had red hair, green eyes and skin so white it was painful to look at in the brutality of the sunlight.

'Hola, Consuelo,' she said, homing in on her amongst all the official faces.

'Hola, Maddy,' said Consuelo, who introduced her to everybody as Madeleine Krugman, Sra Vega's next-door neighbour.

'Is there something wrong with Lucía or Rafael? I saw the ambulance. Can I do anything?'

All eyes were on Madeleine Krugman, and not just because she spoke Spanish with an American accent. She was tall and slender with a full bust, an unstarved bottom and the innate ability to give dull men extravagant imaginations. Only Falcón and Calderón had sufficient testosterone control to be able to look her in the eye, and that required concentration. Consuelo's nostrils flared with irritation.

'We need to get into this house very urgently, Sra Krugman,' said Calderón. 'Do you have a set of keys?'

'I don't, but . . . what's the matter with Rafael and Lucía?'

'Rafael's lying on the kitchen floor not moving,' said Consuelo. 'We don't know about Lucía.'

Madeleine Krugman's short intake of breath revealed a straight line of white teeth broken only by two sharp incisors. For a fraction of a second the invisible plates in the lithosphere of her face seemed to spasm.

'I have the telephone number of his lawyer. He gave it to me in case there was a problem with the house while they were on holiday,' she said. 'I'll have to go back home . . .'

She backed away and then turned to the gate. All eyes fastened on to her rump, which shivered slightly under the white linen of her flared trousers. A thin red belt like a line of blood encircled her waist. She disappeared behind the wall. Male noises, which had been suspended under the bell jar of her glamour, resumed.

'She's very beautiful, isn't she?' said Consuelo Jiménez, annoyed at her own need to draw attention back to herself.

'Yes,' said Falcón, 'and quite different to the beauty we're accustomed to around here. White. Translucent.'

'Yes,' said Consuelo, 'she's *very* white.'

'Do we know where the gardener is?' he asked.

'He's disappeared.'

'What do we know about him?'

'His name is Sergei,' she said. 'He's Russian or Ukrainian. We share him. The Vegas, the Krugmans, Pablo Ortega and me.'

'Pablo Ortega . . . the actor?' asked Calderón.

'Yes, he's just moved here,' she said. 'He's not very happy.'

'That doesn't surprise me.'

'Of course, it was you, wasn't it, Juez Calderón, who put his son in jail for twelve years?' said Consuelo. 'Terrible case that, terrible.

But I didn't mean that when I said . . . although I'm sure that's a contributing factor. There's a problem with his house and he finds the area a bit . . . dead after living in the centre of town.'

'Why did he move?' asked Falcón.

'Nobody in the barrio would talk to him any more.'

'Because of what his son did?' said Falcón. 'I don't remember this case . . .'

'Ortega's son kidnapped an eight-year-old boy,' said Calderón. 'He tied him up and abused him over several days.'

'But didn't kill him?' asked Falcón.

'The boy escaped,' said Calderón.

'In fact it was stranger than that,' said Consuelo. 'Ortega's son released him and then sat on the bed in the soundproofed room he'd prepared for the kidnap and waited for the police to arrive. He was lucky they got to him first.'

'They say he's having a hard time of it in prison,' said Calderón.

'I can't find any pity for people who destroy the innocence of children,' said Consuelo, savagely. 'They deserve everything they get.'

Madeleine Krugman returned with the telephone number. She was now wearing sunglasses as if protecting herself from her own painful whiteness.

'No name?' said Falcón, punching the number into his mobile.

'My husband says his name is Carlos Vázquez.'

'And where's your husband?'

'At home.'

'When did Sr Vega give you this number?'

'Before he went to join Lucía and Mario on holiday last summer.'

'Is Mario the child who slept at your house last night, Sra Jiménez?'

'Yes.'

'Do the Vegas have any family in the Seville area?'

'Lucía's parents.'

Falcón broke away from the group and asked to speak to the lawyer.

'I am Inspector Jefe Javier Falcón,' he said. 'Your client, Sr Rafael Vega, is lying on his kitchen floor incapacitated, possibly dead. We need to get into his house.'

A long silence while Vázquez digested this devastating news.

'I'll be there in ten minutes,' he said. 'I advise you not to try to break in, Inspector Jefe, because it will certainly take you much longer.'

Falcón looked up at the impregnable house. There were two security cameras on the corners. He found two more at the back of the building.

'It seems the Vegas were very security conscious,' he said, rejoining the group. 'Cameras. Bulletproof windows. Solid front door.'

'He's a wealthy man,' said Consuelo.

'And Lucía is ... well, neurotic to say the least,' said Maddy Krugman.

'Did you know Sr Vega before you moved here, Sra Jiménez?' asked Falcón.

'Of course. He told me that the house I eventually bought was going to come up for sale before it appeared on the market.'

'Were you friends or business associates?'

'Both.'

'What's his business?'

'Construction,' said Madeleine. 'That's why the house is built like a fort.'

'He's a client of mine at the restaurant in El Porvenir,' said Consuelo. 'But I also knew him through Raúl. They were in the same business, as you know. They joined forces once on some developments in Triana years ago.'

'Did you know him just as a neighbour, Sra Krugman?'

'My husband is an architect. He's working on some projects for Sr Vega.'

A large silver Mercedes pulled up outside the house. A short, stocky man in a white long-sleeve shirt, dark tie and grey trousers got out. He introduced himself as Carlos Vázquez and ran his fingers through his prematurely white hair. He handed the keys to Falcón, who opened the door with a single turn. It had not been double locked.

The house seemed bleak and freezing after the heat of the street. Falcón asked Juez Calderón if he and the forensics could take a quick look before the Médico Forense started his work. He took Felipe and Jorge to the edge of the tiled floor of the kitchen. They looked, nodded to each other and backed away. Calderón had to prevent Carlos Vázquez from entering the kitchen and contaminating the crime scene. The lawyer didn't look as if he was used to having a hand placed on his chest by anybody but his wife in bed. The Médico Forense, already gloved, was ushered in. While he checked for a pulse and took the temperature of the body Falcón went outside and asked Consuelo and Madeleine if they would be available for interviews later. He made a note that Consuelo was still taking care of Vega's son, Mario.

The Médico Forense murmured into his dictaphone as he checked the ears, nose, eyes and mouth of the victim. He took a pair of tweezers and turned over the plastic bottle which lay close to the body's outstretched hand. It was a litre of drain cleaner.

Falcón backed away down the corridor and checked the downstairs rooms. The dining room was ultra modern. The table was a thick single sheet of opaque green glass mounted on two stainless steel arches. It was fully laid for ten people. The chairs were white, the floor was white, the walls and light fixtures were also white. In the chill of the air conditioning the dining experience must have been like the inside of a fridge, without the clutter of butter trays and old food. It did not seem to Falcón that any entertaining had ever taken place in this room.

The living room by comparison was like the inside of a confused person's head. Every surface was covered in bric-a-brac – souvenirs from around the world. Falcón saw holidays in which Vega obsessively filmed with the latest technology while his wife devastated the tourist shops. On the mid section of the sofa was a cordless phone, a box of chocolates with half a tray uneaten and three remotes for satellite, DVD and video. On the floor was a pair of pink fluffy slippers. The lights were off, as was the television.

Each of the stairs up to the bedrooms was made out of a slab of absolute black granite. He checked the glass-smooth surfaces as he moved slowly upwards. Nothing. The floor at the top of the stairs was made of black granite inlaid with diamonds of white marble. He was drawn to the door of the master bedroom. The double bed was occupied. A pillow lay over the face of the occupant whose arms lay outside the light duvet on the bed. There was a slim band of a wristwatch on an arm flung out as if reaching for help. A single visible foot had bright-red toenails. He went to the bedside and checked for a pulse while looking down on the two depressions in the pillow. Lucía Vega was dead, too.

There were three other rooms upstairs, all with bathrooms. One was empty, another had a double bed and the last belonged to Mario. The ceiling of the boy's room was painted with a night sky. An old, one-armed teddy bear lay face up on the bed.

Falcón reported the second dead body to Juez Calderón. The

Médico Forense was kneeling by Sr Vega's side and working at prising his fingers apart.

'There seems to be a note in Sr Vega's right hand,' said Calderón. 'The body's cooled down quickly in the air con and I want him to get it out without tearing it. Any first thoughts, Inspector Jefe?'

'On the face of it, it looks like a suicide pact. He's smothered his wife and then drunk some drain cleaner, although that's a nasty, lingering way to kill yourself.'

'Pact? What makes you think there was an agreement?'

'I'm just saying that's what it looks like,' said Falcón. 'The fact that the little boy was left out of it might indicate some collusion. A mother wouldn't be able to bear the thought of the death of her own child.'

'And a father could?'

'It depends on the pressure. If there's the possibility of financial or moral disgrace he might not want his male child to see that or live with the knowledge of it. He would see killing him as a favour. Men have killed their entire families because they think they have failed them and that it's better nobody survives bearing their name and its shame.'

'But you have your doubts?' said Calderón.

'Suicide, whether it's a pact or not, is rarely a spontaneous thing and there are some spontaneous elements to this crime scene. First, the door was not securely locked. Consuelo Jiménez had called to say that Mario had fallen asleep so they were sure he wasn't going to return, but they didn't double lock the door.'

'The door was shut, that was enough.'

'If you're about to do something unnatural you would put yourself behind locked doors to make absolutely certain there was no possibility of interruption. It's a psychological necessity. Serious suicides normally take full precautions.'

'What else?'

'The way everything has just been left here: the phone, the chocolates, the slippers. There seems to be a lack of premeditation.'

'Well, certainly on her part,' said Calderón.

'That is a point, of course,' said Falcón.

'Drain cleaner?' said Calderón. 'Why would you take drain cleaner?'

'We may find there was something stronger than drain cleaner in the bottle,' said Falcón. 'The reason? Well, he could be meting out punishment to himself...you know, cleaning himself of all his sins. There's also the advantage of it being noiseless and, depending on what else he's taken, irrevocable, too.'

'Well, that does sound premeditated, Inspector Jefe. So there are both spontaneous and planned elements to these deaths.'

'All right...if they were lying on the bed together holding hands, dead, with a note pinned to his pyjamas then I'd be happy to treat it as suicide. As it stands, I would prefer to investigate the deaths as murder before deciding.'

'Perhaps the note in his hand will...' said Calderón. 'But strange to get dressed for bed before you...or is that another psychological necessity? Getting ready for the biggest sleep of all.'

'Let's hope he was the sort who left his security cameras on and the recorders loaded with tapes,' said Falcón, returning to the pragmatic. 'We should have a look in his study.'

They crossed the entrance hall and went down a corridor by the stairs. Vega's study was on the right with a view of the street. There was a leather chair tilted back behind a desk, with a framed poster of this year's bullfights held during the Feria de Abril hanging on the wall.

The desk was a large, empty, light-coloured piece of wood with a laptop and a telephone. Three drawers on castors sat underneath. Behind the door were four black filing cabinets and at the end of the room the recording equipment for the security cameras. There were no LEDs and the plugs were out of the wall sockets. Each recorder had an unused tape inside.

'This doesn't look good,' said Falcón.

The filing cabinets were all locked. He pulled at the mobile set of drawers under the desk. Locked. He went upstairs to the bedroom and found a walk-in closet, with his suits and shirts to the right and her dresses and a vast number of shoes (some worryingly similar) to the left. A tall set of drawers had a wallet, set of keys and some change on top.

One of the keys opened the drawers under the desk. There was nothing unusual in the top two, but as he pulled on the third drawer something at the back butted up against the ream of paper at the front. It was a handgun.

'I haven't seen many of these,' said Falcón. 'This is a Heckler & Koch 9 mm. You own one of these if you're expecting trouble.'

'If you had one of those,' said Calderón, 'would you drink a litre of drain cleaner or blow your brains out?'

'Given the choice . . .' said Falcón.

The lawyer appeared in the doorway, his dark brown eyes set hard in his head.

'You have no right –' he started.

'This is a murder investigation, Sr Vázquez,' said Falcón. 'Sra Vega is upstairs on the bed, she's been suffocated with a pillow. Any idea why your client should have one of these in his study?'

Vázquez blinked at the gun.

'Seville is one of those curious cities where the wealthy and privileged people of Santa Clara are separated from the drug-ridden disadvantaged ones of the Polígono San Pablo by a small barrio, the paper factory and the Calle de Tesalónica. I imagine he had it for his own protection.'

'Like the security cameras he didn't bother to switch on?' said Falcón.

Vázquez looked at the inert recorders. His mobile went off playing the first few bars of Carmen. The lawmen grinned at each other. Vázquez went down the hall. Calderón closed the door and Falcón knew what he'd suspected as he'd shaken the Juez's hand that morning – there was news and it was relevant to him.

'I wanted you to hear this from me,' said Calderón, 'and not the rumour machine in the Jefatura or the Edificio de los Juzgados.'

Falcón nodded, his larynx suddenly paralysed.

'Inés and I are getting married at the end of the summer,' said Calderón.

He'd known this was coming but the news still rooted him to the floor. It seemed like minutes before his feet, moving at the pace of a diver's on the ocean floor, brought him close enough to shake Calderón's hand. He thought about gripping the judge's shoulder in comradely fashion but the bitterness of his disappointment filled his mouth with the taint of a bad olive.

'Congratulations, Esteban,' he said.

'We told our families last night,' said Calderón. 'You're the first outsider to know.'

'You'll make each other very happy,' said Falcón. 'I know.'

They nodded to each other and disengaged.

'I'll get back to the Médico Forense,' said the judge and left the room.

Falcón went to the window, took out his mobile and thumbed up Alicia Aguado's number from the address book. She was the clinical psychologist he'd been seeing for more than a year. His thumb stroked the call button and a flash of anger helped him to resist pressing it. This could wait until their regular weekly appointment the following evening. They'd covered his ex-wife Inés a million times over and she would just chastise him again for not moving on.

Javier and Inés had settled their differences. It had been a part of the rebuilding process after the Francisco Falcón scandal had broken fifteen months ago. Francisco was the world-famous artist whom Javier had always believed to be his father, but who had been revealed as a fraud, a murderer and not his real father after all. Inés had forgiven Javier even before they'd arranged to meet some months after the media frenzy. It had been his coldness, captured by her terrible rhyming mantra, *Tú no tienes corazón, Javier Falcón.* 'You have no heart, Javier Falcón', that had finished their short marriage. Given his family history it was now clear to her why he should have been deficient in this fundamental human way. Over the last few months of his therapy thoughts of her had subsided, but whenever her name came up there was an unmistakable leap in his stomach. Her terrible accusation still mangled his mind and, in forgiving him she'd become, in his unstable state, someone to whom he had to prove himself.

And now this. Still, Inés had been seeing the judge for nearly a year and a half. They were the new golden couple not just of the Seville legal system, but of Seville society as well. Their marriage was an inevitability, which didn't made the news any easier to bear.

Vázquez appeared on his shoulder in the reflection of the glass. Falcón switched back into professional mode.

'How surprised are you to find your client dead under these strange circumstances, Sr Vázquez?' he asked.

'Very,' he said.

'Where's the licence for his gun, by the way?'

'That's his private affair. This is his house. I'm only his lawyer.'

'But he entrusted you with the keys to his home.'

'He has no family here. When they went away for the summer they often took Lucía's parents, as well. There is someone in my office all the time. It seemed . . .'

'What about the Americans next door?'

'They've been here barely a year,' said Vázquez. 'He rents that house to them. The husband works for him as an architect. He didn't like people to get too involved in his life. He gave them my telephone number in case of emergencies.'

'Is Vega Construcciones his only company?'

'Let's say he's in the property business. He builds and rents out apartments and offices. He constructs industrial property to order. He buys and sells land. He has a number of estate agencies.'

Falcón sat on the edge of the desk, his foot swinging.

'This gun, Sr Vázquez, is not for discouraging burglars. It's a gun for stopping a man dead. Even if you clipped a man on the shoulder with a 9 mm bullet from a Heckler & Koch you'd probably kill him.'

'If you were a rich man who wanted to protect his family and home, would you go out and buy a toy or a serious piece of weaponry?'

'So, as far as you know, Sr Vega is not involved in anything criminal or borderline illegal.'

'Not that I know of.'

'And you can think of no reason why anybody would want to kill him?'

'Look, Inspector Jefe, I'm involved with the legal aspects of my clients' businesses. I rarely get involved in their personal lives unless it has an impact on their business. I know about his company. If he was doing anything else then he was not employing me as his lawyer. If he was having an affair with another man's wife, which I doubt, I wouldn't have known about it.'

'So what is your reading of this crime scene, Sr Vázquez? Sra Vega upstairs, suffocated by a pillow. Sr Vega downstairs, dead with a litre of drain cleaner by his side. While their son, Mario, is in the hands of a neighbour for the night.'

Silence. The brown eyes steadied on Falcón's chest.

'It looks like suicide.'

'At least one of those deaths has to be a murder.'

'It looks like Rafael killed his wife and then himself.'

'Did you ever see any evidence of that level of instability in your late client?'

'How's anybody supposed to know what goes on inside a man's head?'

'So, he wasn't looking at business failure or financial ruin?'

'You'd have to speak to the accountant about that, although the accountant was not the finance director. His knowledge would probably be confined.'

'Who was the finance director?'

'Rafael kept things close to his chest.'

Falcón gave him his notebook. Vázquez wrote down the accountant's name, Francisco Dourado, and his details.

'Is there any scandal brewing that you know of, involving Sr Vega or his company?' asked Falcón.

'*Now* I know you,' said Sr Vázquez, smiling for the first time with astonishingly perfect teeth. 'Falcón. I didn't make the connection before. Well . . . *you're* still here, Inspector Jefe, and my client hasn't gone though anything like you did.'

'But *I* didn't commit any crime, Sr Vázquez. I wasn't facing moral ruin or personal shame.'

'Shame,' said the lawyer. 'Do you think shame still has that sort of power in our modern world?'

'It depends on the society in which you have built your life. How important its opinion is to you,' said Falcón. 'By the way, do you hold Sr Vega's will?'

'Yes, I do.'

'Who is the next of kin?'

'As I said, he has no family.'

'And his wife?'

'She has a sister in Madrid. Her parents live here in Seville.'

'We'll need someone to identify the bodies.'

Pérez appeared in the doorway.

'They've pulled the note out of Sr Vega's hand,' he said.

They went to the kitchen, squeezing past the forensics who were crowding the corridor with their cases, waiting to get on to the crime scene.

The note was already in a plastic evidence bag. Calderón handed it over, eyebrows raised. Falcón and Vázquez frowned as they read it, and not just because its ten words were written in English.

'. . . the thin air you breathe from 9/11 until the end . . .'

2

'Do these words mean anything to you?' asked Calderón.

'Nothing at all,' said Vázquez.

'Does the handwriting look normal to you?'

'It's definitely Sr Vega's . . . that's all I can say.'

'It doesn't differ from his usual handwriting in any way?'

'I'm not an expert, Juez,' said Vázquez. 'It doesn't seem to have been written with a trembling hand, but it is not exactly fluid either. It seems careful rather than dashed off.'

'It's not what I would call a suicide note,' said Falcón.

'What would you call it, Inspector Jefe?' asked Vázquez.

'An enigma. Something that's demanding to be investigated.'

'Interesting,' said Calderón.

'Is it?' said Vázquez. 'We are always given the impression that detective work is *very* exciting. This . . ?'

'If you were a murderer you would normally *not* want to have your work investigated,' said Falcón. 'You would hope to get away with it. You told me earlier that you thought this crime scene looked like a suicide. A killer with a motive would usually try to give that notion authority with a straightforward suicide note and not with something that makes the investigating team think: What's this all about?'

'Unless he was a madman,' said Vázquez. 'One of those serial killers laying down a challenge.'

'Well, first of all, there's no challenge. A half-note in Sr Vega's handwriting is not what I would call a psychotic attempt to communicate. It's too oblique. Secondly, the crime scene does not contain any of the qualities we associate with a psychopathic killer. They are the sort of people who think about body placement for instance.

They introduce elements of their obsessions into the picture. They show that they have been here, that an intricate mind has been at work. There's nothing casual about a serial killer's montage. A bottle of drain cleaner is not left where it fell. Everything has importance.'

'So what normal person would kill a man and his wife and *want* to have it investigated?' asked Vázquez.

'A murderer who had good reason to hate Sr Vega and wanted him to be revealed for the man he was,' said Falcón. 'As you may know, murder inquiries are very intrusive processes. To find the motive we have to conduct a post mortem, not just on the body but on the victim's life. We have to go into everything – business, social, public, private and as personal as we can get. Perhaps Sr Vega himself . . .'

'But, Inspector Jefe, you can never get inside a man's head, can you?' said Sr Vázquez.

'The other possibility is that Sr Vega himself is trying to communicate with us. By balling this note in his fist he may be telling us to investigate the crime.'

'You didn't let me finish,' said Vázquez. 'The one thing my job has taught me is the three voices of man: the public one to address the world, the private one he keeps for his family and friends, and the most troubling one of all – the voice inside his own head. The one he uses to talk to himself. Successful people like Sr Vega have very powerful inner voices and something I've noticed about that kind of person . . . he never lets anybody have access to it – not his parents, not his wife, not his first-born child.'

'That's not the point –' said Falcón.

'The point is that we get insights,' said Calderón, cutting in. 'A man's actions, the way he behaves with people . . . different people, it all tells us something about him.'

'In my experience, they tell you what *he* wants you to think,' said Vázquez. 'Let me show you something about Sr Vega and you give me your insight. Can we walk across this kitchen floor yet?'

Felipe and Jorge were brought in to check and clear a corridor across the kitchen floor. Falcón gave Vázquez a pair of latex gloves. They crossed the kitchen to a door on the other side which opened on to a room whose three walls were made up of floor-to-ceiling stainless steel fridges. Hanging on the clear wall was an impressive array of knives, choppers and saws. The white tiles of the floor were pristine and gave off the faint smell of a pine detergent. In the middle of the room was a wooden table with a top thirty centimetres thick. Its bleached surface was a crosshatching of cuts and notches with a declivity in the middle, its edge furred from constant use. Falcón felt a strange sense of dread looking at that table.

'And this is where he keeps the bodies, is it, Sr Vázquez?' asked Calderón.

'Look in the fridges and freezers,' said the lawyer. 'They're full of bodies.'

Calderón opened a fridge door. Inside was a half-carcass of beef with hooves removed. The visible meat was a deep, dark red, almost black in parts where it wasn't pearled with membrane or covered in thick, creamy yellow fat. The fridges on either side contained several lambs and a pink pig. The latter's head had been removed and hung on a hook, ears stiff, eyes closed with long white lashes making it look at restful sleep. The other doors opened on to freezers with cuts of frozen meat packaged and stored in baskets or just thrown into the dark frosty depths.

'What do you make of that?' asked Vázquez.

'He wasn't a vegetarian,' said Calderón.

'He enjoyed butchering his own meat,' said Falcón. 'Where did he get it from?'

'From specialized farms up in the Sierra de Aracena,' said Vázquez. 'He didn't think there was a single butcher in Seville who had the first idea about handling meat, neither hanging it nor cutting it up.'

'Does that mean he used to be a butcher?' asked Falcón. 'Do you know when and where that was?'

'All I know is that his father used to be a butcher before he was killed.'

'Before he was killed? What does that mean? He was murdered or –?'

'That was the expression he used to describe the death of his parents. "They were killed." He never offered an explanation and I didn't ask for one.'

'How old was Sr Vega?'

'Fifty-eight years old.'

'So, born in 1944... five years after the Civil War ended. They didn't die in wartime,' said Falcón. 'You don't know when they were killed?'

'Is this relevant, Inspector Jefe?' asked Vázquez.

'We're building a picture of the victim's life. It would have had a significant effect on Sr Vega's mental state if, say, they died in a car accident when he was still a boy. If they were murdered, that would be something else altogether. That leaves unanswered questions and, especially if there was no retribution, it could breed a determination, not necessarily to find out why, which could be beyond his capabilities, but to prove something to himself. To find out who he was in this world.'

'My God, Inspector Jefe, 'said Vázquez, 'perhaps it's your own experience that's made you so eloquent on the matter but I'm sorry I can't help you with that kind of information. I'm sure there are records . . .'

'How long have you known him?' asked Calderón.

'Since 1983.'

'Was that here . . . in Seville?'

'He wanted to buy a plot of land. It was his first project.'

'And what had he been doing before that?' asked Falcón. 'Butchery doesn't buy you very much land.'

'I didn't ask him. He was my first client. I was twenty-eight years old. I didn't want to do or ask anything that might lose me the work.'

'So his background didn't bother you – the possibility that he might rip you off?' asked Falcón. 'How did you meet?'

'He came in off the street one day. You probably don't know this about business, Inspector Jefe, but you have to take risks. If you want to be sure about everything you don't set up your own practice . . . you work for the State.'

'Did he have an accent?' asked Falcón, ignoring the slight.

'He spoke in Andaluz, but it didn't sound as if he was born to it. He'd been abroad. I know he spoke American English, for instance.'

'You didn't question him about any of that?' asked Falcón. 'I mean, over lunch or a beer, not in an interrogation room.'

'Look, Inspector Jefe, I just wanted the man's business. I didn't want to marry him.'

The Médico Forense put his head round the door to say he was going upstairs to look at Sra Vega's body. Calderón went with him.

'Was Sr Vega married when you first met him?' asked Falcón.

'No,' said Vázquez. 'There were no divorce proceedings, although

I think he produced a death certificate of a previous spouse. You'll have to ask Lucía's parents.'

'When did they marry?'

'Eight . . . ten years ago, something like that.'

'Were you invited?'

'I was his *testigo*.'

'A trusted man in *every* respect,' said Falcón.

'What do you make of my client's hobby?' asked Vázquez, wanting to take back control of the interview.

'His parents "were killed". His father was a butcher,' said Falcón. 'Perhaps this is his way of keeping a memory alive.'

'I don't think he liked his father that much.'

'So he *did* give you some personal revelations?'

'Over the last . . . nearly twenty years I've gleaned some small pieces of information. His father being hard on his only son was one of them. A favourite punishment was to make his son work in the cold store in just a shirt. Rafael suffered from arthritis in his shoulders, which he put down to that early treatment.'

'Perhaps butchery gives him a sense of control. I mean, not just because he's good at it but because he's reducing something large and unmanageable down to comprehensible and usable pieces,' said Falcón. 'And that's the work of the constructor. He takes the vast and complex architect's plans and dismantles them into a series of jobs involving steel, concrete, bricks and mortar.'

'I think the few people who knew about his hobby found it more. . . sinister.'

'The idea of the urbane businessman hacking his way down the spine of a dead beast?' said Falcón. 'I suppose, there *is* a certain brutality to the work.'

'A lot of people who had dealings with Sr Vega *thought* they knew him,' said Vázquez. 'He understood what made people tick and he had learnt how to charm. He had an instinct for a person's strengths and weaknesses. He made men feel interesting and powerful, and women, mysterious and beautiful. It was shocking to see how well it worked. I realized some time ago that I didn't know him . . . at all. It meant that he trusted me, but only with his business, not with his private thoughts.'

'You were his testigo, that's a little more than a business relationship.'

'You know there was a business element to his relationship with Lucía . . . or rather Lucía's family.'

'They had land?' asked Falcón.

'He made them very wealthy people,' said Vázquez, nodding.

'And not very inquisitive about his mysterious past?'

'I only wanted to show you that being his testigo did not imply a more intimate relationship . . .'

'Than he had with his wife?'

'You'll be talking to Lucía's parents, I'm sure,' said Vázquez.

'How was he with his son, Mario?'

'He loved his son. The child was very important to him.'

'It seems odd that he should have waited until he was over fifty before starting a family.'

Silence, while Vázquez riffled through his lawyerly mind.

'I can't help you there, Inspector Jefe,' he said.

'But I'm making you think.'

'I mentioned the death certificate. I was just going over other conversations.'

'You met him when he was nearly forty years old. He had money enough to buy land.'

'He had to borrow as well.'

'Still, someone of that generation, with that sort of money, would normally have a family.'

'You know, he never talked about his life, that part of it before he and I met.'

'Apart from his father's butchery business.'

'And that only came up because of the planning permission needed to build this room when he renovated the house. I saw the drawings. It needed an explanation.'

'When was that?'

'Twelve years ago,' said Vázquez. 'But I didn't get the full family history.'

'He told you how he was punished by his father.'

'It was just fragments. There was no major discussion.'

Felipe, the older of the two forensics, put his head round the door.

'Do you want to talk about this now, Inspector Jefe?'

Falcón nodded. Vázquez gave him his card and the house keys and said he'd be in Seville for at least another week before the August holidays. As he turned to leave he told Falcón to open the door on the other side of the butcher's room. It gave on to the garage, in which there was a brand-new silver Jaguar.

'He took delivery of that last week, Inspector Jefe,' said Vázquez. '*Hasta luego*.'

Falcón joined the forensics in the kitchen. Felipe was watching Jorge working his way around the foot of the kitchen units.

'What have we got?' asked Falcón.

'Nothing so far,' said Felipe. 'The floor has been recently cleaned.'

'The work surfaces?'

'No, there are prints all over those. It's just the floor,' said Felipe. 'You'd have thought with a litre of drain cleaner in his guts he'd have gone into convulsions. You ever had gallstone trouble, Inspector Jefe?'

'Fortunately not,' he said, but he caught the glimmer of horror in Felipe's eye. 'Don't they say it's the closest a male can get to the pain of childbirth?'

'I told my wife that and she reminded me both her babies were nearly four kilos each and that a gallstone is about nine grammes.'

'There's very little sympathy in the pain stakes,' said Falcón.

'I thrashed around on the bathroom floor like a lunatic. There should be latent prints everywhere.'

'Fingerprints on the bottle?'

'One set, very strong and clear . . . which is surprising, too. I wouldn't have thought Sr Vega would buy his own drain cleaner. There should be others.'

'It must have been doctored with something stronger, or with poison, or he must have taken pills. Conventional drain cleaner would take some time, wouldn't it?'

'Strange way to do it, if you ask me,' said Jorge, from the foot of the kitchen units.

'Well, I think this points to what we all saw when we first took a look at the crime scene,' said Falcón.

'It didn't look right,' said Felipe.

'I thought it was "off", too,' said Jorge.

'Nothing you can put your finger on?' said Falcón.

'It's always the same with these scenes,' said Felipe. 'It's what's missing that matters. I took one look at the floor and thought: No, I'm getting nothing from that.'

'Did you hear about the note?'

'Weird,' said Jorge. '"... the thin air you breathe..." what's that?'

'Sounds pure,' said Falcón.

'And the 9/11 stuff?' asked Jorge. 'We're a long way from New York.'

'He was probably bankrolling al-Qaeda,' said Felipe.

'Don't joke about it,' said Jorge. 'Anything can happen these days.'

'All I know is that this is wrong,' said Felipe. 'Not so wrong that I'm totally convinced that he was murdered, but wrong enough to make me suspicious.'

'The position of the bottle?' asked Falcón.

'Had it been me, I'd have drunk it and flung it across the room,' said Jorge. 'There should be droplets everywhere.'

'And there aren't any, except at the point where the bottle lay just over a metre from the body.'

'But there *are* some drops?'

'Yes, they've dripped from the neck of the bottle.'

'Any between the body and the bottle?'

'No,' said Felipe, 'which again is odd, but not... impossible.'

'Just as he could have thrashed around on the floor wiping away any latents and droplets with his dressing gown?'

'Ye-e-es,' said Felipe, unconvinced.

'Give me some conjecture, Felipe. I know you hate it, but just give me some.'

'We only deal in facts here,' said Felipe, 'because facts are the only things that stand up in court. Right, Inspector Jefe?'

'Come on, Felipe.'

'I'll say it,' said Jorge, getting to his feet. 'We all know what's missing from this crime scene and that is... a person. We're not sure what they did, or whether they were involved even. We just know that somebody was here.'

'So we have a phantom,' said Falcón. 'Any of you believe in ghosts?'

'Now they really don't go down well in a court of law,' said Felipe.

3

Wednesday, 24th July 2002

Consuelo Jiménez opened the door to Javier Falcón and led him down the corridor to her L-shaped sitting room overlooking a manicured lawn, whose greenness was lurid in the bleaching sunlight. The water in the blue pool, with its necklace of white tiles, trembled against its confinement pushing silky rhomboids towards the garden house, whose walls and roof were blasted by purple bougainvillea.

Falcón stood in front of the floor-to-ceiling sliding doors with his hands clasped behind his back, feeling self-consciously official. Consuelo sat on the sofa dressed in a tight cream silk skirt and a matching blouse. They were tense but oddly comfortable with each other.

'Do you like bougainvillea?' she asked.

'Yes,' he said, without thinking, 'it gives me hope.'

'I'm beginning to find it trite.'

'Perhaps you see too much of it here in Santa Clara,' said Falcón. 'And framed by these windows it looks like a painting that says nothing.'

'I could have a man endlessly diving naked into the pool and call it my Hockney *vivant*,' she said. 'Can I get you anything? I've made some iced tea.'

He nodded and looked at her figure as she went to the kitchen. His blood stirred at the sight of the muscles in her calves. He glanced around the room. There was a single painting on the wall of a large cerise canvas with a dark blue widening stripe diagonally across it. The surfaces of tables and a sideboard contained photographs of her children – individuals and grouped. Apart from a dark blue sofa which turned a right angle with the L-shaped room and an armchair there was little else. He turned back to the facile garden thinking that she'd mentioned Hockney because this barrio, in the incessant sunshine, was much more like California than Andalucía.

Consuelo Jiménez handed him an iced tea and pointed him into the armchair. She lounged on the sofa, nodding her foot at him, her low-heeled sandal hanging from her toes.

'It doesn't feel like Spain out here,' said Falcón.

'You mean we're not falling over each other like a basket of puppies.'

'It's quiet.'

They sat in silence for a moment – no traffic, no church bells ringing, no whistling, no handclapping down the streets.

'Double-glazing,' she said. 'And I live with noise all the time in the restaurants. I live my Spanish life three times over while I'm there so when I'm out here it's like . . . the afterlife. I'd have thought you'd be the same, doing what you do.'

'I prefer to be in the midst of things these days,' said Falcón. 'I've done my time in limbo.'

'I'm sure in that massive house of your father's you don't exactly feel in . . . I mean, not your father . . . Sorry.'

'I still refer to Francisco Falcón as my father. It's a forty-seven-year habit which I haven't been able to break.'

'You've changed, Inspector Jefe.'

'Call me Javier.'

'Your style is different.'

'I cut my hair. I've given up suits. There's been a relaxation of standards.'

'You're not so intense,' she said.

'Oh, I am. I've just realized that people don't like it, so I hide it. I've learnt to keep smiling.'

'I had a friend whose mother gave her the advice: "Keep moving, keep smiling." It works,' said Consuelo. 'We live in an age of glibness, Javier. When was the last time you had a serious conversation?'

'I have them all the time.'

'With someone other than yourself.'

'I've been seeing a clinical psychologist.'

'Of course you have, after what you've been through,' she said. 'But that's not conversation, is it?'

'Very little of it,' he said. 'Sometimes it's like an absurd self-indulgence, other times vomiting.'

She snatched at the cigarettes on the table, lit one up and sank back satisfied.

'I'm annoyed with you,' she said, pointing at him with the lit cigarette. 'You never called me and we were supposed to have dinner . . . remember?'

'You moved house.'

'Does that mean you tried?'

'I haven't had much time,' he said, smiling.

'Smiling doesn't work with me,' she said. 'I know what it means. You'll have to learn some new strategies.'

'Things have been coming to a head,' he said.

'In the therapy?'

'Yes, that, and I have legal problems with my sister Manuela. My half sister.'

'She's the acquisitive one, I seem to remember.'

'You've read all the scandal.'

'You'd have to have been in a coma to avoid it,' she said. 'So what does Manuela want?'

'Money. She wanted me to write a book about my life with Francisco, including all the journals, and my take on the murder case that brought it all to light. Or rather she wanted me to work with her journalist boyfriend, who would ghost the book for me. I refused. She got angry. Now she's working on proving that I'm not the rightful heir to Francisco Falcón's house, that I am not his son . . . You see how it goes.'

'You have to fight her.'

'She has very different mental processes. She thinks how Francisco used to think, which was probably why he never liked her,' said Falcón. 'She's a manipulator and a public relations expert which, combined with her energy, ambition and wallet, is lethal.'

'I'll buy the dinner.'

'It's not that bad. It's just something that adds to the background pressure of life.'

'What you need is some foreground pleasure, Javier,' she said. 'That brother of yours, the bull breeder, Paco. Is he any help to you?'

'We get on well. There's been no change there, but this kind of thing is not his strength. He needs Manuela, too. She's his vet and one word to the authorities about any possible threat of BSE in his herd and he'd be finished.'

'You are remarkably sane.'

'Thank you,' he said, and decided not to tell her that it was probably the drugs.

'But, having disdained it, I now think you *are* in need of some glibness and fun.'

Silence. Falcón tapped his notebook. A sad inevitability compressed her lips. She smoked it away.

'Bring on the questions, Inspector Jefe,' she said, beckoning him to her.

'You can still call me Javier.'

'Well, Javier, at least you've learnt a few things.'

'Like what?'

'How to ease somebody . . . or rather how to ease a suspect, into an interrogation.'

'Do you think you're a suspect?' he asked.

'I'd like to be one so that we can relive the detective/suspect dynamic,' she said drily.

'And how do you know it was murder?'

'Why are you here, Javier?'

'I investigate any death that is not by natural causes.'

'Did Rafael die of a heart attack?'

Falcón shook his head.

'So it's murder.'

'Or a suicide pact.'

'Pact?' she said, stubbing out the cigarette. 'What pact?'

'We found Sra Vega dead upstairs, suffocated by her pillow.'

'Oh my God,' she said, looking over her shoulder. 'Mario.'

'Sr Vega had drunk a litre of drain cleaner, which was probably either boosted or poisoned, or he'd taken pills beforehand. We'll have to wait for the Médico Forense's report.'

'I can't believe it.'

'You mean you didn't think he was the suicidal type?'

'He appeared so connected to life. His work, the family . . . especially Mario. He'd just bought a new car. They were going away on holiday . . .'

'Was Sr Vega there when you called last night about Mario?'

'I spoke to Lucía. I assumed he was there but I don't know.'

'Where were they going on holiday?' asked Falcón.

'Normally they go to El Puerto de Santa María but this time they thought Mario was old enough so they'd rented a house in La Jolla near San Diego and they were going to take him to Sea World and Disneyland.'

'Florida would have been closer.'

'Too humid for Lucía,' she said, lighting another cigarette and shaking her head, staring at the ceiling. 'We've got no idea what goes on in people's heads.'

'His lawyer didn't mention any of this.'

'He might not have known about it. Rafael was the type who kept his life compartmentalized. He didn't like overlaps, one thing bleeding into another. Everything had to be separate and in its place. I got all the holiday stuff from Lucía.'

'So he was a control freak?'

'Like a lot of successful businessmen.'

'You met him through Raúl?'

'He was very supportive after Raúl was murdered.'

'He let Mario sleep over?'

'He liked my boys, too.'

'Was it a regular thing, Mario sleeping over?'

'At least once a week. Normally on a weekday night or over the weekend in the summer when I have more time,' she said. 'The only thing he wouldn't allow was for Mario to go in the pool.'

'Surprising that Sr Vega didn't have a pool.'

'There was one there but he filled it in and turfed it over. He didn't like them.'

'Did anybody else know about the arrangement with Mario?'

'They might have if they were nosey enough,' she said. 'Don't you find all this incredibly tedious, Javier?'

'In my experience it's through the minutiae of everyday life that you find out about how people really live. The small details lead to bigger things,' he said. 'Some years ago I was beginning to find it dull, but now, strangely, I find it quite riveting.'

'Since you restarted your own life?'

'Sorry?'

'I didn't mean to be so intrusive.'

'I'd nearly forgotten ... but that's your style, isn't it, Doña Consuelo?'

'You can dispense with the Doña, Javier,' she said. 'And I'm sorry. It was a thought that should have remained a thought.'

'I come across a lot of people who think things about me,' he said. 'Because of my story I've become public property. The only reason I don't get accosted more is that people have too many questions. They don't know where to start.'

'All I meant was that, from my own experience, when the foundations of your life collapse it's the everyday things that begin to matter. They hold things together,' she said. 'I've had a lot of rebuilding to do myself since we last met.'

'New life, new home . . . new lover?' he asked.

'I deserved that,' she said.

'It's just my job.'

'But was that a personal inquiry or solely for the purposes of your investigation?'

'Let's say both,' said Falcón.

'I have no lover and . . . if this is where you're leading to, Rafael was not interested in me.'

He played that back in his mind and found no nuances.

'Let's get back to the minutiae,' he said. 'When did you last speak to the Vegas?'

'I spoke to Lucía at about eleven p.m. to tell her that Mario had fallen asleep and I'd put him to bed. There was some mothers' talk and that was it.'

'Was it any longer than usual?'

Consuelo blinked as her eyes filled. Her mouth crumpled around the cigarette. She spat the smoke out, swallowed hard.

'It was the same as always,' she said.

'She didn't ask to speak to the boy or . . .'

Consuelo leaned forward, dug her elbows into her thighs and wept. Falcón got to his feet, went to her and gave her a handkerchief. He patted her between the shoulder blades.

'I'm sorry,' he said. 'The minutiae lead to bigger things.'

He took the cigarette from her hand and crushed it out in the ashtray. Consuelo recovered. Falcón returned to his chair.

'Since Raúl's death I get very emotional about children. All children.'

'It must have been hard for your boys.'

'It was, but they showed remarkable resilience. I think I felt more for their loss than they did. It's surprising the route that grief takes,' she said. 'But now I find myself constantly pledging money to kids who've been orphaned by AIDS in Africa, to children who've been exploited in India and the Far East, to street children in Mexico City and São Paulo, the rehabilitation of boy soldiers...It just pours out of me and I have no idea why this should suddenly have happened.'

'Didn't Raúl leave some money to Los Niños de la Calle, the street children charity?'

'I think it was something deeper than that.'

'Guilt money for...Arturo? That son of his who was kidnapped and never seen...'

'Don't start me off again,' she said. 'I can't stop thinking about that.'

'OK. Something else,' he said. 'Lucía has a sister in Madrid, doesn't she? She should be able to look after Mario.'

'Yes, she's got two children, one who's Mario's age. I'll miss him,' she said. 'Losing your father is bad enough, but to lose a mother as well is a catastrophe, especially at that age.'

'You adapt,' said Falcón, feeling the stab of his own experience. 'The survival instinct hasn't been undermined. You accept love from wherever it comes.'

They stared at each other, minds orbiting around the concept of the parental void, until Consuelo went to the bathroom. As the taps ran Falcón slumped back in his chair, already exhausted. He had to find the stamina for this work again or perhaps try to find new ways of keeping the worlds he pried into at a distance.

'So what do you think happened in that house last night?' said Consuelo, face repaired.

'It looks as if Sr Vega smothered his wife and then killed himself by drinking a bottle of drain cleaner,' said Falcón. 'Official cause of death will be established later. If the scenario is as it appears we'll expect to find pillow material under Sr Vega's fingernails...that sort of thing, which will give us –'

'And if you don't?'

'Then we'll have to look deeper,' said Falcón. 'We're already... puzzled.'

'By the new car and the fact he was going on holiday?'

'Suicides rarely advertise what they're about to do. They carry on as normal. Think how many times you've heard the relatives of victims say, "But he seemed so calm and normal,"' said Falcón. 'It's because they've made up their minds and it's given them some peace at last. No, we're puzzled by the scenario and by the strange note.'

'He wrote a suicide note?'

'Not exactly. In his fist he had a piece of paper on which was written in English "... the thin air you breathe from 9/11 until the end..."' said Falcón. 'Does that mean anything to you?'

'Well, it's not explaining anything, is it?' she said. 'Why 9/11?'

'One of the forensics said he was probably bankrolling al-Qaeda,' said Falcón. 'As a joke.'

'Except... aren't we being led to believe that anything is possible these days?'

'Did Sr Vega seem unstable to you in any way?'

'Rafael seemed to be *completely* stable,' said Consuelo. 'Lucía was the unstable one. She was a depressive, with occasional bouts of manic compulsive behaviour. Have you seen her wardrobe?'

'A lot of shoes.'

'Many of them were the same design and colour, as were her dresses. If she liked something she'd buy three straight off. She was on medication.'

'So, if he was in crisis, given his nature, he would be unlikely to turn to anyone outside the family and he wouldn't have been able to talk to his wife.'

'The restaurant business has taught me not to judge people's lives from the outside. Couples, even crazy ones, have ways of communicating, some of which are not attractive, but they work.'

'What about their domestic situation? You saw that, too.'

'I did, but a third party always changes the dynamics. People start behaving.'

'Is that a general or specific observation?'

'I meant it specifically but it can be applied generally,' she said. 'And that felt like the second time you've tried to insinuate that I might have been having an affair with Sr Vega.'

'Did it?' said Falcón. 'Well, I didn't mean to be specific. I was just thinking that under those stressful circumstances *a* lover might have been a possibility, and that would have changed mental and marital landscapes.'

'Not Rafael,' she said, shaking her head. 'He's not the type.'

'Who is the type?'

She tapped a cigarette on the box, lit it and blew smoke at the glass.

'Your Inspector Ramírez is the type,' she said. 'Where is he, by the way?'

'He's taken his daughter to have some medical tests.'

'Not serious, I hope.'

'They don't know,' said Falcón. 'But you're right about Ramírez, he was always a player . . . combing his hair for the secretaries in the Edificio de los Juzgados.'

'Maybe the work he did gave him an eye for the vulnerable,' she said. 'That's another definition of the type.'

'But not, apparently, Rafael Vega. The Butcher.'

'You said it. That's a pastime that really doesn't go with love-making: "Do you want to see my latest cuts?"'

'What did you make of all that?'

'I used him. His beef always tasted better. Almost all the steaks served in my restaurants are cut by him.'

'And psychologically . . ?'

'It ran in the family. I don't think it's any more than that. If his father had been a carpenter . . .'

'Of course, some spare-time cabinet making. But butchery . . ?'

'It gave Lucía the creeps, but then . . . she had her sensitivities.'

'She was squeamish, as well?'

'Squeamish, nervous, depressed, unable to sleep. She used to take two sleeping pills a night. One to knock her out and then another when she woke up at three or four in the morning.'

'Bulletproof windows,' said Falcón.

'She needed total silence to sleep. The house was hermetically sealed. Once you were inside there was no sense of the outside world. No wonder she was a little crazy. Sometimes when she opened the door I expected a rush of air as if the pressures were different inside.'

'In a world of glibness and fun she doesn't sound like much fun,' said Falcón.

'There you go again, Javier. That's number three,' she said. 'Anyway, she was glib. She used the material and the trivial to hold her life together. She found relationships complicated. Even Mario could be too much for her at times, which was why she was so happy for him to come over here. But that's not to say he wasn't the focus of her life.'

'So how did Sr Vega fit into his family?'

'I don't think they were expecting a child. I didn't see them much at that time, but I seem to remember it was a shock,' she said. 'Anyway, a marriage changes after a child. Perhaps you'll find that out for yourself one day, Javier.'

'You pretend not to understand what I'm doing but you know I have to do this. I have to look for the weaknesses and vulnerabilities in a situation,' said Falcón, sounding oversensitive even to himself. 'My questions can be ugly, but then it's not so nice to have a double murderer out there leaving a crime scene to look like a suicide pact.'

'It's OK, Javier, I can take it,' said Consuelo. 'Despite the attractions of the detective/suspect dynamic I'd rather you eliminated me from your inquiries with whatever ugly questions you have to ask. I have a good memory and I did not enjoy being accused of Raúl's murder.'

'Well, these are just the preliminaries. I'm hoping for some harder facts on which to base my suspicions about the way in which the Vegas died. So you'll be seeing me again.'

'I look forward to it.'

'How did you get into the grounds of the Vegas' house?'

'Lucía gave me the code to open the gate.'

'Did anybody else know that?'

'The maid. Probably Sergei. I've no idea, but the Krugmans' garden butts on to the Vegas' and there's a gate at the bottom, so they would have access. As for Pablo Ortega, I don't know.'

'Sergei?' said Falcón. 'You said he was a Russian or Ukrainian. That's a bit unusual.'

'Even you must have noticed the number of Eastern Europeans around these days,' said Consuelo. 'I know it's wrong, but I think people prefer them to Moroccans.'

'What do you know about Madeleine Krugman?'

'She's friendly in the way that Americans are . . . immediately.'

'You could say the same of the Sevillanos.'

'Perhaps that's why we get so many Americans here every year,' said Consuelo. 'I'm not complaining, by the way.'

'She's an attractive woman,' said Falcón.

'Rafael's never had it so good in your eyes,' she said. 'Anyway, all men think Madeleine Krugman is attractive – even you, Javier. I saw you looking.'

Falcón flushed like a fifteen year old, grinned and ran through a range of displacement activity. Consuelo gave him a sad smile from the sofa.

'Maddy knows her power,' she said.

'So she's the femme fatale of the barrio?' asked Falcón.

'I'm trying to edge her out,' said Consuelo, 'but she's got a few years on me. No. She just knows that men melt around her. She does her best to ignore it. What's a girl supposed to do when everybody from the gas man to the fishmonger to the Juez de Instrucción and the Inspector Jefe de Homicidios seem to have lost control of their lower jaws?'

'What about Sr Krugman?'

'They've been married a long time. He's older.'

'Do you know what they're doing here?'

'Taking a break from living in America. He works for Rafael. He's designing, or has designed, a couple of his projects.'

'Were they taking a break after 9/11?'

'That happened while they were here,' she said. 'They were living in Connecticut, he was working in New York and I think they just got bored . . .'

'Children?'

'I don't think so.'

'Have you been to any social occasions there?'

'Yes . . . Rafael was there, too.'

'But not Lucía?'

'Too much for her.'

'Any observations?'

'I'm sure he was probably interested in the idea of having sex with her because that's what travels through every man's brain when they see Maddy Krugman, but I don't think it happened.'

There was a loud bellow from upstairs, the terrible noise of an animal in pain. It shot up Consuelo's spine and jerked her to her feet. Falcón scrambled out of his chair. Feet rumbled down the stairs. Mario in a pair of shorts and shirt came running down the corridor. He had his arms held out from his puny body, his head thrown back, eyes closed, mouth open in a silent scream. The famous war photograph of the napalm attack on a Vietnam village snapped into Falcón's mind but not focused on the central figure of a naked Vietnamese girl running down the road. It was on the boy in front of her, his black mouth stretched open, crammed full of horror.

4

Wednesday, 24th July 2002

In his passport photo Martin Krugman, without his beard, looked his age, which was fifty-seven years old. With the beard, which was grey and had been allowed to grow untrimmed, he looked beyond retirement age. Life had been kinder to Madeleine Krugman who was thirty-eight and looked no different from her passport photo taken when she was thirty-one. They could have been father and daughter, and many people would have preferred it that way.

Marty Krugman was tall and rangy, some might say skinny, with a prominent nose which, face on, was blade thin. His eyes were set close together, well back in his head and operated under eyebrows which his wife had given up trying to contain. He did not look like a man who slept much. He drank cup after cup of thick espresso coffee poured from a chrome coffee-maker. Marty was not dressed for the office. His shirt was nearly cheesecloth with a blue stripe, which he wore like a smock outside his faded blue jeans. He had Outward Bound sandals on his feet and sat with an ankle resting on his knee and his hands clinging on to his shin as if he was pulling on an oar. He spoke perfect Spanish with a Mexican inflexion.

'Spent my youth in California,' he said. 'Berkeley, doing Engineering. Then I took some years out in New Mexico painting in Taos and taking trips down to Central and South America. My Spanish is a mess.'

'Was that in the late sixties?' asked Falcón.

'And seventies. I was a hippy until I discovered architecture.'

'Did you know Sr Vega before you came here?'

'No. We met him through the estate agent who rented the house to us.'

'Did you have any work?'

'Not at that stage. We were playing it fast and easy. It was lucky that we met Rafael in the first few weeks. We got talking, he'd heard of some of my New York stuff and he offered me some project work.'

'It was *very* lucky,' said Madeleine, as if she might have flown the coop if it hadn't worked out.

'So you came here on a whim?'

Maddy had changed out of the white linen trousers into a knee-length skirt which flared out over her cream leather chair. She crossed and uncrossed her very white legs several times a minute and Falcón, who was sitting directly opposite her, annoyed himself by looking every time. Her breasts trembled under her blue silk top with every movement. Hormonal sound waves seemed to pulse out into the room as her blue blood ticked under her white skin. Marty was impervious to it all. He didn't look at her or react to anything she said. When she spoke his gaze remained fixed on Falcón, who was having trouble finding a resting place for his own eyes with the whole room now an erogenous zone.

'My mother died and I inherited some money,' said Maddy. 'We thought we'd take a break and be in Europe for a while . . . visit our old honeymoon haunts: Paris, Florence, Prague. But we went to Provence and then Marty had to see Barcelona . . . get his Gaudí fix, and one thing led to another. We found ourselves here. Seville gets into your blood. Are you a Sevillano, Inspector Jefe?'

'Not quite,' he said. 'When did all this happen?'

'March last year.'

'Were you taking a break from anything in particular?'

'Just boredom,' said Marty.

'Your mother's death, Sra Krugman . . . was that sudden?'

'She was diagnosed with cancer and died within ten weeks.'

'I'm sorry,' said Falcón. 'What was boring you in America, Sr Krugman?'

'You can call us Maddy and Marty if you like,' she said. 'We prefer to be relaxed.'

Her perfect white teeth appeared behind her chilli-red lips in a two centimetre smile and were gone. She spread her fingers out on the leather arms of the chair and switched her legs over again.

'My job,' said Marty. 'I was bored with the work I was doing.'

'No you weren't,' she said, and their eyes met for the first time.

'She's right,' said Marty, his head slowly coming back to Falcón.

'Why would I be working here if I was bored with my job? I was bored with being in America. I just didn't think you'd be interested in that. It's not a detail that's going to help you find out what happened to the Vegas.'

'I'm interested in everything,' said Falcón. 'Most murder has a motive . . .'

'Murder?' said Maddy. 'The officer on the gate told me it was suicide.'

'Self-murder,' said Falcón. 'If that's what it was. It's all motivated, which means I'm interested in everybody's motives for doing anything. It is all indicative.'

'Of what?' asked Maddy.

'A state of mind. Degrees of happiness and disappointment, joy and anger, love and hate. You know, the big emotions that make things happen and break things down.'

'This guy doesn't sound like a cop,' said Marty in English, throwing the line over his shoulder to his wife.

Her eyes were on Falcón, digging deep, excavating his cranium in a way that made him think that he must look like somebody she knew.

'What was so wrong with America that you had to leave?' asked Falcón.

'I didn't say anything was wrong,' said Marty, bracing his shoulders as if he was at the start of the Olympic sculls final. 'I was just bored with the grind of daily life.'

'Boredom is one of our strongest motivations,' said Falcón. 'What did you want to get away from? What were you looking for?'

'Sometimes the American way of life can be a rather enclosed world,' said Marty.

'There are a lot of Sevillanos who've hardly been outside Andalucía, let alone Spain,' said Falcón. 'They don't see the need for it. They don't think there's anything wrong with their enclosed world.'

'Maybe they don't question it.'

'Why should they when they live in the most beautiful place on earth?'

'Have you ever been to America, Inspector Jefe?'

'No.'

'Why not?' asked Marty, indignant.

'It's the greatest nation on earth,' said Maddy, bright, cheerful and ironical.

'Probably...' said Falcón, thinking it through as he spoke, 'because what I'd be looking for there has gone.'

Marty slapped out a beat on his shin, delighted.

'What would that be?' asked Maddy.

'What had transfixed me as a boy...which was all those black-and-white noir movies of the forties and fifties. They were the reason I became a detective.'

'You'd be disappointed,' said Marty. 'Those streets, that life, those values...we've moved on from them.'

'You've made a big mistake here, Inspector Jefe,' said Maddy. 'America is Marty's favourite topic. We get out of there and suddenly that's all he wants to talk about. He wakes me up at night because he has to tell me his latest theory. What was it last night, honey?'

'Fear,' said Marty, his dark peepers flashing from deep in his head like tropical birds escaping into the jungle.

'America is a society based on fear,' said Maddy flatly. 'That's the latest. It's sad that he thinks he's the first one to think them.'

'Well, now, I suppose, in the post September 11th world...'

'Not just now,' said Marty. 'It's *always* been fear.'

'Forget the pioneering spirit,' said Maddy, hurling her hand over her shoulder.

'There have always been pioneers,' said Marty. 'The strong and fearless men...'

'This is very interesting,' said Falcón, seeing his mistake now. 'And it would be fascinating were it not for the fact that I have a double death to investigate.'

'You see, he's not *that* interested in your motives,' said Maddy, and Marty flicked a dismissive finger at her. 'And by the way, Inspector Jefe, he still thinks it's the greatest nation on earth, despite...'

'When did you last speak to the Vegas?' asked Falcón.

'I spoke to him yesterday evening about seven o'clock in the office,' said Marty. 'It was a technical conversation, nothing personal. He was businesslike, professional...the usual.'

'Were you aware of any financial difficulties that might have put pressure on Sr Vega?'

'He was always under pressure. It's the nature of construction. There's a lot to think about: the building, the machinery, materials and labour, budgets and money...'

'And you?' Falcón said, turning to Maddy.

'Me?' she replied, coming out of some deep, distracting thought.

'The last time you spoke to Sr Vega?'

'I don't . . . I can't think,' she said. 'When would that have been, honey?'

'Dinner last week,' he said.

'How were the Vegas then?'

'Rafael came on his own,' said Marty.

'As usual,' said Maddy. 'Lucía always cancelled at the last minute. The kid or something. She didn't like these dinners of ours. She was a traditionalist. You only go to dinner at someone else's house if they're family. She found it awkward. She had no conversation, except about Mario and I've never had children, so . . .'

'She was neurotic,' said Marty.

'How did Sr Vega and his wife get along?'

'He was very *loyal* to her,' said Maddy.

'Does that mean love no longer came into it?'

'Love?' she said.

Marty stared at her, nodding, his nose sawing through the chill air, as if willing her to conclude what she'd embarked on.

'Don't you think loyalty is a part of love, Inspector Jefe?'

'I do,' said Falcón. 'But you seem to have separated loyalty from the whole, as if that was all that remained.'

'Don't you think that's the nature of a marriage . . . or of love, Inspector Jefe?' she said, 'That time degrades it, wears away at passion and ardour, the thrill of sex . . .'

'For Christ's sake,' said Marty in English.

'. . . the intensity of interest you have in what the other says or thinks, the wild hilarity of the smallest jokes, the deep, unquestioning admiration of physical beauty, intelligence, moral certitude . . .'

'Yes,' said Falcón, his insides starting to bind up, as they did sometimes in therapy sessions with his psychologist, Alicia Aguado. 'That's true . . .'

He sat back, let his intestines have some room, wrote some gibberish down in his notebook, wanted to get out of there.

'So, are you saying, Sra Krugman, that the Vegas' marriage, in your opinion, was strong . . . ?'

'I only observed that he was loyal to her. She was an unwell and, at times, an unhappy woman, but she was the mother of his child and that had considerable weight with him.'

The ground seemed to firm up under Falcón's chair as the business at hand reasserted itself.

'Sr Vega liked to control things,' said Falcón.

'He had firm ideas about how things should be done and he had a very disciplined mind,' said Marty. 'I never saw further into his corporation than was necessary for me to do my work. He didn't attempt to involve me in anything outside my own project. He would even ask me to leave his office if he was going to talk about other jobs on the phone. He was very concerned about hierarchy, the way things were reported to him, who did what and the chain of command. I don't have any direct experience of this, but his style seemed military to me, which is no bad thing on a construction site. People can get killed very easily.'

'In life, too' said Maddy.

'What?' said Marty.

'He liked to control things in life, too. The gardener, his family, his meat,' she said, chopping her hand down on to her knee.

'It's odd then that he'd come over here for dinner,' said Falcón. 'If he was going to put himself in the hands of others, I'd have thought he'd prefer a restaurant.'

'He understood it as an American thing,' said Marty.

'He liked it,' said Maddy, shrugging her shoulders so that her loose breasts shifted under the silk. Her legs slipped to one side and she rubbed them together, as if taming an itch.

I bet he did, thought Falcón.

'A controlling man might kill himself if his carefully constructed world was about to fall apart due to financial ruin or a shaming scandal. It could also collapse because of an emotional involvement that went wrong. News of the first two scenarios, if they existed, will break soon enough. Do you know anything about the third possibility?'

'Do you think he was the type to have affairs?' Marty asked his wife.

'Affairs?' said Maddy, almost to herself.

'He would have left a note,' said Marty. 'Did he?'

'Not a conventional one,' said Falcón, and gave them the text.

'That seems almost a little too poetic for someone like Rafael,' said Maddy.

'What about the 9/11 reference?' said Falcón. 'You must have talked about that with him.'

Maddy rolled her eyes.

'Sure,' said Marty. 'We talked about it endlessly, but as an item of current affairs. I really don't understand its significance in this context.'

'Why kill your wife?' asked Maddy, which relieved Falcón, who didn't want Marty's theories on 9/11 at this stage of his inquiry. 'I mean, if you're suffering like that, kill yourself by all means, but don't leave your kid with no parents.'

'Maybe he thought Lucía would not be able to survive without him,' said Marty.

'That would be true,' she said.

'Do you always allow this much conjecture into your investigations, Inspector Jefe?' asked Marty.

'No,' said Falcón, 'but the situation in the Vegas' house was sufficiently enigmatic that I have to keep an open mind until I get a full forensic report and the pathology of the bodies. Also the closest person to Sr Vega, his wife, is dead, too. I have to rely on people who knew him peripherally – socially or in business.'

'Lucía's parents should be able to help you,' said Marty. 'They were around there almost every Sunday for lunch.'

'Did you ever meet them?'

'I met them once,' said Maddy. 'They weren't. . .er. . .very sophisticated people. I think he used to be a farmer.'

'How long have you been married?' asked Falcón.

'Twelve years,' she said.

'How did you meet?' he said, a question he'd found himself asking every couple he'd met over the last year.

'It was in New York,' said Marty. 'Maddy was showing a collection of her photographs at a gallery which was owned by a friend of mine. She introduced us.'

'And I never went back to my apartment,' said Maddy.

'Are you still a photographer?'

'She's taken it up again since we left the States,' said Marty, steamrollering over Maddy's negative.

'What do you photograph?'

'People,' she said.

'Portraits?'

'Never.'

'She photographs people in their unconscious moments,' said Marty.

'He doesn't mean when they're sleeping,' she said, her eyes flashing with irritation.

'When they don't know the camera is there?' asked Falcón.

'One step further than that,' said Marty. 'When they believe themselves to be completely alone.'

'That makes me sound like a snoop,' she said. 'I'm not a –'

'Yes, you are,' said Marty, laughing.

'No, I'm not,' she said, 'because that implies that I'm interested in what people are doing, and that's not it.'

'What is *it*?' asked Marty. Then, turning to Falcón, he added, 'She never shoots me.'

'It's the internal struggle,' she said. 'I hate it when you make me say these things. It's just not –'

'Have you got any shots of Sr Vega?' said Falcón.

They left Marty on the sofa and went upstairs. One of three bedrooms had been converted into a darkroom. While Maddy looked through her contact sheets Falcón checked the books on the shelves and pulled out one with Madeleine Coren on the spine. There was a photograph of her on the inside flap – a creamy beauty with sparkling eyes, challenging the camera to come closer. She had the dazzle of youth then, which had been skimmed down by life's natural damage to its present translucence. There was still something of the celebrity about her, that quality that film producers look for: not beauty, but watchability. She absorbed things from around her – available light, unused energy and anything anybody might want to give. Falcón opened the book, tore himself away from her profile. He could feel his bone marrow weakening.

Her photographs at first seemed to be about loneliness: old people sitting on park benches, a young man standing at a rail overlooking a river, a woman in a towelling robe on a roof terrace in Manhattan. Gradually, as the camera's eye moved closer, other things became evident: contentment on the old person's face, possibility in the young man's eyes, dreaminess in the woman's face.

'They're facile, those early ones,' said Maddy. 'The idea was just a gimmick. I was only twenty-two. I didn't know anything. Take a look at these –'

She handed him six black-and-white prints. The first three showed Rafael Vega in a white shirt and dark trousers, hands in pockets, standing on his well-clipped lawn. The camera was looking over his shoulder at his profile. His jaw was tight. Falcón waited for the shot to tell him something. Then he saw what it was.

'He's barefoot.'

'That was 14th January this year.'

'What was he doing?'

'That's not the point . . . remember,' she said. 'I'm not a snoop. Look at these. They're taken down by the river. I go there a lot. I can sit with a big zoom lens on a tripod and people will stop on Calle Bétis and the bridges. I pick up a lot of contemplative looks. People go to the river for a reason . . . don't they?'

The three shots she gave him were close-ups of head and shoulders. In the first Rafael Vega was wincing, in the second he was gritting his teeth, eyes screwed up, and in the third his mouth had cracked open.

'He's in pain,' said Falcón.

'He was crying,' said Maddy. 'There's saliva at the corners of his mouth.'

He gave her back the photos. They were intrusive and he didn't like them. He returned her book to the shelf.

'And you didn't think any of this was worth mentioning before?'

'This is my work,' she said. 'This is how I express myself. I wouldn't have shown you them if Marty hadn't pushed me.'

'Even though it could have a bearing on what happened in the Vegas' house last night?'

'I answered your questions – the last time we spoke, how the Vegas got along, whether he was having an affair. I just didn't relate any of that to these shots because the point is that we should never know about them. They were not taken for the purposes of investigating causes.'

'Why were they taken?'

'These are shots of people suffering in intensely private moments, but out in the open. They have chosen not to hide in their homes but to walk it out of themselves in the presence of other human beings.'

Falcón remembered the hours he'd spent walking the streets of Seville in the past fifteen months. The contemplation of the fundamentals of his existence were too unsettling for the confines even of his sprawling house on Calle Bailén. He'd walked it all out of himself, stared it all into the sloe-black waters of the Guadalquivir, shaken it all off into the empty sugar sachets and cigarette ends on the floors of anonymous bars. It was true. He had not sat at home with his horrors piling up in his mind. There was solace in the wordless company of strangers.

Maddy was standing close to him. He was aware of her smell, the body under its thin sheath of silk, the exquisite pressure, the flimsiness of the barrier. She hovered, expectant, confident of her ability. Her white throat trembled as she swallowed.

'We should go back downstairs,' said Falcón.

'There was something else I wanted to show you,' she said, and led him across the corridor to another bedroom, which had a bare tiled floor and more of her photographs on the walls.

His attention was grabbed by a colour shot of a blue pool with a white necklace of tiles in a green lawn with a purple flame of bougainvillea in one corner and a white cushioned lounger in the other. A woman sat on the lounger in a black bathing costume under a red hat.

'That's Consuelo Jiménez,' he said.

'I didn't know you knew her,' said Maddy.

He went to the window. Across the road Consuelo's garden was visible.

'I had to get up on the roof for the angle,' she said.

To his left he could see the Vegas' entrance and driveway through the trees.

'Do you know what time Sr Vega came back home last night?'

'No, but it was rarely before midnight.'

'You wanted to show me something?' he said, turning back in to the room.

On the back wall behind the door, framed in black, was a print 75 cm by 50 cm of a man staring down from a bridge, under which it was clear his whole life was flowing. The features of the man did not compute at first. There was too much going on in the face. It was a shock for him to discover that he was looking at himself – a Javier Falcón he'd never seen before.

5

Wednesday, 24th July 2002

Back at the crime scene next door everybody had moved upstairs into the Vegas' bedroom. Calderón had already signed off the *levantamiento del cadáver* for Sr Vega. The body was in a bag on a trolley in the hallway, waiting in the air conditioning to be loaded on to the ambulance and taken down to the Instituto Anatómico Forense on Avenida Sánchez Pizjuan.

The crime scene team were now congregated around the bed, looking down at Sra Vega, hands behind backs, solemn as if in prayer. The pillow was off her face and had been put in a plastic bag and leaned against the wall. Her mouth was open. The top lip and teeth were set in a snarl as if she'd left life bitterly. Her lower jaw was off centre.

'She'd been hit once with the right hand,' Calderón explained to Falcón. 'The jaw's dislocated . . . Probably knocked her unconscious. The Médico Forense thinks it was done with the flat of the hand, rather than a closed fist.'

'What was the time of death?'

'Same time as the husband: three, three thirty. He can't be more accurate than that.'

'Sra Jiménez said she used sleeping pills, two a night, to knock herself out. She must have woken up and had to be subdued before being suffocated. Is there any link between this death and Sr Vega's yet?'

'Not until I get them back to the Instituto,' said the Médico Forense.

'We're hoping for some sweat or saliva on the upper side of the pillow,' said Felipe.

'This strengthens your case for an unknown murderer, Inspector Jefe,' said Calderón. 'I can't see a husband dislocating his wife's jaw.'

'Unless, as I said, she woke up, perhaps got out of bed just as Sr Vega came in full of intent. She might have seen something different in him, become hysterical and he felt the need for violence,' said Falcón. 'I'm still keeping an open mind on this. Any ghosts in here?'

'Ghosts?' asked Calderón.

'Something that makes a crime scene look "off", not as it should be,' said Falcón. 'We all had the same feeling about Sr Vega's body in the kitchen. Somebody else had been there.'

'And here?'

Jorge shrugged.

'She was murdered,' said Felipe. 'Nobody was trying to make this scene look like anything else. Whether it was Sr Vega remains to be seen. All we've got is the pillow.'

'What did the neighbours have to say?' asked Calderón, moving away from the others in the room.

'We have some conflicting views,' said Falcón. 'Sra Jiménez has known Sr Vega for some time and did not consider him the suicidal type. She also noted the new car and said he was about to go on holiday to San Diego. Sra Krugman, however, showed me these photographs, taken recently, of Sr Vega in private, clearly distressed and possibly unstable. She let me have this contact sheet.'

Calderón looked over the images, frowning.

'He's barefoot in his garden in January,' said Falcón. 'And there's another one of him crying down by the river.'

'What's she doing, taking these photographs?' asked Calderón.

'It's her work,' said Falcón. 'The way she expresses herself.'

'Taking shots of people's private distress?' said Calderón, raising an eyebrow. 'Is she weird?'

'She told me that she was interested in the private, inner struggle,' said Falcón. 'You know, that voice that Sr Vázquez talked about. The one nobody ever hears.'

'But what's she doing with it?' asked Calderón. 'Recording the face but not the voice . . . I mean, what's the point?'

'The voice is loud in the head but silent to the outside world,' said Falcón. 'She's interested in the distressed person's need to be out in the open . . . amongst his fellow strangers, walking his pain out of himself.'

They exchanged a look, left the room and went into Mario's bedroom. Calderón gave him back the contact sheet.

'What's all that bullshit about?' said Calderón.

'I'm telling you what she said.'

'Is she getting some . . . vicarious experience from this?'

'She's got a photograph of *me* on her wall,' said Falcón, still seething. 'A blow-up of *me* staring down into the river from the Puente de Isabel II, for God's sake.'

'She's like some paparazzo of the emotions,' said Calderón, wincing.

'Photographers are strange people,' said Falcón, who was one himself. 'Their currency is perfect moments from real life. They define their idea of perfection to themselves and then pursue it . . . like prey. If they're lucky they find an image that intensifies their idea, makes it more real. . .but in the end they're capturing ephemera.'

'Ghosts, internal struggles, captured ephemera . . .' said Calderón. 'This is unusable stuff.'

'Let's wait for the autopsy. That should give us something tangible to work with. In the meantime I'd like to find Sergei, the gardener, who was physically the closest person to the crime scene and discovered the body.'

'There's another ghost,' said Calderón.

'We should search his rooms down at the bottom of the garden.'

Calderón nodded.

'Maybe I'll go across and take a look at Sra Krugman's photographs while you search the gardener's rooms,' said Calderón. 'I want to see these shots full size.'

Falcón tracked the judge with his eyes back to the second crime scene. Calderón exchanged words with the Médico Forense, rolling his mobile in his hand like a bar of soap. He trotted down the stairs in a hurry. Falcón shrugged away the unsettling thought that Calderón seemed oddly self-conscious and keen, which was not part of his usual knowing style.

As he sweated his way down the unshaded lawn Falcón noticed a pile of blackened paper in the grill on the paved barbecue area. The uppermost paper had been crumpled and was thoroughly burned so that it disintegrated at the touch of his pen. Beneath it were pages that had not been so completely consumed by fire, on which there was discernible handwriting.

He called Felipe down to the garden with his forensic kit. He looked it over wearing his custom-made magnified goggles.

'We're not going to save much of this,' he said, 'if anything.'

'They look like letters to me,' said Falcón.

'I can only make out partial words, but the writing has that rounded look of a female hand. I'll take a shot of it before we wreck it.'

'Give me the partial words you can see.'

Felipe called out some words which at least confirmed the language as Spanish and he took a couple of shots with his digital camera. The blackened paper collapsed as he dug in deeper with his pen. He found a partial line *'en la escuela'* – in the school – but nothing else. At the bottom of the pile he came across paper of a different quality. Felipe lifted some filigree remains from the blackened flakes.

'This is a modern photograph,' he said. 'They're very flammable. The chemicals blister as the paper underneath burns and all that's left is this. Older photographs don't burn so easily. The paper is thicker and higher quality.'

He teased out some paper which was glossy black and curled at the edges but still white in the middle. He turned it over to reveal a black-and-white shot of a girl's head and shoulders. She was standing in front of a woman whose presence had been reduced to a ringed hand resting on the girl's clavicle.

'Can we date it?'

'This sort of stock hasn't been used commercially in Spain for years, but it could have been developed privately or come from abroad where they are still using that kind of stuff. So . . . tricky,' said Felipe. 'The girl's hairstyle looks a bit old-fashioned.'

'Sixties, seventies?' asked Falcón.

'Maybe. She certainly doesn't look like a girl from the pueblo. And the woman's hand on her shoulder doesn't look as if it's done any manual labour. I'd have said they were well-off foreigners. I've got some cousins out in Bolivia who look a bit like this, you know, just not up to date.'

They bagged the piece of photograph, found some shade and cleaned themselves up.

'You burn old letters and photographs if you're putting your house in order,' said Felipe.

'Or your head,' said Falcón.

'Maybe he *did* kill himself and we're just imagining things.'

'Why would you burn this sort of stuff?' said Falcón. 'Painful memories. A part of your life you don't want your wife to find out about . . .'

'Or a part of your life you don't want your *son* to find out about,' said Felipe, 'when you die.'

'Perhaps it could be dangerous material if it falls into the wrong hands.'

'Whose hands?'

'I'm just saying, you burn this sort of thing to get rid of it because it's either painful, embarrassing or dangerous.'

'It could just be a picture of his wife as a girl,' said Felipe. 'What would that mean?'

'Have we tracked down Sra Vega's parents yet?' asked Falcón. 'They should really be looking after the boy, rather than Sra Jiménez.'

Felipe told him that Pérez was working on it. They went down to the gardener's house. The door was not locked. The two rooms were stuffy, airless and stripped of all possessions. The mattress was half off the bed as if he kept something under there, or perhaps just slept on it outside. The only other furniture in the bedroom was an upturned box, used as a bedside table. The kitchen had a gas ring and bottle of butane. There was no fridge and only dried food out on a sideboard.

'The staff didn't see much of the Vega luxury,' said Felipe.

'Better than living in Tres Mil Viviendas,' said Falcón. 'Why run?'

'Allergic to police,' said Felipe. 'These guys get asthmatic when they see 091 on the wall of the phone booth. A dead body . . . well, you don't hang around waiting for the disaster to happen, do you?'

'Or he might have seen something or someone,' said Falcón. 'He must have been aware of Sr Vega burning his papers, probably saw him standing out in the garden in his bare feet. Maybe he even saw what happened last night.'

'I'll take some prints and run them through the computer,' said Felipe.

Falcón walked back up to the house, his shirt sticking to his back. He called Pérez on his mobile.

'Where are you?' asked Falcón.

'Now, I'm in the hospital, Inspector Jefe.'

'I left you searching the garage and the outside of the house.'

'I did that.'

'What about all the burnt papers in the barbecue?'

'They were burnt. I made a note of it.'

'Did you hurt yourself?'

'No.'

'What are you doing in the hospital then?'

'Sra Jiménez sent the maid over, saying she was having trouble with the boy, Mario. She thought it would be good for him to see a familiar face, get the grandparents over.'

'Did you speak to Juez Calderón about this?'

'Yes.'

'He didn't mention it to me.'

'He had other things on his mind.'

'Like what?'

'He's not going to tell me, is he?' said Pérez. 'I could see he was preoccupied, that's all.'

'Just tell me why you're in the hospital,' said Falcón, who had never quite got used to Pérez's maddening style of working and reporting.

'I arrived at the apartment of Sr and Sra Cabello, who are the parents of Sra Vega,' he said. 'They're both in their seventies. They let me in. I tell them what's happened and Sra Cabello collapses. I thought it was shock, but Sr Cabello says she has a weak heart. I call an ambulance and give her first aid. She's stopped breathing. I have to give her heart massage and mouth to mouth, Inspector Jefe. The ambulance arrives and fortunately has a defibrillator on board. She's now in intensive care and I'm sitting here with Sr Cabello. I've called his other daughter and she's on her way down from Madrid on the AVE.'

'Have you spoken to Sra Jiménez?'

'I don't have a number for her.'

'Juez Calderón?'

'His mobile's turned off.'

'Me?'

'We're talking now, Inspector Jefe.'

'All right, good work,' said Falcón.

Back in the cool of the house Falcón's insides felt like smouldering wreckage. Everybody was standing around impatiently. Both bodies were bagged and lying on stretchers in the hallway.

'What are you waiting for?' asked Falcón.

'We need Juez Calderón to sign off the levantamiento del cadáver,' said the Médico Forense. 'We can't find him.'

Falcón called Sra Jiménez on his way over to the Krugmans to tell her about Sra Vega's parents and the imminent arrival of Lucía's sister from Madrid. Mario had collapsed with exhaustion and was now sleeping. She asked him over for a drink in the heat.

'I've still got things to do,' he said.

'I'll be here all day,' she said. 'I'm not going to work.'

Marty Krugman answered the door stretching as if he'd been dozing on the sofa. Falcón asked after the judge. Marty pointed upstairs and dragged himself back to his sofa, barefoot, his jeans hanging off his backside. Falcón followed the sound of voices speaking English. Calderón was quite fluent and had the eagerness of a leaping puppy.

'Yes, yes,' he said. 'I can see that. The sense of deracination is palpable.'

Falcón sighed. Art conversations. He knocked on the door. Maddy tore it open with a sardonic smile on her face. Calderón's eyes behind her right shoulder were staring, wild with dilated pupils. It put Falcón on the back foot for a moment.

'Inspector Jefe,' she said. 'Juez Calderón and I were having *such* an interesting conversation, weren't we?'

Falcón apologized for interrupting but the judge was needed to sign off the second body. Calderón pulled himself together piece by piece, as if he was picking up his clothes in a strange woman's bedroom.

'Your mobile was switched off,' said Falcón.

Maddy raised an eyebrow. Calderón looked around the room to make sure he was leaving nothing incriminating. He gave an uncomfortably protracted goodbye speech whilst holding on to Sra Krugman's hand, which he kissed at the end. He shambled down the stairs like a schoolboy with a decent report in his satchel and stopped halfway.

'You're not coming, Inspector Jefe?'

'I've a question for Sra Krugman.'

Calderón made it clear he would wait.

'You must go off and do your work, Juez,' said Maddy, giving him a dismissive little wave.

A herd of emotions ravaged Calderón's face. Hope, delight, disappointment, longing, jealousy, anger and resignation. They left him trampled. He stumbled down the remaining stairs unable to co-ordinate his feet.

'Your question, Inspector Jefe?' she said, her look as level as the sea's horizon.

He asked to see the shots of Sr Vega in his garden again. She went into the darkroom and laid the prints out on the table. Falcón pointed to the top corner of the shots.

'Smoke,' he said.

'He was burning stuff,' she said. 'He quite often burnt papers down there.'

'How often?'

'Since the beginning of the year . . . quite a lot.'

'And all your shots are . . .'

'From this year,' she said. 'Although he didn't become a regular down at the river until March.'

'You *knew* he was disturbed by something,' said Falcón, annoyed by her now.

'I told you, it's not my business,' she said. 'And you seem to be confused yourself as to whether it's suicide or murder.'

He turned without a word and headed for the door.

'He's a very sensitive and intelligent man, the Juez,' she said.

'He's a good man,' said Falcón. 'And he's a happy man, too.'

'They're a rarity once they get over thirty,' said Maddy.

'Why do you say that?'

'I see more men down at the river than I do women.'

'Women have a talent for remaining connected to the world,' said Falcón. 'They find it easier to talk.'

'There's no secret to it,' said Maddy. 'We just get on with it. Men, like Marty for instance, get sidelined by trying to answer unanswerable questions. They allow things to complicate in their minds.'

Falcón nodded and set off down the stairs. She stood at the top, folded her arms across her chest and leaned against the wall.

'So, why is the Juez so happy?'

'He's getting married later this year,' said Falcón, without turning.

'Do you know her?' she asked. 'Is she nice?'

'Yes,' said Falcón, and he turned to the door.

'Lighten up' she said in English. '*Hasta luego*, Inspector Jefe.'

6

❧❧❧

Falcón understood those words perfectly and he strode back to the Vegas' house in a fury that was only broken by the sight of the maid walking off towards Avenida de Kansas City. He caught up with her and asked her whether she'd bought any drain cleaner recently. She hadn't, ever. He asked her when was the last time she'd cleaned the kitchen floor. Sra Vega, who was obsessed with the idea that Mario would catch germs from a dirty floor, had insisted that it was done three times a day. Mario had already gone across to Consuelo Jiménez's house before she cleaned the floor for the last time yesterday evening.

The ambulance containing the two bodies pulled away as he arrived back at the Vegas' house. The front door was open. Calderón was smoking in the hallway. Felipe and Jorge nodded to him as they left with their forensic kits and evidence bags. Falcón closed the door behind them against the heat.

'What did you ask her?' said Calderón, pushing himself away from the wall.

'I saw from the barbecue that Vega had been burning papers. I wanted to see if he was burning anything in the shots she had taken of him,' said Falcón. 'He was.'

'Is that all?' said Calderón, both accusing and mocking.

Falcón's anger came back to him.

'Did *you* get anywhere with her, Esteban?'

'What do you mean?'

'You were over there for half an hour with your mobile switched off. I assumed you were talking about something with an important bearing on the investigation.'

Calderón dragged hard on his cigarette, drew in the smoke with a rush of air.

'Did *she* say what we talked about?'

'I heard you talking about her photographs as I came up the stairs,' said Falcón.

'They're very good,' said Calderón, nodding gravely. 'She's a very talented woman.'

'You're the one who called her a "paparazzo of the emotions".'

'That was before she talked to me about her work,' he said, flicking his cigarette fingers at Falcón. 'It's the thinking behind the photographs that makes them what they are.'

'So they're not *Hola!* with feelings?' said Falcón.

'Very good, Javier. I'll remember that one,' said Calderón. 'Anything else?'

'We'll talk after the autopsy reports have come out,' said Falcón. 'I'll meet Sra Vega's sister off the AVE and take her to Sra Jiménez later this evening.'

Calderón nodded without knowing what Falcón was talking about.

'I'll talk to Sr Ortega now . . . he's the other neighbour,' said Falcón, unable to resist the sarcasm.

'I know who Sr Ortega is,' said Calderón.

Falcón went to the front door. By the time he turned back Calderón was already lost in labyrinthine thoughts.

'I meant what I said this morning, Esteban.'

'What was that?'

'I think you and Inés will be very happy together,' said Falcón. 'You're very well suited.'

'You're right,' he said. 'We are. Thanks.'

'You'd better come with me,' said Falcón. 'I'm going to lock up now.'

They left the house and parted ways in the drive. Falcón shut the electric gates with a remote he'd picked up from the kitchen. The entrance to Ortega's house was to the left of the Vegas' driveway and covered by a large creeper. He watched Calderón from its shade. The man hovered by his car and appeared to be checking his mobile for messages. He headed off in the direction of the Krugmans' house, stopped, paced about and gnawed on his thumbnail. Falcón shook his head, rang Ortega's bell and introduced himself over the intercom. Calderón threw his hands up and went back to his car.

'That's the way, Esteban,' said Falcón to himself. 'Don't even think about it.'

The smell of raw sewage had already reached Falcón's nostrils as he stood by the gate. Ortega buzzed him in to a stink gross enough to make him gag. Large bluebottles cruised the air as threatening as heavy bombers. Brown stains crept up the walls of the corner of the house where a large crack had appeared in the façade. The air seethed with the busy richness of decay. Ortega appeared from around the side of the house which overlooked the lawn.

'I don't use the front door,' said Ortega, whose hand grip was bone-cracking. 'As you can tell, I have a problem with that side of the house.'

Pablo Ortega's whole body expressed itself in that handshake. He was compact, unyielding and electric. His hair was long, thick and completely white and fell below the neck of his collarless shirt. His moustache was equally impressive, but had yellowed from smoking. Two creases ran from the *entradas* of his hairline to his eyebrows and had the effect of pulling Falcón into his dark brown eyes.

'You've only just moved in, haven't you?' asked Falcón.

'Nine months ago . . . and six weeks later, this shit happens. The house used to have two rooms built over a cesspit, which holds the sewage for the four houses you can see around us. Then the previous owners built another two rooms on top of them and, with the extra weight, six *fucking* weeks after they sold me the house, the roof of the cesspit cracked, the wall subsided and now I've got the shit of four houses bubbling up through the floor.'

'Expensive.'

'I have to take down that side of the house, repair the cesspit, strengthen it so it can take the additional weight and then rebuild,' said Ortega. 'My brother sent somebody round who's told me I'm looking at a bill for twenty million, or whatever the fuck that is in euros.'

'Insurance?'

'I'm an artist. I didn't get round to signing the vital piece of paper until it was too late.'

'Bad luck.'

'I'm an expert in that particular commodity,' he said. 'As I know you are. We've met before.'

'We have?'

'I came to the house on Calle Bailén. You were seventeen or eighteen.'

'Most of Seville's artistic community passed through that house at some stage or other. I'm sorry I don't remember.'

'Bad business, that,' said Ortega, putting a hand on Falcón's shoulder. 'I'd never have believed it. You've been through the media mill. I've read everything, of course. Couldn't resist it. Drink?'

Pablo Ortega was wearing blue knee-length shorts and black espadrilles. He walked with his feet splayed and had immense, bulbous calf muscles, which looked as if they could support him through long stage runs.

They entered round the back of the house through the kitchen. Falcón sat in the living room while Ortega fetched beer and Casera. The room was chill and odourless apart from the smell of old cigar butts. It was stuffed full of furniture, paintings, books, pottery, glassware and rugs. On the floor leaning against an oak chest was a Francisco Falcón landscape. Javier looked at it and felt nothing.

'Charisma,' said Ortega, returning with beer, olives and capers, and nodding at the painting, 'is like a force field. You don't see it and yet it has the power to suspend everybody's normal levels of perception. Now that the world has been told that the emperor has no clothes it's easy, and all those art historians that Francisco so despised are endlessly writing about what an evident departure the four nudes were from his other work. I'm with Francisco. They're contemptible. They delighted in his fall but do not see that now all they're doing is writing about their own failures. Charisma. We are kept in such an ordinary state of boredom that anybody who can light up our life in any way is treated like a god.'

'Francisco used to substitute the word "genius" for "charisma",' said Falcón.

'If you have mastered the art of charisma you don't even need genius.'

'He certainly knew that.'

'Quite right,' said Ortega, guffawing back into the armchair.

'We should get down to business,' said Falcón.

'Yes, well I knew something was going on when I saw that rat-faced bastard out there, smug and comfortable in his expensive light-weight suit,' said Ortega. 'I'm always suspicious of people who dress well for their work. They want to dazzle with their carapace while their emptiness seethes with all forms of dark life.'

Falcón scratched his neck at Ortega's melodrama.

'Who are we talking about?'

'That ... that *cabrón* ... Juez Calderón,' said Ortega. 'It even rhymes.'

'Ah yes, the court case with your son. I didn't...'

'He was the cabrón who made sure that Sebastián went down for such a long time,' said Ortega. 'He was the cabrón who pushed for the maximum sentence. That man is just the letter of the law and nothing else. He is all sword and no scales and, in my humble opinion, for justice to be justice you have to have both.'

'I was only told about your son's case this morning.'

'It was everywhere,' said Ortega, incredulous. 'Pablo Ortega's son arrested. Pablo Ortega's son accused. Pablo Ortega's son blah, blah, blah. Always Pablo Ortega's son ... never Sebastián Ortega.'

'I was preoccupied at the time,' said Falcón. 'I had no mind for current affairs.'

'The media monster ate its fill,' said Ortega, snarling and scoffing at the end of his cigar.

'Do you see your son at all?'

'He won't see anybody. He's shut himself off from the rest of the world.'

'And his mother?'

'His mother walked out on him ... walked out on us, when he was only eight years old,' said Ortega. 'She ran off to America with some fool with a big dick ... and then she died.'

'When was that?'

'Four years ago. Breast cancer. It affected Sebastián very badly.'

'So he knew her?'

'He spent every summer with her from the age of sixteen onwards,' said Ortega, stabbing the air with his cigar. 'None of this was taken into consideration when that cabrón...'

He ran out of steam, shifted in his chair, his face crumpled in disgust.

'It *was* a very serious crime,' said Falcón.

'I realize that,' said Ortega, loudly. 'It's just that the court refused to accept any mitigating circumstances. Sebastián's state of mind, for instance. He was clearly mentally deranged. How do you explain the behaviour of someone who kidnaps a boy, abuses him, lets him go and then gives himself up? When his time came to defend himself in court he said nothing, he refused to dispute any point of the boy's statement . . . he took it all. None of that makes any sense to me. I am not an expert, but even I can see he needs treatment, not prison, violence and solitary confinement.'

'Have you appealed?'

'It all takes time,' said Ortega, 'and money, of course, which has not been easy. I had to move from my house . . .'

'Why?'

'My life was made impossible. They wouldn't serve me in the cafés or the shops. People would cross the street if they saw me. For my son's sins I was being ostracized. It was intolerable. I had to get out. And now here I am . . . alone with only the shit and stink of others for company.'

'Do you know Sr Vega?' asked Falcón, seizing his opportunity.

'I know him. He introduced himself about a week after I moved in here. I rather admired him for that. He knew why I'd ended up here. There were photographers in the street. He walked straight past them, welcomed me and offered me the use of his gardener. I asked him over for a drink occasionally and when I had the trouble with the cesspit he gave his opinion, sent round a surveyor and costed it all out for me for nothing.'

'What did you talk about over drinks?'

'Nothing personal, which was a relief. I thought he might be . . . you know, when people come round to your door and want to be your friend. I thought he might have a prurient interest in my son's misfortunes or want to associate himself with me in some way . . . there are plenty of people out there who'd like to add another dimension to their social standing. But Rafael, despite his apparent charm, was enclosed . . . everything went in but not a lot came out on a personal level. If you wanted to talk about politics, that was a different matter. We talked about America after September 11th, for instance. That was interesting because he was always very right wing. I mean, he thought José María Aznar a little too communist for his liking. But then the World Trade Centre came down and he maintained that the Americans had that coming to them.'

'He didn't *like* Americans?' asked Falcón.

'No, no, no, que no. He *liked* Americans. He was very friendly with that couple from next door. Marty is working for him and I'm sure Rafael was interested in fucking his wife.'

'Really?'

'No, I was just being mischievous, or perhaps giving you a more general truth. We'd all like to fuck Maddy Krugman. Have you seen her?'

Falcón nodded.

'What do you think?'

'Why did he think the Americans had it coming to them?'

'He said they were always messing about in other people's politics and when you do that things blow up in your face.'

'Nothing specific then, just bar talk?'

'But quite surprising, given that he liked Americans and he was going there on holiday this summer,' said Ortega, kissing the end of his cigar. 'Another thing he said about Americans was that they're your friends while you're useful to them, and as soon as you stop making money for them or giving them help, they drop you like a stone. Their loyalty is measured, it has no faith in it. I think those were his words.'

'What did you make of that?'

'Judging by his vehemence it seemed to come from direct experience, probably in business, but I never found out what that was.'

'How often have you seen him this year?'

'Two or three times, mostly to do with the cesspit.'

'Did you notice any difference in him since last year?'

Silence, while Ortega smoked with narrowing eyes.

'Has he killed himself?'

'That's what we're trying to determine,' said Falcón. 'So far we have discovered that there was a change in him at the end of last year. He became more preoccupied. He was burning papers at the bottom of his garden.'

'I didn't notice anything, but then our relationship was not intimate. The only thing I remember was in the Corte Inglés in Nervión one day. I came across him picking over leather wallets or something. As I approached to say hello he looked up at me and I could see he was completely spooked, as if I was the ghost of a long-lost relative. I veered away and we didn't speak. That was probably the last time I saw him. A week ago.'

'Have you noticed any regular visitors to the house or any unusual ones?' said Falcón. 'Any night-time visitors?'

'Look, I know I'm here all the time, especially these days with the work not coming my way, but I don't spend my days looking over the fence or squinting between the blinds.'

'What *do* you do with your time?'

'Yes, well, I spend an uncomfortable amount of it inside my own head. More than I should or want to.'

'What did you do last night?'

'I got drunk on my own. A bad habit, I know. I fell asleep right here and woke up freezing cold from the air conditioning at five in the morning.'

'When I asked you about visitors to the Vegas, I didn't mean anything . . .'

'Look, the only regulars I saw were Lucía's parents and the tough bitch from across the road who used to take care of the kid occasionally.'

'The tough bitch?'

'Consuelo Jiménez. You don't want to cross her, Javier. She's the kind that only smiles when she's got a man's balls in a vice.'

'You've had some disagreements?'

'No, no, I just recognize the type.'

'What type is that?' asked Falcón, unable to resist the question.

'The type that doesn't like men but is unfortunately not a lesbian and finds they have to go to men for their demeaning sexual needs. This leaves them in a permanent state of resentment and anger.'

Falcón chewed the end of his pen to stop himself smiling. It sounded as if the great Pablo Ortega had offered his outstanding services and been rebuffed.

'She likes children, that one,' said Ortega. 'She likes little boys running around her legs. The more the better. But as soon as they grow hair . . .'

Ortega grabbed a great tuft of his white chest hair and flicked his head up in disdain. It was a perfect cameo, in which male foolishness and female pride met in the same body. Falcón laughed. Ortega basked in the acclaim from his audience of one.

'You know,' he said, topping up his glass with Cruzcampo, offering it to Falcón who refused, 'the best way to meet women?'

Falcón shook his head.

'Dogs.'

'You have dogs?'

'I have two pugs. A big, burly male called Pavarotti and a smaller, darker-faced female called Callas.'

'Do they sing?'

'No, they crap all over the garden.'

'Where do you keep them?'

'Not in here with my collection all over the floor. They'll cock their leg over a masterpiece and I'll do something unforgivable.'

'Your collection?'

'You don't think I live in this sort of mess all the time? I had to move my collection in here when the cesspit cracked,' said Ortega. 'Anyway, let me finish with the dogs. Pugs are the perfect way to start talking to a lone woman. They're small, unthreatening, a little ugly and amusing. Perfect. They always work with women and children. The children can't resist them.'

'Is that how you met Consuelo Jiménez?'

'*And* Lucía Vega,' he said, winking.

'Perhaps you don't realize this . . . I should have made it clear . . . Sra Vega has been murdered.'

'Murdered?' he said, getting to his feet, beer spilling into his lap.

'She was suffocated with her pillow . . .'

'You mean he killed her and then himself? What about the boy?'

'He was at Sra Jiménez's house at the time.'

'My God . . . this is a tragedy,' he said, going to the window, thumping it with his fist and looking out into the garden for some reassurance.

'What you were saying about Sra Vega . . . You didn't have an affair with her, did you?'

'An affair?' he said, terrible things now occurring to him. 'No, no, no que no. I just met her on that little bit of park, walking the dogs. She's not really my type. She was rather fascinated by my celebrity, that was all.'

'What did you talk about?'

'I don't remember. I think she'd seen me in a play or . . . What *did* we talk about?'

'When did this happen?'

'March some time.'

'You winked when you mentioned her name.'

'That was just some ridiculous braggadocio on my part.'

Falcón's pen hovered over his notebook. He was running some memory footage of fifteen months ago through his mind. The photographs that Raúl Jiménez had hanging on his wall behind his desk in the apartment in the Edificio Presidente. Celebrities who'd dined at his restaurants, but also the people from the town hall, the policemen and the judiciary. And that was where he'd seen Pablo Ortega's face before.

'You knew Raúl Jiménez,' said Falcón.

'Well, I occasionally ate at his restaurants,' said Ortega, relieved.

'I remember you from one of his photographs he kept at home . . . celebrities and important people.'

'I can't think how that happened. Raúl Jiménez loathed the theatre . . . Unless, of course, that's it, my brother, Ignacio, *he* knew Raúl. My brother's company installs air-conditioning systems. Ignacio would ask me to receptions when he wanted to impress people. That must have been it.'

'So you knew Consuelo Jiménez before you moved here?'

'By sight,' said Ortega.

'Have you ever managed to interest Sra Krugman in your dogs?'

'My God, Javier, you're a different breed to the other policemen I've had to deal with.'

'We're just people.'

'The ones I've spoken to are much more methodical,' said Ortega. 'That's an observation, not a criticism.'

'Murder is the greatest aberration of human nature, it brings out some ingenious subterfuges,' said Falcón. 'Methodical thinking does not survive well in that illusory world.'

'*Acting* is the most ingenious subterfuge of all time,' said Ortega. 'Sometimes it's so ingenious we end up not knowing who the fuck we are any more.'

'You should meet some of the murderers I've put away,' said Falcón. 'Some of them have perfected the art of denial to the degree of absolute truth.'

Ortega blinked at that – a horror he hadn't considered before.

'I have to go,' said Falcón.

'You asked me about Sra Krugman and the dogs,' he said, a little desperately.

'She doesn't look like a dog person to me.'

'You're right . . . Now, if I'd had a leopard in a diamond collar . . .'

They left via the sliding doors into the garden. Ortega walked Falcón round to the front gate. They stood in the quiet street away from the stink. A large black car rolled slowly past before picking up speed heading in the direction of Avenida de Kansas City. Ortega followed it with his eyes.

'You know you were asking me about unusual visitors to the Vegas' house?' he said. 'That car's reminded me. That was a BMW 7 series and there was one of those parked outside their house on 6th January.'

'La Noche de Reyes.'

'Which is why I remember the date,' said Ortega. 'But I also remember it because of the nationality of the occupants. These guys *were* unusual. One was huge – fat, powerful, dark-haired and brutal looking. The other one was still heavy and muscular, but he looked a little more human than his friend and he was fair-haired. They spoke and I don't know what was said, but because I'd been to St Petersburg last year I knew that they were Russians.'

Consuelo Jiménez's three children and Mario were playing in the pool in the late afternoon. The screaming, shouting and indefatigable mutual bombardment arrived heavily muffled through the double glazing. Only the occasional patter of water on the glass reminded them of the severity of the child artillery barrage. Javier nursed another beer. Consuelo was halfway down a glass of tinto de verano, a mix of red wine, ice and Casera. She smoked, clicking her thumbnail. Her foot, as always when distracted, was nodding.

'I see you've let Mario join in,' said Falcón.

'I thought it best to let him lose himself in play for a bit,' she said. 'The swimming ban was Rafael's obsession and there doesn't seem much point...'

'I can't remember when I had that kind of energy,' said Falcón.

'There's nothing more beautiful than a child, eyes stung with chlorine, lashes spiked, body trembling under towel with hunger and tiredness. It overwhelms me with happiness.'

'You don't mind me claiming my drink now?' said Falcón. 'When I come back with Mario's aunt...I mean, I'll have to take her back to her parents' house, it wouldn't be the same.'

'As what?'

'As seeing you like this.'

'I have one major advantage over everyone else in this investigation of yours,' said Consuelo. 'I know how you work, Inspector Jefe.'

'You *did* invite me for a drink.'

'We're all part of your world now,' she said. 'Helpless under your merciless observation. How did you get on with the others?'

'I've just spent the last hour or so with Pablo Ortega.'

'Performing, as ever,' said Consuelo. 'I could never marry an actor. I'm a monogamist and they can make a bed feel very crowded.'

'I wouldn't know.'

'No actresses before you married that little truth-seeker... What was her name? Inés. Of course...'

Consuelo stopped.

'Sorry, I should have remembered about Juez Calderón.'

'This is the first time I've worked with him since your husband's murder,' said Falcón. 'He told me today that he and Inés were getting married.'

'Doubly insensitive of me,' said Consuelo. 'But, my God, that's going to be quite a truth-seeking union. A juez *and* a fiscal. Their first born is going to have to become a priest.'

Falcón grunted out a laugh.

'There's nothing you can do about it, Javier,' she said. 'You might as well laugh.'

'Lighten up,' said Falcón. 'That's what Sra Krugman told me to do.'

'She's not exactly a comedy show herself.'

'Has she shown you her photographs?'

'So *sad*,' said Consuelo, making the face of the unhappy clown. 'I've had all that bullshit up to here.'

'Juez Calderón was rather impressed by them,' said Falcón.

'By her ass, you mean.'

'Yes, even all the many Pablo Ortegas stepped down off the pedestal of his ego to pant at her.'

'I knew you had it in you,' said Consuelo.

'I'm angry with Maddy Krugman,' he said. 'And I don't like her.'

'When a man says that it normally means he fancies her.'

'I'll be joining a long queue.'

'And Juez Calderón will be in front of you.'

'You noticed.'

A spectacular bomb by one of the children drenched the window. Consuelo went outside and told them to calm down. Falcón was aware of Mario looking at her as if she was a goddess. She came back in. By the time she'd closed the door the madness had restarted.

'It's a pity that *they* have to become *us*,' she said, looking back to the pool.

'You're not so bad,' said Falcón, the crass words out of his mouth so fast he stared bug-eyed at them, like a disgrace on the carpet. 'I mean, when I said that . . . I meant you were . . .'

'Relax, Javier,' she said. 'Drink some more beer.'

Falcón gulped down the Cruzcampo, bit into a fat olive and put the stone in the tray.

'Did Pablo Ortega ever make a pass at you?' he asked.

'Was that what you were trying to do then?'

'No, that was . . . that was me thinking something and it coming out.'

'Yes, well . . . "You're not so bad,"' she said, quoting him back. 'You'll have to do a lot better than that to improve your sex life. What did Pablo Ortega tell you?'

'How he used his dogs to chat up women.'

'You talked about him panting after Maddy and chatting up women, but I've always assumed he was a closet gay, or maybe just not that interested in sex,' she said. 'The kids love Pavarotti and Callas, but he's never made a pass at me, and I imagine you wouldn't miss a pass from Pablo Ortega when it happened.'

'Why do you think he's gay?'

'It's just a feeling that comes off him when he's with women. He likes them, but he's not interested in them sexually. It's not just me. I've seen him with Maddy as well. He's not panting. He's showing off. He's reminding everybody that he's still potent but it's got nothing to do with sex.'

'He referred to you as a tough bitch,' said Falcón. 'I thought it was because you'd turned him down.'

'Well, I *am* a tough bitch, but I've never been one with him. In fact I've thought that we always got on very well,' she said. 'Since he moved out here he's been coming round for drinks, playing football with the kids, swimming . . .'

'It was unmistakably sexual. He said you only smiled when you had a man's balls in a vice – that sort of thing.'

Consuelo spurted laughter, but she was annoyed, too.

'I can only think that he believes that this is manly talk and that it would never get back to me,' said Consuelo. 'He's underesti-mated your capacity for intimacy, Javier. But then I suppose intimacy between a cop and a . . . whatever. He probably thought he was safe.'

'He knew Raúl, didn't he?' said Falcón. 'I remember seeing him in the photographs behind the desk in your old apartment, but not in the celebrity section.'

'Pablo's brother was the connection,' she said. 'Ignacio had worked for Raúl.'

'I'd like to see Raúl's photographs again, if that's possible.'

'I'll let them know at the office,' she said.

The commercial world of cars – Repsol, Firestone, Renault – flashed past as he drove down Avenida de Kansas City. While the buildings beyond the windscreen throbbed with expended energy, Falcón puzzled over his intimacy with Consuelo Jiménez. He felt comfortable with her. Despite what she referred to as the detective/suspect dynamic, she was now integrated into his past. He thought about her sitting on her sofa in the cool of her house, nodding her foot at the glass, laughing with the children as she rubbed them down with their towels, leading them off to the kitchen for food while he drove into the writhing beast of the metropolis which, beaten by heat, lay panting in its pen.

A sign outside the Estación de Santa Justa at the end of Avenida de Kansas City told him it was 44°C. He parked and staggered through the torpid air into the station. He called Pérez, who told him that he'd persuaded Sr Cabello to leave his wife in intensive care. He was now in Sr Cabello's apartment in Calle de Felipe II in El Porvenir, waiting for the first female member of the Grupo de Homicidios, Policía Cristina Ferrera, to replace him.

Falcón stood at the gates of the platform for the Madrid AVE, with a handwritten piece of paper asking for Carmen Ortiz. A woman with black hair and big brown eyes floating in a pale frightened face approached him. She had two children with her and 'distraught' seemed a mild adjective for her condition.

He drove back to Santa Clara. Carmen Ortiz talked at full tilt all the way, primarily about her husband, who was on a business trip to Barcelona and wouldn't be able to fly down until the following morning. The children sat looking out of the windows as if they were being moved to a more secure prison. Falcón murmured encouragement while Sra Ortiz flooded out the silence.

Consuelo came to the door with Mario clamped to her like a chimpanzee. The boy, after the swim, had retreated into a vulnerable silence. He transferred himself to Carmen with a swiftness that showed his need for human contact. Carmen amazed them with her limitless memory for all kinds of detail from her journey. Consuelo listened, knowing Carmen Ortiz's purpose, which was not to allow one moment's silence in which the calamity of the day could jam its wedge and lever time open to reveal Mario's future of despair and loneliness.

They went to the car. The whole family sat in the back. The children stroked Mario as if he was a damaged kitten. Consuelo leant in and kissed him hard on the head. Falcón almost heard the physical wrench as she pulled back from the car. He knew about the sickening sense of plummet that was forming in the boy's stomach as he started his free fall into motherless chaos. The routine of love was over. The woman who made you has gone. He was filled with pity for the boy. He drove off with his bruised cargo back into the pulsating city.

He took them up to Sr Cabello's apartment, carrying the luggage. They arrived in the apartment like nomads. Sr Cabello sat in a rocking chair with unblinking eyes. His grandchildren animated his lips to a tremble. Mario kicked and fought to hold on to his aunt. Pérez had gone. Falcón and Ferrera withdrew and a whimpering sense of impending doom welled up in the destroyed family.

They went down in the lift. Ferrera sighed with her head to one side as if the pain of the exchange had found its way into her neck and cricked it for good. They drove in silence into the centre of town where Falcón was going to drop her off. She shut the car door and walked back to a crossing. Falcón pulled out and drove around the Plaza Nueva. He turned right into Calle Mendez Nuñez and waited by El Corte Inglés. As he veered away from the Plaza de la Magdalena and prepared to turn down Calle Bailén his mobile went off.

'I don't want to sound like an idiot in my first week,' said Cristina Ferrera, 'but I think you're being followed. It was a blue Seat Cordoba two cars behind you. I got the plates.'

'Phone them through to the Jefatura and get them to give me a call,' said Falcón. 'I'll check it out.'

In the fading light he could still distinguish colour and he picked out the Seat, now only a single car behind him, as he eased past the Hotel Colón. He drove past the tile shop just before his house and turned up the short driveway and parked between the orange trees. He got out. The blue Seat stopped in front of him. It seemed to be a full car. He walked towards it and the car, in no hurry, pulled slowly away. He even had time to see the plates before it turned left past the Hotel Londres on the corner.

The Jefatura called him on his mobile and told him that the registration number reported by Cristina Ferrera did not match a blue Seat Cordoba. He told them to report it to the traffic police to see if they could get lucky.

He opened up the doors to his house, parked the car and closed them. He felt uneasy. His flesh crawled. He stood in the patio and looked around, listening as if he might be being burgled. The noise of distant traffic came to him. He went to the kitchen. Encarnación, his housekeeper, had left him some fish stew in the fridge. He boiled some rice, warmed the stew and drank a glass of cold white wine. He ate facing the door in a strange state of expectancy.

After eating he did something that he hadn't done for a long time. He picked up a bottle of whisky and a tumbler of ice and went to his study. He'd installed a grey velvet chaise longue he'd moved down from one of the upstairs rooms. He lay down on it with a good measure of whisky in the glass, which he rested on his chest. He was exhausted by the day's events but sleep, for many reasons, was a long way off. Falcón drank the whisky more methodically than he approached any of his investigations. He knew what he was doing – it takes some purpose to blot out damage. By the bottom of the third glass he'd worked over Mario Vega's new childhood and Sebastián Ortega's difficult life with a famous father. Now it was Inés's turn. But he was lucky. His body wasn't used to this level of alcohol and he quietly passed out with his cheek on the soft grey pelt of the chaise longue.

7

Thursday, 25th July 2002

The heat did not back off during the night. By the time Falcón arrived at the Jefatura at 7.30 a.m. the street temperature was 36°C and the atmosphere as oppressive as an old régime. The short walk from his car to the office with a hangover like a hatchet buried in his head left him gasping, with odd flashes of light going off behind his eyes.

At one of the desks in the outer office he was surprised to find Inspector Ramírez already at work, two thick fingers poised over the computer keyboard. Falcón had always doubted that he and Ramírez would ever be friends since he'd taken the job that Ramírez had thought should have been his. But he'd been getting on better with his number two in the last four months since he'd started full-time work again. While Falcón had been suspended from duty due to depressive illness, Ramírez had seized the opportunity for command with both hands, only to find that he didn't like it. Its pressures did not suit his personality. Not only did he lack the necessary creative streak to launch a new investigation, but he could be explosive and divisive. In January Falcón had returned to part-time work. By March he had been reinstated as Inspector Jefe full time and Ramírez had been grateful. These developments had reduced the tension within the squad. They now rarely used each other's ranks in addressing each other in private.

'My God,' said Ramírez, 'what happened to you?'

'Buenos días, José Luis. It was a bad day for children, yesterday,' said Falcón. 'I got friendly with the whisky again. How did it go at the hospital?'

Ramírez stared up from the desk and Javier had the vertiginous experience of teetering over two dark, empty lift shafts which led directly to this man's pain and intolerable uncertainty.

72

'I haven't slept,' said Ramírez. 'I've been to early-morning Mass for the first time in thirty years and I've confessed my sins. I've prayed harder than I've ever done in my life – but it doesn't work like that, does it? *This* is my penance. I must watch the sufferings of the innocent.'

He breathed in and covered his cheeks with his hands.

'They're keeping her in for four days to conduct a series of tests,' he said. 'Some of these tests are for very serious conditions like lymphatic cancer and leukaemia. They have no idea what the problem is. She's thirteen years old, Javier, thirteen.'

Ramírez lit a cigarette and smoked with one arm across his chest as if he was holding himself together. He talked about the tests as if he'd already confirmed to himself that she had something serious and the terrible words of future treatment were creeping into his vocabulary – chemotherapy, nausea, hair loss, crashing immune system, risk of infection. Footage came to Falcón's lurid mind of huge-eyed children beneath the perfect domes of their fragile craniums.

His cigarette suddenly tasted foul to Ramírez, who crushed it out and spat the smoke into his lap as if it was responsible for his child's health. Falcón talked him down, reminded him that these were just tests, to stay calm and positive and that he could take any time off that he needed. Ramírez asked to be put to work to stop his endlessly revolving thoughts. Falcón brought him into his office, took another two aspirin and briefed him on the Vega deaths.

Pérez and Ferrera turned up just after 8 a.m. The other two squad members, Baena and Serrano, were out doing a door-to-door. Falcón decided to move on two fronts. He would conduct a house search at the Vega property while Ramírez made a start on Rafael Vega's place of business, interviewing the project managers, the accountant and visiting all the construction sites. They would also have to work on finding the missing gardener, Sergei, and getting more information on the Russians seen by Pablo Ortega on La Noche de Reyes visiting the Vegas' house.

'Where do we look for Sergei?' asked Pérez.

'Well, you can find out if there are any Russians or Ukrainians working on Vega's building sites and ask them, for a start. I doubt he's unique.'

'If we want to search Vega's office, from what you've said about Vázquez, we're going to need a warrant.'

'And we won't get one from a judge unless we can prove suspicious circumstances, for which we'll have to wait until we get the autopsies,' said Falcón. 'I'm going to have to take someone from Lucía's family down to the Instituto to identify the bodies. I'll pick them up probably around midday and see if that scrap of photograph we found in the barbecue means anything to any of them.'

'So until then we rely on the kindness of Sr Vázquez?' said Ramírez.

'He's already told me to talk to the accountant and given me his details,' said Falcón, who turned to Ferrera. 'Did you get anything more on those number plates?'

'What plates?' asked Ramírez.

'Somebody followed me home last night in a blue Seat Cordoba.'

'Any ideas?' asked Ramírez, while Ferrera called the traffic police.

'Too early to say, but they didn't seem too bothered by me or that I saw their plates.'

'They were reported stolen off a VW Golf in Marbella,' said Ferrera. 'Nothing more.'

Falcón and Ferrera picked up the crime scene photographs from Felipe and Jorge and went down to the car. Cristina Ferrera always dressed as if she was about to disappear without trace. She never used make-up and had one piece of jewellery: a crucifix on a chain. Her face was wide and flat with a nose that calmed the traffic of freckles across it. She had watchful brown eyes that moved slowly in her head. She made no physical impact and yet she had a strong presence which had impressed Falcón in her interview. Ramírez had passed over her photograph on the grounds of looks alone, but Falcón's curiosity was piqued. Why should an ex-nun want to become a member of a murder squad? Her prepared answer was that she wanted to be part of a group that was engaged on the side of Good against Evil. Ramírez had warned her that there was nothing theological about murder work, that in fact it was illogical – the result of breakdowns and short circuits in society – and nothing to do with chariot battles in heaven.

'The Inspector Jefe was asking for my reasons as someone who'd been thinking of becoming a nun,' she'd said, coolly. 'It was my naïve belief then that the next best institution after the Church where I could do some good was the police force. My ten years on the streets of Cádiz have taught me that that is possible only on rare occasions.'

Falcón had wanted to give her the job there and then, but Ramírez wasn't finished.

'So why did you leave your *vocation*?'

'I met a man, Inspector. I fell pregnant, we got married and had two children.'

'In that order?' asked Ramírez, and Ferrera had nodded without taking her brown eyes off him.

So, a fallen angel, too. A Bride of Christ who'd found herself more mortal boots. Falcón had made his decision. The transfer from Cádiz had been slow but the few days she'd been with his squad had convinced him that he'd made the right choice. Even Ramírez had taken her out for a coffee, but that was how things changed. Ramírez, with his daughter's mystery illness, had found himself searching for spiritual sustenance rather than the corporeal version he usually hunted for amongst the courts' secretaries, the bar flirts, shopgirls and even, so Falcón suspected, some of the hookers that crossed his path.

Ferrera drove. Falcón preferred to lose himself in vague thoughts that might lead to better ideas. They drove to Santa Clara in silence. Falcón liked her for that resistance to the Andaluz gene for talking non-stop. His thoughts moved in a slow sickly loop. How men were changed by crisis. Ramírez had gone to church. Falcón had never been attracted to it. It made him feel fraudulent. He, like Sr Vega, had gone to the river, whose draw, he had to admit, was not always positive. There had been times when it offered him an alternative solution and he'd had to pull back and rush home to the comfort of whisky.

They pulled up outside the Vegas' house. Falcón used the remote to open the gates to the driveway. The air conditioning was still on in the house. He gave Ferrera a guided tour of the two crime scenes, the rest of the house and the garden with Sergei's accommodation. He profiled the two victims as they progressed. They returned to the crime scenes and went through the police photographs. Falcón filled in what he knew about the lead up to the crisis, but did not particularly emphasize murder or suicide. He wanted Ferrera to look at the crime scenes from the point of view of a woman, to think herself into Lucía Vega's mind by going through her effects and then relive her actions.

He went into Vega's study and sat at the desk below the bullfight poster. The laptop had been removed and was in the lab. There was only the phone and the tape outline of the position of the laptop on the desk. He looked down the list of pre-programmed numbers on the phone. There were office numbers and Vázquez's direct line as well as the Krugmans' and Consuelo's. The last number was void. He picked up the phone and pressed it.

'*Dá . . . zdrastvutye, Vasili,*' said a voice, clearly expecting someone else on the line.

'Your telephone number has been selected in our grand draw,' said Falcón. 'I'm happy to inform you that you and your wife have won a prize. All you have to do is give me your name and address and I will tell you where to go to pick up your wonderful prize.'

'Who are you?' asked the voice in heavily accented Spanish.

'Name and address first, please.'

A hand went over the receiver. Muffled voices came down the line.

'What's the prize?'

'Name and –'

'Tell me the prize,' he said brutally.

'It's a watch for you and your –'

'I've got a watch,' he said, and slammed down the phone.

Falcón made a note to ask Vázquez about these Russians. The desk drawers revealed nothing unusual. The Heckler & Koch had been removed for tests. He opened up the filing cabinets with the keys he'd found the day before. He flicked through the files for telephone, bank, insurance. They were catching on something underneath – a leather-bound loose-leaf diary and address book.

The diary was private. The entries were minimal. Most of the time there was just an 'X' marked next to the hour and they were mostly night-time meetings. Falcón went back to Noche de Reyes and found that there was an 'X' marked there, too. The first daytime meeting was in March with 'Dr A'. In June there were meetings with Dr A and another with Dr D. In the address section he found a list of doctors – Médicos Álvarez, Diego and Rodríguez. He flicked through the diary and found that Dr R was the last doctor to see Vega. He called and arranged to talk to him around midday.

He went through the address section of the book, which contained only names and telephone numbers. Raúl Jiménez's name was there but had been crossed out. As he turned the pages, names he knew leapt out at him. A lot of them he vaguely recalled from the Raúl Jiménez murder investigation – people from the town hall and public works. There was one name though that really took him back to that turbulent time – Eduardo Carvajal. Again it had been crossed out. Like Raúl Jiménez, he was dead. Falcón had never found what linked the two men. All he'd discovered was that Jiménez had rewarded Carvajal via a fake consultancy company during Expo '92 and, at the time of his death in a car crash in 1998 on the Costa del Sol, Carvajal was about to face trial on charges relating to a paedophile ring.

Ortega's name was also in the book and the last name to stand out was one that had him pacing around the house, reminding himself that there was no art on the walls of any significance. Ramón Salgado, who had been one of Seville's best-known art dealers, was also in the book, crossed out. Maybe Vega Construcciones had invested in art or bought a piece for their headquarters, but there was also that disturbing memory of the child pornography they'd discovered on Salgado's hard disk after his brutal murder. In these circles everybody knew each other, links in a golden chain of wealth and influence. Another question for Vázquez.

There were no Russian names in the book. He put it back in the filing cabinet. He moved on to another cabinet which contained box files full of blueprints and photographs of buildings. In the bottom drawer of the third cabinet there was a box file with no reference number. It said simply *Justicia*. In the file there were pages, mostly in English and mostly from this year, which had been extracted from the internet on a range of subjects but primarily concerned with an international system of justice. There were also newspaper articles on the International Criminal Court, the Tribunal that it was designed to replace, the crusading Spanish judge Baltasar Garzón and also the intricacies and possibilities within the Belgian legal system for bringing international war criminals to justice.

The doorbell sounded in the hall. He locked up the cabinet and went to answer it. Sra Krugman was wearing a black linen top and a skirt, bias-cut, with a scarlet silk sash hanging down the side. On the end of her long white arm was a plastic thermos jug.

'I thought you might like some coffee, Inspector Jefe,' she said. 'Spanish strength. None of your American sock water here.'

'I thought there'd been a coffee revolution in America,' he said, thinking other things.

'The levels of penetration have been uneven,' she said. 'It cannot be guaranteed.'

He let her pass, closed the door to the grotesque heat. He didn't want this intrusion. Maddy fetched cups and saucers. He shouted upstairs to Ferrera but she didn't want any coffee. They went into Vega's office and sat at the desk. Maddy smoked and flicked ash into her saucer. She made no attempt at conversation. Her physical, or rather, sexual presence filled the room. Falcón still felt nauseous and he had nothing to say to her. His mind raced as he drank the coffee.

'Do you like bullfights?' she asked, looking above his head just as the silence had reached screaming point.

'I used to go a lot,' he said, 'but I haven't been since . . . for well over a year now.'

'Marty wouldn't take me,' she said, 'so I asked Rafael. We went on several occasions. I didn't understand it, but I liked it.'

'A lot of foreigners don't,' said Falcón.

'I was surprised,' she said, 'at how quickly the violence became tolerable. When I saw the first picador's lance go in I didn't think I'd be able to take it. But, you know, it sharpens your sight. You don't realize how soft focus everyday life is until you've been to a bullfight. Everything stands out. Everything is defined. It's as if the sight of blood and the prospect of death wakes up in us something atavistic. I found myself tuning into a different level of awareness, or rather an old one, that the boredom in our lives has gradually smothered. By the third bull I was quite used to it, the brilliance of the blood welling up from a particularly deep lance wound and cascading down the bull's foreleg wasn't just bearable but electrifying. We must be hard-wired for violence and death, don't you think, Inspector Jefe?'

'I remember a sort of ritualistic thrill on the faces of the Moroccans in Tangier when they killed a sheep for the festival of Aid el Kebir,' said Falcón.

'Bullfighting must be an extension of that,' she said. 'There's ritual, theatre, thrills . . . but there's something else, too. Passion, for instance and, of course . . . sex.'

'Sex?' he said, the whisky lurching in his stomach.

'Those beautiful guys in their tight costumes performing so gracefully with every muscle in their bodies, in the face of terrible danger . . . possible death. That is the ultimate in sexiness, don't you think?'

'That's not the way I see it.'

'How do you see it?'

'I go to see the bulls,' said Falcón. 'The bull is always the central figure. It's his tragedy and the greater his nobility the finer his tragedy will be. The torero is there to shape the performance, to bring out the bull's noble qualities and in the end to dispatch him and give us, the audience, our catharsis.'

'You can tell I'm an American,' she said.

'That's not how everybody sees it,' said Falcón. 'Some toreros believe that they are there to dominate the bull, even to humiliate it and showcase their masculine prowess in the process.'

'I've seen that,' she said, 'when they thrust their genitals at the bull.'

'Ye-e-s,' said Falcón nervously. 'Quite often the spectacle is a travesty, even in the best arenas. There have been Ladies Only nights and other . . .'

'Decadence?' said Maddy, filling in.

'Greek tragedy is quite rare these days,' said Falcón, 'whereas soap opera isn't.'

'So how are we supposed to keep ourselves noble in such a world?'

'You have to concentrate on the big things,' said Falcón. 'Like Love. Compassion. Honour . . . that sort of stuff.'

'It sounds almost medieval now,' she said.

Silence. He heard Ferrera leave the house. She walked in front of the study window.

'You said something to me yesterday in English?' he said, wanting to get rid of her now.

'I don't remember,' she said. 'Did it make you angry?'

'Lighten up. You told me to lighten up.'

'Yes, well, today's a different day,' she said. 'I read your story on the internet last night.'

'Is that why you've come over this morning?'

'I'm not here to scavenge – whatever you might think of my photographs.'

'I thought the stories of your subjects, the causes of their internal struggle, were not your concern.'

'This isn't about my work.'

'Unfortunately this is about mine. I have to get on, Sra Krugman. So, if you'll excuse me . . .' he said.

The front doorbell rang. He went to open it.

'I locked myself out, Inspector Jefe,' said Ferrera.

Maddy Krugman sauntered out between them. Ferrera followed Falcón to the study where he sat back in the chair.

'Tell me,' he said, staring out of the window, wondering what Maddy Krugman was after.

'Sra Vega was a manic depressive,' said Ferrera.

'We know she had trouble sleeping.'

'There's quite a range of drugs in *his* bedside table.'

'That was locked, as I remember, and the keys are here.'

'Lithium, for instance,' said Ferrera. 'He was probably handing the drugs out to her . . . or so he thought. I found a duplicate key in her wardrobe, along with a secret stash of eighteen sleeping pills. There's plenty of evidence of obsessive-compulsive behaviour in there, too. I also found a lot of chocolate in the fridge and more ice cream in the freezer than a small child could possibly eat.'

'What about her relationship with her husband?'

'I doubt they were having sex, given her condition and the fact that he was handing out the drugs to her,' said Ferrera. 'He was probably getting his sex from elsewhere . . . but that didn't stop her buying an extensive range of sexy underwear.'

'What about the child?'

'She had a picture of her and the child just after the birth on her bedside table. She looks fantastic – radiant, beautiful and proud. I think it's a photograph she looked at a lot. It reminded her of the woman she used to be.'

'Postnatal depression?'

'Could be,' said Ferrera. 'She didn't go out much. There's stacks of mail-order catalogues under the bed.'

'She let the child sleep over at a neighbour's house quite often.'

'Difficult to cope when your life runs away from you like that,' said Ferrera, her eyes dropping to the lipstick-smeared coffee cup. 'Was she that neighbour?'

'No, another one,' said Falcón, shaking his head.

'She didn't look the mothering type.'

'So what do *you* think happened here?' asked Falcón.

'There's enough despair in this house to lead you to believe that having decided to kill himself he would have had to kill her to put her out of her misery.'

'Why did he dislocate her jaw?'

'To knock her out?'

'Doesn't that seem too violent? She was probably groggy with sleep anyway.'

'Perhaps he did it as a way of finding the violence in himself,' said Ferrera.

'Or perhaps she heard the death agonies of her husband and surprised the murderer, who then had to deal with her,' said Falcón.

'Where's the pad Sr Vega wrote his note on?'

'Good question. It hasn't been found. But it's possible that it was an old piece of paper he had in his dressing-gown pocket.'

'Who bought the drain cleaner?'

'Not the maid,' said Falcón.

'Do we know when it was bought?'

'Not yet, but if it was from a supermarket it won't be much help.'

'It looks as if Sra Vega was on her own that night, indulging herself as usual,' said Ferrera. 'She spends a lot of time on her own and she's well prepared for it.'

'You're always on your own with mental illness,' said Falcón.

'She has a box of her favourite videos and DVDs. All romantic stuff. There's a DVD still in the machine. She gets the call from her neighbour so the child is taken care of. She has no responsibilities. When did her husband get home?'

'I'm told it was normally quite late . . . around midnight.'

'That would fit: put off coming home to the despair for as long as possible,' said Ferrera. 'Sra Vega probably didn't like seeing him anyway. She heard the car . . . or maybe not through these windows. So she more likely heard him come into the house from the garage. She turned off the DVD and ran upstairs leaving her slippers. He eventually joined her in bed, or at least . . .'

'How do you know he joined her? His pillow was undented in the crime scene shots.'

'But the sheets and covers were pulled out . . . so he might have been about to join her . . .'

'And then been distracted by something else.'

'Do we know from the phone company if there were any more calls after the neighbour rang about the child?'

'Not yet. You can work on that when we get back.'

'The only other oddity I've come across is that in the crime scene photographs he's got his watch on with the face on the outside of his wrist, but in the photos I've seen elsewhere in the house he always wore it with the face on the underside of his wrist.'

'What do you conclude from that?'

'It either worked its way round in his struggle with himself or an assailant,' said Ferrera, 'or the watch has come off and been put back on his wrist by somebody who doesn't know how he wears it.'

'Why would someone want to do that?'

'Well . . . if it came off as a result of a struggle with an assailant whose ultimate aim was to make this look like a suicide it would be less indicative of another person's presence if the watch was on his wrist rather than on the floor.'

'What sort of a strap did his watch have?'

'It seems to be a metal bracelet type, which can come off easily in a struggle or just as easily work its way round a wrist, so . . .'

'Whatever . . . that was a good piece of observation,' said Falcón. 'It might not help us form a case for murder, but it is indicative of the strange circumstances of the crime scene. Now all we've got to do is find the incontrovertible proof that will convince Juez Calderón that we have a case. We know Sr Vega was burning things at the bottom of the garden. What does that imply to you?'

'He was getting rid of things in preparation for something.'

'They were personal things, letters and photographs, and they caused him great distress.'

'So he didn't want them discovered. He was hiding them and now . . .'

'If you were Sr Vega and you wanted to hide something, where would you put it?'

'In my territory – either here in my study or in the butcher's room.'

'I've searched the study,' said Falcón.

They went into the butcher's room. Ferrera turned on the harsh neon lights and Falcón walked around the wooden chopping block putting on latex gloves. They opened up the first freezer cabinet and he started taking out the blocks of meat. When all the meat was out of the cabinets Ferrera crawled into the dark frozen holes with a pen torch in her mouth and a knife to scrape away at the frost on the sides of the freezers. At the back in a corner of the second freezer she found what they were looking for. A plastic package encrusted in ice. She passed it out. They returned the meat to the cabinets.

The package was a small freezer bag with a wire twist at its neck. Inside was an Argentinean passport issued in Buenos Aires in May 2000 in the name of Emilio Cruz. The photo was of Rafael Vega in a pair of old-fashioned heavy-framed glasses. There was also a single key with no label.

'This was an escape route,' said Falcón. 'What are the implications of that?'

'Well, if he had an escape route into the life of Emilio Cruz,' said Ferrera, 'then he'd probably already escaped into the life of Rafael Vega.'

'So we now check Vega's ID card right back to its original issuing office,' said Falcón.

8

Thursday, 25th July 2002

In Consuelo Jiménez's office they sorted through her husband's old photos, finding ones that included Pablo Ortega and/or Rafael Vega. They headed out of the old city to Dr Rodríguez's surgery, which was in a barrio next to Nervión. On the way the Médico Forense called Falcón to say that the autopsies were complete and both bodies ready for identification. Ferrera called Carmen Ortiz and told her to prepare herself to go down to the Instituto Anatómico Forense.

Dr Rodríguez was running late and Falcón sat down with *El País*. He skimmed past a photo of six drowned Moroccans on the beach at Tarifa, victims of another failed attempt to get into Europe. His eye settled on an article about the trial of Slobodan Milosevic at the International Criminal Tribunal in the Hague, or rather a sidebar which was giving an update on a strange continuing phenomenon. Since the beginning of July, when the Rome Statute of the permanent International Criminal Court had entered into force, the Americans, for reasons that were not clear, had been persuading governments who had signed the treaty to declare that they would not press or put up for trial any US citizen for prosecution by the ICC. They gave a list of the countries wavering under American pressure but no more information. The nurse called him in to Dr Rodríguez's consulting room.

The doctor was in his late thirties. He dried his hands on paper towels while inspecting Falcón's credentials. They sat. Falcón told him of Sr Vega's death. The doctor pulled up Vega's file on the computer.

'On 5th July this year you had an appointment with Sr Vega,' said Falcón. 'As far as I can tell, that was the only time you saw him this year.'

'It was the only time ever. He was a new patient. His records came to me from Dr Álvarez.'

'His diary showed that he had an appointment with a Dr Diego before he came to you.'

'The notes came from Dr Álvarez. Maybe he saw a Dr Diego and decided that he wasn't right for him.'

'Was there any indication from the consultation or the notes sent to you by Dr Álvarez that Sr Vega was suicidal?'

'He had some hypertension, but nothing catastrophic. He was suffering from anxiety and he described a number of incidents which sounded like classic panic attacks. He assumed the cause was from pressure of work. According to Dr Álvarez's notes he'd been suffering mild anxiety since the beginning of the year, but it wasn't sufficiently serious to prescribe anything.'

'Did Dr Álvarez mention that Sr Vega's wife had an advanced mental illness? She was taking lithium.'

'He didn't, which I presume means he didn't know about it,' said Rodríguez. 'That would certainly have contributed to Sr Vega's stress.'

'Do you know why Sr Vega stopped seeing Dr Álvarez?'

'There's nothing specific in the notes, but I noticed that Dr Álvarez had been recommending some psychological therapy. When I put this to him myself he was very resistant to the idea, so it's possible they had a disagreement about that.'

'So the mild anxiety was probably developing into something more serious and he was hoping for a different approach from you?'

'My approach was to reduce his anxiety with a mild drug and then, when he was feeling more in control, persuade him into some form of therapy.'

'Did he talk about any sleep problems?'

'He mentioned a sleepwalking incident. His wife had woken up at three in the morning to see him leaving the bedroom. When she questioned him about it the next day he had no recollection of it.'

'So he did talk about his wife?'

'When describing that incident, yes, but he also said his wife could not be relied upon because she took sleeping pills. There was some-thing else that had happened, which had convinced him that the sleepwalking had occurred, but he wouldn't be drawn on it,' said Rodríguez. 'It was the first consultation, remember. I thought there would be time to coax things out of him later.'

'Did you think he was a danger to himself?'

'Obviously I didn't. Mental disturbances of the sort he was suffering are not uncommon. I have to make decisions on the basis of a snapshot of a man's life. He was not extremely agitated, nor was he preternaturally calm – those two extremes being indicators of danger. There was no history of depression. He had come to me from someone else. He seemed to be trying to tackle his problem. He wanted something to reduce his level of anxiety and he didn't want another panic attack. These are all positive signs.'

'It sounds as if he wanted a quick fix. No therapy.'

'Men are more resistant to the idea of discussing their private thoughts or shameful deeds with someone else,' said Rodríguez. 'If their problems can be solved with a pill, so much the better. There are plenty of doctors who believe we are bundles of chemicals and that psychopharmacology is the answer.'

'So, in your opinion, Sr Vega was troubled but not suicidal?'

'It would have been good to have known about his wife,' said Rodríguez. 'If you have pressure at work and no respite at home and possibly no love . . . that is a situation that can tip a troubled mind into despair.'

Falcón sat wedged into the corner of the car, Ferrera driving. He was already questioning his instincts on day two of the investigation. So far there was no conclusive evidence to support a murder inquiry. The suicide option was looking stronger with every interview. Even if there were no matching fibres from the pillow found under Sr Vega's fingernails that was still only an indicator that somebody else might have been there. It wasn't positive proof.

Ramírez called from the offices of Vega Construcciones to say that Sergei was a legal immigrant and Serrano and Baena now had a photograph and were circulating with it around Santa Clara and the Polígono San Pablo.

The Cabellos lived in the penthouse of a block built in the seventies in the upmarket barrio of El Porvenir, opposite the bingo hall on Calle de Felipe II.

'You're never too rich to play bingo,' said Falcón, as they went up to the apartment where Carmen Ortiz was having a hysterical attack. She was in the bedroom with her husband, who had arrived from Barcelona that morning. The Ortiz children, with Mario between them, were sitting on the sofa, subdued. It was the old man, Sr Cabello, who'd answered the door. He led them into the sitting room. Ferrera knelt down with the children and had them playing and giggling in a matter of moments. Sr Cabello went to find his daughter but returned with his son-in-law. They went into the kitchen.

'She doesn't want to see the bodies,' said the son-in-law.

'They'll be behind a glass panel,' said Falcón. 'They'll look as if they're asleep.'

'I'll go,' said Sr Cabello, composed and determined.

'How is your wife?' asked Falcón.

'Stable, but still in intensive care, unconscious. I'd appreciate it if you could take me to the hospital afterwards.'

Falcón sat in the back of the car with Sr Cabello while Ferrera took on the pre-lunch traffic. The old man rested his worker's hands in his lap and stared straight into the intricacies of Ferrera's pinned-up plait.

'When was the last time you saw Lucía?' asked Falcón.

'We were there for Sunday lunch.'

'With Sr Vega?'

'He came for lunch. He'd been out driving his new car.'

'How was your daughter?'

'I think you already know by now that she was not well. She has not been well since Mario was born,' he said. 'It was never easy to see her in that state, but there was nothing extraordinary about that particular lunch. It was the same as always.'

'I am going to have to ask you some questions which might be painful,' said Falcón. 'You are the closest family and it is only through you that we can begin to understand the domestic situation between your daughter and Sr Vega.'

'Did he kill her?' asked Sr Cabello, turning his wounded eyes on Falcón for the first time.

'We don't know. We're hoping for clarification from the autopsy. Do you think he could have killed her?'

'That man was capable of anything,' said Sr Cabello, with no drama, mere fact.

Falcón waited in silence.

'He was a cold man,' said Sr Cabello, 'a ruthless man, a man that never allowed anyone too close. He never talked about his dead parents, or any member of his family. He did not love my daughter, even before her problems when she was a beautiful young woman... when... when she...'

Sr Cabello closed his eyes to memories, his jaw muscles worked over his grief.

'Were you aware of any difference in your son-in-law's behaviour since the beginning of this year?'

'Only that he was even more withdrawn than usual,' said Sr Cabello. 'Whole meals would pass in silence.'

'Did you remark on it?'

'He said it was work, that he was managing too many projects at once. We didn't believe him. My wife was sure he had a woman somewhere and it had all gone wrong.'

'Why did she think that?'

'No reason. She's a woman. She sees things I don't see. She sensed that the trouble was in the heart and not the head.'

'Was there anything specific that led you to believe that he had a mistress?'

'He was not often at home with Lucía. She would go to bed before he arrived back from whatever he was doing and sometimes he would be gone by the time she woke up,' said Sr Cabello. 'So there was that, and the way he had always been with our daughter.'

'His neighbours said that Mario appeared to be very important to him.'

'That is true. He was very fond of the boy... and Lucía found it difficult to cope with his energy as that *puta* of a disease took hold of her mind,' said Cabello. 'No, I don't say that he was all bad, and certainly he would not have appeared bad to an outsider. He understood the necessity for charm. It was only by living close to him that you saw his true nature.'

'When did you spend time with him?'

'On holidays down at the coast. He was supposed to be relaxed then, but in many ways he was worse. Constant company made him uneasy. I think the idea of family made him sick.'

'Do you know what happened to his parents?'

'He said they were killed in a car accident when he was nineteen years old.'

'You know more than his lawyer.'

'He wouldn't tell Carlos Vázquez that sort of thing.'

'He told him that his father had been a butcher,' said Falcón. 'And how he used to punish him.'

'You've seen the room he has in his house,' said Cabello. 'He gave Carlos Vázquez an explanation. He never told me what his father had done to him. You see, he is not a normal man. He is at heart a suspicious man, because he believes that people are like he is himself.'

'Lucía didn't like the butchery?'

'That only started after Mario was born. Before then she didn't mind.'

'Were you surprised that she wanted to marry him?'

'It was a difficult time.'

They were stopped at a traffic light. An African boy walked between the cars, hatless in the full sun, selling newspapers. Sr Cabello seemed to need movement to get himself talking. The lights changed.

'As I told you, Lucía was a beautiful woman,' said Cabello, embarking on a story that he'd built inside himself over years. 'There was no shortage of men who wanted to marry her . . . and she married a man whose father had a large farm outside Córdoba. They went to live in a house on the farm and they were very happy, until Lucía did not conceive. She went for tests. They told her that there was nothing wrong with her and that perhaps they should consider IVF. The husband refused. Lucía always thought that he was afraid to find that *he* had a problem. Things were said in the heat of the moment that could not be undone and the marriage was dissolved. Lucía came back to live with us. She was twenty-eight years old by now and had missed out on the best of her generation.

'I still owned these pieces of agricultural land in and around Seville. They weren't big pieces of land, but some of them were strategic – without them an area could not be successfully developed. A lot of developers knocked on my door and one of the most persistent was a nameless person represented by Carlos Vázquez.

'Lucía had been working for the Banco de Bilbao. They had a caseta at the Feria de Abril every year. Lucía was a beautiful dancer. She lived for the Feria de Abril and went every night, all night. She looked forward to that time of year. It was a week in which she could forget about all her problems and be herself. That's where she met him. He was an important client at the bank.'

'He was twenty years older than her,' said Falcón.

'She'd missed out on her own generation. All the eligible men were taken. She had no interest in what was left. Then an important man took an interest in her. Her superiors at the bank were happy about it. They started to take notice of her. She was promoted. He was already wealthy. He had found his place in the world. There was certainty with him. All these things were very seductive to someone who thought they'd been left on the shelf.'

'What did you think?'

'We told her to make sure that a man of that age still wanted to have a family.'

'Were you surprised that he hadn't been married before?'

'But he had been married before, Inspector Jefe.'

'Yes, I forgot, Sr Vázquez mentioned a death certificate that had to be supplied.'

'We know only that she came from Mexico City. She might have been Mexican, but we're not sure. As always with Rafael, we were told the minimum that was relevant to us.'

'Were you concerned that his reticence was because of a criminal past?'

'Well now, Inspector Jefe, you have uncovered my shame. I was prepared to overlook his reticence. My financial circumstances then were not like they are now. I had land, but no job. Capital, but no income. Rafael Vega solved those difficulties for me. He made me a partner in a business that paid a large sum of money for several plots of my land. We built apartments financed by the Banco de Bilbao and rented them out. He made me wealthy and gave me an income. That's how an old farmer like me lives in a penthouse in El Porvenir.'

'What did Sr Vega get out of it, apart from your daughter's hand in marriage?'

'One of the other plots I sold to him separately was the key that unlocked a very large development for him in Triana. And there was a second plot, which one of his competitors wanted very badly. When that plot came into Rafael's hands they had to sell out to him. It meant that he could be more generous to me than any other developer.'

'So, he didn't *have* to marry your daughter?' said Falcón. 'He was offering you a very sweet deal anyway.'

'I have the mentality of a farmer. That land was only going to go to someone who would marry my eldest daughter. I am old-fashioned and Rafael is a traditionalist. He knew the key to unlock the problem. His meeting of Lucía was no accident. It is my shame that I allowed the business to cloud my judgement of the man. I had no idea how cold a brute he would be to her.'

'Was he violent?'

'Never. If he had beaten her, that would have been the end of it,' said Cabello. 'He reduced her. I mean he . . . this is difficult . . . he was reluctant to perform his marital duties. He implied it was her fault, that she was not making herself attractive to him.'

'One thing . . . did the death certificate of his previous wife give a cause of death?'

'Accidental. He told us she drowned in a swimming pool.'

'Did he have any children from this previous marriage?'

'He said not. He said he wanted children . . . so it was strange that he didn't want to do what was necessary to make them happen.'

'Did you know of any previous relationships here, before he met Lucía?'

'No. Lucía hadn't heard of any either.'

Falcón took out the plastic sachet containing the partial photograph of the girl that Vega had burnt at the bottom of the garden.

'Do you recognize this person?'

Cabello put on glasses, shook his head.

'She looks foreign to me,' he said.

They arrived at the Instituto on Avenida Sánchez Pizjuan and parked in the hospital grounds. Falcón found the Médico Forense, who showed them into the room for the body identification and left them there for a few minutes. Sr Cabello started to pace the room, nervous at what he'd let himself in for – his daughter dead on the slab. The Médico Forense returned and opened the curtains. Sr Cabello stumbled forwards and had to put a hand up on the glass to steady himself. With the fingers of his other hand he dug into his skull through his thinning hair as if he was trying to tear this unnatural image from his brain. He nodded and coughed against the violence of the emotion. Falcón drew him away from the glass. The Médico Forense supplied the paperwork and Sr Cabello put his signature to his daughter's death.

They went outside into the fierce heat and light whose savagery had sucked all colour from everything so that the trees seemed vague, buildings merged with the white sky and only dust looked as if it belonged in this place. Sr Cabello had shrunk in his suit; his thin neck, loose in its collar, jumped and gasped as he tried to swallow what he'd just seen. Falcón shook his hand and eased him into the car. Cristina Ferrera took the old man round to the hospital entrance. Falcón called Calderón and arranged a meeting for seven o'clock to discuss the autopsies.

He went back into the chill of the morgue. He sat with the Médico Forense in his office, the two autopsy reports open on the desk. The doctor puffed on a Ducados whose smoke was sucked up into the air conditioning unit and spat out into the crushing heat.

'Let's start with the easy one,' said the doctor. 'Sra Vega was suffocated to death by the application of a pillow over her face. She was probably unconscious while this was happening, due to a severe slap across the face which dislocated her jaw. It's probable that the heel of the hand made contact with her chin.'

The Médico Forense gave an unintentionally comical slow-motion replay of the blow, his cheek, jowl and lips shunting to one side into a slobbery air kiss.

'Very graphic, Doctor,' said Falcón, smiling.

'Sorry, Inspector Jefe,' he said, more self-conscious now. 'You know how it is. Long days in the company of dead people. The heat. The holidays nearly, nearly there. The family already at the coast. I forget who I'm with sometimes.'

'It's all right, carry on, Doctor. You're helping me,' said Falcón. 'What about time of death? It's important for us to know if she died before or after Sr Vega.'

'I'm not going to be much help to you on that. Their deaths occurred within the same hour. Their body temperatures were nearly the same. Sra Vega was only slightly warmer. The ambient temperatures were the same in the kitchen and the bedroom, but Sr Vega was lying bare chested on a tiled floor while his wife was in bed with her face under a pillow. I wouldn't be able to stand up in court and say with any conviction that she'd died after her husband.'

'All right, what about Sr Vega?'

'He died directly as a result of the ingestion of a corrosive liquid. Cause of death was a combination of effects on his vital organs. He'd suffered renal failure, liver and lung damage . . . It was a real mess in there. The composition of what he ingested is interesting. I seem to remember it was a regular brand of drain cleaner . . .'

'That's right: Harpic.'

'Well, normally those gels are a mixture of caustic soda and disinfectant. The caustic element would be about a third of the contents. Of course, that would do your system no good at all, but it would take time for it to kill a grown man in good health. This product killed him in less than quarter of an hour because it had been powerfully boosted with hydrochloric acid.'

'How easy is that to get hold of?'

'Any hardware store would sell it to you under the name of muriatic acid. It's used for cleaning cement off paving stones, for instance.'

'We'll check his garage,' said Falcón, making a note. 'There's no going back once you've ingested something that strong?'

'Irreparable damage would be done to the throat, digestive tract and, in this case, the lungs as well.'

'How did it get into the lungs?'

'It's very difficult to tell what damage was caused by force or violence and what was caused by the corrosiveness of the liquid. I would say that he, or someone else, had rammed the bottle down his throat. Under those circumstances some of the liquid would inevitably find its way into the lungs. There's evidence of corrosive action in the nasal passages, so product was being coughed up. With the mouth occupied by the bottle the only way out was via the nose.'

'You seem to think he could have accomplished this on his own.'

'I have to say that's doubtful.'

'But not impossible?'

'If you were going to kill yourself in this horrible way I imagine that you would try and put yourself beyond rescue by making sure you ingested as much of the product as possible in the first moments. I think there would be a certain amount of nervousness involved, too . . . and that would cause you to ram the neck of the bottle down your throat. That of course would also set off the gagging mechanism. I think it would be a messy business, unless there was someone holding the bottle in place and holding the victim steady as well.'

'The floor was clean apart from some droplets close to the neck of the bottle.'

'There was spotting on his chest and clothes, but nothing like the quantities you'd expect if he gagged and spurted it out all over.'

'Any evidence of holding – marks on arms, wrist, neck, head?'

'Nothing on the wrists. There are burn marks on the arms in the crooks of his elbows, but the dressing gown had slipped down and it's possible that happened as he writhed in agony on the floor. There are marks on the head and neck, and claw marks on the throat. I would say they are self-inflicted. He had product on his hands. But the marks could just as easily have been made by someone holding him in a kind of neck lock.'

'You know what I'm trying to do here, Doctor,' said Falcón. 'I've got to go back to Juez Calderón and show him conclusive proof that someone else was in the room with Sr Vega, who was responsible for his death. If I can't do that there may well be no murder inquiry. Now, if I'm not mistaken, you think, like me and the forensics, that it was probably murder.'

'But conclusive proof of another party's presence is more difficult,' said the Médico Forense.

'Is there anything that would link Sr Vega to the death of his wife?'

'I didn't find anything. Sr Vega had only his own tissue under his fingernails from clawing at his throat.'

'Anything else?'

'What's the psychological profile of the victims?'

'She was suffering from mental illness,' said Falcón. 'He doesn't seem to have been suicidal, but there are questionable aspects to his mental state.'

Falcón gave a brief resumé of what he'd been told by Dr Rodríguez and how disturbed Vega had been since the beginning of the year.

'I see what you mean,' said the Médico Forense. 'This could go either way.'

'To balance that, the victim had a 9mm handgun, a surveillance system he didn't use and bulletproof windows.'

'Expecting trouble.'

'Or just a nervous, wealthy person close to the Polígono San Pablo.'

'And the unused surveillance system?'

'Nerves again,' said Falcón. 'Maybe his mentally ill wife was paranoid. She showed off to her neighbours about the windows. Or possibly Vega himself wanted to discourage outsiders but not leave a record of people who came to the house.'

'Because he's involved in something criminal?'

'A neighbour saw some Russian visitors who didn't look like they'd come from the Bolshoi.'

'There's plenty of talk about the Russian mafia these days, especially down on the Costa del Sol, but I didn't know they'd reached Seville,' said the Médico Forense.

'This is a nasty way to die, isn't it, Doctor?'

'Revenge or punishment, maybe an example to others. What about his sex life?'

'His father-in-law says he was reluctant to perform his marital duties . . . ever, even before his wife got depressed. The mother-in-law reckoned he was having an affair which went wrong, which was why he'd been so withdrawn since the beginning of the year,' said Falcón. 'Is there anything else I should know?'

'Just one curious thing. He's had some cosmetic surgery done to his eyes and neck. Nothing extraordinary, just bags removed from under the eyes, and skin removed from the neck to tighten up and reveal the jawline.'

'Everybody's having cosmetic surgery these days.'

'That's true, and this is the curious thing. The work is pretty old. Difficult to say exactly how old, but more than ten years.'

9

Thursday, 25th July 2002

On the way back to the Jefatura Falcón drove while Ferrera read the autopsy reports. It was lunchtime, the temperature had now reached 45°C. There was no one on the streets. Cars bulldozed the heat down the shimmering tarmac. When they arrived at the Jefatura he told Ferrera to leave the reports on Ramírez's desk and they would reconvene at 6 p.m.

The heat had broken Falcón's appetite. At home he managed a bowl of gazpacho, of which Encarnación made a daily supply. He could not find the energy, with the heat crammed into every corner of the house, to look through the Jiménez photographs he'd brought in from the car. He went upstairs, stripped and showered and collapsed into the air-conditioned cool of his bedroom. His brain wavered and released images of the day. He lurched into sleep and a recurring dream where he entered a public toilet which was pristine until he flushed it, whereupon it started filling up with sickening quantities of shit until it overflowed. He found himself trapped and had to climb the walls of the cubicle, only to find all the other toilets were doing the same thing so that he felt a rush of nausea followed by a deep animal panic. He woke up, his hair full of sweat and his mind inexplicably latched on to Pablo Ortega until he remembered the actor's cesspit problem.

It was 5.30 p.m. The shower drilled the muck out of his hair and head. His mind tripped forwards and backwards under the pummelling water. He knew why he had dreamt the dream – another investigation, his own past and the past of others all rucked up by the tragedy. What he was unprepared for was his mind's next leap, which told him that he should go and visit Pablo Ortega's son, Sebastián, in prison. This would be nothing to do with his investigation, just a separate mission. The idea made him feel good.

Something creaked open in his chest. He felt more able to breathe.

He took the Jiménez photographs into the study and pulled out the shots of Pablo Ortega. There was one of Pablo smiling and talking to two men. One of these men was obscured by people in the foreground and the other man he did not know. He took the photo with him, put it on the passenger seat.

Ramírez was typing up his report on his interviews in Vega's offices and the latest on the search for Sergei. Falcón told him about the passport in the name of Emilio Cruz and the key. Ramírez took down the details.

'I'll e-mail this to the Argentinean Embassy in Madrid, see what they make of it,' said Ramírez. 'And I'll put a trace right back to the original issuing office on Rafael Vega's ID.'

'Can we get something on that before the weekend?'

'Not in July, but we can try.'

'Any news on Sergei?'

'He was seen some time in the last couple of weeks in a bar on Calle Alvar Nuñez Caleza de Vaca with a woman who was not Spanish and talked the same language as him. The woman had been seen there before and the barman thought she came from the Polígono San Pablo. He also thought she was a hooker. We've got a full description and Serrano and Baena are working with it now.'

Falcón listened to his messages, staring at the photograph he'd brought up from the car. Calderón had postponed their meeting until the following morning. He put a call through to Inspector Jefe Alberto Montes from GRUME (Grupo de Menores), who was responsible for crimes against children, and asked if he could pass by for an informal chat. Ferrera arrived as he was leaving and he told her to work on the phone numbers listed beside calls in and out of the Vegas' house and Rafael Vega's mobile, and then join Serrano and Baena looking for the woman seen with Sergei.

'What about the key we found with the passport in Vega's house?'

'Sergei is more important at this stage. We need a witness,' said Falcón. 'Work on the key if you have time. Start with the banks.'

On the way up to Montes's office he dropped in on Felipe and Jorge in the lab. He talked them through the autopsies. They looked dismal. They had nothing to offer from the crime scene. The pillow had been clean of any sweat or saliva. The only curious thing they'd come across was to do with the note in Vega's hand.

'As his lawyer said, it's clearly his own handwriting, but we thought it interesting that he should describe it as "careful" so I looked at it under the microscope,' said Felipe. 'It's traced over.'

'What do you mean?'

'He'd written it before, which left an indent on the page beneath, then he'd gone back to the pad and traced over the indent . . . as if he wanted to see what had been written.'

'But *he'd* written it in the first place?' said Falcón.

'I can only tell you the facts,' said Felipe.

Alberto Montes was in his early fifties, overweight, with bags under his eyes and a nose that had exploded from excessive drinking. He'd undergone a psychological assessment at the end of last year because of the drinking problem and had somehow got through it. He was looking at early retirement now and seemed anxious to get there. He had been with the Grupo de Libertad Sexual, which investigated adult sex crimes, and GRUME for over fifteen years and held an encyclopaedic knowledge of names and the horrors attached to them. He sat turned away from his desk, looking out of his second-floor window, smoking and presumably thinking of future freedom. He strained water from a plastic cup through his thick moustache as if he was wishing it was whisky. As Falcón reached his desk he swivelled in his chair and refilled the plastic cup.

'Kidney stones, Inspector Jefe,' he said. 'They get me every summer. I've been told to drink six litres of water a day. What can I do for you?'

'Eduardo Carvajal,' said Falcón. 'Remember him?'

'He's burnt on my heart, that guy. He was going to make me famous,' said Montes. 'Why has his name suddenly reappeared?'

'I'm investigating the deaths of Rafael and Lucía Vega.'

'Rafael Vega . . . the constructor?' said Montes.

'Do you know him?'

'I don't get invited to his caseta in the Feria, but I know who he is,' said Montes. 'Did somebody kill him?'

'That's what we're trying to find out. While I was going through his address book I came across Carvajal and it was a name that rang bells from that case I investigated last year – he was known to, and a friend of, Raúl Jiménez. I didn't have time to dig him up then so I thought I'd try now,' said Falcón. 'How was he going to make you famous?'

'He said he was going to give me all the names of everybody who'd been a part of his paedophile ring . . . ever. He promised me the biggest coup of my career. Politicians, actors, lawyers, councillors, businessmen. He said he would bring me the golden key which would open up high society and reveal it for the rotten, stinking egg it really was. And I believed him. I genuinely thought he was going to come through with the information.'

'But he died in a car crash before he could deliver.'

'Well, he came off the road,' said Montes. 'It was late at night, there was alcohol in his system and it was a very tricky series of bends from Ronda to San Pedro de Alcántara . . . but we'll never know.'

'What does that mean?'

'All this is pretty well known, Inspector Jefe. By the time I'd been notified, he'd been buried and the car was a block in a breaker's yard about that big –' said Montes, holding his hands fifty centimetres apart.

'But some people were convicted, weren't they?'

Montes held up four fat fingers with a cigarette burning amongst them.

'And they couldn't help you in the same way that Carvajal could?'

'They only knew each other. They were one cell in the ring,' said Montes. 'They're careful, these people. It's no different to a terrorist outfit or a resistance movement.'

'How did you get to them in the first place?'

'I'm ashamed to have to tell you it was through the FBI,' said Montes. 'We can't even crack our own paedophile rings.'

'So it was international?'

'That's the internet for you,' said Montes. 'The FBI were running a sting operation. They found a couple in Idaho who were managing a child porn site and they took it over. They picked up addresses from all over the world and informed the local authorities in each country. It's good to know that there are a lot of scared paedophiles out there, but I don't think we'll pull in any of the people that Carvajal knew. I'm sure that's all finished.'

'Why?'

'Carvajal was the key man. He was procuring. They knew him. He knew them. But they didn't know each other. There's nothing to hold it together.'

'But what was Carvajal doing out of custody on his own?'

'That was part of the deal negotiated with his lawyer. He was going to pull all the different cells together and we were going to scoop the lot in a series of raids.'

'Did you find out how he was procuring?'

'Not that it did us much good,' said Montes, nodding. 'It was something that was just starting then. The Russian mafia involvement in people trafficking. Prostitution became a big thing for them because they could control the supply. To control the drugs trade they had to fight for territory because they didn't have home-grown heroin or cocaine, but with prostitution they had the goods from the word go. And what's more they found that it was less dangerous and just as lucrative. There was a Romanian girl in here last week who'd been bought and sold seven times. Believe me, Inspector Jefe, we've come full circle and we're back in the slave-trade era.'

'Do you mind just giving me a little resumé about that?'

'The ex-Soviet states are full of people. A lot of them are able and intelligent – university lecturers, technical college instructors, builders, public servants – but hardly any of them can make a living in the post Soviet era. They're trying to live off fifteen to twenty euros a month. We in Europe, and especially in countries like Italy and Spain, don't have *enough* people. I've read reports saying that Spain needs an extra quarter of a million people a year just to keep the country functioning and pay taxes so that the state has money to give me a pension. Supply-and-demand economies are the easiest to understand and are immediately exploited.

'You need a visa to get into Europe. I've heard a lot of Ukrainians cross the border into Poland and get their visas from the embassies in Warsaw. Portugal offers visas quite easily. Spain, because of our Moroccan problem, is more difficult, but it's easy enough to enrol in a language school or something like that. Of course, you need help to do this. This is where the mafia steps in. They will facilitate your journey. They will get you a visa. They will arrange transport. They will charge you a minimum of a thousand dollars per head . . . I can see you're thinking, Inspector Jefe.'

'Fifty people on a bus, less a few thousand in expenses,' said Falcón. 'It's not difficult to see how well that works.'

'They're taking at least forty-five thousand dollars a busload,' said Montes. 'But it doesn't stop there because with a bit of intimidation these are people who can also be put to work for you when they reach their destination. The mafia gangs pick them off. The women and children go into prostitution and the men go into forced labour. It's happening everywhere – London, Paris, Berlin, Prague. A friend of mine was on holiday outside Barcelona last month and on the road going into Roses there was a line of beautiful girls waving him down . . . and they weren't hitchhikers.'

'What sort of work do the men get put into?'

'Factory work, sweatshops, building sites, warehouses, driving jobs – anything menial. They're even in the greenhouses in the flat-lands out towards Huelva. There are girls out there, too.'

'Four or five years ago prostitution was something you came across only if you wanted to, or if you took a wrong turn in the city. The red-light districts were confined. Now you can go to a garage in the middle of nowhere and find a girl "working".'

Montes lit another cigarette while crushing out the one he'd been smoking.

'Now I know that I'm too old for this work. It's not a challenge any more. It's something that's become overwhelming, something that's got the better of me,' said Montes. 'You said you had another question, Inspector Jefe. Hurry up before I lose myself in despair and throw myself into the car park.'

Falcón faltered over that because he could see the man's weariness, feel his ingrained fatigue and colossal disappointment.

'Just kidding, Inspector Jefe,' said Montes. 'I'm too close to the end. I feel sorry for the mid-career guys. They've got a long haul.'

'I was going to ask you about Sebastián Ortega, but it can wait for another time.'

'No, no . . . it's no problem, really, Inspector Jefe. I just need my annual holiday,' said Montes. 'Sebastián Ortega – what about him?'

'Pablo Ortega is Rafael Vega's next-door neighbour. The Juez de Instrucción on the case is Esteban Calderón.'

'Aha, yes, well, I shouldn't bring those two together in the same room.'

'What happened? It sounds like a strange case.'

'Which version did you hear?'

'I see ... it's that complicated,' said Falcón. 'I heard that he kidnapped the boy, sexually abused him over a number of days and released him. He then waited for the police to come and arrest him.'

'That's what they pinned on him in court – abduction and sexual assault, which was why Juez Calderón and the fiscal managed to get him put away for twelve years,' said Montes. 'I didn't work the case, so this is only what I heard, but I know it's true. Having said that, the only video statement you'll see in the file is the official one used in court,' said Montes. 'First of all, Sebastián Ortega did not make life easy for himself. He said nothing about what he'd done. He never put his own version of events out there. So, when there's nothing to contradict, people feel they have an imaginative licence.

'Question number one: why did he abduct the boy? Question number two: why did he have a specially prepared room in which to keep his prisoner? Question number three: why did he tie the boy up? And the answer to all those questions, in the minds of the investigators and prosecutors, was that Sebastián Ortega planned and carried out his action in order to give himself the opportunity to sexually abuse this boy at will. Except ... he didn't.'

'He didn't what?'

'He didn't sexually abuse him ... or rather there was no evidence of it, and the boy also said that Sebastián Ortega didn't touch him in that way,' said Montes. 'Then, I think, the judge had a word with the investigators, who spoke to the boy's parents. And in the subsequent video the victim's statement became more persuasive or imaginative, whichever you prefer.'

'So what was the purpose of the abduction?'

'They knew each other. They were from the same barrio. I hesitate to call them friends because of the age difference, but that is more or less what they were. So Sebastián Ortega didn't exactly have to abduct him. He invited him to his flat. Then things got a bit strange, as far as I can make out. He kept him in this closed-off room he had already built and tied him up. But in the initial interview the boy said that, although he was frightened by Ortega's strangeness, he was not hurt or touched in a sexual manner.'

'I don't get it,' said Falcón. 'So what did Sebastián do?'

'He read children's stories to him. He sang songs ... he wasn't a bad guitarist, apparently. He made him meals, let him drink as much Coca Cola as he wanted.'

'Why did he tie him up?'

'Because the boy said he had to go home or his father would be angry.'

'And this went on for some days?'

'Everybody outside was going crazy looking for the boy. The parents even called Sebastián, who said he was sorry but he hadn't seen the boy . . . Manolo was his name, I think. Then one day he just gave up . . . He let the boy go, sat on the bed and waited for retribution.'

'And none of this came out in court?'

'Some of it did, but obviously the prosecution's emphasis was not the same as mine. They made Sebastián out to be more aggressive and predatory.'

'What do you make of it?'

'I think Sebastián Ortega is a disturbed young man who should probably not be in prison. He did something wrong, but not twelve years' worth of wrong.'

'And your investigators?'

'The real story was too strange. If you were experienced you could possibly handle it in such a way as to bring the truth to light, but it was summer, the two investigators were young and they were uncertain and that made them malleable. The media interest in the case because of Pablo Ortega introduced some pressure. They didn't want to appear stupid and, like Juez Calderón, they were excited by a high-profile conviction.'

'What do you think of the Juez's role in this case?'

'None of my business . . . officially,' said Montes. 'But personally I think his vanity got the better of him. He was riding high after your case. The media coverage of that was incredible. He's young, good-looking, good family with all the right connections and . . . Yes, well, that's it.'

'What were you going to say?'

'I only just remembered in time about his new wife . . . I'm sorry.'

'So that's got out already, has it?'

'We knew it before he did.'

'Do you think Juez Calderón knew the reality of the case?'

'I don't know *what* went through his mind. There were lots of unofficial discussions about it between him and my men. He *said* that he thought the whole thing was a ludicrous fantasy planted in the boy's head by a manipulative brute. The court would not believe a word of it. He said it would be better for the boy to give a clearer and less ambiguous account of what had happened to him. The investigators talked to the parents and the boy did what he was told.'

'Where were you in all this?'

'Off sick. Hernia operation.'

'It doesn't sound as if justice was done.'

'To be fair, as I told you earlier, Sebastián Ortega did not contest any of the facts that came out in the boy's video interview shown in court. He did not defend himself at all. There should be the possibility of an appeal, but as far as I know Sebastián Ortega does not want that. I get the impression that for some reason Sebastián is where he wants to be.'

'Do you think he should get some psychological help?'

'Yes, but he won't. I'm told he doesn't speak any more. He's gone into solitary confinement and communicates the absolute minimum.'

Falcón stood up to leave.

'Tell me, do you recognize any of the men in this photograph?' he said, and laid down the Ortega shot on Montes's desk.

'My God, there he is, the *hijo de puta*. That's Eduardo Carvajal. And if I'm not mistaken he's talking to Pablo Ortega and somebody I can't see,' said Montes. 'I should get him out of my sight unless you want to see a grown man cry, Inspector Jefe.'

'Thanks for that,' said Falcón, picking up the photograph.

They shook hands and he headed for the door.

'What work did Eduardo Carvajal do, by the way?' he said, reaching for the door handle.

'He was a property consultant,' said Montes, whose face had turned haggard again after its relative calm during the Ortega discussion. 'He used to work for Raúl Jiménez, here in Seville in the construction business, until the late seventies, early eighties. He was from a wealthy family who had a lot of property in the Marbella area. When he left Raúl Jiménez he developed that land and sold it off. He made contacts. He knew all the right people. He started finding holiday companies plots of land to build hotels. He had the town halls eating out of his hand, so all the building permissions and the licences went through and he had the connections for the finance. He made a fortune.'

'So his big promise to you was entirely believable?'

'Completely.'

Falcón nodded, opened the door.

'On the Ortega case,' said Montes. 'I don't attach any blame to my men – which doesn't mean I haven't spoken to them about how to handle it next time, but you need to be strong to stand up to the sort of gilded personality that is Juez Calderón.'

'And it's his job to put together a case that will give the fiscales the best chance of success in court,' said Falcón. 'That's where very tricky moral decisions have to be made and Juez Calderón is a very able man.'

'You like him, Inspector Jefe,' said Montes. 'I'd never have thought it.'

'I've only worked with him once . . . on the Raúl Jiménez case. He handled it very well. He handled *me* very well when I was not in a fit state to be running an investigation.'

'Success changes a man,' said Montes. 'Some people are destined for a very high form of it. Others, like me, have reached their level and have to be content with it or go mad. Juez Calderón isn't even forty years old and yet he's achieved things that some judges never do in an entire career. It's a hard act to maintain . . . to reach even greater heights. Sometimes things have to be forced a little so that the star's distinctive glow retains its brightness. Judgement is affected by ambition and mistakes get made. People like that fall very hard and fast. Do you know why, Inspector Jefe?'

'Because people like to see them broken,' said Falcón.

'I think there are plenty of people out there waiting,' said Montes.

10

Thursday, 25th July 2002

On the way back downstairs he stopped off and picked up Sebastián Ortega's file to take back home with him. In the office Ramírez was still hammering out his report with his big intrusive forefingers. Cristina Ferrera had spoken to the phone company and found that the last call received at the Vegas' house had been from Consuelo Jiménez at around 11 p.m. She'd typed up her report and left. Falcón sat opposite Ramírez, who glared at the screen like a critic inserting exquisitely savage remarks into a review.

'Anything I should know about Rafael Vega's business?'

'He employed Russian and Ukrainian labour,' said Ramírez. 'Some legal like Sergei, some not.'

'How did you find out about the non-legal labour?'

'They didn't turn up for work today – or rather they were told to go away when they did, and that left two projects with skeleton crews.'

'What about the offices?'

'Vázquez wouldn't let us search without a warrant, but he was quite accommodating about Sergei.'

'Did he have anything to say about the labour force?'

'Not his concern. He wasn't running Vega Construcciones day to day. He was just the lawyer ... with a non executive role on the board, which, since Vega's death, has become executive.'

'Did you see the accountant – Sr Dourado?'

'The Golden Boy. Yes, we saw him. He explained the business to us and showed us the accounts.'

'Did he explain how the illegal labour force was being dealt with in the numbers?'

'We're not at the specifics stage of the investigation. We were talking in more general terms about structure, finding out if the company was solvent, if there were any financial time bombs, or if there was some nasty penalty clause from a project which was eating into profits.'

'Talk me through the structure of the company.'

'Vega Construcciones is the holding company for a collection of separate projects. Each project is a company with its own board, comprising a representative from Vega Construcciones, someone from the investors/venture capitalists, and someone from the financial institution providing the backing. I suppose it's to stop a fuck-up in one project bringing down the whole company,' said Ramírez. 'Anyway, the holding company has shown a decent profit for the last three years and there didn't seem to be anything going badly wrong with any of the current projects. There was no catastrophe pending. If it was a business problem that resulted in his death, it's more likely to have been something to do with the partners in the projects.'

'Did you see any names?'

'Not yet,' said Ramírez. 'How did it go at the Instituto?'

'Take a look when you're finished. There's nothing really meaty in there that would persuade a judge that it was definitely a murder. We're going to have to work hard to find a motive from Vega's three closest neighbours, who all seemed to be benefiting from their relationship with him and who were all at home last night asleep, as you'd expect. That's why we have to find Sergei. He was closest to the crime scene. If anybody saw anything, he did.'

'I haven't had a good look at that passport yet, but someone who's totally innocent doesn't keep a false document in their freezer,' said Ramírez. 'You've already had people drifting past your front door with stolen plates, and the smell of Russians is very strong down at Vega Construcciones. So we know there's something in this case that's not right. We're finding things out every day. Eventually one of those things will be a motive.'

'I've got to go,' said Falcón, looking at his watch.

'Oh, yes, shrink night tonight. Maybe I'll have to start seeing her,' said Ramírez, grinning, tapping his temple. 'She can help me straighten out my noodles.'

'Still no news on your daughter?'

'Not until they're completely finished.'

Falcón drove home. He needed another shower and time to relax before he saw Alicia Aguado. As he came into the house he had the same sense of unease he'd had the night before. He found himself listening again.

He dumped the Ortega file in his study and went upstairs, showered and changed into jeans and a black T-shirt. He came back down to the kitchen and drank water. He went to his study and lay down on the chaise longue. He did some breathing exercises and was beginning to feel quite calm when he was transfixed by something alien on the pinboard above his desk which he hadn't seen earlier. He got up slowly, as if stealth was important. He walked in a crouch to his desk and leaned against it. On the board was a photograph of Inés. It had been stuck there by a pin with a red plastic head which pierced her throat.

By 9.30 p.m. he was sitting in the S-shaped chair in Alicia Aguado's consulting room. She put her fingers to his wrist. She needed this technique even more now that she'd lost the last vestiges of her sight to retinitis pigmentosa.

'You're tired,' she said.

'I'm at the end of the second day of a new investigation,' he said. 'A double death and lots of emotional upheaval.'

'You're anxious again.'

'I had another "shit" dream during my siesta,' said Falcón. 'They always come in the afternoons.'

'We've talked about them before,' she said. 'So what are you anxious about?'

'The shit dream was different this time. I woke up with a clear idea in my head and a sense of purpose.'

He told her about the Sebastián Ortega case, what he knew about it at the time of the dream (including the state of Pablo Ortega's house), and what he discovered subsequently from Montes.

'Is that a common occurrence?'

'Quite often evidence that's not admissible in court shows unquestionable proof of a defendant's guilt,' said Falcón defensively. 'Police and prosecutors will then use nuance and emphasis to secure the "right" conviction.'

'But that's not the case here, is it?' said Aguado. 'A victim has been manipulated to give an exaggerated account of what happened to him. Who was the judge on the case?'

'The conviction was never in doubt. What they wanted to secure was the maximum sentence, but...I don't want to get into specifics and personalities,' said Falcón. 'The point was that I didn't know about that before the dream and yet I woke up with a strong sense of wanting to help this young man, who is not connected to me in any way.'

'That's good,' said Aguado.

'I think so, too. It's the most boring thing about depression – the time you have to spend with yourself,' said Falcón. 'I'm glad to be breaking out of my self-absorption.'

'What drew you to Sebastián Ortega's predicament?'

'There are some interesting connections there. Pablo Ortega knew Francisco Falcón. He was a friend of his. He had even met me before, when I was eighteen, but I didn't remember him. Like Francisco, he's charismatic and someone who can summon up tremendous fury. He also said things which I subsequently found out were not true. It was quite difficult to disentangle the truth from performance. It's possible that he is hiding things from himself. In a later interview someone said that they'd always assumed that he was either homosexual or asexual.'

'My God...we *are* talking about Pablo Ortega the actor, aren't we?'

'Yes, but don't go ringing the *Diario de Sevilla*,' said Falcón. 'He'd kill himself if that broke.'

'I can see the comparisons with your own situation,' she said.

'I think I've subconsciously identified with Sebastián, which is why I want to help him.'

'Because?'

'Because I want to help myself.'

'This is good, Javier,' said Aguado. 'I just want to go back to Pablo Ortega...'

'That stuff about him being homosexual – there's no proof. It was just something that this particular interviewee had always assumed to be the case.'

'That's not what concerns me,' she said. 'Why was Pablo Ortega so angry?'

'He was furious at Juez Calderón...'

'So he was the judge on Sebastián Ortega's case as well?'

'You found me out.'

'I thought there was something more complicated at work there.'

'If there is, I don't know *what* it is.'

'I remember you saying while you were investigating the Jiménez murder that you liked Juez Calderón. You told me that he was one of the first people you'd considered a possible friend since your training in Barcelona.'

'That was before I knew he was seeing Inés.'

Her fingers jumped off his pulse as he said her name.

'Has something happened with Inés?'

'Yesterday he told me they were getting married,' said Falcón. 'I nearly called you.'

'We've dealt with Inés.'

'I thought we had.'

'You were expecting them to get married,' said Alicia Aguado. 'And you told me that you'd accepted it.'

'The concept, yes.'

'And the reality was different?'

'I was surprised at how bitterly disappointed I was by the news.'

'You'll get over it.'

'That's why I didn't call you,' said Falcón. 'But just before I came out to see you this evening I found a photograph of her stuck up on the noticeboard above my desk with a red pin through her throat.'

Silence. Falcón thought he felt Alicia shiver.

'Did *you* stick it up there?' she asked.

'That's what concerns me,' said Falcón. 'I don't know.'

'Do you think you might have done it subconsciously?' asked Aguado.

'I don't even recognize the photograph.'

'What about the other prints?'

'I bought a digital camera last week. Work has been slack until yesterday and I've been out on the streets taking snaps, getting used to the technology and then downloading stuff on to the computer, erasing shots, printing out others, throwing some stuff away. You know, playing around with it. So. . .I. . .I just can't be certain. Maybe I did snap her without realizing it. We don't live that far from each other. I see her occasionally in the street, as you do in Seville.'

'How else could it have got on to your noticeboard?'

'I don't know. I did get very drunk last night and passed out . . .'

'You shouldn't let this worry you,' said Aguado.

'But what do you think it means?' said Falcón. 'I don't like the idea that my mind is operating independently of me. This was what was happening to one of the victims in my investigation.'

Falcón explained Vega's bizarre note, how he'd traced over it.

'The positive side of this incident is that it seems to indicate that by pinning Inés by her throat to your board you're releasing yourself from this hold you believe she has over you.'

'Well, that's one interpretation,' said Falcón. 'There could be some darker ones.'

'Don't dwell on it. You're on the move. Keep up the momentum.'

'All right, let's talk about something else – Sebastián Ortega. What do you think about his behaviour, psychologically? Why did he do what he did?'

'I'd need to know a lot more about him and the case before I ventured an opinion on that.'

'My theory is that he was reliving an ideal,' said Falcón. 'He was being to the boy what he'd wanted his father to be to him.'

'I can't comment.'

'I'm not asking you for a serious professional opinion.'

'And I don't give amateur ones.'

'OK, so what shall we talk about that's not Inés?'

'Talk to me some more about Juez Calderón.'

'I don't know what I think about him any more,' he said. 'I'm confused. Initially I was attracted by his intelligence and sensitivity. Then I found out that he had a relationship with Inés, which I couldn't and can't talk about with him. Now they're getting married. I've watched his star consistently rising, but then I hear from others that it's vanity propelling this trajectory . . .'

'I think you missed something out.'

'I don't think so.'

'Has Juez Calderón done something to you?'

'Not to me,' said Falcón. 'I can't talk about it yet.'

'Not even to your clinical psychologist, who you've been seeing for over a year?'

'No . . . not yet. I can't be certain about it,' said Falcón. 'It could have just been a moment's madness, now forgotten, or there could be clearer intent.'

'To do someone wrong?'

'Not wrong exactly . . . although it would be wrong,' said Falcón. 'All I can promise you is that it has nothing to do with me.'

The appointment finished soon after. Before walking Javier to the door she deviated to a cabinet, fumbled around and took out a dictaphone.

'I don't mind thinking about Sebastián Ortega for you,' she said. 'My summer is quiet. Since my blindness has become complete I've been getting agoraphobic. The idea of hundreds of people on the beach, and me amongst them, makes me feel nervous. I'm staying in town, despite the heat. Put everything you know down on tape and I'll listen to it.'

She gave him the dictaphone and some tapes. Javier shook her cool white hand, their professional relationship never having got beyond this formality, apart from some madness on his part in the early stages of treatment. But this time she pulled him to her and kissed him on both cheeks.

'Good night, Javier,' she said, as he walked down the stairs. 'And remember: the important thing is that you're a good man.'

Falcón left the coolness of her consulting room and stepped into the thick heat in the street. He walked and did what Alicia had told him not to do. He dwelt on that photograph of Inés pinned to his board. Without thinking, he crossed a road and found himself in front of the Old Tobacco Factory, which had now been incorporated into the university. He'd overshot the Edificio de los Juzgados where he'd parked the car. He crossed Avenida del Cid and backtracked through the walkways of the Palacio de Justicia. Someone called his name. The sound of the voice was like a woman's hands coming up his chest from behind. The skipping heels on the pavement told him before he'd turned that he was going to see Inés.

'Congratulations,' he said, his lips fluffing the word.

She looked blank as they kissed hello.

'Esteban told me yesterday,' said Falcón.

She put her hand to her mouth as if that would obscure her memory struggle and then rolled her eyes.

'I'm sorry. I wasn't thinking,' she said. 'Thank you, Javier.'

'I'm very happy for you,' he said. 'Isn't it a bit late for you to be working?'

'Esteban told me to meet him here at 9.30. Have you seen him today?' she asked.

'He postponed our meeting until tomorrow.'

'He's always here at this time of night. I don't know what could. . .'

'What did the security guard say?'

'That he left at six and hasn't been back.'

'You've tried his mobile?'

'It's switched off. He switches it off all the time now. Too many people want to talk to him,' she said.

'Well . . . can I give you a lift somewhere?'

Inés left a message with the security guard and they got into Falcón's car. They drove down Cristobal Colón and agreed to have a tapa in El Cairo on Reyes Católicos.

They sat at the bar and ordered beers and a tapa of piquillo peppers stuffed with hake. He asked her about the wedding. She spoke with her mind only half on the job, looking at every face that walked by the window. Falcón sipped his beer and murmured encouragement until she turned on him and gripped his knee with her long white manicured nails.

'Has he been all right?' she asked. 'You know . . . in his work.'

'I don't know. I've been working this case with him out in Santa Clara, but only since yesterday.'

'Santa Clara?'

'At the end of Avenida de Kansas City.'

'I know where Santa Clara is,' she said, annoyed, but her irritation instantly broke and she was staring at him with her big brown eyes in the way that she did when she wanted something. 'He said . . . he said . . .'

'What, Inés?'

'Nothing,' she said, and released his knee. 'He seems a little anxious recently.'

'Only because he's made it official now: the announcement.'

'What difference does that make?' she said, hanging on Falcón's every syllable, desperate for insight into the male psyche.

'You know . . . total commitment . . . no going back.'

'He was committed before.'

'It's official . . . confirmed to the world. It can make a man nervous, that sort of thing. You know, The End of Youth. No more playing around. Family. Adult responsibilities – all that stuff.'

'I see,' she said, not seeing it at all. 'You mean there's doubt?'

'No, no, no que no,' said Falcón. 'There's no doubt, just a nervousness at the prospect of change. He's thirty-seven, never been married before. It's just a reaction to the future physical and emotional upheaval.'

'Physical?' she said, sitting on the edge of her seat.

'You're not going to stay in his apartment, are you?' said Falcón. 'You'll get a house . . . start a family.'

'Did Esteban talk to you about this?' she said, searching his face for the least sign of a tic.

'I'm the last person . . .'

'We'd always said that we'd buy a place in the centre of town,' she said. 'We wanted to be in the old city in a big house like yours . . . maybe not so mad and enormous, but in that classic style. I've been looking for months . . . mostly at old properties that need work, and guess what Esteban said last night?'

'That he's found somewhere?' said Falcón, unable to stop the thought flashing through his mind that Inés had only married him for his house.

'That *he* wants to live in Santa Clara.'

Falcón stared into those big frightened eyes and felt something like slow-motion wreckage forming in his mind. Consonants caught in his throat like fish bones.

'Exactly,' she said, leaning back, almost in triumph, 'it's the antithesis of what we'd always talked about.'

Falcón drained his beer, ordered more, stuffed the pepper into his mouth messily.

'What does it mean, Javier?'

'It means,' he said, hurtling towards tragic revelations and veering off at the last moment, 'it means that it's part of the emotional upheaval. When everything in your life changes at once . . . you change with it . . . but more slowly. I know. I've become an expert in these matters of change.'

She nodded, gulping the words down into her chest where she could treasure them until her eyes flickered and she shot off the bar stool and leapt at the door.

'Esteban!' she roared down the street, better than any fishwife.

Calderón stopped as if he'd been knifed in the chest. He turned and Falcón expected to see the hilt jutting out of his ribs, but instead he saw – in the moments before Calderón could compose his face – fear, loss, contempt and a strange wildness, as if the man had been lost for days in the mountains. Then the judge smiled and the radiance shone out of him. She went to him. He went to her. They kissed madly in the street. An old couple sitting in the window nodded their approval. Falcón blinked at the fraudulence on display.

Inés hauled him into the bar. Calderón's step faltered as he saw Falcón perched on his bar stool. The three of them explained everything to each other twice without listening to a word. Beers shot down throats. Topics came and went. Inés and Calderón left after minutes. Falcón studied the sinew standing out of Inés's forearm as she gripped her fiancé's shirt. It was desperate. She was never letting go of this one.

The bill came. He paid it and drove home. Every light turned to red. The cobbles jolted his insides. Despite his tiredness he had no patience for bed. He went to his study and booted up the computer. He went through all the shots he'd taken since the weekend. He kept looking at the snap of Inés, seeing if it fitted with any of the others, seeing if he could remember it. It didn't help. He found the whisky, poured himself a single glass and left the bottle in the kitchen.

He was about to shut the computer down when he remembered Maddy Krugman telling him that she'd read his story on the internet. He logged on and entered her name into a search engine. There were several thousand hits, mostly for a political commentator called John Krugman and a journalist for the *New York Times* called Paul Krugman. Falcón entered Madeleine Coren into the search engine. There were only three hundred hits and he quite quickly started to find references to her photographic work. They were mainly old articles and a few reviews of her exhibitions, but they always featured a shot of the stunningly beautiful young Madeleine Coren, who looked cool, unapproachable and dressed exclusively in black. He was butting up against his boredom when a small piece from the *St Louis Times* caught his eye. FBI murder inquiry: Madeleine Coren, photographer, has been helping the FBI with their inquiries into the murder of Iranian-born carpet dealer Reza Sangari. The article appeared under the local news section and was dated 15th October 2000.

Madeleine Coren in FBI Murder Inquiry

The New York photographer Maddy Coren has been helping
the FBI with their murder inquiry following the discovery of
Reza Sangari's bludgeoned body in his Lower East Side apart-
ment. The FBI could not reveal why they were talking to Ms
Coren in connection with the Iranian carpet dealer's murder.
They have only stated that no charges have been brought
against the thirty-six-year-old photographer whose latest show
'Minute Lives' has just moved from the St Louis Art Museum.
John and Martha Coren, who still live in Belleville, St Clair
would make no comment on their daughter's FBI interview.
Maddy Coren currently lives in Connecticut with her husband,
the architect Martin Krugman.

The journalist's name was Dan Fineman and after reading it
through a few times Falcón began to pick up the slightly mischievous tone of the piece. Its newsworthiness was hardly worth the
column inches. He entered 'Minute Lives' into the search engine
and a review came up with the headline 'Short on content. Small in
stature.' The by-line was the same Dan Fineman. A man with a
grudge.

Falcón typed Reza Sangari into the search engine. His murder
had been well covered at a local and national level, and from these
articles he was able to piece together the full story.

Reza Sangari was just thirty years old. He was born in Tehran.
His mother was from a banking family and his father originally ran
his own carpet factory until they left prior to the Iranian revolution
in 1979. Reza was brought up in Switzerland but went to the USA
to study Art History at Columbia University. After graduation he
bought a warehouse on the Lower East Side from which he developed his carpet import and sales business. He converted the second
floor into an apartment, which was where his dead body was found
on 13th October 2000. He had been murdered three days earlier;
he had taken two blows to the head with a blunt instrument, which
had not killed him, but he had fallen sideways on to a brass bedstead
which had. The weapon that caused the first wounds was never
found. Because of the wide-ranging nature of the investigation and
Sangari's international client list the FBI took over from the New

York homicide cops and contacted all his clients and social acquaintances. They found he was seeing a number of women but not one in particular. There was no evidence of a break-in and nothing obvious had been stolen. There was nothing missing from the inventory. The FBI had been unable to develop any suspects in the case despite extensive interviews with the women he was seeing at the time of his death. Some of the names of these women had crept into the media because they were famous. They were: Helena Valankova (dress designer), Françoise Lascombs (model) and Madeleine Krugman. The last two were married women.

11

Friday, 26th July 2002

Falcón woke up and reached for a pen and notebook which he kept by the bed to record his dreams. This time he wrote:

She could have found out about the other women and done it.

He could have found out she was having an affair and done it.

Or it could be nothing at all.

He allowed his brain the run of this circuit for a few minutes and then wrote:

He could have killed Reza S. and not told her.

She could have killed Reza S. and not told him.

Or there could be some complicity.

Or it could be nothing at all.

He'd slept badly. The Ortega file was all over the bed, along with Alicia Aguado's dictaphone and tapes. He'd been up for hours, too spooked to go to sleep, and had recorded the Ortega file as he read it. Before he got under the shower he checked the strip of paper he'd stuck over the door. It was unbroken. At least he hadn't been sleepwalking. He let the water pummel his head and some of his frustration left him as a new possibility about Inés's photograph came to him.

The heat in the gallery outside his room smothered him. He looked down on the trickling fountain. He rippled past the pillars on his way to the kitchen. He ate a round of fresh pineapple and some toast drizzled with olive oil. He took his pills. His mind roved around the loneliness of the house. Inés had called it 'mad and enormous', which it was – a sprawling, illogical, labyrinthine expression of the state of Francisco Falcón's bizarre mind.

It came to him with a clarity that must have been obvious to everyone except himself, caught up in his months of self-absorption:

Why live here any more? This is not your house and it will never be your home. Let Manuela have it. The only reason she's pursuing you through the courts is that she'd have to sell everything and take on a huge mortgage to be able to afford it.

He felt free. He started to punch out Manuela's number on his mobile and stopped himself just in time. He'd go through his lawyer, Isabel Cano. No sense in presenting things to Manuela on a plate. When people did that she just demanded more. The mobile rang.

'We have a meeting here at 9 a.m.,' said Calderón, tense and businesslike. 'I'd like you to come to that alone, if you don't mind, Javier.'

On the way to the Jefatura he dropped off the tapes at Alicia Aguado's consulting room in Calle Vidrio. Before going to his office he took the photograph of Inés to the lab along with some blank stock that he'd been using to print out his snaps. He asked Jorge to run a test to see if the paper was the same. Back in his office he read through the reports left on his desk. He collected all the necessary papers for his meeting and put them in his briefcase, separate from his internet findings about Madeleine Krugman née Coren. He put the photograph of Pablo Ortega and Carvajal in there as well. He wanted to see the actor's reaction to it. He called Isabel Cano: still no answer from her office. Ramírez and Ferrera turned up as he was leaving. He told Ramírez that Calderón wanted to see him alone and that he should keep trawling through Vega's offices while the rest of the squad went door-to-door looking for Sergei and/or the mystery woman he'd been seen talking to.

The Edificio de los Juzgados was building up for an active morning. The stink of humanity sweating in hope and fear had reached an animal intensity and there was no air-conditioning unit in the world that could cope. Falcón went up to Calderón's first-floor office, which overlooked the car park and the El Prado de San Sebastián bus station. The judge was smoking. There were six butts already in the ashtray, each one smoked down to the filter. Falcón closed the door. Calderón's eyes were smudged dark underneath. He still had the intense look of someone returning to civilization after an experience in the wild. Falcón laid the autopsies and police reports in front of him and sat down.

Calderón read fast, his lawyer's brain taking in the large quantities of detailed information. He sat back with a freshly lit cigarette and sized up Falcón. He seemed on the brink of saying something personal but veered away from it as if this might be too confrontational too early.

'What do you make of all this then, Javier?' he asked. 'The foundations for the building of a murder case haven't exactly been laid by these autopsies. I'm surprised the Médico Forense wasn't prepared to commit himself more at this stage.'

'Officially,' said Falcón. 'Unofficially, like all of us at the Jefatura, he's extremely doubtful that it was suicide, which is why he doesn't want to release Sr Vega's body for burial just yet.'

'Let's look at the mental states of the deceased,' said Calderón. 'Sra Vega had a serious enough condition that she was taking lithium. Her husband was not only behaving strangely, as we've seen in Madeleine Krugman's photographs, but had also been to see two, possibly three doctors about his anxiety.'

Falcón knew that Calderón had wanted to say her name, had felt the need for its sweetness on his lips and tongue. It decided him that the internet downloads in his briefcase should stay there.

'The crime scene . . .' Falcón started.

'Yes, the crime scene,' said Calderón. 'That seems to be explicable in any number of ways. Suicide or murder, with between one and three people involved in the deaths. You have no suspects. There's not even the vaguest mention of a motive in any report. You have no witnesses. Sergei the gardener is still missing.'

'We're working on that. We have a photo ID and we know he was seen talking to a woman in a bar near the Vegas' house quite recently. We're also going door-to-door in Santa Clara and the Polígono San Pablo,' said Falcón. 'As far as motive goes, we're going to have to work hard on the Russian angle and –'

'Let's not get too excited about the Russians until we know who they are and we've seen the extent of their involvement from the accountant's reports. I know there's a lot of money-laundering going on in Marbella and places along the Costa del Sol, but so far all we've had here in Seville is a sighting by Pablo Ortega of a few Russians making a social visit seven months ago.'

'I was followed home on Wednesday night by a blue Seat with plates stolen in Marbella, and there's Russian and Ukrainian illegal labour on Vega's building sites,' said Falcón. 'There are enough questions over the state of the crime scene, the state of the body, the deceased's relationship with his son and potentially harmful outside influences to justify further inquiry.'

'OK, I take your point about the Russians. Let's try and work that up into something,' said Calderón. 'Sticking with the suicide angle for the moment, what about the boy?'

'Vega's domestic circumstances were not totally desperate. Even Sr Cabello, who has no love for his son-in-law, conceded that Vega was very fond of the boy,' said Falcón.

'He drank acid rather than shoot himself with a gun, which could indicate that he was punishing himself for unknown sins and protecting his son from possibly seeing a violent death. Maybe he killed himself precisely because there was something he couldn't bear his son to know about him,' said Calderón. 'If you had a son, Javier, what could you not bear him to know about you?'

'If he knew that I was a war criminal, I'd find it difficult to face him,' said Falcón. 'The difference between the war criminal and the murderer is that self-knowledge could be possible. Once history had moved on, the war criminal might see that he had been persuaded through a combination of political thought, national fervour and fear to have gone from being an ordinary man to becoming a merciless killer with a sense of duty to the régime and self-righteousness. Later in life, especially if he was being hunted down, he might reflect on what he'd done and feel a deep sense of shame. I could not imagine looking into my son's eyes and have him know that I was capable of such mercilessness.'

Silence. More smoking from the judge.

'We're doing what two law men should never do,' said Calderón.

'Back to business,' said Falcón. 'We found a false passport in one of Vega's freezers. It's Argentinean in the name of Emilio Cruz. We're checking that out and Rafael Vega's ID.'

Calderón nodded, crushed out his cigarette, lit another.

'Vázquez said that Vega's parents were "killed", implying they did not die of natural causes,' said Falcón. 'Who were they? What happened to them? That could be interesting.'

'For background, yes,' said Calderón.

'And there something else that's not in the report. I found a file in Vega's study entitled *Justicia*. Inside there were articles and downloads on criminal courts such as the ICC –'

'There's your war crimes, Javier.'

'– Baltasar Garzón and the Belgian justice system,' said Falcón. 'This is very specific material for someone in the construction industry, even if he did have an interest in current affairs. Put this together with the strange note in his hand at time of death and the false passport, and maybe we're looking at someone who had sensitive information which could do damage to people.'

'Both the Krugmans and Ortega mentioned some anti-American sentiment in their interviews,' said Calderón.

'It didn't seem to be as general as that. I think Vega's anger was more directed towards government. Marty Krugman even said he was pro-America.'

'Whatever, I only mentioned that because the US administration are against the ICC, which is directly related to the post 9/11 world, and there's Vega's weird note, as you said.'

'I read something about that in *El País* yesterday, but I didn't understand why.'

'The bland reason is that the US government doesn't want any of its citizens unfairly prosecuted,' said Calderón. 'The more piquant reason is that the world after 9/11 is in need of more policing. The cops are the US military. The Americans want to reserve the right to decide what's fair. They also don't want any member of the administration indicted for war crimes. They are the most powerful nation on Earth, they're exerting influence wherever they can. Plenty of people don't like their tactics – "If you don't support us, we'll cut military aid." But it's a complex world. Just as one person's freedom fighter is another's terrorist, so one person's fair military target is another's atrocity.'

'Then don't you think an interesting line of inquiry could be to look at why Vega had the remotest interest in the ICC and other judicial systems?'

'I don't know what he was expecting from it, because the ICC only came into being on 1st July this year and it can't look at crimes committed before that date. The Belgian justice system and Baltasar Garzón just means you've got to steer clear of Europe if you're worried about being indicted or arrested. So don't narrow your vision too much, Javier,' said Calderón. 'Keep concentrating on the details as well. Has any muriatic acid been found on the property?'

'Not yet. We haven't been able to fully search the property. My squad is spread all over the place trying to find Sergei as well as looking into Vega's business.'

'You know what I'm looking for: motive, suspect, reliable witness,' said Calderón. 'What I don't want to hear about are things that weren't there. If you don't find any muriatic acid it's only an indicator, it doesn't mean anything. No more . . . ghosts.'

Calderón did a passable imitation of a man drowning at his desk.

'This is why we don't like talking about our hunches in front of judges.'

'I'm being glib,' said Calderón. 'I know you're concentrated on the realities and the facts, but at the moment all we've got is nuance and hint – Russian mafia involvement, Vega's obsession with international courts, the Carvajal paedophile ring . . .'

'We haven't discussed that yet.'

'It's just names in an address book. Some of them are crossed out. There's no meat, Javier. There aren't even skeletons in here, they're just phantasms.'

'There you go again.'

'You know the meat I'm looking for and I'm not letting you launch a full murder investigation until I get it,' said Calderón. 'We'll reconvene for a case update early next week and if you still can't bring me anything that stands up in court then we'll have to move along.'

Calderón sat back, lit another cigarette – the man smoking more than Javier could remember – and became lost in his own thoughts.

'You wanted to see me alone,' said Javier, just to nudge Calderón out of his groove.

'Apart from not wanting Inspector Ramírez thumping me into submission –'

'He's more subdued these days,' said Falcón. 'His daughter's undergoing tests in the hospital.'

'Nothing serious, I hope,' said Calderón, on automatic, the news shooting past him while his mind wrestled with his own predicament. 'I didn't know that you and Inés were still in contact.'

'We're not,' said Falcón, who then gave an absurdly elaborate explanation of how he came to be in El Cairo with her.

'Inés seemed very nervous,' said Calderón.

'Look what happened the last time she got married,' said Falcón, opening his hands, opting to look ridiculous. 'She seemed to be worried that you were having doubts. I –'

'Why would she think I was having doubts?' asked Calderón, and Falcón felt the diamond bits of the judge's drilling mind cut into him.

'She thought you seemed nervous, too.'

'And what did you say to that?'

'That it was quite natural for a man to feel nervous under these circumstances. I myself had felt the same nervousness,' said Falcón. 'And nervousness is easily misinterpreted as doubt.'

'Did you doubt?' asked Calderón.

'I never doubted her,' said Falcón, the sweat streaming down his back.

'That wasn't the question, Javier.'

'I probably did doubt. In retrospect I was probably afraid of change, of my incapacity . . .'

'For what?'

Falcón's chair creaked as he writhed on the skewer of the judge's questions.

'I was a different man then, more distant,' said Falcón. 'That's why I go to the shrink.'

'And now?'

With that last light inquiry, Calderón's cycle was complete. Falcón was almost grateful to receive the implicit warning that he should keep his nose out of the judge's private life.

'It's a long haul,' he said.

Falcón sat at his desk replaying the dialogue. He was relieved that he hadn't brought up the internet downloads about Maddy Krugman. That might have turned Calderón savage. The judge knew that Falcón had seen something. But under their delicate personal circumstances Falcón couldn't start talking about Maddy's involvement in the FBI inquiry until he was certain of the facts. He pitied the two lives he saw on their way to destruction as he dialled his lawyer, Isabel Cano.

She agreed to see him for a maximum of ten minutes. He drove to her small office on Calle Julio César and made his way past the three law students in the outer office. She greeted him in her bare feet. He sat down and laid out his proposal to her for cutting a deal with Manuela.

'Are you out of your mind, Javier?'

'Not always,' he said.

'You now want to give her everything we've been fighting over for the last six months. You're prepared to take a loss of, God knows, half a million euros. Why don't we throw in the contents as well?'

'That's not a bad idea,' said Falcón.

She leaned over the desk at him, long black hair, dark brown, almost black eyes, a beautiful, fierce and haughty Moorish look that could wither most of the fiscales in the courts at a hundred metres.

'Is that shrink still tinkering about in your head?'

'Yes.'

'Has there been a change in medication?'

'No.'

'You're still taking the drugs?'

He nodded.

'Well, I don't know what's going on in there, but it must be very loud,' she said.

'I don't want to live in that house any more. I don't want to live with Francisco Falcón. Manuela does. She's obsessed by the place . . . but she doesn't have the money.'

'Then she can't have it, Javier.'

'Just think about it.'

'I've thought about it and rejected it – instantly.'

'Think some more.'

'That's your ten minutes,' said Isabel, putting on her shoes. 'Walk me to my car.'

The law students fired questions at her as she strode through the office. She ignored them all. Her heels cracked across the marble foyer.

'I've got another question for you,' said Falcón.

'Let's hope it's cheaper than the last,' she said, 'or you won't be able to afford me.'

'Do you know Juez Calderón?'

'Of course I do, Javier,' she said, stopping dead in the street so Falcón knocked into her. 'Ah, now I get it. You're emotionally distraught about him and Inés. Let's forget this meeting ever happened and when you're calm we'll –'

'I'm not *that* emotionally distraught.'

'So what is it about Juez Calderón?'

'Does he have a reputation?'

'As long as your arm . . . longer than your leg . . . longer than this street.'

'I mean . . . with women.'

Falcón, who was staring eagerly into her face, saw all her fierceness disappear to be replaced by a vast hurt, which surfaced like a harpooned whale and disappeared. She turned away and pointed her keys at her car, whose lights flashed back.

'Esteban has always been a hunter,' she said.

She got in the car and pulled away, leaving Falcón on the pavement thinking that Isabel Cano had been happily married for more than ten years.

12

On the way to Ortega's house he took a call from Jorge, who told him that the paper used for the Inés print was of a different make and quality to the blank stock he'd given him. The news momentarily elated him until he realized that this proof of his sanity must also mean that someone had got into his home and planted the photo. Not only that, they also knew about him and his particular vulnerability. His blood felt sharp in his veins but he calmed his paranoia with the thought that everybody knew about him. Since the Francisco Falcón scandal his story was public property.

Pablo Ortega was coming back from walking his dogs. Falcón buzzed down his window as he drew alongside and asked if he could spare a few minutes. Ortega nodded grimly. Falcón pulled the photograph out of his briefcase. Ortega held the gate open for him. The stink from the cesspit was as thick as a mud wall. They went around the house and into the kitchen. The dogs drank noisily.

'I've had some good news about the cesspit,' said Ortega, unable to sound delighted by it. 'One of my brother's contractors thinks he can rebuild without having to knock down all the rooms and he could do it for five million.'

'That's good,' said Falcón. 'I'm glad it's going to work out for you.'

They went into the living room and sat down.

'I might have some more good news for you,' said Falcón, wanting to keep things positive. 'I'd like to help with Sebastián's case.'

'It's no use you helping from the outside if Sebastián doesn't want to be helped from the inside.'

'I think I can help there, too,' said Falcón, taking the risk that

Aguado would agree. 'I have a clinical psychologist who's looking at his case and might be prepared to talk to him.'

'A clinical psychologist,' said Ortega, slowly. 'And what would he talk to Sebastián about?'

'*She* would try to find out why Sebastián felt the need to incarcerate himself.'

'He didn't incarcerate himself,' said Ortega, leaping to his feet, throwing out a big dramatic hand. 'The state incarcerated him with the help of that cabrón Juez Calderón.'

'But Sebastián didn't defend himself. He seems to have welcomed his punishment and failed to offer anything that might have reduced his sentence. Why?'

Ortega dug his fists into his expansive waist and drew in a massive breath as if he was about to blow the house down.

'Because,' he said, very quietly, 'he was guilty . . . It was just his mental state at the time that was in question. The court decided he was sane. I dispute that.'

'She will find that out from him,' said Falcón.

'What will she talk to him about?' said Ortega. 'The boy has a fragile mind as it is. I don't want her stirring up more trouble. He's already in solitary confinement. I don't want him feeling suicidal.'

'Have there been any reports from the prison that he might be?'

'Not yet.'

'She's very good at her work, Pablo. I don't think this will do him any harm,' said Falcón. 'And while she helps him clarify things, I'll look at various elements of the case . . .'

'Like what?'

'The boy he kidnapped – Manolo. I should talk to his parents.'

'You won't get anywhere there. The Ortega name cannot be spoken in that house. The father has suffered some sort of collapse. He can't work any more. They spread malicious gossip so that the whole barrio has turned against me. I mean, that is why I am here, Javier . . . and not there.'

'I *have* to talk to them,' said Falcón. 'It was the seriousness of Manolo's testimony that resulted in such a heavy prison sentence for Sebastián.'

'Why should he change it?' said Ortega. 'It's his testimony.'

'That's what I have to find out: whether it *was* his testimony or something that he was encouraged to say by others.'

'What's that supposed to mean?'

'He's a very young boy. At that age you do what you're told.'

'You know something, Javier, don't you?' said Ortega. 'What do you know?'

'I know that I want to help.'

'Well, I don't like it,' said Ortega. 'And I don't want it to rebound on Sebastián.'

'It can't get any worse for him, Pablo.'

'It'll stir things up...' said Ortega, repeating his fear. He started out angry but then softened. 'Can you just let me think about it for a bit, Javier? I don't want to rush into these things. It's delicate. The media has only just fallen silent. I don't want them on my back again. Is that all right?'

'Don't worry, Pablo. Take your time.'

Ortega blinked at the photograph whose corner Javier was flicking. 'Anything else?' he asked.

'I was confused,' said Falcón, throwing back the pages of his notebook, 'as to your relationship with Rafael Vega. You said: "I knew him. He introduced himself about a week after I moved in here." Does that mean you *did* know him before you moved here, or that you've only known him since you've lived in Santa Clara?'

Ortega was staring at the photograph face down on the table in front of Falcón as if he was a poker player and it was a draw card whose suit and number he wouldn't mind knowing.

'I did know him before,' he said. 'I suppose I should have said he reintroduced himself. I met him at some party or other. I can't remember whose...'

'Once, twice, three times?'

'It's not so easy for me to remember. I meet so many...'

'You knew Consuelo Jiménez's late husband,' said Falcón.

'Yes, yes, Raúl. That would have been it. They were in the same business. I used to go to the restaurant in El Porvenir. That's what it was.'

'I thought the connection was your brother and his air-conditioning systems?'

'Yes, yes, yes, now I've got it. Of course.'

Falcón gave him the photograph, watching his face as he did so.

'Who are you talking to in that photograph?' asked Falcón.

'God knows,' said Ortega. 'The one you can't see is my brother. I know that from his bald head. This guy... I don't know.'

'It was taken at one of Raúl Jiménez's parties.'

'That doesn't help. I went to dozens of functions. I met hundreds of . . . All I can say is that he wasn't from my profession. He must be in the construction industry.'

'Raúl divided his friends up into celebrities and . . . useful people for his businesses,' said Falcón. 'I'm surprised you didn't appear in his celebrity photographs.'

'Raúl Jiménez thought Lorca was a brand of sherry. He'd never been near a theatre in his life. He'd like to think of himself as a friend of Antonio Banderas and Ana Rosa Quintana, but he wasn't. It was all a publicity stunt. I was a . . . No, let's be accurate: I occasionally gave support to my brother by turning up at functions. I knew Raúl and I'd met Rafael, but I wasn't exactly a friend.'

'Well, thank you for explaining that,' said Falcón. 'I'm sorry to have taken up your time.'

'I'm not sure what you're investigating here, Javier. One moment we're talking about Rafael's suicide, the next you make it sound as if he's been murdered, and now you're looking at Sebastián's case. And that photograph . . . that must have been taken years ago, before I put on all this weight.'

'There's no date on it. All I can tell you is that it was taken before 1998.'

'And how do you know that?'

'Because the man you're talking to died in that year.'

'So, you already *know* who he is?'

Falcón nodded.

'I feel as if I'm being accused of something here,' said Ortega, 'when it's just that my memory has been shot to pieces since this business with Sebastián. I've never used a prompter in my life and then twice in the last year I've come to in front of the camera or on the stage, wondering what the hell I'm doing there. It's . . . ach . . . you don't want to know. It's silly stuff. Nothing a cop would be interested in.'

'Try me.'

'It's as if reality keeps breaking through the illusion I'm trying to create.'

'That sounds plausible. You've been through a difficult time.'

'It's never happened before,' said Ortega. 'Not even after Glória left me. Anyway, forget about it.'

'Not all the work I do is about putting criminals behind bars, Pablo. We're servants of the people, too. That means I also try to help.'

'But can you help me with what's going on in here?' he said, tapping his forehead.

'You have to tell me first.'

'Do you know anything about dreams?' said Ortega. 'I have this one where I'm standing in a field with a cool wind blowing at the sweat on my face. I'm in an incredible rage and my hands are hurting. The palms are stinging and the backs of my fingers feel bruised. There's the sound of traffic and I find that my hands are causing me not physical pain but great personal distress. What do you make of that, Javier?'

'It sounds as if you've been hitting somebody.'

Ortega looked through him, suddenly deep in thought. Falcón said he'd let himself out, but there was no reaction. As Falcón reached the gate he realized that he'd forgotten to ask about Sergei. He went back but stopped at the corner of the house because Ortega was standing on the lawn with his hands reaching up to the sky. He sank to his knees. The dogs came out and snuffled around his thighs. He stroked them and held them to him. He was sobbing. Falcón backed away.

The Vegas' garage with its brand-new Jaguar was cleaner than Sergei's accommodation and Falcón knew that there wasn't going to be any muriatic acid anywhere near this car's paintwork. He went down the garden to the barbecue, thinking that Sergei must have had a place where he kept his gardening tools. There was nothing unplanned about this area of the garden. It had been built by a man who understood how to grill meat. Behind the barbecue area there was thick, almost tropical growth. He went round the back of Sergei's quarters and saw that there was a path into this jungle, which obscured a brick shed. He was furious that this hadn't appeared in Pérez's report on his search of the garden.

He found a key in the garage and waded back through the thickening heat. The shed was full of sacks of charcoal and the usual barbecue paraphernalia. Sergei kept his tools at one end, along with some small quantities of building materials. On a shelf above there was paint and other liquids, one of which was an opened plastic bottle of muriatic acid with a centimetre left in the bottom. Falcón went back to the car for an evidence bag and used a pen through the loop handle to lift the bottle into it. As he worked, the light dimmed in the shed.

'You're on your own today, Inspector Jefe,' said Maddy Krugman, startling him.

She stood in the doorway, backlit. He could see every curve and crux of her figure through the diaphanous material of her dress. He looked down at her zebra-skin sandals. She leaned against the door jamb, arms folded.

'I prefer it that way, Sra Krugman,' he said.

'You look like a loner to me,' she said. 'Thinking things out, piecing things together. Building the picture in your head.'

'You're keeping a careful eye on me.'

'I'm bored,' she said. 'I can't go out to take my photographs in this heat. There's nobody around down at the river anyway.'

'Is your husband still working for Vega Construcciones?'

'Sr Vázquez and the finance people called him last night and said that he should continue to manage his projects,' she said. 'They don't seem to be pulling the plug . . . just yet. Would you like some coffee, Inspector Jefe?'

They walked out into the sunlight. She checked the contents of his evidence bag. He locked the shed.

'We can cut through here to our place,' she said, leading him towards a break in the hedge by Sergei's quarters.

Falcón went back to the house, put the evidence bag inside the garage and shut the door. He followed her through the hedge and up the garden to her house thinking about how he was going to introduce Reza Sangari into the mix.

He sat on the sofa in the chill of the living room while she made the coffee. Her sandals had low heels on them which clicked softly on the marble floor. Even out of the room there was still this subliminal sexual presence. She poured the coffee and lowered herself on to the other end of the sofa.

'You know what it feels like out here when I'm all on my own day after day?' she said. 'It feels like I'm in limbo. It's one of those weird incongruities of life that I've found my social life has improved one hundred per cent since Rafael died. He used to be just about our only guest. But now you come around and yesterday I spent some time with Esteban . . .'

'Juez Calderón?'

'Yes,' she said. 'He's a nice guy and very cultured, too.'

'When did you see him?'

'I ran into him in town in the morning and we met up later and had an evening together,' she said. 'He took me to some odd bars in the centre that I would never go into by myself. You know, those places with a thousand *jamones* hanging from the ceiling, sweating into those conical plastic cups over the heads of fat guys with their black hair combed back in brilliant rails, smoking cigars and adjusting their trousers every time a woman walks by.'

'What time was that?'

'You can't stop being a detective, can you?' she said. 'It was about six until ten o'clock.'

She crossed her legs. Her dress slipped back towards her lap. She kicked the sandal off her foot.

'I saw that you had a show called "Minute Lives",' said Falcón. 'What was that about?'

'Or "M*i*nute Lives",' she said, rolling her eyes. 'I never like that stupid title. It was my agent's idea. They like things to be catchy and commercial. I've got the book upstairs, if you'd like to see.'

She stood and flipped the hem of her dress out with her finger-tips.

'It's OK, 'said Falcón, wanting to keep this on the ground floor. 'I just wanted to know the subject matter.'

She walked over to the sliding doors and put her hands up on the glass and looked out into the garden. Again the light streamed through her clothes. Falcón squirmed. Everything seemed to be calculated.

'They were shots of very ordinary people taken at work or in their homes. They were people in a big city with small lives and the shots were just clips of their life story – your imagination was supposed to do the rest.'

'I read a review of the show,' said Falcón. 'It was by somebody called Dan Fineman. He didn't seem to like it.'

He watched the back of her head, her neck and shoulders as his words crept into her mind. She was as still as a night animal with a host of predators. She turned suddenly and with an intake of breath came back for her coffee. She lit a cigarette and thumped her back into the sofa.

'Dan Fineman was an asshole I knew from high school. He always wanted to fuck me but he made my flesh crawl. He never aspired to anything greater than writing for the *St Louis Times* and when he got there he took his revenge.'

'He wrote another article about you,' said Falcón. 'You might not have seen it.'

'That was the only show I ever did in St Louis. First and last.'

'This wasn't to do with the arts. It was a local news story.'

'I only went back to St Louis to see my parents for Thanksgiving and Christmas.'

'When did you say your mother died?'

'I didn't,' she said, 'but it was on December 3rd 2000. You know who you remind me of, Inspector Jefe?'

'Americans only seem to know one Spaniard and I don't look anything like Antonio Banderas.'

'Columbo,' she said, not thinking this at all but wanting to get back at him. 'A much better-looking Columbo. You ask a load of questions that don't seem to have any bearing on the case and then, bang, you nail the culprit.'

'Fictional police work is always more entertaining than the real thing.'

'Marty said from the beginning that you weren't like any cop he'd ever seen.'

'And I suppose he'd have come across quite a few in the months before you arrived here?'

She rested her chin on her thumb and tapped her nose with her finger.

'You never said what Dan Fineman wrote about, Inspector Jefe.'

'How you were helping the FBI with their inquiries into the murder of your ex-lover, Reza Sangari.'

'You're a very thorough person,' she said.

'You looked me up on the internet,' said Falcón. 'I looked you up.'

'Then you won't need to ask me anything,' she said. 'And, anyway, none of it's relevant to what happened to the Vegas.'

'Have you had any other affairs since you've been married to your husband?' he asked.

She narrowed her eyes, pursed her lips and smoked about two centimetres in a single drag.

'Are you seriously trying to put me and Rafael together, Inspector Jefe?' she asked. 'Is that how your mind works? You see a pathetically obvious pattern in things and your policeman's brain snaps the two together.'

Falcón sat still, his eyes fixed on her, waiting for the cracks to appear. Instead, something dawned in her face and she sat up on the edge of the sofa.

'I've got it,' she said. 'How stupid of me. Columbo – disconnected questions. This is about the judge, isn't it? You think I'm embarking on an affair with Juez Calderón. And, yes, I read the story . . . Javier Falcón. His fiancé is your ex-wife. Is that what this is all about?'

There was some colour in Maddy Krugman's cheeks. She was angry. Falcón wouldn't have minded blocking out the glare coming from her green eyes, the flames of her red hair. He realized that the two of them were prepared to hurt each other and she didn't mind the idea of that.

'Now that I've discovered that your motive for leaving America was a little more complicated than you've led me to believe, I have to look at things from a different perspective.'

'So what was all that stuff about Esteban?'

'You mentioned him, not me,' he said. 'I was interested because he decided to postpone a meeting he had with me yesterday. I now find out it was because he was with you.'

'Do you still love your ex-wife, Inspector Jefe?'

'That's got nothing to do with anything.'

'Why are you so curious about Esteban?' she asked. 'It shouldn't be any of your business what he does with his private life. And you shouldn't give a damn about your ex-wife . . . but you do.'

'They're getting married. I'm under no illusions.'

'You've given yourself away, Inspector Jefe,' she said. 'You're under no illusions, but you wouldn't mind the chance, I bet.'

'You're like a defence lawyer putting words into the mouth of a prosecution witness.'

'And you've got nobody to object to,' she said, looking sadly around the living room before fixing on him again, 'Any woman over the age of twenty would take one look at Esteban Calderón and know him for what he is.'

'Which is?'

'A ladies' man who's always looking,' she said. 'You don't see it because you're not the type. I hope your ex-wife isn't a romantic.'

'And what if she is?'

'She'd be under the illusion that she could make that kind of man change,' she said. 'But I can promise you one thing . . . she knows what he's like. No woman could miss it. Why do you think Esteban was around here with his tail wagging on the first day of your investigation?'

'How does your husband take that sort of thing?' asked Falcón.

'Marty's got nothing to worry about,' she said. 'He trusts me.'

'How did he take Reza Sangari?'

Silence, while Maddy stubbed out the cigarette with a dozen precise little stabs at the ashtray.

'We nearly didn't make it through,' she said, looking up with her eyes magnified by impending tears. 'That was my first and last affair.'

'Were you still seeing Reza Sangari when he was murdered?'

She shook her head, slowly.

'Did you contemplate leaving your husband for Reza Sangari?'

She nodded.

'And what happened?'

'That is private,' she said.

'I'm sure you had to tell the FBI everything . . . or did they respect your privacy?'

'It upsets me. I don't want to talk about it.'

'Did you find out about the other women?' asked Falcón, riding over her sensitivities.

'Yes,' she said. 'They were younger than me. They had more resilience.'

'And why, when you see so clearly what sort of a man Esteban Calderón is, did you not spot Reza Sangari?'

'I made the crucial mistake of falling completely and madly in love with him.'

She paced the room, her nerves getting the better of her.

'I used to go into New York City twice a week,' she said. 'I had work from a couple of magazines and I used a studio which happened to be close to Reza's warehouse. He came to the studio one day with a model I was using for a shoot. The model was flying out to LA straight afterwards. Reza asked me out to lunch. By the end of that afternoon we'd had food, wine and he'd made love to me on a pile of pure silk carpets from Qom. That's what it was like. Nothing was ordinary. He was beautiful and I fell for him like I've never fallen for anybody in my life.'

'The model you were using that day, was her name Françoise Lascombs?'

'Yes.'

'She must have been around once she came back from LA. Didn't you see her?'

'Reza was very good at keeping all aspects of his love life separate. And you know how it is with these men – when you were with him you were the only person in the world who mattered. I wasn't thinking of anybody else and certainly not the invisible competition.'

'But you did find out about them?'

'About six months after we started, when I was so in love with him I didn't know what to do with myself, I went into the city on an odd day. I didn't intend to see him but inevitably I ended up at his warehouse. As I went for his doorbell a woman came out and I recognized that happy spring in her step. I didn't go up. I went across the street and stood in a doorway. I was shaking. I don't know whether you know what that sort of betrayal is like – a really appalling sense of breakage. My organs felt lacerated. It took me an hour to stop shaking. Then I decided I would go up and finish with him and, as I crossed the street, another woman converged on his door. I couldn't believe it. I didn't go up. I somehow managed to get home and collapsed. I never saw him again and then somebody killed him over a weekend and they took four days to find the body.'

'And they never found the murderer?'

'It was a long and painful investigation. Never was so much pressure put on so many relationships by the death of one man. The media were on top of it too, because Françoise Lascombs had just become Estée Lauder's girl. The FBI probably had about ten suspects, but they couldn't pin it on any of them. Then they discovered his coke habit. He had something like two hundred grammes in his apartment. I never knew about it, but I suppose he had to be on something just to maintain that lifestyle. They thought that something must have gone wrong in a deal.'

'What do *you* think?'

'I think about a lot of things – what the affair did to Marty, what it did to me, and I think about Reza and the madness of those months – but I don't let myself think about his end, who killed him or why, because that's where insanity lies.'

'You never suspected Marty?'

'You're kidding – the weekend he was killed I was still struggling to be without Reza. I couldn't bear to be on my own. Marty and I were drunk and stoned and watching old movies. Then, on the Wednesday, the FBI came calling and everything changed.'

'Well . . . it explains your fascination with the internal struggle.'

'It also explains why I'm disdainful of everything I did before I came here,' she said. 'Dan Fineman was right. I remember his headline, it played on the title of the show: "Short on content, small in stature".'

'You said Sr Vega used to come here for dinner . . . quite often on his own,' said Falcón. 'That's unusual for a Spanish man with a family.'

'You're so transparent, Inspector Jefe,' she said. 'And you've insinuated that before.'

'These aren't trick questions, Sra Krugman,' he said. 'Nor do they necessarily imply any impropriety on your part. I'm just asking if you think he was in love with you, or infatuated with you, as a lot of men seem to be.'

'But not you, Inspector Jefe. I've noticed that,' she said. 'Perhaps your lust is directed elsewhere . . . maybe that's it, yes, maybe you just don't like me . . . Your friend Consuelo doesn't like me either.'

'My friend?'

'Or is she a little more passionate than a friend?'

'Do you think Sr Vega was interested in you sexually?' asked Falcón, shouldering through her insinuations. 'You went to see bullfights together.'

'Rafael liked to be accompanied by a pretty woman. That's it. Nothing happened. In the same way that nothing ever happens with the gas man either.'

'Did you know if you had an effect on Sr Vega's mind?'

'You think *I* was the cause of his disturbed state,' she said. 'You think he was burning papers down the bottom of his garden because of *me*. You're crazy.'

'He was a man trapped in difficult marital circumstances. He had a wife who was severely depressed, but they had a son together they both loved. He wasn't going to break up his family, but his relationship with his wife was limited by her condition.'

'It's a plausible theory . . . except I think I was a side attraction for Rafael. His main interest was talking things over with Marty. I mean, Marty would always meet us after the bullfight for tapas, then we'd have dinner and, I'm telling you, those two were still talking long after I went to bed.'

'About what?'

'Their favourite topic. The United States of America.'

'Had Sr Vega lived in America?'

'He spoke American English and he talked about Miami a lot, but he didn't react well to direct questions, so I'm not sure. But Marty's convinced that he'd lived there. Unlike most Europeans, he wasn't full of the usual clichés on the American way of life,' she said. 'He enjoyed talking with Marty because Marty isn't that interested in personal details. Marty was happy to talk about theories, thoughts and ideas without having to know where the guy lived or his favourite colour.'

'Did they talk in Spanish or English?'

'Spanish until they got on the brandy, and then English. Marty's Spanish fell apart with alcohol.'

'Did Sr Vega ever get drunk?'

'I was in bed. Ask Marty.'

'When was the last time Sr Vega and Marty had one of these evenings?'

'The really long sessions happened during the Feria. They'd be up until dawn then.'

Falcón finished his coffee, got to his feet.

'I don't know whether I'll invite you again, if all you're going to do is interrogate me,' she said. 'Esteban doesn't interrogate me.'

'It's not his job to interrogate you. I'm the one who has to go digging in the dirt.'

'And you find out a few things about Esteban on the way.'

'His private life is not my concern.'

'You're used to keeping yourself in tight, aren't you, Inspector Jefe?'

'It's best not to let my sort of job and social life bleed into each other.'

'Very funny, Inspector Jefe,' she said. 'You do have a social life, then? Most cops don't. I understand their lives are full of broken relationships, separations from their kids, alcoholism and depression.'

Falcón couldn't help thinking that he scored two, maybe three, out of four.

'Thank you for your time,' he said.

'We should try meeting socially, just to see if we really get along without all this stuff getting in the way,' she said. 'I'm interested in the cop with artistic vision. Or is your mind made up about me? I'd hate you to think I was some stereotype, like the femme fatale.'

'I'll go back the way I came,' he said, heading for the sliding doors out into the garden, and he could tell he'd annoyed her.

'Columbo always left his last question for the doorstep,' she said to the back of his head.

'I'm not Columbo,' he said, and sealed her back in with the sliding door.

13

Friday, 26th July 2002

On the way back to pick up the evidence bag containing the bottle of muriatic acid, his mobile vibrated in his pocket.

'*Digame*, José Luis,' he said.

'They've found a Ukrainian hooker in the Polígono San Pablo who they're pretty sure is Sergei's mystery friend,' said Ramírez. 'She doesn't speak much Spanish, but she reacted to the photo of Sergei when they showed it to her.'

'Take her down to the Jefatura and get a translator,' said Falcón. 'Don't interrogate her until I get there.'

'It's nearly lunchtime.'

'Do what you can.'

Back in the Jefatura, Nadia Kouzmikheva, dressed in a black miniskirt, a white halter-neck top and flat shoes with no stockings, paced the floor of the interrogation room while Policía Carlos Serrano watched her through the pane of glass in the door. She'd already gone through three of his cigarettes and he was hoping that the translator was a smoker and would arrive soon.

Ramírez and Falcón walked down the corridor with a female Russian translator from the university. Serrano opened the door for them. Introductions were made. The two women sat together on one side of the table, the men on the other. The translator lit a cigarette. Ramírez looked over his shoulder as if there might be a waiter. Serrano opened the door.

'Another ashtray, Carlos,' Ramírez said.

Falcón explained the purpose of the interview while looking at Nadia's passport and finding the visa, which still had six months to run. The Ukrainian girl's shoulders relaxed a couple of microns.

'She's enrolled in a language school,' said Ramírez.

'We're not here to make your life difficult,' said Falcón to the girl. 'We need your help.'

In the passport photo her hair was dark brown. The roots were still visible under the rough peroxide job she'd presumably done herself. She had green eyes under blue eye shadow which did not quite obscure the fact that her left eye was recovering from some damage. Her skin was white and blotchy as if she had not seen the sun for some months. She had fresh bruises on her upper arms. He smiled to encourage her. She smiled back, revealing a tooth missing from behind the incisor. He positioned the photo of Sergei in the middle of the table.

'Where do you come from in the Ukraine?' he asked.

The translator repeated the question to the side of the girl's head.

'Lvov,' she said, playing with her cigarette in red chapped fingers.

'What did you do in Lvov?'

'I worked in a factory until it closed. Then I did nothing.'

'Sergei came from Lvov . . . Did you know him?'

'There's nearly a million people in Lvov,' she said.

'But you knew him,' said Falcón.

Silence. More smoking through trembling lips.

'I can see that you are afraid,' said Falcón. 'I can see that you have been beaten by the people you have been working for. They are probably threatening your family, too. We won't interfere with any of that if you don't want us to. We only want to know about Sergei because he was working for someone who is now dead. He is not a suspect. We want to talk to him to see if he has any information for us. I would like you to tell us how you know Sergei, when you last saw him and what he said to you. Nothing will leave this room. You can return to your apartment when you want.'

He didn't take his eyes off her. She'd learnt some ugly lessons about human beings and she was staring back at him to see if there were cracks in his nature – any faltering, any shift of gaze, any tell-tale tic – that might mean more pain for her. She looked at her watch, a cheap, pink plastic thing with a big flower for a face.

'I have thirty-eight minutes to get back to my apartment,' she said. 'I'll need a little money to keep people quiet about where I've been.'

'How much?'

'Thirty euros will be enough.'

Falcón unfolded a twenty and a ten and laid them on the table.

'Sergei and I are friends. We come from the same village outside Lvov. He used to work in a technical college teaching mechanics. He earned twenty-seven euros a month,' she said, looking down on the money that Falcón had given her so easily. 'I was earning seventeen euros a month. It wasn't so much a living as a slow death. Sergei came to see me one day, very excited. He'd heard from friends that Portugal was a good place to go to get into Europe, that in Europe you could earn twenty-seven euros a day. We went to the embassy in Warsaw to get our visas and that's where we met the mafia. They got us our visas, they arranged transport. You paid in dollars – eight hundred each. We already knew about the rumours that the mafia were big in Lisbon. We had heard that they take you off the bus, beat you and put the young women into prostitution and the men into slave labour until they've paid off a never-ending debt. So we decided that we would not go to Lisbon. The bus stopped at a service station outside Madrid. I met a Russian girl there in the toilets. She told me not to go to Lisbon and gave me a cigarette. She introduced me to a Spanish man who said he could get me work in a restaurant in Madrid. I asked if he could get Sergei some work and he said that he could wash dishes, no problem. They pay six hundred euros a month. We left the bus.'

She shrugged, stubbed out the cigarette and Ramírez gave her another.

'There was no restaurant. We were taken to an apartment where we were told we could stay. They left us there saying they would be back in the morning. Later there was a knock on the door and three big Russians came in. They beat us up very badly and took our passports. All three men raped me. Sergei was taken away. I was locked in the apartment. Every day men came to have sex with me and left without a word. After three months the three Russians came back with another Russian. He made me strip and inspected me as if I was an animal. He nodded and left. I had just been sold. They brought me to Seville and put me in a flat. They treated me very badly for six months and then things got a little better. I was allowed to leave the apartment to work in a club. I served drinks and did . . . other things. They gave me my passport but dislocated my finger,' she said, holding up her hand, 'so that I would remember . . . They needn't have bothered. I was scared anyway. Too scared to run – and where would I go with no money and looking like this? They told me my family's address and what they would do to them. They also told me that they had Sergei here and what would happen to him if I ran.'

She asked for water. Serrano brought in a chilled bottle. She smoked hard. The translator didn't look as if she'd be able to bear much more of Nadia's story.

'I am allowed a little money for food and cigarettes. I am trusted, but one mistake and I'm beaten and locked up in the apartment,' she said, pointing at her eye. 'This was from my last mistake. They saw me in a bar talking to Sergei. It was the second time I'd seen him. We met by accident one night and he told me where he worked.'

'How long ago was that?'

'Six weeks,' she said. 'I was beaten and locked up for two weeks.'

'But you saw him again?'

'Twice. Two weeks after I got out I found the house where he worked. We just talked. He told me what had happened to him. The work he'd had to do on the building sites – dangerous work where men died – how much he hated Europe and wanted to get back to Lvov.'

'Did he tell you who he worked for?'

'Yes, I don't remember the name. It wasn't important. He was the owner of the construction sites where Sergei had worked.'

'When was the second time?'

'Wednesday morning he came to the apartment and told me to get my things . . . that we were leaving. He said that the man he worked for was dead on the floor of his kitchen and that he had to run.'

'Why did he have to run?'

'He said he didn't want to go back to the building sites. He said we had to be quick, that the police were going to come and he had to move very fast.'

'Did he have money?'

'He said he had enough money. I don't know how much that was.'

She blinked, tried to swallow but couldn't. She sipped the water. Ramírez gave her another cigarette.

'You didn't go?' said Falcón.

'I couldn't. I was too scared. He said goodbye and that was it.'

'Can you remember exactly what he said when he told you his employer was dead?'

She put her face in her hands, pressed the fingertips into her forehead.

'He just said he was dead.'

'Did he say he'd been murdered?'

'No . . . he was dead, that's all.'

'And since then – has anybody been to see you about Sergei?' asked Falcón.

She pointed at the bruises on her arms.

'They knew Sergei would come to see me,' she said. 'They held me down and did some things to me, but I couldn't tell them anything. All I knew was that he had gone.'

She looked up at the clock, nervous.

'What did they ask you?'

'They wanted to know why Sergei had run and what he'd seen, and I told them that he'd only seen a dead man lying on the floor. That was it,' she said. 'Now I have to go.'

Falcón called Serrano in, but he'd already left and been replaced by Ferrera. He told her to get the girl back to the bar on Calle Alvar Nuñez Caleza de Vaca in twenty-three minutes. Ramírez gave her his cigarettes. She grabbed the money, stuffed it down the front of her skirt and left.

The translator struggled to fill in the receipt, as if the last quarter of an hour had removed some of the purpose from her life. Ramírez reminded her of the confidentiality agreement she'd signed. She left. Ramírez smoked in silence, his legs braced on either side of his chair.

'It's our job to listen to that,' he said, 'and do nothing. That's what we're paid for.'

'Go and take a look at Alberto Montes,' said Falcón. 'He's had those stories up to here.'

'I don't know how your meeting went with Calderón this morning,' said Ramírez, 'but that has clarified one thing. We definitely have Russian mafia involvement in this case.'

He stubbed out his cigarette in the cheap tin ashtray. They walked back up to the office. Ramírez jangled his car keys.

'I'll put some men on the bus stations this afternoon, check the airport, send Sergei's photograph down to the ports and e-mail the Policía Judiciária in Lisbon,' said Ramírez, and left for lunch.

Falcón stood at the window. Ramírez appeared below him and walked the length of the main block of the Jefatura to his car. In the adjoining block of offices Falcón could see another man standing at his window looking down at the same dull scene – Inspector Jefe Alberto Montes. Falcón's mobile vibrated. Isabel Cano wanted to talk to him in her office sometime before 9 p.m. He said he would do his best and shut the phone down.

Montes opened his window and looked down the two floors into the car park. Falcón took another call. Consuelo Jiménez asked him to dinner that night at her house in Santa Clara. He agreed without thinking because he was so fascinated by Montes, who was now leaning out of the window, both elbows on the ledge. Nobody opened their window to 45°C heat in an air-conditioned office. Montes's head turned. He backed away and closed the window.

Falcón went home for lunch. The heat and Nadia's story had ruined his appetite, but he managed two bowls of chilled gazpacho and a chorizo sandwich. He spoke to Encarnación to find out if she'd let anybody in the house yesterday. She said she hadn't but that she had left the front doors open for an hour in the morning to try and circulate some air. He went up to bed and drifted off into a doze in which his mind played back disturbing versions of the day's interviews, which culminated with a view into a cell whose walls bore the faint, bloody prints of human hands. He dragged himself to the shower to wash away the appalling sense of dread that had accompanied the last image. The water poured through his hair and over his lips and the thought came to him that it was time to stop being the detective monk and to immerse himself in life.

On the way to the Jefatura he took a call from Alicia Aguado, who'd already listened to the Sebastián Ortega tapes. She was interested in talking to him if Pablo Ortega was happy and the prison authorities amenable.

Falcón told her about the discussion he'd had with Pablo Ortega that morning, how the actor had been reluctant to allow something that might result in the deterioration of Sebastián's already fragile state of mind.

'Well, there's bound to be some history between those two,' she said. 'Just as there was between Sebastián and his mother who abandoned him twice, in divorce and death. I'm sure Pablo Ortega knows that if his son is willing to talk to us they'll both end up on the couch. The expression he used – "stirring things up" – won't just be in his son's mind, and that will be making him uncomfortable. Perhaps I should meet him. He's probably got some fame paranoia and won't like it if just anybody starts rummaging about in his private thoughts.'

'I'm going out that way this evening. I'll drop in and see him again,' said Falcón.

'I'm free tomorrow morning, if he wants to have an informal meeting.'

From the car park of the Jefatura he could see that the offices of the Grupo de Homicidios were full. Everybody was reporting back after a long week on the hot streets. As he headed for the rear entrance he glanced up at Montes's office and found the man standing there at his window. His stomach was straining against his white shirt, his tie was down his chest. Falcón gave him a short wave. He did not react.

The noise coming from his office had the excitement of the impending weekend, August and the holiday season about it. The squad was about to lose Pérez, Baena and Serrano for two weeks, which was going to mean a lot more footwork for the three left behind. He expected to find them all in shorts with cold beers in their hands in full readiness, but they were sitting on desk corners, smoking and chatting. Falcón stood at the door, smiling and nodding.

'Inspector Jefe!' shouted Baena, as if he was three beers ahead of the game.

Pérez and Serrano gave extravagant salutes. He was going to have to wait until Pérez came back from holiday before he tore a strip off him about failing to search the Vegas' garden properly.

'So the holidays have started,' said Falcón.

'We filed our reports,' said Pérez. 'We spent the whole afternoon out at the bus stations and Santa Justa. Carlos even went out to the airport for you as a going-away present.'

'No Sergei?'

'The girl was as close as we got,' said Serrano.

'That guy's just going to disappear,' said Baena. 'I would if I had the Russian mafia chasing my ass.'

'Did you have any luck with the other residents of Santa Clara?'

'Hardly anybody was around,' said Pérez. 'Cristina called all the private security companies and most of the people are away. Those we did interview had seen nothing.'

'Did you manage to start work on the key we found in Vega's freezer?'

'Not yet. By the time I'd dropped Nadia off the banks were all shut.'

'OK. Start work on that on Monday morning,' said Falcón. 'What about the ID trace on Rafael Vega?'

'Nothing yet, but Cristina and I had an interesting talk down at Vega Construcciones this afternoon,' said Ramírez, 'with Golden Boy, the accountant. He was responsible for getting the computer system installed and he's been having a closer look at some of the projects.'

'What is Golden Boy in Vega Construcciones?' said Falcón. 'Is he just Francisco Dourado, accountant, or is he something more?'

'He thinks he should have been made the finance director by now . . . but he hasn't,' said Ramírez. 'Rafael Vega was not prepared to let go of the money, or rather, he was not happy for someone to know that much about his business.'

'So he's the book-keeper.'

'Exactly, but since Vega's death he's had freedom of access. He had it before, but he was too scared about getting caught. As I said, he knows the computer system inside out and Vázquez isn't IT savvy enough to stop him.'

'So what are we looking at?' said Falcón. 'Do we have any names for a start?'

'Vladimir Ivanov and Mikhail Zelenov,' said Ferrera, handing over two photos and profiles of the Russians. 'These came through just now from Interpol.'

Vladimir Ivanov (Vlado) had a tattoo on his left shoulder, was fair-haired, blue-eyed with a scar under his jawline on the right side of his face. Mikhail Zelenov (Mikhas) was dark and heavy (132 kg) with green eyes that were just slits in the fat of his face. Their illegal activities covered the full spectrum of mafia activity – prostitution, people-trafficking, gaming, internet fraud and money-laundering. They both belonged to one of the main mafia gangs – Solntsevskaya – which had more than five thousand members. Their sphere of operation was the Iberian peninsula.

'On the two projects which those guys are involved in, there are two sets of books,' said Ramírez. 'The first ones have been prepared by Dourado, based on figures given to him by Vega. The second set have been kept by Vega himself and they show how the projects are really being run.'

'Money-laundering has arrived in the Seville construction industry,' said Falcón.

'The Russians are pretty well financing the whole thing. They supply all labour and materials. Vega Construcciones supplies the architect, the engineers and the supervising site workers.'

'So, who owns the building and what did Rafael Vega get out of it?'

'The ownership details are with Vázquez,' said Ramírez. 'All property deeds and deals are handled by him. We haven't moved on him yet. I thought we should talk first. All we know at the moment is that it's a joint project, with all the cash coming from the Russians and the expertise from Vega . . . There has to be some balancing out somewhere.'

'Vega *is* providing the shell through which the whole thing can work,' said Falcón. 'So that's significant. But we'll have to fix up a meeting with Vázquez tomorrow. The two of us.'

'What about me?' asked Ferrera. 'I was involved in this part of the investigation, too.'

'I know you were, and I'm sure you've done good work,' said Falcón. 'But Vázquez needs to feel the full weight of seniority in this case. We might even have enough to apply for a search warrant. I'll call Juez Calderón.'

'So what am I going to be doing?' said Ferrera.

'We're losing three men as from tonight,' said Falcón. 'By tomorrow morning we'll all be foot soldiers.'

'But I'll be the only one actually on my feet.'

'We have to find Sergei. He's sixty hours ahead of us now, which means we've probably lost him, but he, at the moment, is our only possible witness. There's got to be one last push at his possible escape routes. I'll ask Juez Calderón if we can put his photo in the press.'

Falcón dismissed them, told them all to go to the bar La Jota and he'd buy them a beer. They filed out. He held Ferrera back.

'I've just had another thought,' he said. 'You got on well with Sr Cabello. I want you to go back to him, and it's going to have to be tonight, because José Luis and I need to go into Vázquez with the information tomorrow morning. I want you to find out from him which properties he sold to Rafael Vega and, in the case of the strategically placed ones, which developments they opened up.'

Falcón drove her to the bar La Jota and bought his round of beers. He called Calderón, no answer. He left the squad in the bar and, on the way to Isabel Cano's office, dropped in on Edificio de los Juzgados. It was silent. The security guard said that Calderón had left at 7 p.m. and that he hadn't seen Inés. Falcón called Pablo Ortega and asked if he could stop by his house to show him some photographs.

'You and your photographs,' said Ortega, irritably. 'As long as you make it quick.'

Isabel Cano's office was open but empty. He knocked on the desktop and she shouted from her office for him to come in. She was sitting at her desk with her heels off, smoking. Her head was thrown back and her hair spilled down the black leather chair. She smiled at him out of the corner of her face.

'Thank God for the weekend,' she said. 'Have you recovered your marbles yet?'

'If anything, the idea has consolidated in my mind.'

'Cops,' she said, wincing at their mental incapacity.

'We lead very sheltered lives.'

'But it doesn't mean you've got to be stupid,' said Isabel. 'Please don't make me capitulate when I've only just started on Manuela. It's bad for my image.'

'Can I sit down?'

She waved vaguely at a chair with her cigarette fingers. Falcón liked Isabel Cano but sometimes she could be abrasive. There was no subject too delicate not to be slapped on the table and filleted like so much fish.

'You know what I've been through, Isabel,' he said.

'Actually, I don't,' she said, surprising him. 'I can only imagine what you've been through.'

'Well, that'll do,' said Falcón. 'The fact is I feel like a man who's lost everything. All the things that made me human were brought into question. People need a living structure to give themselves a sense of belonging. All I have is memory, which is unreliable. But what I do have is a brother and a sister. Paco is a good man who will always do the right thing. Manuela is complicated for a whole bunch of reasons but which all boil down to the fact that she didn't get the love she wanted from Francisco.'

'I don't feel sorry for her and nor should you,' said Isabel.

'But despite what I know about Manuela – her avarice, possessiveness and covetousness – I *need* her to be my sister. I need to hear her call me her *hermanito*, her little brother. It's sentimental, illogical and offensive to your legal mind . . . but it's the way it is.'

Isabel's leather chair creaked. The air conditioning breathed. The city slumped in silence.

'And you think you'll get it by giving her the house?'

'By coming to an agreement on the house, which I no longer want to live in, I will open up the possibility. If I don't, I will have to bear the brunt of her hate.'

'You might *think* you need her, but she *knows* she doesn't need you. You have become dispensable because you are no longer a full-blood relative. You are just a barrier,' said Isabel. 'When you give people like Manuela something, all they want is more. They are incapable of love. Your gift will not give what you crave, but it will create resentment, lending her hate more purpose.'

Each sentence was like a slap across his face, as if she was bringing a hysteric back to reality.

'You're probably right,' he said, shaken by her verbal brutality, 'but my nature dictates that I have to take a risk and hope you're proved wrong.'

She threw up her hands and said she'd draft a letter for him to read. He offered to take her for a drink and a tapa in El Cairo but she declined.

'I'd offer you a drink here, but I don't keep any in the office,' she said.

'Let's go to El Cairo, then,' said Falcón.

'I don't want what we're going to talk about now to have any chance of local broadcast.'

'Have we got anything else to talk about?'

'What you mentioned to me this morning.'

'Esteban Calderón,' said Falcón, sitting back down.

'Did you ask me about him now because he's going to get married to Inés?'

'They announced it on Wednesday,' he said.

'Do you remember who handled your divorce with Inés?'

'You did.'

'So why is Esteban's history any business of yours?'

'I'm concerned . . . for Inés.'

'Do you think that Inés is some kind of innocent little sweetie who needs to be protected?' said Isabel. 'Because I can tell you she's not. This house you're so keen to give away to Manuela . . . I had to fight tooth and nail to stop Inés from claiming half of it. You don't have to worry about *her*, she knows everything there is to know about Esteban Calderón, I can assure you.'

Falcón nodded as small worlds, previously closed to him, opened up.

'You called Esteban a hunter this morning. What's he hunting?'

'Difference. He doesn't know that yet,' said Isabel. 'But that's what he's always been looking for.'

'And what is this *difference*?'

'Someone whose face he cannot read and whose mind he doesn't understand,' said Isabel. 'Women have always thrown themselves at Esteban. They've tended to be women from his professional life. They all have legal minds. He knows their architecture from the moment they walk into the room. He plays with them in the hope that they will not be as they seem. Then he finds that they're the same as all the others and he gets bored. The hunt starts again. He's doomed to the relentless movement of a shark, that man.'

Falcón drove out of the darkening city, the real world brutalized by the heat seemed very distant as his hands shifted automatically from gear stick to steering wheel within the cool cockpit of the car. The street lights sliced shadows across the window as he drove down the banks of oleander on Avenida de Kansas City. Neon made promises out of the darkness and high palms held up the tent of the night sky. Nothing reached him apart from the red and green of the traffic lights. He lived in his head while his automaton drove him to Santa Clara. Isabel's words about Calderón and Inés ran through his mind like a news bar in lights. Falcón knew he'd been through a patch of madness, but now he was confronting the extraordinary lunacy of the perfectly sane people around him.

The only thing they had not discussed was the brief glimpse she'd given Falcón that morning of the hurt that had come to the surface at the mention of Calderón's name. He now realized that it had nothing to do with Calderón himself. The judge had become insignificant in Isabel's mind. What had surfaced was the memory of her betrayal as a wife and mother, who had been prepared to jeopardize her husband and family. What she'd shown him was the savage regret which had been lashed to that memory.

He had to pull off the Avenida de Kansas City beneath the red hovering neon of La Casera to take a call from Cristina Ferrera, who'd spoken to Sr Cabello. Falcón opened up his city map and marked off the plots of land Cabello had sold to Vega and the two major developments that were opened up by their sale. Before he hung up he told her to keep an eye on Nadia.

It was only after this call that he began to wonder what he was doing going for dinner with Consuelo.

14

Friday, 26th July 2002

As he pulled up outside Pablo Ortega's house he remembered Montes standing at his window. He should have asked him about the Russians. He called the Jefatura and got a mobile number for Montes.

Montes answered the call. From the background noise he was clearly in a bar, and in their first exchange revealed himself to be very drunk.

'This is Javier Falcón from the Grupo de Homicidios,' he said. 'We spoke yesterday . . .'

'Did we?'

'In your office. We spoke about Eduardo Carvajal and Sebastián Ortega.'

'I can't hear you,' said Montes.

Music and voices blared.

'Shut the fuck up!' Montes roared, to total indifference. '*Momentito.*'

Traffic noise. A car horn.

'Can you hear me, Inspector Jefe?' said Falcón.

'Who are you?'

Falcón started again. Montes apologized elaborately. Now he remembered perfectly.

'We also talked about the Russian mafia.'

'I don't think so.'

'You explained the people-trafficking business.'

'Ah, yes, yes, the people . . . business.'

'I have a question. There are two Russians who are connected to my investigation into the death of Sr Vega, the constructor – you remember?'

Silence. He shouted Montes's name.

'I'm waiting for the question,' Montes said.

'Do the names Vladimir Ivanov and Mikhail Zelenov mean anything to you?'

Concentrated nasal breathing came over the ether.

'Did you hear me?' asked Falcón.

'I heard you. They don't mean anything to me, but my memory is not what it should be. I've had a couple of beers, you see, and I'm not at my best tonight.'

'We'll talk Monday then,' said Falcón, and hung up.

Falcón had a strong sense of circling, as if he was a bird of prey high up in the thermals and there were things going on down in the terrestrial world that could be of interest. He leaned against the roof of his car, tapping his forehead with his mobile. It was unusual for Montes, a married man, to be drunk early on a Friday evening in a crowded bar, probably alone. Was that an evasive reaction to the two names? Had he seemed drunker at the end of the conversation than he was at the beginning?

Ortega buzzed him into his stinking, flyblown courtyard. He wasn't as edgy as he'd been on the phone because he'd reached the affable stage of drunkenness. He was wearing a voluminous white shirt untucked over blue shorts. He offered Falcón a drink. He himself was sipping from a massive glass of red wine.

'Torre Muga,' he said. 'Very good. Would you like some?'

'Just a beer,' said Falcón.

'A few prawns with your beer?' he asked. 'Some jamón . . . Iberico de bellota? I bought it today in the Corte Inglés.'

Ortega went to the kitchen and came back fully supplied.

'I'm sorry I was sharp with you on the phone,' he said.

'I shouldn't be bothering you with these things on a Friday night.'

'I only go out at the weekend if I'm working,' said Ortega, who had been completely smoothed out by the excellence of the Torre Muga. 'I'm a very bad member of the audience. I see all the techniques. I never lose myself in the play. I prefer reading books. I'm sorry if I'm rambling, this is my second glass and, as you can see, they are quite some glasses. I must find a cigar. Have you read a book by . . . it'll come to me.'

He found the cigar box amongst the clutter.

'Cohibas,' he said. 'I have a friend who goes to Cuba regularly.'

'No, thank you,' said Falcón.

'I don't give away my Cohibas easily.'

'I don't smoke.'

'Take one for a friend,' said Ortega. 'I'm sure even cops have friends. As long as you don't give it to that cabrón Juez Calderón.'

'He's not a friend,' said Falcón.

Ortega slipped the cigar into Falcón's top pocket.

'Glad to hear it,' he said, moving off. '*A Heart So White*. That was the book. Javier Marías is the author. Have you read that?'

'Some time ago.'

'I don't know how I could forget the title. It's from *Macbeth*, of course,' said Ortega. 'After Macbeth has killed the king he returns with the bloody daggers, which he is supposed to have left in the servants' quarters. His wife is furious and tells him he has to go back. He refuses and *she* has to go. When she returns, she says:

'"My hands are of your colour; but I shame
To wear a heart so white."

'Her guilt at this stage is only a colour and not yet a stain. She is ashamed of her innocence in the matter. She wants a share in his guilt. It's a wonderful moment because, of course, by Act V it's "out damned spot" and "all the perfumes of Arabia will not sweeten this little hand". Why am I telling you this, Javier?'

'I have no idea, Pablo.'

Ortega took two huge gulps of red wine, which leaked out of the corners of his mouth. Drops of red appeared on his white shirt.

'Hah!' he said, looking down at himself. 'You know what that is? *That* is a filmic moment. This only happens in the movies, never in real life. Like . . . oh, come on, there must be hundreds . . . I can't think now.'

'*The Deer Hunter*.'

'*The Deer Hunter*?'

'A couple get married before the guy goes off to be a soldier in Vietnam. They drink out of a double cup and the wine spills on her bridal dress. It prefigures –'

'Yes, yes, yes. It prefigures something terrible,' said Ortega. 'An embarrassment at dinner. Extra bleach in the washing. Awful, awful things.'

'Can I show you these photographs?'

'Before I lose all visual–oral linkage you mean?'

'Er . . . yes,' said Falcón.

Ortega roared with exaggerated laughter.

'I like you, Javier. I like you very much. I don't like many people,' he said, and stared out into the dark lawn, the unlit swimming pool. 'I don't like . . . anybody in fact. I've found the people I've dealt with in my life . . . lacking. Do you think that's something that happens to celebrities?'

'Fame attracts a certain type of person.'

'Fawning, obsequious, deferential, flattering sycophants.'

'Francisco Falcón hated them. They reminded him of his fraudulence. They reminded him that the only thing he wanted more than fame was real talent.'

'We want people to love us for what we are not, for what we pretend to be . . . Or in my case all those people I've pretended to be,' said Ortega, who was becoming more dramatic by the moment. 'I'm wondering if, at my death, I'll drop to the floor and, like a mad Touretter, all the characters I've ever portrayed will pour out of me in a compressed babble to silence, leaving only a husk to be blown here and there in the wind.'

'I don't think so, Pablo,' said Falcón. 'You've got a lot to lose to become a husk.'

'I'm just layers,' he said, not listening. 'I remember Francisco said: "The truth about an onion, Pablo, is nothing. You tease open that last bit of onion skin and that's what you find – nothing."'

'Well, Francisco was a man who knew his onions,' said Falcón. 'Human beings are a little more complicated. You tease them open –'

'And what *do* you find?' said Ortega, looming over Falcón, anxious with anticipation.

'That we're defined by what we hide from the world.'

'My God, Javier,' said Ortega, sucking in a vast quantity of Muga. 'You should try some of this wine, you know. It's really very, very good.'

'The photographs, Pablo.'

'Let's get that out of the way.'

'When you told me you saw two Russians going into Sr Vega's house on Noche de Reyes, were these the men?'

Ortega took the shots and went to hunt down his spectacles.

'I haven't seen your dogs tonight,' said Falcón.

'Oh, they're asleep, those two, all curled up in their pug fug. It's a good life . . . the canine one,' said Ortega. 'I never showed you my collection, did I?'

'Another time.'

'I am not defined by what I hide, but what I *show* to the world,' said Ortega, his arm sweeping slowly around the room where his collection lay on tabletops and up against the walls. 'You know the worst thing you can say to a collector?'

'That you don't like a piece?'

'No . . . that you *do* like *one* particular piece,' said Ortega. 'I have a Picasso drawing. It's nothing special but you can't mistake it. I divide the people I show my collection into two groups. The ones who gravitate to the Picasso with the words, "Now I *do* like that," and the ones who realize that a collection is about the whole. There, Javier, I've saved you some embarrassment.'

'I'll make a point of telling you how much I *love* the Picasso.'

Ortega held up his spectacles with a roar as if he'd won the European Cup. He put his face into them almost warily, as if it might be some hair-trigger trap he'd set for himself.

'The ones who gravitate to the Picasso are the ones who are attracted to celebrity. They see nothing else.'

'Have you ever shown your collection to someone who's looked at the whole and found it . . .'

'Lacking?' said Ortega. 'Nobody has ever had the nerve to say that to my face. But I know there have been some.'

'Perhaps that means you've had the nerve to express *everything* through your collection. The good and the bad. We've all got something we're ashamed of.'

'You must see it, Javier,' he said urgently. 'The Actor's Collection.'

Ortega confirmed that the two men in the shots were the Russians he'd seen going into Vega's house back in January. He hurled the photographs back to Falcón and refilled his glass. He sucked on his Cohiba, which he still hadn't lit. The wine spots on his shirt had burgeoned with the sweat from his chest. He tore off his glasses.

'You remember our talk about Sebastián this morning?' said Falcón. 'Have you thought any more about that?'

'I *have* thought about it.'

'The clinical psychologist I told you about – a woman called Alicia Aguado. She's unusual.'

'How?'

'First of all, she's blind,' said Falcón, and told Ortega about her Chinese pulse-taking technique. 'I told her about your concerns for Sebastián. She thought it would be a good idea to meet. She realizes that famous people don't like intruders.'

'Bring her over,' said Ortega, charming and amenable. 'The more the merrier.'

'How about tomorrow?'

'Coffee,' he said. 'Eleven o'clock. And perhaps when you've taken her home you'd like to come back and I'll show you everything you need to know in the clear light of day.'

Consuelo Jiménez was wearing a long, blue crepe dress and gold sandals. Her bare arms were brown and muscular. She was keeping up the gym, and not just at a social level. She sat him in the living room, overlooking the sloppy blue ingot of the lit pool, and gave him a chilled glass of manzanilla. She put a tray of olives, pickled garlic and capers out on the table and kicked off her sandals. The ice in her tinto de verano clicked on the sides of the glass.

'Guess who came to see me this morning, full of wheedling charm and flattery?'

'Pablo Ortega?'

'For one of the great actors of yesterday he's a little too easy to encapsulate,' she said. 'It must mean he's got a limited range.'

'I've never seen him on the stage,' said Falcón. 'Did you let him in?'

'I let him suffer in the heat for a bit. I was interested to hear what he had to say for himself. He didn't bring his two stage props along – Pavarotti and Callas. So I knew he hadn't come to entertain the boys.'

'Where are your boys?'

'They're with my sister. She's taking them off to the coast tomorrow and they're too riotous for dinner. They'd want to see your gun.'

'And what did Pablo Ortega want?'

'To talk about Rafael's death and your investigation, of course.'

'I hope you didn't reveal my . . . indiscretion.'

'I used it,' she said, lighting up a cigarette, 'but not in an overt way. I just made him feel as if he was sitting on a bad sofa. He left more uncomfortable than when he arrived.'

'I'm taking a look at his son's court case,' said Falcón.

'Personally, I think the sentences for child abuse are too lenient,' said Consuelo. 'Once a child's been damaged in that way they can never recover. Their innocence has been taken away, and I think that's not so different to murder.'

He told her what Montes had explained to him about the manipulation of the boy's statement and Sebastián Ortega's refusal to defend himself.

'Well, that doesn't exactly renew my faith in the justice system,' she said. 'But I saw that glimmer of vanity in Juez Calderón when he was working on Raúl's case.'

'Did you see anything else in him?'

'Like what?'

'What we were talking about before . . . like, say, Ramírez.'

'You mean, on the lookout for opportunities?' she said. 'Well, I spotted him as unmarried and therefore a free agent.'

'Yes, I suppose that's different.'

'Oh, I see, you're asking me why, since he's announced his engagement to your little truth-seeker, is he sniffing around Maddy Krugman?'

'Is there such a thing as pre-marital infidelity?'

'He was there this afternoon,' she said. 'As you know, I don't keep regular hours. I'm here when most people are at work or, in the case of Juez Calderón, when he *should* be at work.'

'Was Marty there?'

'I assumed it was to do with the investigation into Rafael's death,' she said, shaking her head.

'That would not be normal procedure.'

'He doesn't seem the sort to give a shit about normal procedure,' said Consuelo. 'Anyway, why should it bother you? You're not still interested in Inés?'

'No, I'm not,' he said, as if to emphasize it to himself.

'Liar. Don't make the same mistake twice, Javier,' she said. 'I know it's a deeply ingrained human trait, but it should be resisted, because all the pain that was there the first time round will be present and correct the second time round . . . and then doubled.'

'I keep hearing from women with the powerful voice of experience.'

'Listen to them,' she said, standing up and slipping on her sandals. 'I'm going to give you some food now and I don't want any more talk about these fools in love or your investigation.'

She served jamón on toast with salmorejo, crostini of grilled red peppers with an anchovy fillet, gambas al ajillo, octopus salad and piquillo peppers stuffed with saffron rice and chicken. They drank a cold red Basque rioja. Consuelo ate as if she'd starved herself all day and Falcón found the appetite that the summer heat had previously suppressed.

'You are allowed that shameful final piquillo pepper,' she said, lighting a cigarette. 'There will now be a pause before the main course.'

'I read in a magazine review that you knew how to do everything in your restaurants,' he said.

'It's all simple stuff done well,' she said. 'I don't understand those restaurants with a menu the size of a novel but which can't cook any of the dishes properly. Never spread yourself too thinly . . . neither in life, nor in love.'

'I'll drink to that,' he said, and they clinked glasses.

'A question –' she said. 'Not about your investigation, but it is connected to what happened . . . before. It's something I think about every day since Raúl's past came out.'

'I know what you're going to ask.'

'You do?'

'I've thought about it myself.'

'Go on, then.'

'What happened to Arturo?' said Falcón. 'Is that it? What happened to Raúl's little boy?'

Consuelo came round the table and took his face in both her hands and kissed him hard on the lips. The voltage slammed through his spine and earthed itself down the chair legs.

'I knew it,' she said, and let him go, running her fingertips across his cheeks so that nerves flashed all over his body.

Falcón wondered if this physical invasion had changed him. He saw himself, hair frizzed and clothes smoking. He had the taste of her on his mouth. Things started up inside him, small bits of machinery which turned cogs and ran belts setting bigger wheels in motion, thrusting drive shafts forward, which were geared to pull back some vast unused piston, rusted into its chamber.

'Are you all right, Javier?' she asked as she reached her end of the table. 'I'll get the main course while you decide how we're going to find out what happened to Arturo Jiménez.'

He gulped down half a glass of wine which nearly choked him. Stay calm. Consuelo returned with two grilled pieces of steak an inch thick. Blood oozed from the meat into a potato confection and a salad. More Basque rioja was put in his hand and a corkscrew. He pulled the cork, poured the wine. He wanted to get her down on the floor amongst the chair legs, find out what was under the blue crepe. Stay calm. He watched her waist, hips, buttocks move around the table. His eyeballs felt hot. His cooling system was shot. She sat back down.

He drank. He was drunk.

'How are we going to find Arturo?' she asked, unaware of the turmoil on the other side of the table. 'I've never even been to Morocco.'

'We should go,' he said, the words out of his mouth before he could stop them.

'What are you doing this summer?'

'I'm free in September.'

'Then in September we shall go,' she said. 'The estate of Raúl Jiménez can pay the expenses.'

'This steak is fantastic.'

'Hand cut by Rafael Vega,' she said.

'My God, he knew what he was doing.'

'You're not concentrating,' she said.

'There's too much happening to me at once,' he said, slugging down more wine. 'I think I'm reaching critical mass.'

'Don't go off in here,' she said, 'I've just had the decorators in.'

He laughed, poured more wine.

'We should start a charity,' he said, 'which specifically looks for missing children.'

'There must be one already.'

'We'll use retired policemen. I know just the man. He's the Inspector Jefe of the Grupo de Menores and he's coming up for retirement.'

'Slow down, Javier,' she said. 'You're talking too much, you're eating too quickly, you're drinking like a fish.'

'More wine?' he asked. 'We *need* more wine.'

'You'll be drunk and incapable if . . .'

Their eyes met across the table and stuff that was far too complicated to be talked about was instantly understood. Falcón dropped his knife and fork. Consuelo stood up. They kissed. She pushed her hands up under his shirt. All sorts of personal hygiene matters tore through his brain. He eased the zipper down her back, ran his finger along the furrow of her spine and encountered no underwear. His thighs shuddered. Her hands found his back. Adrenalin careered around his system.

Steady on, he thought, or I won't have even got out of my trousers. She saved him.

'Not here,' she said. 'I don't want *la puta americana* nosing around with her camera.'

She led him upstairs, holding him by the wrist.

'You know I haven't done this for a long time,' he said, following the two dimples in her lower back.

'Nor have I,' she said. 'Perhaps we should turn up the air conditioning.'

15

❦❦❦

In bed Consuelo Jiménez was as he had expected her to be – exciting, demanding and unrelenting. In one of the several cigarette breaks she'd revealed that this had been her first sex since she'd been with Basilio Lucena on the night her husband, Raúl, had been murdered. Since then she'd been concentrated on the children.

'I had an AIDS test, too,' she said, 'when I found out about Basilio's promiscuity. You know, I haven't had much luck...'

Falcón turned his head on the pillow to find her dark eyes close to him.

'It was negative,' she said.

This was how they'd talked, which had fascinated Falcón. He couldn't remember lying in bed with a woman and talking about anything and everything. Even in the two big relationships in his life, lying in bed had never been a time for honesty but for some acting role whose lines he wasn't sure of and a part he was not suited to.

They woke up early and stickily in the morning. Consuelo took him off for a shower and soaped him up with her body so that he had to support himself on the glass doors. She took advantage of his arousal, thrusting down on him so that the whole structure shuddered. They dressed looking at each other.

He stood in her kitchen with a coffee and toast drizzled with olive oil. His legs felt brand new, straight out of the factory. He didn't have even the scintilla of a hangover and yet three bottles of Basque rioja stood empty by the bin. Still he looked at her wordlessly, with big, risky things going through his head.

'I'd like to see you again,' he said.

'I'm glad we've got that out of the way,' she said. 'Since the invention of the mobile phone women haven't had to spend the day waiting, but now we know for certain that he didn't call.'

'You'll have to tell me how I can fit into your life,' he said.

'Yours is more complicated than mine.'

'You have children.'

'They're going away.'

'You'll follow them.'

'Later in August.'

'I have no control over my time at the moment,' he said. 'Something happens and I have to react.'

'Then call me when you have some time to spare,' she said. 'Unless . . . it's all taken up talking to your lawyers about Manuela so that you can't have dinner with me.'

He smiled. He was falling in love with her humour, her directness. He told her his idea about selling the house to Manuela and what Isabel Cano had advised.

'Take her advice,' said Consuelo. 'The best you can expect from Manuela is respect, and you get that by driving a hard bargain. I'll say this once, Javier, and then it's finished. You can listen or ignore. Get a valuation on the house, offer her a private sale less the agent's commission, and give her a week to respond before you put it on the open market.'

He nodded. This was what he needed in his life – simplification. He pulled her to him, kissed her through the smell of coffee and toast.

It was 9.30 a.m. He called Ramírez on his mobile.

'Have you made an appointment to see Carlos Vázquez this morning?' asked Falcón.

'What about the search warrant from Juez Calderón?'

'I couldn't get hold of him,' said Falcón. 'And I checked his office last night.'

'Then we'll just have to try and talk it out of Vázquez,' said Ramírez. 'I'll call you when I've set up the meeting with him. I've just put Sergei's face up on the computer – national and international.'

Falcón called Alicia Aguado to ask her if he could pick her up and bring her out to Santa Clara to meet Pablo Ortega later that morning. On the way back into town Ramírez told him that Vázquez would be in his office until midday. Falcón took down the address and said he'd meet him there in fifteen minutes.

He took a call from Cristina Ferrera.

'Nadia's gone,' she said. 'Two guys came round last night and picked her up and they didn't bring her back.'

'Has that happened before?'

'She's always back in the apartment by five or six in the morning,' said Ferrera. 'What do I do?'

'Unless there's someone who's prepared to give you a detailed description of the two guys – which I doubt – there's nothing you can do,' said Falcón.

Carlos Vázquez's offices were in the Edificio Viapol in a soulless part of the city on the edge of San Bernardo. Ramírez was waiting for him at the entrance. They went up in the lift. Ramírez stared into the side of his face.

'What are you looking at, José Luis?'

'You,' he said, grinning. 'I heard it in your voice. Now I've seen you in the same clothes you were wearing yesterday, it's confirmed.'

'What, exactly?' he said, thinking he'd be able to brazen this out.

'I am the expert,' said Ramírez, holding his huge fingers to his chest, nearly offended by his boss's effrontery. 'I can tell, even over the phone, that you've finally come to the end of a drought.'

'What drought?'

'Is it true . . . or am I a liar?' said Ramírez, laughing. 'Who is it?'

'I don't know what you're talking about.'

Ramírez's big, dark, mahogany face took up Falcón's vision. The individual rails of the Inspector's black pomaded hair stood out pin sharp.

'It wasn't la americana, was it? I've heard about her from Felipe and Jorge. They said she'd leave a man as hollow as a spare suit.'

'I think we should concentrate on what we're going to say to Carlos Vázquez, José Luis.'

'No, no, no, she's not the one. La americana is Juez Calderón's latest squeeze.'

'Who did you hear that from?' said Falcón. 'The guy's just announced his engagement, for God's sake.'

Ramírez laughed, a mirthless guffaw. The lift stopped. They went into Vázquez's offices to be confronted by a large painting of an abstract city-scape – vague lights and building outlines coming through fog. It struck Falcón that this was the sort of piece that Ramón Salgado might have sold.

'I'll lead this discussion,' said Falcón. 'I don't want you to instigate anything, because I know things you don't, José Luis. It's important.'

'And I know things you've never even thought about,' said Ramírez.

Falcón wanted to know what those things were, but one of Vázquez's junior lawyers was already on top of them. They were shown into Vázquez's office, which had a view of the back of the buildings on Calle Balbino Marrón. Vázquez asked them to sit down while he continued to read through a document. There was a large map of Seville behind him on which the locations of various projects were shown in different coloured squares. Vázquez threw the papers in an out-tray and sat back. Falcón introduced Ramírez and Vázquez took an instant dislike to him.

'So I'm getting the full weight of the homicide squad,' he said.

'That painting in your reception area,' said Falcón. 'Who's it by?'

'That's an interesting question,' said Vázquez, lost for a moment.

'He likes to get warmed up first,' said Ramírez, smiling.

'It's by a German called Kristian Lutze. I understand it's an abstract of Berlin. He's done another one of Cologne which hangs in the foyer of Vega Construcciones.'

'How did you and Sr Vega acquire them?'

'Through an art dealer here in Seville called Ramón Salgado. He . . . of course, you know, he was murdered.'

'How did Sr Vega know Ramón Salgado?'

Ramírez slumped in his chair, bored.

'I don't know,' said Vázquez.

'Not through you?'

'I have to confess that it's not really my interest. It was a gift from Rafael,' said Vázquez. 'I like cars.'

'What sort of cars?' asked Ramírez.

They looked at him. He shrugged.

'Can I smoke?' he asked.

Vázquez nodded. Ramírez lit up, sat back, hands behind his head.

'Is this social,' asked Vázquez, annoyed, 'or something else?'

'Sr Vega was running two projects with Russian partners,' said Falcón. 'Vladimir Ivanov and Mikhail Zelenov.'

'They aren't strictly partnerships,' said Vázquez. 'Vega Construcciones was contracted by two Russian clients to provide technical help. They were being paid for architectural plans, site engineers, gang supervisors and some equipment. On completion of the structure Vega Construcciones were also to be involved in the interior planning – air conditioning, electrics, lift installation, plumbing . . . that kind of thing.'

'These are unusual projects for Vega Construcciones,' said Falcón. 'Normally they do all the physical work while the partners supply the necessary finance and . . . in recent times, as far as I know, they've always retained a controlling percentage in the projects.'

'That's true.'

'Who owned the land on which the two Russian projects were being built?'

'The Russians themselves. They came to Rafael with the proposal,' said Vázquez. 'They are not Seville-based. Sr Zelenov has had some projects in Marbella and Sr Ivanov is in Vilamoura in the Algarve. It was easier for them to contract the work out than start up their own companies.'

'Are they linked, these Russians?' asked Falcón. 'Do they know each other?'

'I . . . I don't know.'

'So you dealt with them separately?' said Falcón.

'Two unusual deals with different Russians out of the blue,' said Ramírez, interested now.

'What's the point you're making?'

'All you've got to do is answer the questions,' said Ramírez.

'Could you show us on that map behind you where the two Russian projects are located?' asked Falcón.

Vázquez pointed out two green squares which were amongst a mass of orange. Falcón flipped through his notebook and went up close to the map.

'And what is unique about those two locations?' asked Falcón.

Vázquez looked at the map like a schoolboy who knows the right answer but whose confidence has been shattered by a brutal teacher.

'Even I can see it,' said Ramírez.

'I don't see what this has got to do with Rafael Vega's death,' said Vázquez, angry now.

'Just answer the question,' said Ramírez, putting a big meaty elbow on the desk.

'They are both in locations where all the other projects are being developed by Vega Construcciones,' said Falcón.

'So what?' said Vázquez.

'We've spoken to Sr Cabello. He pointed out that, of the properties he brought to Vega Construcciones on the back of his daughter's marriage to Rafael Vega, two held the key to the development of whole areas. One area owned by Vega Construcciones and the other by another developer, who without Sr Cabello's plot would be unable to develop it. When Sr Vega came into ownership that developer had to sell out to Sr Vega or . . . *friends* of Sr Vega. That's what those two Russian plots have got in common.'

Silence, apart from some flamboyant smoking by Ramírez, who was enjoying his boss's magic show.

'This is admirable footwork on your part, Inspector Jefe,' said Vázquez. 'But are we any closer to understanding what happened to Sr Vega?'

'Sr Vega's Russian friends were known mafiosi. We think they were using these projects to clean up cash they'd been making from people-trafficking and prostitution. Why was Sr Vega involved with these people and why was he giving them extremely advantageous deals?'

'You can't possibly prove any of this.'

'Perhaps your office was involved in the property deals. Possibly you have the deeds here and a record of payments made?' said Falcón.

'You could remind yourself now,' said Ramírez.

'The only documents I have are the contracts for the building of the projects, which are in the archives, and the person who runs that is on holiday.'

'So the property deals were done direct between the original owner of the land and the Russians?' said Falcón. 'Did Sr Vega ask the original owner to give the Russians a sweet deal, which he would make up to them elsewhere?'

'I really don't know, Inspector Jefe.'

'But we could have a look at the sale details of the other plots – which I assume, as Sr Vega's lawyer, you *were* involved in – and make a comparison of the prices paid,' said Falcón. 'You *do* have those details here, don't you, Sr Vázquez?'

'I told you, the person who runs the archives is . . .'

'It doesn't matter. We can, of course, talk to the original owners of the plots. That's just the fine detail that the court will require,' said Falcón. 'What we'd like to know is why Sr Vega was involved with these Russians and expediting their money-laundering operations.'

'I don't know how you can justify that remark,' said Vázquez. 'There are two projects with these Russians. There are two contracts. There are two clear sets of books which show the financial involvement of both parties.'

'We've been around to see these projects,' said Ramírez. 'They were looking a little bare of people without the illegal labour.'

'That's the Russians' problem, not Vega Construcciones.'

'In that case,' said Ramírez, 'maybe you can tell us why Sr Vega kept another set of books for these two projects – the official version for tax purposes and his private version, which was the reality.'

'You might also venture an opinion on why Sergei, the gardener, has disappeared since the discovery of the body,' said Falcón. 'And why Sr Vega was getting social visits from his Russian clients at his home on Noche de Reyes, for instance. Doesn't that sound a little more intimate than the usual business partner?'

'All right, all right, you've proved your point,' said Vázquez. 'You've discovered a Russian *connection*. But that is all. If you want to know things about that relationship then I can't help you because I don't know anything. All I can say is . . . ask the Russians, if you can find them.'

'How do *you* contact them?'

'I don't. I drew up the contracts. They were returned to me by Vega Construcciones, signed and stamped,' said Vázquez. 'And you won't find anybody in their offices who's spoken to them either.'

'They must have phone numbers, addresses, bank accounts?' said Ramírez.

'*You* think they're the Moscow mafia.'

'We know they are.'

'Well, maybe they are. And maybe they had good reason to kill a man who was facilitating their business needs, but I can't think what that reason would be,' said Vázquez. 'And I doubt you'll ever find out if there *was* a reason and that they *did* kill him. These people keep themselves well removed from the situation. As I said, I've never met them. So, Inspector Jefe, Inspector. . .it's all in your hands now. You know as much as I do. Now, I think that concludes our business for this morning so . . . please excuse me.'

On the way down in the lift Ramírez jangled the change in his pocket. Falcón told him to get Cristina Ferrera to find the names of the original owners of the two plots sold to the Russians.

'That's police work for you,' said Ramírez, punching Ferrera's number into his mobile. 'One moment you think you've got them nailed and the next they've disappeared over the horizon.'

'What things do you know that I've never even thought about?' asked Falcón, remembering Ramírez's earlier comment.

'Even if we do find Sergei and he has seen something . . . what's he going to tell us?' said Ramírez, regretting his loose talk now.

'We were talking about Juez Calderón on the way up in the lift and you said that you knew things that I'd never even thought about, José Luis.'

'It was nothing . . . just something to say.'

'It didn't sound like that,' said Falcón. 'It sounded as if it was something about Juez Calderón that was personal to me.'

'It's nothing . . . forget it,' said Ramírez.

Ferrera came on the line and Ramírez relayed Falcón's message about the plots of land.

'Tell me, José Luis. Just tell me,' said Falcón. 'I'm not mad any more. I'm not going to throw myself into the traffic if you –'

'All right, all right,' said Ramírez, as the lift reached the ground floor. 'I'll ask you a question and you see if you can tell me the answer.'

They left the building and stood facing each other in the sweltering street.

'When did Juez Calderón and Inés start seeing each other?' said Ramírez.

16

Saturday, 27th July 2002

Back at home, in the cool of his bedroom, Falcón stripped off the clothes that had marked him out to Ramírez as an amateur. He stood under the shower and stared out through the fogged glass doors and thought about the way Isabel Cano had spoken to him about Inés – 'an innocent little sweetie'. She knew. Those words that Inspector Jefe Montes had used about Calderón: 'You like him, Inspector Jefe. I'd never have thought it.' He knew. Felipe and Jorge. Pérez, Serrano and Baena. The whole of the Edificio de los Juzgados and the Palacio de Justicia. They all knew. That's what happens to you when you're buried in your own life. You don't see anything. You don't even see that someone else is fucking your wife under your nose. He shook his head as he remembered that horrible algebra that the police psychologist had made him use. When did you split up with your wife? When did you last have sex with her? If we separated in July then it must have been May. That was May 2000.

He dressed and left the house. He needed another coffee before he went to pick up Alicia Aguado. He bought *El País* and went to the Café San Bernardo and ordered a café solo at the bar. Cristina Ferrera called from the Vega Construcciones offices giving him the details of the original owner of the plots who'd sold out to the Russians. Unfortunately the man was on holiday in South America and would not be back until September. She also mentioned that the accountant had hacked into Vega's address book and had found a number for the Russians. A single number for both Russians and it was in Vilamoura in the Algarve, Portugal.

He closed down the phone and tried to read his newspaper, but this time, rather than the humiliation of learning about a tawdry affair running through his mind, he found memories of last night surfacing. The sight of Consuelo astride him, the small strip of her pubic hair hovering over him. Her unswerving stare as she eased him into her. Her words: 'I want to see you inside me.' Christ. His throat was too tight for him to swallow. The newsprint blurred. He had to shake himself back into real life, the café, people sitting around.

Sex mattered to Consuelo. She was good at it. When her orgasm was coming she let out a kind of low, feline growl and when she came it was with a massive grunt of effort, like a sprinter hitting the finishing line. She liked to be on top and when it was over she knelt above him, hair hanging down, some of it plastered to her face, panting, unconscious to the world, her breasts shuddering with each breath. He thought sex with Inés had been good. He thought they had hit it off in bed. But now he realized there had been something withdrawn about her, something held back. It was as if she couldn't let herself go to the animal edge of her being. Something in her head told her that this was not quite how she should behave.

Was that true? Is this what the mind does when you've been drawn to another partner? Persuade you that the last one wasn't up to much? Maybe that was what Calderón had seen as well. That with Inés there is none of that difference that Isabel Cano spoke about. Inés is beautiful, intelligent and attractive, but he knows how it's all going to unfold. And it was at that moment, just as his mobile had started to vibrate in his pocket, that he realized it was over. It was none of his business. It didn't matter to him any more. He didn't give a shit about Inés or Calderón or what the hell happened to them in their miserable lives. Something gave way inside him. He had a physical sensation of release, of tension breaking, of ropes flying off and whipping back into the night. He grinned and looked around himself at the whole café's magnificent unconcern and then took the call from Alicia Aguado asking him where the hell he was.

Because this wasn't a consultation they kissed hello and she immediately noticed a difference in him.

'You're happy,' she said.

'A few things have fallen into place.'

'You've had some sex.'

'I don't believe you can tell that,' he said. 'And anyway, this isn't an appointment.'

They drove out to Santa Clara for the meeting with Pablo Ortega. There was no answer when Falcón rang the bell by the gate, but he noticed that the wooden door had been left open. They coughed at the stench from the cesspit which Falcón had warned her about. Aguado held on to Falcón's elbow as they made their way to the kitchen on the other side of the house. There was no sign of Ortega and it was past eleven o'clock.

'He's probably walking the dogs,' said Falcón. 'We'll take a seat in the shade by the pool and wait for him.'

'I don't know how he can live with that stink.'

'Don't worry, you don't notice it inside. He's had that part of the house sealed off.'

'Walking into that everyday would make me suicidal.'

'Well, Pablo Ortega is not a happy man.'

He sat her down at the table by the pool and walked along the edge towards the deep end. He stood on the small diving board and looked down. There seemed to be a sack sitting on the bottom. He found a pole lying by the side of the pool. It had a net at one end and a hook at the other.

'What are you doing, Javier?' asked Alicia, concerned by his silent activity.

'There's a sack in the bottom of the pool. Something like an old fertilizer bag.'

The sack was heavy. He had to push it along the bottom to the edge of the pool and then drag it down to the shallow end where he pulled it out. It must have weighed thirty kilos. He undid the twine at the neck of the sack and gasped at its horrific contents.

'What is it?' said Alicia, on her feet, disorientated by the sounds he was making, panicked.

'It's Pavarotti and Callas,' said Falcón. 'Ortega's dogs. This doesn't look good.'

'Someone has drowned his *dogs*?' she said.

'No,' he said. 'I think he's drowned his own dogs.'

Falcón told her to stay sitting by the pool. He went to the kitchen door, which was shut but not locked. He opened it and the horrific stink of the cesspit was thick in the room. There were two empty bottles of Torre Muga on the table. He went into the sitting room where there was another empty bottle of wine and the box of Cohibas Ortega had offered him last night. No glass. The smell of raw sewage was more powerful and he realized that the seal to the other part of the house had been broken. The door to the hallway was open and across the corridor the door to the room with the cracked cesspit was ajar.

On the floor in the corridor was an empty bottle of Nembutal with no top. He pushed the door open. There were wooden boards and plastic sheeting thrown against the wall, which had a large subsidence crack in it. A hole in the floor had been opened up by workmen so that they could inspect the damage. Fragments of Ortega's shattered wine glass were all over the bare concrete and tiles. There was a burnt-out cigar stub as well. In the hole, just below the surface of the sewage, was the white and yellow sole of Pablo Ortega's right foot. Falcón called the Jefatura on his mobile. He specifically asked that Juez Calderón be notified as the death might be relevant to the Vega case. He also asked for Cristina Ferrera but instructed that Ramírez should be left alone.

He backed out of the room and went up the corridor to the master bedroom. On the smooth untouched burgundy cover of the bed were two letters, one addressed to Javier Falcón and the other to Sebastián Ortega. He left them where they were and went back to Alicia Aguado, who was still sitting by the pool, very frightened. He told her that Pablo Ortega appeared to have committed suicide.

'I can't believe this,' said Falcón. 'I saw him last night and he was on his way to becoming very drunk, but he was affable, charming, generous. He even said that after our meeting today he was going to show me his collection.'

'His mind was made up,' said Alicia, who was holding on to herself as if she was freezing cold in 42°C.

'Damn,' said Falcón to himself, 'I can't help feeling responsible for this. I've stirred things up and it's –'

'Nobody is responsible for another person killing themselves,' said Alicia firmly. 'He has a whole history that won't have been changed, or even particularly stirred up, by talking to Javier Falcón for a couple of hours.'

'Of course, I know that. I suppose what I mean is that I've precipitated it by pushing him too hard.'

'You mean you weren't just talking to him about Sebastián?'

175

'I thought he had information that might help my investigation.'

'Was he a suspect?'

'Not exactly a suspect. I could just see that I was making him nervous. The questions I was asking him, whether they were about his son or the Rafael Vega case, for some reason disturbed him.'

'Just out of interest, from the psychological point of view,' she said, 'how did he kill himself?'

'He got drunk, took some sleeping pills and drowned himself in the cracked cesspit.'

'He's planned it out pretty carefully, hasn't he?' she said. 'Drowning the dogs –'

'I asked after his dogs last night,' said Falcón. 'He said they were sleeping. He'd probably already killed them.'

'Any suicide note?'

'Two letters: one to me and the other to his son. I've left them until the Juez de Guardia gets here.'

'He knew you were going to be the first person in here this morning,' she said. 'No nasty surprises for anybody but the professional. The gate and doors conveniently left open. He thought it all out down to the last detail of throwing himself in the cesspit.'

'What do you mean?'

'I thought you said that part of the house was sealed off.'

'I did.'

'So he went to the trouble of breaking the seal because it was psychologically important for him to drown himself in shit . . . his own shit,' she said. 'I'm sure the pills and alcohol would have done the job on their own.'

'Alcohol can induce vomiting.'

'All right. So he was making sure of it as well . . . but he could have used the pool. Less private, but it was good enough for his dogs.'

'Assuage my guilt, Alicia. Give me a theory,' he said.

'As you know, there's been a build-up of events even before you started coming to see him about Rafael Vega,' she said. 'His son has been jailed in a high-profile case for a nasty crime. He himself was ostracized by his community so that he had to leave his apartment, and there's a story behind that which you still don't know. He's moved here to a place which, on the face of it, suits him. A garden city, a wealthy community, peace and quiet. But it didn't turn out like that. He felt dislocated and craved the involvement of the barrio. The house he bought developed an unpleasant and antisocial problem. To us that would seem an irritating and expensive inconvenience, but to Pablo Ortega it probably achieved some sort of significance in his mind. Then his neighbour died . . .'

'He wanted to know if Sr Vega had committed suicide.'

'So it was already on his mind,' said Alicia. 'I've left out the fact that his son didn't want to see him either . . . another isolating factor. Then Javier Falcón arrived on the scene, perceiving an injustice in Sebastián's case and wanting to help. As you know, from your own experience, you can't help without stirring things up. And what came to the surface of Pablo Ortega's mind? Whatever it was, he didn't want to know about it. He didn't think it worth staying alive to face it. So, not only does he *not* bring the difficult things to the surface, he actually submerges himself. He drowns his memories in his own ordure. His sweet and innocent dogs did not get that treatment.'

Falcón shook his head in dismay.

'You were asking him about his son, Javier, and you said you were putting pressure on him through your investigation. What did you suspect him of having done?'

'I don't want to talk about that just yet. It would help if you came to this with an open mind,' he said. 'That is, if you want to be involved. It doesn't have to be any of your business.'

'I'm involved,' she said. 'I'd like to know what the letters say. And it might be interesting to know what he had in his collection.'

A patrol car pulled up outside the house.

'We've got to do our work first,' he said. 'But I don't think this will take very long.'

An ambulance parked up behind the patrol car. Felipe and Jorge turned up a few minutes later, along with the Juez de Guardia, Juan Romero. There was a quick conference about the relevance of this suicide to the Vega case. Calderón called Romero who gave him Falcón's verbal report. It was decided to treat them separately. Cristina Ferrera arrived in time to hear the decision.

Falcón gave them a tour of the crime scene via the dead dogs by the pool and the interior of the house. Felipe took the crime scene shots while Jorge inspected the dogs and scraped meat from between their teeth. Ferrera checked the telephone for messages and asked the phone company for a breakdown of calls in and out. She searched for a mobile.

The ambulancemen came in and decided that Ortega's body had been weighted to keep it submerged and would have to be winched out via a pulley in the ceiling. They went to get a block and tackle. Felipe and Jorge moved in and bagged all the evidence before moving on to the bedroom. The Médico Forense arrived and sat chatting with Alicia Aguado by the pool while he waited for the body to be lifted out.

Felipe handed over the letters to Falcón unopened in evidence bags. The ambulancemen chipped away at the ceiling until they found a reinforced concrete beam and started drilling. Falcón took the letters into the sitting room to read. Ferrera hadn't found the mobile. He sent her out to speak to the neighbours to see what Ortega's movements had been in the last twenty-four hours.

PRIVATE AND CONFIDENTIAL

27th July 2002
Dear Javier,

I think you must have realized now that I chose you and I am sorry if this has upset you. You are the professional and, as I said, I like you and I want this, the last scene of my final act, to pass safely into your hands.

Just in case there is some doubt, or some opportunistic burglar has happened on the scene and messed up my tragedy, I would like to declare unequivocally that I have taken my own life. This was not a snap decision. It was certainly not provoked by any recent developments but is a culmination of events. I have come to the end of my road and found it a cul-de-sac, with no possibility of retracing my steps and doing all the things that I should have done. It was a dead end with only one exit and I chose it with clear eyes, if not a clear conscience.

My reasons for having taken my own life are the only reasons a suicide can have. I am weak and I am selfish. I have neglected my son. This has been the stamp of all my family and personal relationships and has happened prob-

178

ably because I am consumed by vanity. The reward for this is my loneliness. My son is in prison. My family have grown tired of me. My community has thrown me out. My profession has shunned me. Vanity, in case you do not know this, requires an audience. Life inside my bubble has become intolerable. I have no one to perform to and therefore I am no one.

It probably seems absurd that someone of my fame and in my comfortable circumstances should have chosen this end. I can feel myself on the brink of a long and rambling explanation, but it would only be the Torre Muga speaking. My apologies for the inconvenience, Javier. Please give the other letter to my son, Sebastián. I hope you succeed in helping him where I have so singularly failed.

Con un abrazo,
Pablo Ortega

PS I never showed you my collection. Please enjoy it at your leisure.

PPS Please inform my brother, Ignacio. His number is in the address book on the kitchen table.

Falcón read the letter through several times until his thoughts were interrupted by the sound of an electric winch. He stood at the door as Ortega's stained and bloated body emerged from under the floor. The masked ambulancemen pulled him away from over the hole and lowered him on to the concrete. He had a large flat rock taped to his chest and another one shoved down his blue shorts. Falcón called in the Médico Forense and asked Felipe to take more shots. He went to sit with Alicia Aguado and read her Ortega's letter.

'I don't think he's as drunk as he makes out.'

'There were three empty bottles of Muga in there.'

'They weren't inside him when he wrote this letter,' she said. 'He's stated his guilt, but he's been very careful not to admit to anything. The denial that his suicide has anything to do with "recent developments" seems to be important. *He* is in denial. He cannot face up to whatever it is that he believes will be revealed by these recent developments.'

'The only recent developments I know about are Rafael Vega's death and me volunteering to help his son.'

Cristina Ferrera came back from talking to the few neighbours she could find. Ortega had walked his dogs yesterday morning. He'd been out in his car twice at about 11 a.m. and 5 p.m. Both trips were for about an hour and a half each.

'Would you bother to walk your dogs if you were going to kill them?' asked Falcón.

'It seems to have been a routine,' said Ferrera. 'His neighbour walked his dog at the same time. And even condemned men get fed and exercised.'

'Killing them is to do with his admitted selfishness and vanity. They were a part of him, only he knew how to love them,' said Alicia Aguado. 'You saw him yesterday morning before he went out, Javier. What did you talk about then?'

'I was interested in his relationship with Rafael Vega, how he knew him, whether he'd met him through Raúl Jiménez and whether he knew any of the people around those men. I had a photograph of him with some people at a party which seemed to unnerve him. I also talked to him about his son's case. Then I left, but – no, that's not quite right. He told me about a recurring dream, then I left, but I came back to ask him about something I'd forgotten and I saw him sink to his knees in the garden, weeping.'

Alicia Aguado asked about the dream and he described Ortega's vision of himself in a field with his hurting hands.

'I read your report of your first meeting,' said Ferrera. 'He was very different then.'

'Yes, he was much more the actor. Most of that interview was performance,' said Falcón. 'He was more serious in subsequent talks. The pressure was building.'

'What were you being accusatory about, Javier?' asked Aguado.

'I don't want to talk about it until I've got it clear in my mind,' he said. 'I've got a lot more work to do on that.'

Jorge called Falcón over for a crime scene conference. They were convinced it was suicide. They had found nothing to lead them to believe it happened any other way. Ortega's fingerprints were over everything. Juan Romero asked the Médico Forense for his opinion.

'Time of death was about 3 a.m. Cause was drowning. There was a single mark on his forehead which probably happened as he fell into the hole. My pre-lab inspection verdict is that he committed suicide.'

Juez Romero signed off the levantamiento del cadáver. Falcón told him that he would inform the next of kin as the dead man had requested. The paramedics removed the body and those of the two dogs. Felipe and Jorge left. Falcón told Ferrera to follow up on the phone numbers on Monday and let her go. He went to the kitchen, found the address book and called Ignacio Ortega on his mobile, which was turned off. He told Romero they would delay telling the press about Ortega's death until his brother had been informed.

The ambulance and cars moved off towards Avenida de Kansas City. A patrol car remained with an officer to keep an eye on the house. The news announcement of Ortega's death might arouse public interest. Falcón offered to take Alicia Aguado home but she was keen to hear a description of the Ortega collection mentioned in the suicide letter.

The collection, which Ortega had moved into the living room when the cesspit cracked, was distributed around one end of the room, the small pieces on tables, the bigger carvings on the floor and the paintings leaning up against the walls. There was a sheet of paper taped to an antique table in the living room listing all the pieces in the collection with their purchase dates and prices. Falcón ran his eye down the eighteen pieces on the list to the Francisco Falcón painting he'd seen on his first visit.

'This is interesting,' he said. 'Ortega bought the Francisco Falcón painting on 15th May 2001. That was *after* he'd been revealed as a fraud. And he picked it up for a quarter of a million pesetas.'

'What did they used to sell for?'

'He'd have had to pay around two million,' said Falcón. 'It was a good buy because they've come back up again now. The old-fashioned collectors wanted to get rid of everything they had by Francisco Falcón when the news first broke. But now there's a different market for the work. They're a sort of post-modern crowd who have a new take on "What is real art?" Between them and the infamy hunters and the celebrity criminal ghouls they've rebuilt the price.'

'So he knew Francisco, but only bought one of his paintings once he'd been exposed,' said Aguado. 'That's telling us something.'

He told her about the Picasso drawing of a centaur and how Ortega used it as a test.

'Talk me down the list,' she said. 'I'll stop you if I need more information.'

'Two carved African ebony figures of boys holding spears, Ivory Coast. One mask, Zaire.'

'Describe the mask, Javier,' she said. 'Actors are experts on masks.'

'It's sixty centimetres long, twenty wide. It has red hair, two slit eyes and a long nose. There's pieces of bone and shards of mirror stuck in the mouth like teeth. It's a pretty terrifying thing, but beautifully shaped. Bought in New York in 1996 for nine hundred and fifty dollars.'

'It sounds like a witch doctor's mask. Carry on.'

'The next four are Meissen figurines, all male.'

'I hate figurines,' she said.

'One mirror, full length with a rococo gilt frame. Paris. 1984. Nine thousand francs.'

'Something to look at himself in with a halo of gold.'

'A Roman glass bottle, opaque with the colours of the rainbow. A set of eight silver coins, also Roman. One gilt chair – Louis XV. London 1982. For which he paid nine thousand pounds.'

'That's expensive enough to be his throne.'

'One horse, bronze at full gallop – Roman. One bull's head – Greek. One shard of pottery of a boy running – Greek. A piece by Manuel Rivera called *Anatomía en el Espejo*.'

'Anatomy through a mirror? What's that?'

'Metal fabrics on wood. Mirror image. Difficult to describe,' said Falcón. 'There's also a painting here by Zobel called *Dry Garden* and an Indian erotic painting.'

'What sort of eroticism?'

'A pretty graphic depiction of a man with an oversized penis having sex with a woman,' said Falcón. 'And that's it.'

'A very complicated man with his figures, masks and mirrors,' she said. 'Is there any indication as to how the collection was originally set out?'

Falcón looked through the drawers of the antique desk and found a series of photographs of the collection, each one dated on the back. In all of them Pablo Ortega was seated on the Louis XV chair. He found the most recent shot, which included all the pieces except the Indian erotic painting and the Zobel. Then he realized that the Zobel was positioned so that Ortega was looking at it and the Indian

182

painting was such a recent acquisition it hadn't been included. He described the layout to Alicia Aguado.

'He seems to be showing us the Beauty and the Beast. The mask from Zaire is both. All the pieces on one side seem to be the stuff of beauty, nobility and magnificence: Picasso's centaur, the bull's head, the galloping horse, the running boy. I'm simplifying it because there are complications. Centaurs are monsters, too. What's the boy running away from? There are the coins and the beautiful, but empty, Roman bottle. Also the Rivera painting reflected in the gilt mirror. I don't understand that.'

'And the other side?'

'The fraudulent Francisco Falcón. Ortega spent his life pretending. The beautiful figurines locked in porcelain – the actor in his roles. And the inference of "I am as hollow as they are". The mirror is a hard, reflective thing that gilds his narcissism.'

'And the black ebony boys?'

'I don't know – guarding his secrets or keeping them?'

'And why is he always looking at the *Dry Garden*?'

'That's probably his vision of death – beautiful but desiccated,' she said. 'You know you can't use any of this in court, Javier.'

'No,' he said, laughing at the absurdity. 'I'm just hoping for an insight. Pablo told me he had everything on show in this collection. He had nothing to hide. What's your overall impression?'

'It's a very male collection. The only female figure is in the Indian erotic painting. Even the non-human pieces are masculine: horses, bulls and centaurs. What happened to his wife, Sebastián's mother?'

'She died of cancer but – this is interesting – not before she'd run off . . . and I'll quote Pablo directly on this . . . not before she'd "run off to America with a guy with a big dick".'

'Oh dear,' said Alicia, in mock dismay. 'Trouble in the bedroom. Now I'm wondering with all these mirrors, masks and figures whether the biggest role he ever played was himself in his own life, pretending to be a strong, powerful, sexually potent male when in fact . . . he wasn't.'

'Maybe it's time for us to speak to his son,' said Falcón.

17

❦❦❦

On the way to the prison, which was outside Seville in Alcalá, Falcón called the director, whom he knew well, and explained the situation. The director was at home but said that he would make all the necessary calls. The prisoner would be made available to him on his arrival and there was no problem about bringing Alicia Aguado in with him. He made it clear that a prison psychologist would also have to be present and a nurse, in case Sebastián Ortega had to be sedated.

The prison, out on a burnt piece of landscape on the road to Antequera, oscillated so violently in the waves of heat shimmering off the ground that at times it completely disappeared to the eye. They drove through the outer gates, between two chain-link fences topped by razor wire, and up to the prison walls, where they parked.

After the brutality of the heat outside the security checks in the cool, institutional corridors were a relief. As they came closer to where the prisoners were kept the stink of incarcerated men became more powerful. The air ticked with bored minds bent on compressing time while they rebreathed the strong hormonal brew of bottled frustrations. They were taken to a room with a single high window which was barred on the outside. There was a table and four chairs. They sat. Ten minutes later the prison psychologist on duty came and introduced himself.

The psychologist knew Sebastián Ortega and believed him to be harmless. He explained that the prisoner was not totally silent but rarely said any more than the bare minimum. A nurse would be along in a moment and they were prepared for all eventualities including violence, although he didn't think it would come to that.

Two guards brought Sebastián Ortega in and sat him down at the table. Falcón had not seen a photograph of him before this meeting and so was unprepared for the man's beauty. He had none of the physical traits of his father. He was slim, 1.85 metres, with blond hair and tobacco coloured eyes. He had high, fragile cheekbones, which didn't look as if they could survive much prison violence. He moved with a slow grace and sat with his long-fingered artistic hands resting on the table in front of him. He used the fingers of one hand to polish each individual nail of the other. The prison psychologist made the introductions. Sebastián Ortega did not take his eyes off Alicia Aguado for one moment and when the psychologist had finished he leaned forward slightly.

'Excuse me,' he said, in a high, almost girlish voice, 'but are you blind?'

'Yes, I am,' she replied.

'*That's* an affliction I wouldn't mind,' he said.

'Why?'

'We believe too much in what our eyes tell us,' he said. 'They draw us into enormous disappointments.'

The prison psychologist, who was standing at the side of the table, explained to him that Falcón had come here to give him some news. Ortega did not acknowledge him but sat back, nodded, and left his fidgeting hands on the table.

'I'm sorry to have to tell you, Sebastián, that your father died at three o'clock this morning,' said Falcón. 'He took his own life.'

There was no reaction. More than a minute passed while the good-looking face remained unmoved.

'Did you hear the Inspector Jefe?' asked the psychologist.

A single nod and a lowering of the eyelids. The prison officials looked at each other.

'Do you have any questions for the Inspector Jefe?' asked the psychologist.

Sebastián breathed in and shook his head.

'He wrote this letter to you,' said Falcón, laying it down on the table.

Sebastián's hand snapped out of its small unconscious task to bat the letter to the floor. As it skittered over the tiles, tension grew in his body – tendons and sinew stood out in his wrists and forearms. He gripped the edge of the table as if he was trying not to fall backwards and the table shook with a muscular spasm. His face started to break up and with a terrible sob he shunted the chair out from under him and fell to his knees. His features were contorted with pain, eyes squeezed shut, teeth bared. Alicia Aguado put her hands out, feeling the air in front of her. Sebastián's body convulsed once more and he fell to the floor.

Only at this moment did any of the men in the room react. The chairs and table were pulled out of the way and they all stood over Sebastián, who had now gone foetal, holding himself. His head writhed against the polished floor and he coughed up great dry sobs of emotion, as if chunks of pumice were lodged in his chest.

The nurse knelt, opened his bag and took out a syringe. The guards hovered. Alicia felt her way around the table and reached out for Sebastián's trembling frame.

'Don't touch him,' said one of the guards.

She put a hand out which found the back of Sebastián's neck. She stroked him, whispered his name. The convulsions smoothed out. He relaxed his grip on his shins. The sobbing up until that moment had been dry, but now he wept like Falcón had never seen anybody weep before. Tears and saliva poured out of him. He tried to get his hands to his face to hide this awful outpouring, but he seemed to be too weak. The guards stepped back, no longer disturbed, just slightly embarrassed. The nurse replaced the syringe in the bag. The psychologist weighed the situation and decided to let it continue.

After ten minutes of sustained weeping Sebastián rolled on to his knees and buried his face in his arms on the floor. His back shuddered. The psychologist decided that he should be taken back to his cell and given a sedative. The guards tried to get him to stand but he had no strength in his legs. He was unmanageable in this state and they put him down on the floor and went to get a wheelchair. Falcón retrieved the letter and gave it to the psychologist. The guard returned with a trolley from the prison hospital. Sebastián was wheeled away.

The psychologist decided he'd better read the letter to see if the contents would disturb Sebastián any more. Falcón could see that there were very few words on the page.

Dear Sebastián,
I am more sorry than I can ever possibly say. Please forgive me.
Your loving father,
Pablo

Falcón and Alicia drove out of the bleached landscape of the prison and back into the crushing heat of the city. Alicia Aguado stared out of the window, the lifeless terrain flickered past her unseeing eyes. Questions came to Falcón but he didn't ask them. After that emotional display, everything seemed banal.

'Even after all these years,' said Alicia, 'I'm still astonished by the terrifying power of the mind. We have this organism sitting in our heads which, if we allow it, can completely destroy us to the point where we will never be the same again . . . and yet it's ours, it belongs to us. We have no idea what we've got sitting on our shoulders.'

Falcón said nothing. She wasn't looking for a reply.

'You witness something like that,' she said, flapping her hand in the vague direction of the prison, 'and you cannot imagine what has gone on in that man's mind. What has passed between him and his father. It was as if the news of his father's death went straight to the core of his being and ripped him open and out came all these incredibly powerful, uncontainable, polarized emotions. He was probably barely alive, just existing on automatic. He'd put himself in prison, in solitary confinement. His personal contact is almost zero. He's ceased to function as a human being, and yet the mind still has to find a way out.'

'Why do you think he's relieved to be there, as your friend was saying?'

'I suppose he'd got to the point where he was afraid of what his uncontrollable mind might do.'

'Do you think you can talk to him?'

'Well, I'm here at Sebastián's moment of crisis – his father's suicide – and I think we've formed a bond. If the prison authorities let me, I'm sure I can help him.'

'I know the prison director,' said Falcón. 'I'll tell him your work could be valuable to my investigation into Vega's death.'

'But you *do* think that there's a connection?' she said. 'This whole thing with Pablo . . . I can hear your brain chewing it over.'

'I know, but I'm just not sure what it is.'

He dropped Alicia Aguado off at her house and had another go at contacting Ignacio Ortega, whose mobile was still switched off.

Consuelo called him and asked if he wanted to meet for lunch at Casa Ricardo, a bar halfway between her restaurant and Falcón's home. He decided to drop the car at home and walk. He parked between the orange trees and went to open the doors. As he reached for his keys a woman called to him from across the street. Maddy Krugman had just come out of a shop which specialized in hand-painted tiles. Her casual behaviour did not persuade him that this was an accidental meeting.

'So this is your house,' she said, as they stood between the two files of orange trees that led up to the wooden doors. 'The famous house.'

'The infamous house,' he said.

'That's my favourite shop in Seville,' she said. 'I think I'm going to take their entire stock back to New York with me.'

'Are you leaving?'

'No, not immediately,' she said. 'But in the end. You know, we all go back to where we started.'

He wasn't sure what she meant or that she knew either. He toyed with the possibility of wishing her well on her shopping trip and disappearing into his house, but he couldn't quite find the rudeness to do it.

'Would you like to see inside the infamous house?' he said. 'I could offer you a drink.'

'That's very nice of you, Inspector Jefe,' she said. 'I've been out shopping. I'm exhausted.'

They went in. He sat her down under the arches of the patio in front of the trickling fountain and went to fetch a bottle of La Guita and some olives. When he came back she was across the patio looking through the glass doors at some of Francisco Falcón's paintings of Seville.

'Are these . . ?'

'They're his real work,' he said, giving her a glass of manzanilla. 'He didn't have to cheat to do these. He was better than that, though. This was his subconscious mind belittling him. If he'd kept at it he'd have painted bare-breasted gypsies and doe-eyed children piddling into fountains.'

'What about your work?'

'I don't have any.'

'I read that you were a photographer.'

'I was interested in the concept of photography as memory,' he said. 'I had no talent for the art. What about you? How do you see it? What do you see as the point of photographing disturbed and anguished people?'

'What bullshit did I give you before?'

'I don't remember ... probably something about capturing the moment,' said Falcón, remembering that, in fact, that had been *his* bullshit.

They walked back to the table. He leaned against a pillar. She sat, crossed her legs and sipped the manzanilla.

'I'm empathizing,' she said, and Falcón knew he wasn't going to hear anything that would make any difference to him. 'When I see people like that I remember the prison of my own anguish and the pain I caused Marty. There's an emotional response. I was surprised, once I started looking, how many of us there were out there. The shots are of individuals, but once you assemble them in a room they become like a tribe. They are an expression of the reality of the human condition. Shit – it doesn't matter how hard I try it always sounds like gallery talk. Don't you find that? Words have a way of flattening things out.'

He nodded, bored by her already. He wondered what Calderón saw in her, apart from the blue veins under the white skin, cold as marble. This one was living life out as a project. Falcón stifled a yawn.

'You're not listening to me,' she said.

He came round to find her standing quite close to him, close enough for him to see the red blood spots in the green of her iris. She licked her lips, applying some natural gloss. Her sexuality, in which she was so confident, shimmered beneath the silk of her loose blouse. She moved her head, a slight tilt, to tell him that he could kiss her now, while her eyes said that this could turn into something frantic on the marble flags of the patio if he wanted. He turned his head away. He was slightly revolted by her.

'I was *half* listening,' he said, 'but I've got a lot on my mind and I'm meeting someone for lunch, so I should really be getting on.'

'I must go, too,' she said. 'I have to get back.'

Her hands trembled with rage as she picked up her bag of hand-painted tiles. He thought she might throw them at his head, one by one. There was something destructive in her nature. She was like a spoilt child who would break things just so that others couldn't enjoy them.

The walk to the front door was punctuated by the anger of her heels on the marble. She kept ahead of him so that he couldn't see her humiliation while she gathered up the fragments of the face she had lost and rearranged them into disdain. He opened the door, she shook his hand and headed off towards the Hotel Colón.

The Casa Ricardo was on Hernan Cortés at the meeting of three streets. It was a bar that could only exist in Seville, where the religious and the secular constantly rub shoulders. Every centimetre of the walls in the bar and small restaurant at the back was covered in framed photographs of the Virgin, the brotherhoods and all the paraphernalia of Semana Santa. The sound system played processional marches from Holy Week while people leaned against the bar drinking beers, eating olives and jamón.

Consuelo was waiting for him at a table in the back with a chilled half-bottle of manzanilla. They kissed each other on the mouth as if they'd been lovers for months.

'You look tense,' she said.

He tried to think of something other than Pablo Ortega, which he couldn't talk about.

'It's just developments. We keep finding things out about Rafael Vega that make him more of a mystery man.'

'Well, we all knew he was a secretive guy,' said Consuelo. 'I once saw him leave his house in his car, the Mercedes he had before he bought the Jaguar. And an hour later I was in town at a traffic light and this old dusty Citroën or Peugeot Estate pulls up alongside me and in the driver's seat was Rafael. If it had been anybody else I'd have knocked on the window and said hello, but with Rafael, I don't know . . . you just didn't intrude on Rafael.'

'Did you ever ask him about it?'

'First of all he never responded to direct questioning and, anyway, so what if he's in a different car? I just assumed it was an office car he used for going out to building sites.'

'You're probably right, it's nothing. You get to the point where every little thing has meaning.'

They ordered a *revuelto de bacalao*, some clams and langoustines, a bright orange bowl of salmorejo and grilled red peppers spiked with garlic. Consuelo filled their glasses. Falcón calmed down.

'I've just had a . . . confrontation with Maddy Krugman.'

'That puta americana didn't come to your house on your day off?' asked Consuelo.

'She ambushed me in the street,' he said. 'That's the third time. She's come round twice when I've been to the Vegas' house. . .offering coffee, wanting to talk.'

'*Joder*, Javier, she's stalking you.'

'There's something of the vampire about her, except she doesn't feed on blood.'

'My God, you let her get that close?'

'I think she feeds on what she doesn't have herself,' said Falcón. 'Her talk is full of arty phraseology about "empathizing", and "emotional response" and "the prison of her anguish", but she has no idea what they mean. So when she sees people who are really suffering she photographs it, captures it to try and make it hers. When I lived in Tangier the Moroccans believed that photographers were stealing their souls. And that's what Maddy Krugman does. She's sinister.'

'You're making her sound like your prime suspect.'

'Maybe I'll send her to the prison of her anguish.'

Consuelo pulled him to her and kissed him hard on the mouth.

'What was that for?'

'You don't have to know everything.'

'I'm an Inspector Jefe, it's in my nature.'

The food arrived. Consuelo released him and poured more manzanilla. Before they started eating he beckoned her forward across the table so that they were cheek to cheek.

'I can't say this too loudly in here,' said Falcón, his lips just brushing her ear, 'but there's another reason why I'm looking a bit tense. It's just that . . . I'm falling in love with you.'

She kissed his cheek, held his hand.

'How do you know?'

'Because when I came in here and saw you waiting for me I've never felt so happy to know that the empty chair was mine.'

'You're all right,' she said. 'You can stay.'

He sat back, held his glass up to her and drank.

They chose a bottle of white wine to drink with the sea bass they'd ordered after the starters.

'I'm sorry, I forgot,' she said, going through her handbag. 'Somebody from your office . . .'

'My office?'

'I assumed he was from the Jefatura. He told me to give you this –' She handed over an envelope.

'Nobody knows I'm here,' said Falcón, 'except you. Tell me what he said again.'

'He said, "I understand you're meeting Inspector Jefe Falcón here. Could you please make sure he gets this." And he gave me that envelope.'

'He was Spanish?'

'Sevillano.'

Falcón turned the white envelope over in his hands. It was very thin. He held it up to the light and could see that it had a single item in it. He knew it was another threat and shouldn't be opened in front of Consuelo. He nodded and put it in his pocket.

He took a taxi home and went straight to his study where he kept latex gloves. He used a paper knife to open the envelope and shook out a photograph which had been folded into a single sheet of paper.

Nadia Kouzmikheva's naked body was very white with the flash from the camera. She was blindfolded and tied to a chair with her arms painfully stretched over the back. On the grimy wall behind her was a single handprint the colour of rust and in black was written: *El precio de la carne es barato.* The price of meat is cheap.

18

Saturday, 27th July 2002

The sunlight was still bright in the cracks of the wooden shutters as he lay on his bed with the thought of Nadia, blind and vulnerable, sharp in his mind. He'd overcome his initial reaction of horror and brought the analytical part of his brain to bear on the meaning of this latest message. These threats, each one worse than the last, each one digging deeper into his private life and now entangling Consuelo – what was their purpose? The car following him at the end of the first day and the photograph of Inés pinned to his board were designed to unsettle him. They were bold – we can follow you and we don't care if you see us, we can enter your house and we know things about you. The implicit physical threat to Nadia and the inclusion of Consuelo raised the stakes, but what was actually happening here? He gave up on any possibility of sleep and dragged himself to the shower and let the water pummel his head clear of the lunchtime wine. Each threat had only the appearance of boldness. There had been no follow-up to any of them so far. They were trying to distract him . . . but from what?

He started thinking about Rafael Vega and the Russians. The phrase that Vázquez had used – 'facilitating their business needs' – had snagged in his brain. It was a natural process of the mind to think that a man who'd had questionable dealings with Russian mafiosi and subsequently been found dead would probably have been murdered as a result of some disagreement. In this case, though, it seemed illogical. The Russians were reaping enormous advantages from their dealings with Vega. Why kill him?

There was no reason why Falcón shouldn't believe Vázquez when he said that he had not been involved in the property deals and had no way of contacting the Russians directly. This would fit with Vega's compartmentalizing style of management. Pablo Ortega's sighting of the Russians in Santa Clara seemed to indicate that Ivanov and Zelenov only visited Vega at home. The telephone number programmed into his study phone seemed to confirm that they were not part of any office procedure. That would also explain why the surveillance system had been switched off. Both he and they would not want any record of these visits.

Falcón dressed and went down to his study where he'd put both the envelope and photograph of Nadia in an evidence bag. He leaned back in his chair while fury and frustration did their work on his insides. There was nothing he could do about this. To refocus his investigation on the abduction of Nadia would be futile. He began to think that the Russians wanted to distract him from his inquiries into Vega's death because they were anxious to hide a crime far darker than the possible murder of the constructor.

He remembered his failed call to Ignacio Ortega and made another attempt. Ortega's mobile was still turned off and there was no answer from any of the other numbers he'd taken from Pablo's book. He went to his notebook and looked down the list of things he'd planned to do this morning before he'd been sidetracked by Pablo Ortega's suicide. Interview Marty Krugman.

Marty Krugman was in the Vega Construcciones offices on Avenida de la República de Argentina. He was finishing off some drawings on the more powerful computer he had there. He said he'd be quite happy to talk as soon as Falcón could get there. He'd make sure the conserje would let him in. As he spoke Falcón jotted down three topics for Marty Krugman – 9/11, Russians, wife.

The entrance to the Vega Construcciones building was between two large estate agencies which advertised the Vega projects in their windows. The conserje let him in and sent him straight up to Marty Krugman's office.

Marty had his feet up on the desk. He was wearing red basketball pumps. They shook hands.

'Maddy told me you had a conversation about Reza Sangari yesterday,' said Marty.

'That's right,' said Falcón, realizing that the reason why Marty had been so amenable about seeing him on a Saturday evening was that he was angry with him.

'She said you were also implying that she might have been having an affair with Rafael.'

'These questions have to be asked,' said Falcón. 'I was only wondering whether she had had an effect on the stability of Sr Vega's mind.'

'It was a ridiculous question and I resent that you asked it,' said Marty. 'You've got no idea what we went through over Reza Sangari.'

'That's true . . . which was why I had to ask the question,' said Falcón. 'I know nothing about you. I have to find out, and you are understandably reticent about certain dramatic events in your lives.'

'Are you satisfied?' he asked, backing off slightly.

'For the moment . . . yes.'

Marty nodded him into a seat on the other side of the desk.

'Your wife told me you had quite a developed relationship with Sr Vega,' said Falcón.

'Intellectually, yes,' said Marty. 'You know what it's like. There's no fun in talking to somebody who agrees with everything you say.'

'She said that you were surprised by how much you did agree.'

'I never expected to find myself agreeing about anything with the kind of person who thought that Franco had the right idea about communists: that they should all be rounded up and shot.'

'So what *did* you agree on?'

'We shared the same views about the American empire.'

'I didn't know there was one.'

'It's called the World,' said Marty. 'We don't go through all that time-consuming, expensive crap of actually colonizing. We just . . . globalize.'

'This note Sr Vega had in his hand referring to 9/11,' said Falcón, cutting in hard before Marty ran away with the ball. 'Pablo Ortega told me Sr Vega was of the opinion that America deserved what happened on September 11th.'

'We had some violent disagreements about that,' said Marty. 'It's one of the few things I get emotional about. Two friends of mine worked for Cantor Fitzgerald and, like a lot of Americans, and especially multicultural New Yorkers, I didn't see why they or the other three thousand people had to die.'

'But why do you think *he* believed that?'

'The American empire is no different to any other. We believe that the reason we have become so powerful isn't just that we commanded the necessary resources at the right time in history to defeat the only other contender, but also because we are *right*. We broke an entire ideology not with an atom bomb but by the sheer brutality of numbers. We forced the Soviet Union to play our game and bankrupted it. And that's the great thing about our tool of empire – we can invade without physically going in. We can dictate whilst appearing to be a force for the good. Capitalism brings a population under control by giving them the illusion of freedom and choice whilst forcing them to adhere to a rigid principle, which can be resisted only at the cost of personal ruin. There's no Gestapo, no torture chambers . . . it's perfect. We call it Empire Lite.'

Falcón started to break in on the Krugman theory, but Marty held up his hand.

'*Paciencia*, Inspector Jefe, I'm getting to it,' he said. 'Those are the basic ingredients of the American empire and, as you've realized, I've just used what Rafael thought was the Americans' greatest talent – the art of presentation. Truth, fact and reality are Play-doh in the hands of a great presenter. For example, how can we be aggressive if we don't invade? Look at our history as Defenders of the Right against the Forces of Evil. We saved Europe from the Nazis, Kuwait from Saddam.

'Rafael saw that as arrogance, which, when combined with Christian fundamentalism and outright support of the Israelis by the present administration, became too much for the Islamic die-hards. He thought this was the Holy War that both parties had been waiting for; we were going back centuries to the Crusades, except that the arena was now larger and the techniques available more devastating.

'When al-Qaeda hit our symbol of the American empire – and Rafael reckoned that to wake up 250 million people from a state of somnolent comfort you needed a very loud bang – he thought that the truly terrible thing for us was to discover that al-Qaeda knew us better than we did ourselves. They had understood what makes our society tick – *our demand for outstanding presentation and our need to make an impact*. He attached a lot of importance to the time lag between the first plane hitting and the second. It meant that the world media would be there.'

'I'm surprised there wasn't an exchange of blows between you,' said Falcón.

'That was a summary of *his* beliefs about 9/11, not *our* discussions,' said Marty. 'I did a lot of storming out and he talked me back in. There were days when diplomatic relations were cut completely. He was surprised by my anger. He hadn't realized how much anger there was pent up in America.'

'Can you relate any of that to the note that was discovered in Sr Vega's hand?'

'I've been trying to and I can't see it.'

'Your wife says that you're certain he'd lived in America, and that he liked it,' said Falcón. 'And yet he held these views which would annoy plenty of Americans . . .'

'They're not so different to what most Europeans secretly think, Inspector Jefe. That's why a lot of my fellow countrymen now see Europeans as treacherous and envious.'

'Envious?'

'Yes, something else Rafael had an opinion on. He said Europeans don't *envy* the American way – its society is too aggressive for them to be envious of it. And, anyway, envy does not inspire hate. What they are, he said, is *afraid* of Americans and fear *does* inspire hate.'

'What do Europeans fear?'

'That with all our economic might and political strength we have the power to make their efforts irrelevant – you know, the Kyoto agreement, trade tariffs, the ICC –'

'And yet, Sr Vega was relentlessly pro-American.'

'If you're as anti-communist as he was, you have to be,' said Marty. 'The point was he didn't think emotionally. He certainly didn't approve of al-Qaeda. He just saw it as the . . . way things go. Playground bullies eventually get punched on the nose and it always comes from the least expected direction. He also believed that once the rest saw blood they'd dive in afterwards. As far as Rafael was concerned this was the beginning of the end for the American empire.'

'I'm surprised you were prepared to put up with his talk,' said Falcón. 'Your wife kept reminding me that you think it's the greatest nation on earth.'

'It didn't make me want to kill him, if that's what you're implying, Inspector Jefe,' said Marty, looking out from under his eyebrows. 'All you've got to do is look at history. Rafael said that America, like the empires before them, would lash out. They'd have to. But it would either be a wild flailing against something too small to be seen, or they would crush, with excessive force and expensive might, the wrong enemy. There'd be a gradual weakening, followed by economic melt-down. This was where I think he was wrong, because the one thing that America would always pay attention to was the dollar. They would never allow anything to jeopardize that.'

'These discussions went on for a long time. Your wife said until dawn.'

'And as the brandy bottle got emptier and the end of Rafael's cigar got soggier, his ideas got wilder,' said Marty. 'He believed that the American empire would end, not in our lifetime but before the end of the century, and that one of two things would happen. Either the Chinese would take over and stamp an even more rapacious form of capitalism on the world, or there would be a reaction against capitalism's decadence. In which case there would be a religious empire which would come from the most populous nations on earth (rather than our dying nations of retirees) and that it would be Islamic.'

'My God,' said Falcón.

'Allah is great, you mean, Inspector Jefe,' said Marty.

'We've seen from your wife's photographs that Sr Vega was in some sort of crisis that dated from the end of last year. This was confirmed by his doctor. Was there any difference in the way your talks developed around that time?'

'He drank more,' said Marty. 'Sometimes he would pass out for a few minutes. I remember once going over to cover him with a blanket and, just as I reached him, his eyes opened and I could see he was very frightened. He started to plead with me as if he was a prisoner begging not to be taken away for torture, until he remembered who I was and where we were.'

'Sr Ortega mentioned that he seemed very disappointed by the American concept of loyalty,' said Falcón. 'That they were your friends until they no longer had any use for you. Do you know where that came from?'

'In business, I imagine. He never spoke about specifics. He took honour very seriously. He seemed to operate on a strict code, which seemed quite old-fashioned by modern standards. He was dismayed by the more practical American belief: honour's fine until you start losing money, then it all goes out the window.'

'It sounded more personal than that. He wouldn't be such a

successful businessman if he didn't have a more relaxed code of morality as far as money was concerned. There was a business aspect to his marriage arrangement. His code was such that, having given his word, he wouldn't leave his wife because of her mental state, but it was loose enough that he would marry to get his hands on the property in the first place.'

'So, you tell me,' said Marty.

Falcón flipped through his notes.

'Pablo Ortega reported him as saying: "as soon as you stop making money for them or giving them information they drop you like a stone."'

'Well, that sounds weird, like some sort of corporate espionage. Money. Information. If he was into that I don't know where he'd expect to find honour in that world.'

'Or was it politics?' said Falcón. 'Your conversations were primarily political.'

'I can't think that politics would have any bearing on his death here in Seville.'

'Do you know anything about the Russian investors in Sr Vega's projects?'

'I know that there *are* some, but that's all. I'm just the architect. I do the drawings, I manage the practicalities, but I don't meet the investors. That happens at a higher level, a business level.'

'These Russians are known mafiosi and we're pretty sure they're laundering money through Sr Vega's projects.'

'It's possible. That's the nature of the construction industry. But I don't know anything about it. I'm on the creative side.'

'Can you think of any reason why the Russians should want to kill Sr Vega?'

'He was cheating on them? That's normally why you get killed by the mafia. But that will be difficult to prove.'

'We've had threats,' said Falcón. 'Have you been threatened?'

'Not yet.'

If Marty Krugman was nervous he wasn't showing it to Falcón. The basketball pumps stayed up on the desk. He was relaxed.

'Why did you leave America, Sr Krugman?' asked Falcón, moving into the third phase of his interview.

'You've asked me that before.'

'Your answer's going to be different now that Reza Sangari is out in the open.'

'Then you already know the answer.'

'I want to hear you tell it.'

'We decided that if our relationship was going to survive we had to get away from the environment in which it started. We both love Europe. We thought a simple life together would bring us closer.'

'But this isn't a simple life – big city, job, house in Santa Clara.'

'We tried a small house in Provence to start with. It didn't work.'

'And how has it been, working here?'

'This is very personal, Inspector Jefe,' said Marty, 'but if you must know it's been going *fine*.'

'You're nearly twenty years older than your wife. Has that ever presented any problems?'

Marty shifted in his seat, the first sign he'd shown of any discomfort in the whole interview.

'Maddy has an effect on men. A predictable and boring effect. The first connection I made with Maddy was up here –' he said, tapping his forehead. 'I surprised her and I still do. Now, you can call this syndrome whatever you like – father/daughter, teacher/pupil – but all I know is that it works and it will continue to work, because unlike all the other guys I'm not and never have been focused solely on her pussy.'

'So what happened with Reza Sangari was . . . unpredictable,' said Falcón, feeling the tension build in the room.

Marty Krugman sat back in his chair with his long artistic hands folded over his lean stomach. He fixed Falcón with his dark, embedded eyes and nodded.

'Are you a jealous man, Sr Krugman?'

Silence.

'Does it annoy you to see your wife talking to other men, laughing with them, being interested in them?'

More silence.

'Was there something that *surprised* you after you discovered your wife's betrayal with Reza Sangari?'

Marty frowned, searched his head. Leaned forward.

'What is this *something* that you're talking about?'

'That you, the intellectual, the political animal, the man of ideas and thoughts, could be . . . passionate?'

'What happened between Maddy and Reza Sangari was what the French call *un coup de foudre*, a lightning strike that set something on fire and which burnt itself out. By the time somebody killed Reza Sangari whatever happened between him and Maddy was just smoke, ash and embers. That's the nature of passion, Inspector Jefe. It burns hard and fast and consumes too greedily for mere sex to keep it satisfied. So once the sex has run its course the passion flames out and, if you're lucky, you survive the fall.'

'That's true if it was just sex,' said Falcón. 'But if it was something more . . .'

'What are you trying to do here, Inspector Jefe?' said Marty. 'Your probes are in. I can feel them. They're hurting. They're stirring up memories that I'd rather let lie. But what are you getting out of it?'

'Sr Vega used to take your wife to bullfights,' said Falcón, determined to drive his point home. 'How did you feel about that?'

'If two intelligent people want to watch such a disgusting spectacle as the torment of a dumb animal, that is their business and they can do it without me.'

'Your wife told me that she was surprised at how quickly she became accustomed to the sight of blood and the violence,' said Falcón. 'She perceived a sexual aspect to the drama.'

Marty shook his head in disbelief.

'Would you describe your marriage as quite open, Sr Krugman? By that I mean you don't appear to see the necessity of establishing yourself as a couple in society. You're quite happy for your wife to spend time with Sr Vega or other men. She was independent in Connecticut. She had her own work and freedom . . .'

'What "other men"?' said Marty, opening his hands, welcoming the exchange.

'Juez Calderón, for instance,' said Falcón.

Marty blinked at the information. As the name slid cleanly into Krugman's mind, Falcón realized that this was news to him.

'Maddy has different energies and pursuits to mine. She can sit by the river for hours taking photographs. That's her world. She also likes the street and bar life of Seville. I don't have time for that. She likes the animation and constant sense of theatre about the people. I am not someone who can bring that alive for her. Rafael was happy to show it to her, as I'm sure is the judge. I have no desire to stop her enjoying herself. To try would be destructive.'

The words came out like a pre-prepared statement from an administration under pressure.

19

Sunday, 28th July 2002

In the morning Falcón was woken by a call from Ignacio Ortega, who he'd finally managed to contact late the previous night and who had now arrived in Seville. He wanted to visit his brother's house. They arranged to meet at midday.

Falcón and Consuelo had a breakfast of huevos rancheros. She was still stunned after hearing about Pablo Ortega's death. The local news on the radio featured Ortega's suicide and an item about a massive forest fire, which had started last night and was now burning out of control near a town called Almonaster la Real in the Sierra de Aracena. Consuelo turned it off. She didn't need her Sunday ruined any more than it was.

At midday Falcón crossed the road, let himself in to Pablo Ortega's garden and opened up the house. He turned on the air conditioning, shut the door to the room where Pablo had died and jammed a damp towel at its base in an attempt to reduce the terrible stink. He checked the fridge for beer.

Ignacio arrived and knocked at the sliding doors. They shook hands. He looked younger than Pablo, but not by much. He was bald but hadn't made the drastic error of trying to plaster his still dark hair from one side over to the other, although the idea had possibly occurred to him. He was slimmer and fitter than his brother but had no presence whatsoever. This was a man who would disappear in a room and Falcón understood why he'd asked his brother to come to his business functions. He badly needed to borrow some charisma.

Ortega apologized for ruining his Sunday but he'd felt a need to see the place where his brother had died. Falcón said he was going to be busy the following day and mentioned the identification of the body and where that would take place. They agreed a time. Falcón offered him a drink and they opened up a litre bottle of Cruzcampo from the fridge. The beer seemed to make Ignacio emotional. He had to wipe away tears and stare at the floor.

'You were close,' said Falcón.

'He was my only brother,' said Ignacio, 'but I didn't see much of him. He was a famous man travelling the world, while I sold and installed air-conditioning systems. Our paths didn't cross that often.'

'You must have seen him more often since Sebastián's trial. He hasn't been working so much and there's been this problem with the house.'

'That's true,' said Ortega, pulling out a pack of Ducados and lighting one. 'He'd been going through a rough time, but . . . I tried to help him with this problem. I sent someone round the other day. I can't believe . . . it just seems so strange that he's not here.'

'I went to see Sebastián in prison yesterday,' said Falcón.

Ignacio looked up with watery eyes as if he was going to get more information.

'That was a difficult relationship,' he said. 'Father and son.'

'Any reason for that?'

'Our own father . . . he was a very difficult man.'

'In what way?'

'He'd had a hard life,' said Ignacio. 'We don't know what happened to him exactly. There was nobody left to tell us except him, and he never talked about anything. Our mother only told us that his village was caught up in the Nationalist advance during the Civil War and that the Moors did terrible things to people. As far as Pablo and I were concerned the worst thing they did was to let him survive.'

'Pablo was the eldest?'

'Our parents married the year the war ended and Pablo was born the year after that.'

'And you?'

'I was born in 1944,' he said.

'Those were hard times in this part of the country.'

'We had nothing . . . like everybody else had nothing. So it was hard, but nobody was alone in their poverty. That wouldn't explain why our father was so brutal with us. Pablo always bore the brunt of it. He said that it was those years dealing with our father that made him into an actor. It wasn't a great childhood. Pablo said it was why he never wanted kids.'

'But he did,' said Falcón. 'And you?'

'I've got two . . . they're grown up now,' he said.

'Do they live in Seville?'

'My daughter is married and lives in California. My son . . . my son is still here.'

'Does he work with you?'

'No,' said Ignacio, his mouth snapping shut, dismissing the notion.

'What does he do?' asked Falcón, more to be polite than to intrude.

'He buys and sells things . . . I'm not really sure what.'

'You mean you don't see so much of him?'

'He has his own life, his own friends. I think I represent something that he wants to rebel against . . . respectability or . . . I don't know.'

'So what about Pablo's relationship with Sebastián? Was that coloured by the fact that he didn't want children in the first place?'

'Is there a problem here?' asked Ignacio, squinting up from his glass of beer.

'A problem?' said Falcón.

'All these questions . . . very personal family questions,' said Ignacio. 'Is there some doubt about what happened here?'

'Not what, but why it happened,' said Falcón. 'We're interested in what triggered your brother's suicide. It might have a bearing on another case.'

'Which case is that?'

'His next-door neighbour's.'

'I heard about that. There was a piece about it in the *Diario de Sevilla*.'

'You knew him, of course.'

'I . . . I did know him,' said Ignacio, faltering as if this was not something he immediately wanted to admit. 'And I read there was some doubt about what had happened in his case . . . but I don't really see how Pablo's death could possibly be linked.'

'Pablo knew him as well . . . through you.'

'Yes, that's right, Pablo would occasionally come with me to functions in the years when I was trying to get the business off the ground,' said Ortega. 'So why do you think Pablo's suicide was connected to Rafael and Lucía Vega's death?'

'I'm looking at it more from the point of view of strange coincidence at this stage,' said Falcón. 'Three people dead within days of each other in a small barrio like this. That's odd. Did one trigger the other? What were the pressures on Pablo in the lead up to his death?'

'For a start, I can tell you that Pablo couldn't kill a chicken. It was one of our father's abuses that he used to force him to do it.'

'Rafael Vega drank, or was forced to drink, a bottle of acid.'

'Pablo was a completely non-violent person,' said Ignacio.

'So what do you think could have triggered your brother's fatal decision?'

'There must have been a letter, surely?' said Ignacio.

'The way it happened was that he and I arranged to meet here yesterday morning. He wanted me, as a professional, to find the body. There was a letter to me explaining that, and a short note to Sebastián.'

'But nothing written to me?' said Ignacio, puzzled. 'What did he write to Sebastián?'

'He said he was sorry and asked for his forgiveness,' said Falcón. 'Do you know why he should write something like that?'

Ignacio coughed against some involuntary sobbing. He pressed the beer glass to his forehead as if trying to cram it into his brain. He broke out of it and hung his head, staring at the floor, as if he was thinking of something plausible to say.

'He was probably sorry that he hadn't been able to show his son enough love,' said Ignacio. 'It's all tied up with our father. I think the same happened between me and my son. I failed him, too. Pablo used to say that damage was passed from generation to generation and it was difficult to break the cycle.'

'Pablo had theories about this, did he?'

'Because he read all these books and plays he had intellectual ideas about it. He said that it was an atavistic trait of fathers to make themselves unknowable to their sons in order to retain power in the family or tribe. Showing love weakened that position, so men's instincts were for aggression.'

'Interesting,' said Falcón. 'But it avoids the issue, which is much more personal. Suicide is a personal matter, too, and most of the time in my job it doesn't matter why it happened, but in this case I want to find out.'

'So do I,' said Ignacio. 'We all feel blame when something like this happens.'

'That's why my questions have to be personal,' said Falcón. 'What can you tell me about Pablo's relationship with his wife – Sebastián's mother? He wasn't married before, was he?'

'No, Glória was his only wife.'

'When did they marry?'

'In 1975.'

'He was thirty-five.'

'I told him he was leaving it too late,' said Ignacio. 'But he had a career, there were actresses. It was a lifestyle.'

'There were lots of girlfriends before Glória, then?'

Ignacio's hand rasped against his face as he rubbed the nascent bristles. He glanced at Falcón, a quick shift of the eye whites. It lasted only a fraction of a second but it added to Falcón's unease about this man. He began to think that the reason Ignacio had come round here was not so much to mourn his brother or to help Falcón, but to find out how much was known. It nagged at Falcón's mind that Pablo hadn't written a note to his only brother.

'There were a few,' said Ignacio. 'As I said, our paths didn't cross much. I was just an electrician and he was a famous actor.'

'How did Glória persuade him to have a child?'

'She didn't. She just got pregnant.'

'Do you know why she left Pablo?'

'She was a little puta,' said Ignacio, some viciousness on his thin lips. 'She fucked around and then left the country with someone who would give her the fucking she wanted.'

'Are those your own observations?'

'Mine, my wife's, Pablo's. Anybody who met Glória knew her for what she was. My wife saw it from day one. This was a woman who should not be married and she proved it by leaving everybody . . . including Sebastián.'

'And Pablo brought up his son on his own?'

'Well, he went away a lot, so a fair amount of the time Sebastián joined our family.'

'Were your kids the same age?'

'I got married young. Our kids were eight and ten years older,' said Ignacio.

'So after Glória left, you were Sebastián's father a fair amount of the time.'

Ignacio nodded, drank some beer and lit another cigarette.

'That was all twenty years ago,' said Falcón. 'What about Pablo's relationships in that time?'

'I used to see him in *Hola!* magazine with women, but we never met any of them. After Glória we only ever saw him on his own,' said Ignacio. 'You're asking a lot of questions about relationships, Inspector Jefe.'

'Failed relationships can make people suicidal, as can, for instance, the possibility of public shame.'

'Or financial ruin,' said Ignacio, pointing at the room with the cracked cesspit. 'Or the end of a great career. Or the accumulation of all these things in a man about to face retirement, maybe illness and certainly death.'

'Are you surprised he killed himself?'

'Yes, I am. He'd suffered a lot recently with his son's trial, moving house, the building problem here, his fading career, but he was dealing with it all. He was a mentally resilient person. He wouldn't have survived my father's beatings without having reserves. I can't think what would have made him take such drastic action.'

'This is a difficult question,' said Falcón, 'but did you have any reason to question your brother's sexual orientation?'

'No, I didn't,' he said, flat and hard.

'You seem very certain.'

'As certain as I can be,' said Ignacio. 'And remember he was a public figure with photographers on his back. They'd have loved to tell the world that Pablo Ortega was a *maricón*.'

'But if something like that was about to be revealed, do you think he could have taken it? Would that have been enough to tip him over the edge, given his other problems?'

'You still haven't told me how he did it.'

Falcón gave him the gruesome details. Ignacio's body shook with emotion. He became ugly with grief. He buried his face in his hands, the cigarette burning out of the back of his fingers.

'Did Pablo ever show you his art collection?' asked Falcón, to ease him out of his distress.

'He showed it to me, but I didn't take much notice of that arty stuff he was into.'

'Did you ever see this piece?' asked Falcón, drawing the Indian erotic painting out from behind the Francisco Falcón landscape.

'Oof!' said Ignacio, admiring. 'Chance would be a fine thing . . .

But doesn't *that* prove something to you, Inspector Jefe?'

'It's the only painting to feature a woman,' said Falcón, thinking that he'd gone off on the wrong tack here. This was not going to work with Ignacio Ortega.

'The painting in front of it,' said Ignacio, looking around his legs, 'that's got your name on it – Falcón.'

Something lit up in Ignacio's mind and Falcón realized with dismay that he'd possibly ruined the whole interrogation. Nobody had missed the story of Francisco Falcón.

'Now, Pablo did tell me about *that* business,' said Ignacio. 'He knew Francisco Falcón personally . . . and the thing about him was that he *did* turn out to be a maricón. And you're the Inspector Jefe, who, if I remember rightly, was his son.'

'No, he wasn't my father.'

'Now I understand. That's why you think Pablo's a maricón, isn't it? Because your father was one, too. You think they're –'

'He wasn't my father and I don't think that at all. It's a theory.'

'It's rubbish. The next thing you'll be telling me is that Rafael was one, too, and they were having a "relationship" and he couldn't bear –'

'Are you surprised that Pablo didn't leave you a letter?' asked Falcón, trying to retrieve the situation, wanting to needle Ignacio at the same time.

'I am . . . Yes, I am.'

'When was the last time you talked?'

'Just before I went away on holiday,' he said. 'I wanted to know if he'd made any progress on the cesspit, and I had someone in mind who might have a different approach to the problem.'

'When we gave Sebastián the letter from his father he batted it off the table, as if he didn't want to know. Then he broke down very badly and had to be wheeled back to his cell,' said Falcón. 'You were a father to him, as you've said, can you explain any of that? He seems to despise Pablo, and yet he was devastated by his death.'

'I can't tell you any more than I have already,' said Ignacio. 'All I can say is that Sebastián was a very complicated boy. It didn't help that his mother left him. It probably wasn't good for his father to have been away so much. I'm not qualified to explain that sort of reaction.'

'Have you been to see him in jail?'

'Pablo said he wasn't seeing anybody. I sent my wife out to the prison in the hope she could talk to him, but he refused to see her as well.'

'What about before he was sent to prison? He was a young man who didn't need looking after any more when Pablo was away. Did you see him then?'

'We saw him. He came for lunch sometimes when he was at the Bellas Artes . . . before he dropped out.'

'Why did he drop out?'

'It was a pity. Pablo said he was very good. There was no apparent reason. He just lost interest in it.'

'When did Glória die?'

'Some time around 1995 or 1996.'

'Was that when Sebastián finished with his art course? He'd have been about twenty.'

'That's true. I'd forgotten that. He'd been seeing her every year since he was about sixteen. He'd go to the USA every summer.'

'He looked like her, didn't he? More like her than Pablo.'

Ignacio shrugged, a sharp jerk as if a fly was irritating him. Falcón could see the questions building up in the man's head.

'In the letter he wrote to you, Inspector Jefe, did Pablo mention me?'

'He put a note at the bottom asking that you be informed,' said Falcón. 'He might have posted something to you. If he did, we'd be very interested to see it.'

Ignacio, having sat on the edge of his seat the whole interview, eased back into his chair.

'I suppose he could have posted something to his lawyer as well,' said Falcón. 'Do you know which lawyer is holding the will?'

Ignacio hunched forward again at this question.

'Ranz Costa,' he said, his mind elsewhere. 'Ranz Costa did the deed on this property, so I'm sure he's got the will.'

'I suppose he's on holiday?'

'He's my lawyer, too. He doesn't go on holiday until August,' said Ignacio, standing up, putting his beer down, crushing out the cigarette. 'Do you mind if I take a quick look around? Just to see my brother's place and things.'

'The room where he died is still officially a crime scene, so you'd better not go in there,' said Falcón.

Ignacio went off into the house. Falcón waited and went to the corridor. Ignacio was in the bedroom. The door was open a crack. Ignacio was madly searching the room. He went under the bed. He lifted the mattress. He surveyed the room, mouth set, eyes penetrating. He went through the clothes in the wardrobe, checked the pockets. Falcón backed down the hall and resumed his seat.

They left the house soon after. Falcón locked up and watched Ignacio's silver Mercedes disappear into the heat. He went back to Consuelo, who opened the door with the *El Mundo* Sunday magazine hanging from her fingers. They went into the living room where they both collapsed on the sofa.

'How's Ignacio taking it?' she asked.

'Do you know Ignacio Ortega?'

'I've met him at Raúl's construction industry functions. I spent more time with his wife than I did with him. He's a rather uninteresting self-made man with not a grain of culture in him. Given Pablo's talent and intellectual capacity . . . you can barely believe they're brothers.'

'Do you know anything about his son?'

'I know his name is Salvador and that he's a heroin addict. He lives somewhere in Seville.'

'Ah, well, that's a little more than Ignacio was prepared to admit.'

'That's what you find out when you talk to the wife.'

'How is he with his wife?'

'He's not what you'd call a "new man". He's of the macho generation. The wife does what she's told,' said Consuelo. 'She was scared of him. If we were talking and he joined us, she'd shut up.'

'Anyway, it's Sunday,' said Falcón, waving it all away. 'Let's try and forget about it for the rest of the day.'

'Well, I'm glad you came back,' she said. 'I was about to fall into a Sunday depression. You stopped me reading about Russia. No, that's not quite true. I turned on the news to try to stop thinking about Russia and I found myself looking at the forest fire, which didn't help. The noise of it. I've never heard fire before, Javier. It was like a beast crashing through the woods.'

'The fire in the Sierra de Aracena?'

'It's destroyed 2,500 hectares and the wind is still blowing up there,' she said. 'The firefighters say it was arson. You wonder what the matter is with people.'

'Tell me about Russia. I'm interested in Russia.'

'It's more about statistics.'

'They're the worst thing about the news,' said Falcón. 'I think editors have a dictum: "If you haven't got a story, give them a statistic." They know that our imagination will do the rest.'

'These are the Russian statistics,' she said, reading. 'The number of illegitimate births doubled between 1970 and 1995. This meant that by 1997 twenty-five per cent of all births were illegitimate. Most of the illegitimate children were born to single mothers who couldn't keep themselves alive and look after a child at the same time, so they abandoned them. In December 2000 the Orthodox Church reckoned that there were between two and five million vagabond children in Russia.'

'Ah, right, your obsession with children,' said Falcón. 'Two to five million.'

'Now for the only good statistic. The fertility rate in Russia is nearly the lowest in the world. Nearly. And it was then that I realized why this article has been written in a Spanish newspaper because the only country with a fertility rate lower than Russia is . . .'

'Spain,' said Falcón.

'That's why your timing was perfect,' said Consuelo. 'I'd just started on that Sunday thinking, that the whole world has gone wrong.'

'I have a temporary solution to the world crisis.'

'Tell me.'

'Manzanilla. A swim. Paella. Rosado. And a long siesta that goes right through to Monday.'

He woke up in the night disturbed by a vivid dream. He was walking down a path in a dense wood. Coming towards him were two children, a boy and a girl, of around twelve years old who he knew were brother and sister. Walking between them was a totemic bird wearing a frightening mask. As they met, the bird explained: 'I need these two lives.' The look on the children's faces was one of unbearable dread and he felt himself powerless to help. He thought it had woken him up until, as he lay there, he realized that the television was on downstairs. Voices were speaking in American-English. Consuelo was still asleep next to him.

The light from the TV pulsated in the dark as he entered the living room. He turned it off with the remote. It felt warm and he noticed that the sliding door to the pool was open about half a metre.

He turned on the light. Consuelo came down the stairs still half asleep.

'What's going on?'

'The TV was on,' said Falcón. 'Did we leave that door open?'

Consuelo was suddenly awake, her eyes wide open. She pointed and let out a shout as if there was something bad in the room.

He followed her finger. Lying on the coffee table was a group photograph of her children. Someone had drawn a large red cross on the glass.

20

Monday, 29th July 2002

The news told him that the fire was still burning outside Almonaster la Real as Falcón made his way to the Jefatura. Fifty kilometre per hour winds were not making the firefighters' task any easier and they were having to let it burn rather than actively save the forest.

He went straight up to the office of his immediate boss, Comisario Elvira, whose secretary sent him in. Elvira sat at his desk. He was a small, neat man with a pencil moustache and black hair, which he kept in a side parting made with the same laser precision as the Prime Minister's. He was a completely different animal to his predecessor, Andrés Lobo, who seemed to have a greater understanding of the primordial mire from which men came. Elvira was a man who kept his pencils straight.

Falcón gave a verbal report of his weekend's work and put in a request for some discreet police protection for Consuelo Jiménez's children, who were down at the coast near Marbella with her sister.

'Were you staying with Sra Jiménez last night?' asked Elvira.

Falcón faltered. Nothing was sacred in the Jefatura.

'This has not been the first threat since the beginning of the Vega investigation,' said Falcón, evasive on that point. 'I met her for lunch on Saturday and she told me someone from the Jefatura had given her an envelope for me. This photograph was inside.'

Elvira drew the evidence bag towards him and inspected Nadia tied to the chair.

'This Ukrainian woman disappeared after helping us with our inquiries,' said Falcón.

'Anything else?'

'Day one a car with stolen plates followed me to my house. Day two I found a photograph of my ex-wife stuck on the board above my desk at home with a pin through her throat.'

'These Russians are people who seem to know your situation, Inspector Jefe,' said Elvira. 'What are you doing about these threats?'

'I think the design of the threats is to put pressure on me directly,' said Falcón. 'If there had been an initial threat which had been developed I would be more concerned, but each one has been different and specific to my situation. They are trying to distract me from my purpose and get me to refocus my attention away from the Vega inquiry.'

'So you're not tempted to reassign any of your resources?'

'If, by that, you mean will I take responsibility for maintaining the small resource at my disposal on the Vega case, then, yes, I will.'

'Just out of interest, have you eliminated Sra Jiménez from your inquiries?'

'We have no suspect, no witness and no motive.'

'And another thing . . . Pablo Ortega – I understand you took a psychologist there with the intention of trying to help his son. She also accompanied you to the prison. Is there any connection between this case and the Vegas' deaths?'

Silence. Falcón shifted in his chair.

'Inspector Jefe?'

'I don't know.'

'But you think there is . . . something?'

'It needs more work,' said Falcón, 'which means more time.'

'We have confidence in your abilities and we support you in your endeavours,' said Elvira, 'as long as you do nothing to discredit the force. I'll call the Jefatura in Málaga and arrange for an officer to keep an eye on Sra Jiménez's sister and the children.'

Falcón went back down to his office with one of Elvira's comments niggling in his mind. These Russians know your situation. They do. How do they know it?

'Did you find Pablo Ortega's mobile?' Falcón asked Cristina Ferrera, as he passed through to his office.

'I'm working on the numbers now,' she said. 'He seemed to have used his fixed line for incoming calls only. The mobile was his first choice for making calls.'

'I want to know who he spoke to in the hours before he died,' he said.

'What about the key found in Vega's freezer?' asked Ramírez.

'She can work on that afterwards,' said Falcón. 'What about Vega's ID?'

'It's taking time. They've gone as far back as they can with the computer. Now they're working through manually kept ledgers.'

'And the Argentineans?' asked Falcón, as he dialled Carlos Vázquez's number.

'They're short-staffed because of the holidays,' said Ramírez, coming into Falcón's office. 'They've sent the details back to Buenos Aires.'

Falcón showed him the photograph of Nadia Kouzmikheva. Ramírez beat the wall with the side of his fist.

'Somebody handed that in an envelope to Consuelo Jiménez in a bar. They asked her to give it to me,' Falcón said, and then held up a silencing finger. 'I've got a question about company cars in Vega Construcciones,' he said into the phone.

'There weren't any,' said Vázquez. 'Rafael had a policy of no company cars. Everybody used their own and claimed back their expenses.'

'But presumably there were some pool cars that the company personnel could use for jobs?'

'No. Vega Construcciones *used* to own lots of vehicles and equipment, but in the end they became too expensive to run. So, from a few years ago, Rafael cut everything back to just the basic equipment required, got rid of all the vehicles and started hiring whatever was needed. Site engineers, architects – everybody uses their own vehicles.'

'Did Sr Vega keep an old car himself for knocking around on the building sites?'

'Not that I know of.'

Falcón hung up.

'Consuelo Jiménez,' said Ramírez, grinning.

'Don't start, José Luis,' said Falcón, putting a call through to Vega Construcciones.

'Why is Cristina working on Pablo Ortega when we know what happened to him?' said Ramírez.

'Call it instinct,' said Falcón. 'What I want you to tell me is who, in the Jefatura, could be talking to the Russians about me?'

He asked for the building supervisor, who confirmed that no cars were kept in the car park other than those personally owned by employees, and that Sr Vega had only one car, which used to be a Mercedes but was now a Jaguar. He hung up and told Ramírez of the threats made to him so far in the investigation and Elvira's comment.

'Why does it have to be someone from the Jefatura? You've been followed from day one. Anybody could be tapping into your mobile calls. Everybody in Seville knows your story.'

Falcón and Ramírez started calling around the car parks in Seville asking if Rafael Vega or Emilio Cruz held an account with any of them. Half an hour later, the car park under the Hotel Plaza de Armas, on Calle Marqués de Paradas, confirmed that Rafael Vega had an annual account which he paid for in cash.

He set off with Ramírez, who retuned the radio away from the news and a series of interviews with locals talking about the forest fire burning outside Almonaster la Real. Alejandro Sanz's plaintive voice filled the car.

'Any news on your daughter, José Luis?' asked Falcón.

'It's going to take longer than they thought,' he said, and switched the subject. 'This car park is perfect for getting out of town quickly.'

'And nobody would see you,' said Falcón. 'Unless you got caught at the traffic lights on el Torneo.'

'So how did you find out about the car?'

'Consuelo saw him driving it once in town,' said Falcón. 'Do you know a lawyer called Ranz Costa?'

'He's not one of the regular criminal lawyers.'

'See if you can get a meeting with him for later this morning,' said Falcón. 'He's Pablo Ortega's lawyer.'

Ramírez punched the numbers into his mobile. Ranz Costa had an office back across the river in Triana. He said he could fit them in for five or ten minutes any time this morning.

They parked in Calle Marqués de Paradas, picked up some latex gloves and a sheaf of evidence bags and walked down the ramp into the basement car park. The supervisor took them to the car, which was an old blue Peugeot 505 diesel estate. The rear number plate was nearly invisible because of dust.

'He was using this off road,' said Ramírez, snapping on his gloves. 'Felipe can analyse this dust, can't he?'

'Do you keep a key for this?' Falcón asked the supervisor, who shook his head, chewing on a toothpick.

'You want to get in the car?' he asked.

'No,' said Ramírez, 'he wants to unlock your brain to see what that fluttering noise is.'

'He doesn't bite,' said Falcón, 'unless you move suddenly.'

The supervisor removed his very unimpressed face from Ramírez and whistled. Two boys appeared in shorts and trainers and nothing else. The supervisor told them to open the car. One produced a screwdriver and the other unbent a length of wire from his pocket. The kid with the screwdriver jammed it in the door and levered the corner open, the kid with the wire flipped the lock. It took two seconds.

'I like a bit of finesse,' said Ramírez, flexing his gloved hands. 'None of that skeleton-key shit.'

'Did Sr Vega ever ask you to wash the car?'

The supervisor, an expert in the small talents of life, flipped the toothpick from one side of his mouth to the other for an answer.

The car's interior was covered with a thin film of dust, even the passenger and rear seats, indicating that Vega always travelled alone when he used this car. There were documents in the glove compartment, two door keys on a ring with no tag in the ashtray, and a single card for a hostal residencia in a village called Fuenteheridos in the district of Aracena.

They closed the car, told the supervisor not to touch it and that they'd send a truck to pick it up. Ramírez brushed some dust off the bumper into an evidence bag. On the way back to Falcón's car Cristina Ferrera called to say that Pablo Ortega had made four outgoing calls on the Friday evening before his suicide. The two earliest calls had lasted thirty seconds each and were to a builder and someone called Marciano Ruiz. The third call was a twelve minute one to Ignacio Ortega. The last call was to Ranz Costa and had lasted two minutes.

Ramírez called the builder who said that Ortega had called to cancel their meeting. Falcón knew the theatre director Marciano Ruiz so he called him as they went up to Ranz Costa's offices. Ortega had left an obscene message on his answering machine.

'So what's the link between Pablo Ortega's suicide and Vega's death?' asked Ramírez.

'On paper, nothing other than that they knew each other and were immediate neighbours.'

'But your guts are telling you something different?'

They were shown in to Ranz Costa's office. He was a big bear of a man who, even in severe air conditioning, sweated heavily.

'You had a call from Pablo Ortega on Friday evening,' said Falcón. 'What was that about?'

'He thanked me for re-drafting his will and for the copy I'd sent him by courier that afternoon.'

'When did he instruct you to re-draft the will?'

'Thursday morning,' said Ranz Costa. 'I now understand the urgency for the document.'

'Have you spoken to Ignacio Ortega this morning?'

'In fact he called me last night. He wanted to know if his brother had written a letter to me. I said that all communication had been over the phone or in person.'

'Did he ask you about the contents of the will?'

'I started to tell him that his brother had changed the will, but he seemed to know that already. That didn't seem to be his concern.'

'Did the changes benefit him in any way?'

'No,' said Ranz Costa, shifting his weight to the other buttock as client confidentiality began to be infringed.

'You know the next question,' said Ramírez.

'The property in the will was changed to the new house in Santa Clara and Ignacio was no longer to be one of the beneficiaries.'

'Who are the beneficiaries?'

'Primarily Sebastián, who is now to receive everything except for two cash sums to be paid to Ignacio's children.'

'What do you know about Ignacio's son, Salvador?' asked Falcón. 'Apart from the fact that he's a heroin addict living in Seville.'

'He's thirty-four years old. The last address I have for him is in the Polígono San Pablo. I've had to arrange a defence for him twice on drug-dealing charges. He survived the first and I got him a reduced sentence on the second for which he served four years. He was released two years ago and I haven't heard from him since.'

'Do Ignacio and Salvador speak?'

'No, but Pablo and Salvador did.'

'A last question on the will and we'll leave you alone,' said Falcón. 'Ignacio was a wealthy man, I doubt he was expecting any money from his brother.'

'He'd always wanted the Louis XV chair from Pablo's collection.'

Falcón grunted as he remembered Ignacio's professed lack of interest in the collection.

'So why had the brothers fallen out?' asked Ramírez.

'I just do the legal documents,' said Ranz Costa. 'I never involve myself . . .'

He didn't finish. The two lawmen had already left his office.

On the way down from Ranz Costa's office Falcón called Ignacio to remind him about the body identification. He also called Inspector Jefe Montes and said that he'd like to drop by later on that morning and talk about the two Russian names he'd mentioned to him on Friday evening. Montes said he could drop in any time, he wasn't going anywhere.

Falcón took Ramírez back to the Jefatura. He wanted Felipe to analyse the dust sample while Ramírez followed up on the hostal residencia in Fuenteheridos. Falcón drove to the Instituto Anatómico Forense.

Ignacio Ortega and Falcón stood in the room with the curtain drawn over the glass panel. They waited in silence while the body was brought up from the morgue and the Médico Forense prepared the paperwork.

'When did you say was the last time you spoke to Pablo?' asked Falcón.

'The night before I went away,' he said.

'Pablo's mobile telephone company has informed us that you had a twelve-minute call with him on the evening before he died. Can you explain that to me, Sr Ortega?'

Silence while Ignacio looked at the unopened curtain.

'Ranz Costa told us that Pablo changed his will before he died. Do you know what those changes were?'

Ignacio nodded.

'Was that what was discussed in the phone call he made to you on Friday evening?'

Ignacio's head stayed still.

'I was surprised at how you seemed more concerned about whether your brother had written to you, and what he had written to Sebastián, than you were by the fact of his suicide,' said Falcón, thinking this was a man who needed to be riled up.

That turned Ignacio, whose two eyes punched into Falcón's face like industrial riveters.

'You have no right to talk to me like that,' he said. 'I am not one of your suspects. I have not been accused of anything. My brother killed himself. I am dealing with that in my own private way, which is no business of yours. You're as curious to know why he killed himself as I am, but you have no right to poke your nose into my family affairs unless you can prove that I was in some way responsible for my brother's death when I was on the coast at the time.'

'You lied to me about the last time you spoke to your brother,' said Falcón. 'Detectives never like being lied to. We get suspicious and think you have something to hide.'

'I have *nothing* to hide. My conscience is clear. What *family* matters passed between Pablo and me are private.'

'You know, we're thinking of reopening Sebastián's case, as well as giving him some psychological help...'

'You can do what you like, Inspector Jefe.'

The Médico Forense informed them that the body was now ready. Ignacio turned to the curtains, which opened. He confirmed his brother's identity, signed the papers and left without another word or glance in Falcón's direction.

Falcón drove back to the Jefatura with three thoughts knocking around in his head. Why did Ignacio Ortega bother him so much? It was clear he hadn't killed his brother, but there was something locked up in the man's head that made Falcón think that he had some responsibility. How do you crack a hard nut like Ignacio Ortega? And how do you find out what the dead men have locked away in their heads? Police work might be easier if it were possible to download the mind's contents on to screen. The software of life. What would that look like? Fact distorted by emotion. Reality transformed by illusion. Truth painted over by denial. That would take some program to disentangle.

His mobile rang.

'*Diga*,' he said.

'Are you on your way back?' asked Ramírez.

'I'm on the Plaza de Cuba.'

'Good, because Inspector Jefe Montes has just jumped out of his second-floor window and landed on his head in the car park.'

Falcón accelerated down the Avenida de Argentina. His tyres squealed on the hot tarmac as he turned into the Jefatura car park. There was a crowd gathered beneath the window from which he'd seen Montes looking out only last week thinking . . . thinking: has the moment come?

The ambulance lights flashed almost invisibly in the glare of the brutally bleaching light that beat down on the scene in the car park. Women's faces stared out from the dark ground-floor office windows, mouths covered. Men stood at first-floor windows, heads viced in their hands, squeezing out this unnatural image. Falcón pushed through the crowd in time to see the paramedics officially give up on the inert Montes. His shoulder and head looked as if they were buried in dark bloody tarmac soft enough to take this terrible indentation. But Falcón knew from the look of it what that body would reveal on the slab: shattered shoulder, compound fracture of the collarbone, broken neck vertebrae, severed spinal chord, smashed skull, catastrophic brain haemorrhage.

Members of Montes's squad were in the crowd. They were crying. Comisario Elvira came out of the Jefatura and made a carefully designed speech to disperse the crowd. His eyes fell on Falcón. He told him to have photographs taken, the body removed and to make an initial verbal report within the hour. The Juez de Guardia arrived with the Médico Forense.

As the crowd dispersed, Ferrera took three of them off to make witness statements. Falcón told Ramírez to seal off Montes's office. Felipe took the necessary shots. The paramedics removed the body under instruction from the Juez de Guardia. The crime scene cleaners moved in and washed away the blood, which was already congealing in the sun.

As Falcón went up to his office to get a fresh notebook, he had a terrible sense of convergence – Vega, Ortega and now Montes. The homicide squad three men short because of the holiday season. Each death not apparently connected and yet somehow being the precursor of the next.

He found Ferrera, gave her Salvador Ortega's details and told her to speak to someone in the Narcotics squad. A current address was all he wanted. He also told her to check all post offices in the Seville area to see if either Rafael Vega or an Argentinean called Emilio Cruz held a postbox for receiving mail.

'Is this more important than Rafael Vega's key?'

'Did you get anywhere with that?'

'He doesn't have a safe-deposit box in the Banco de Bilbao. That was as far as I got.'

'Work on the key later,' he said. 'It'll take time.'

He picked up his notebook and walked slowly up the stairs to the second floor where Ramírez stood with a master key for Montes's office. The members of GRUME were lined up in the corridor, waiting. Felipe came up from the car park sweating with his camera.

Ramírez opened the door. Felipe took his shots and left. Falcón shut the window. They looked around, sweating, while the air conditioning reasserted itself. On Montes's desk was a sheet of notepaper covered in his handwriting and a sealed envelope addressed to his wife. Falcón and Ramírez moved round to read the writing on the notepaper, which was addressed to 'My Fellow Officers':

It probably seems ridiculous to you that I should have taken my own life so close to retirement. I should have been able to bear the pressure of my job for a little longer, but I could not. This is no reflection on the men and women with whom it has been my honour to work.

I joined the police force with the belief that I could do some good. I had a strong sense of the value of the policeman in society. I have not been able to do the good that I intended. I have felt increasingly powerless to act against the new waves of depravity and corruption which are now sweeping through my country and the rest of Europe.

I have been drinking, hoping that it would dull my senses to what was happening around me. I did not succeed. A growing oppression has weighed down on my shoulders until at times I have felt unable to rise from my chair. I have felt trapped and unable to speak to anyone.

I only ask that you, my friends, protect my family and forgive me for this last disastrous act of mine.

Falcón read the letter out to the squad members crowding the door. The women cried open-eyed, staring in disbelief. He asked if someone who knew Sra Montes would accompany Ramírez to give her the letter and break the news to her personally. Montes's number two stepped forward and he and Ramírez left.

There was nothing of interest in the office and the interviews with the various members of the squad, who were all shaken, were monosyllabic. By the time he'd finished, Ramírez was back, having left the inspector of GRUME with Sra Montes. They sealed Montes's office and went back down to their own, where Cristina Ferrera was on the phone. Falcón told her to check for postboxes in the name of Alberto Montes as well. She nodded and scribbled down the name.

Ramírez followed him into his office and they stood at the window overlooking the car park, which was already clean and dry.

'You think Montes was on the take?' asked Ramírez.

'Some of the words he used in his letter were interesting,' said Falcón. 'Like: "I have not been able to do the good I intended", "powerless against corruption", "growing oppression", "trapped" and finally the phrase that really drew my attention: "protect my family". Why should anybody say anything like that? "Look after" maybe, but "protect"? This was a guy whose subconscious was leaking into his everyday life and he couldn't bear it.'

Ramírez nodded and stared into the car park, imagining himself crumpled, corrupted, damaged beyond repair. The man discarded from life.

'You didn't get the idea that he was on the take from that letter,' said Ramírez. 'So what else do you know?'

'I don't know what I know.'

'Don't start with that shit.'

'I mean it. I think Montes *thought* I knew something,' said Falcón.

'Well, if he *was* on the take, he's looking like the source for any information the Russians have on you.'

'Montes thought I was putting pressure on him, which I wasn't. I was just asking him about these Russians . . . to see if he'd heard of them. Nothing more than that.'

'His mind did the rest,' said Ramírez.

'And now I feel like an archaeologist who's found a few unusual shards of pottery and been asked to rebuild a civilization from them.'

'Tell me the shards,' said Ramírez. 'I'm good at gluing things back together.'

'I'm almost too embarrassed to tell you,' said Falcón. 'They're hints revived from the old Raúl Jiménez case. Some names from Rafael Vega's address book. The Russian mafia involvement in the two Vega Construcciones projects. Their threats. The timing of Ortega's death. The timing of this suicide today. They're not even solid enough to be called shards, and if they are they might not be from the same pot but just dislocated fragments.'

'Let's get some things straight in our heads about Vega,' said Ramírez. 'First of all, he's security conscious: the handgun – which I checked and it wasn't licensed – the bulletproof windows, the surveillance system, even if he didn't use it, the front door . . .'

'The front door which is normally fully locked at night but which we discovered only shut on the morning of his death.'

'As was the back door into his garden, meaning . . .'

'Possibly indicating,' said Falcón, correcting him, 'that Vega let someone into the house late at night whom he knew.'

'All his immediate neighbours knew him socially,' said Ramírez, 'but nobody called first to say they were coming round, if indeed they did.'

'We know from Pablo Ortega that the Russians used to visit him at home,' said Falcón. 'But as Vázquez said, Vega was "facilitating their business needs" so their motive for wanting him removed is not clear. Marty Krugman put up the possibility that Vega was in some way cheating the Russians.'

'Was that based on anything?'

'Speculation. I asked him why the mafia might want Vega dead,' said Falcón. 'We should compare the two sets of books on the Russian projects Dourado told you about.'

'The Russians – and we're pretty sure it is them – are rattled enough to make threats against you and Consuelo Jiménez,' said Ramírez.

'It's heavy-handed stuff if they're worried about a bit of money-laundering.'

'Money makes the mafia tick,' said Ramírez.

'Or is there something worse in the Vega scenario which might come to light in the course of an intrusive murder investigation?'

'I took a closer look at the Argentinean passport he had in the name of Emilio Cruz this morning,' said Ramírez. 'It also had a valid Moroccan visa in it. In fact, there were five Moroccan visas in there. Four had expired without being used. The fifth was valid until November 2002. That means he could have been in Tangier in five hours by car and ferry, even less by air. Somebody who keeps themselves in that state of readiness is used to it.'

'You mean he's trained?' said Falcón.

'The only question is whether it's crime, terrorism or government that's trained him.'

'The compartmentalizing style of management,' said Falcón. 'Nobody knows what anybody else is doing. Krugman talked about the importance of hierarchy, the discipline on the sites. He said he had no experience of it, but that it felt like a military style of working.'

'Maybe he's been militarily trained by a government and is using it for the purposes of crime or terrorism.'

'The only reason we're thinking about terrorism is because of the 9/11 reference in the note he had in his hand,' said Falcón. 'I don't know how much importance we can attach to a note that was traced over from an indentation in his own hand and written in English. Marty Krugman talked to him endlessly about 9/11 and he couldn't make any sense of it.'

Cristina Ferrera knocked on the door.

'There's a postbox in the name of Emilio Cruz in the post office in San Bernardo,' she said. 'But don't get too excited. It's empty and there's been nothing in it since last year.'

'What sort of mail used to arrive there for him?'

'He remembers there being a letter every month with US stamps on it.'

'Anything on Alberto Montes?'

'Nothing yet,' she said, closing the door.

The two men turned back to the window.

'What did the letter to his wife say?'

'"I'm sorry . . . forgive me . . . I've failed . . ." – the usual shit,' said Ramírez.

'Anything about being protected or looked after?'

'At the end he said: "Don't worry, you'll be well looked after,"' said Ramírez. 'Are we being paranoid here?'

'And his second in command, his inspector? Did he have anything to say.'

'Nothing. Shocked by the whole thing.'

'Just like the rest of the squad,' said Falcón. 'If he was on the take, he was doing it on his own.'

'And if he was on the take he's got to keep it somewhere. He's also got to let his wife know where it is and she's got to go and collect it or do something with it.'

'I'm going to make my verbal report to Comisario Elvira now,' said Falcón. 'Find out who Montes used as a lawyer.'

Before Falcón could make his verbal report, Elvira had a photocopy of the letter made and went through it with one of his pencils as if it was a piece of homework. Falcón stuck to the facts in his report and offered no conjecture.

'I'm going to ask you to venture an opinion, Inspector Jefe,' said Elvira, when he'd finished. 'This is the first suicide we've ever had at the Jefatura. There will be media interest. The *Diario de Sevilla* has already called.'

'I only knew Montes by sight until last week,' said Falcón. 'I went to ask him about a man called Eduardo Carvajal, whose name appeared in Rafael Vega's address book and whose name I knew from my investigation into the Raúl Jiménez case last year.'

'I know that name,' said Elvira. 'I was working in Málaga when he was "killed" in that so-called car crash. He was a key prosecution witness in a paedophile case. There was a cover-up, as you probably know. The car was destroyed before it could be investigated and there seemed to be some doubt as to the nature of his head injuries.'

'Montes said that Carvajal was going to make him famous. He'd promised him names. Then he died and, in the end, only four members of the paedophile ring were convicted.'

'I'll tell you something that should not go out of this room,' said Elvira. 'Word came down from politicians to top office here that the Carvajal car accident was not something that should be picked over under any media spotlight.'

'As you can imagine, there were some unpleasant memories for Inspector Jefe Montes at the mention of Carvajal's name,' said Falcón.

'Montes explained that Carvajal was the procurer for the rings and that the source for the children being used was the Russian mafia. There's a link between Rafael Vega and two Russians who are investing in an unusual way in two projects under the umbrella of Vega Construcciones. Interpol subsequently told us that the Russians were known mafiosi. I called Montes to run the names by him on Friday evening. He was drunk. I called him again this morning and he said he was happy to talk about it. Then he jumped out of his office window.'

'According to his psychological assessment, carried out last year, he's had a drink problem since 1998 . . . which was the year of the car crash involving Eduardo Carvajal,' said Elvira. 'He has also not been well in the last eight months.'

'He mentioned kidney stones and a hernia.'

'There was a liver problem, as well, which was making him very sick at times.'

'That adds to the pressure,' said Falcón.

'What do you make of this letter to his squad?'

'I wanted to say one more thing about Montes and Carvajal which relates to the letter,' said Falcón. 'Montes told *me* about the Russian mafia connection. He gave *me* an insight into the mafia people-trafficking business. If he has been corrupted and fears being discovered – which, if I'm not mistaken, is what we're talking about here – why should he be giving me that information? When I read the letter I got the feeling that the pressure of not telling had become so great that it was coming out anyway. He hasn't "been able to do the good he intended", which could mean that he has done bad. The "corruption" is possibly what's happened to him. The "oppression" is his guilt. He feels "trapped" and "unable to speak" because he's working against everything he believed in. And the last line about "protect my family" implies some kind of danger to them. I think Inspector Jefe Montes was a good man who made, or was forced to make, a very bad choice and he deeply regretted it.'

'I've asked for your opinion and you've given it to me,' said Elvira. 'It's unusable, of course. Now I want your proof. You realize that this will be unpleasant, Inspector Jefe?'

'You might want to talk to Comisario Lobo about the political implications within the Jefatura of what I would propose,' said Falcón, 'which is that we should look closely at Sra Montes's movements in the next few days.'

21

Monday, 29th July 2002

Now that Alicia Aguado's involvement in Sebastian Ortega's case was out in the open, Falcón decided to speak to Elvira about his intentions. It had occurred to him that his case for using her was weak and the prison director would obviously prefer to use his own psychologists for the work. He pushed Elvira into speaking to the director on his behalf, citing Alicia Aguado's rapport with the prisoner and her belief in her ability to draw information out. Elvira looked at him steadily throughout, as if he barely believed a word he was saying. He acquiesced silently. Falcón also asked that, due to the shortage of manpower in his squad, somebody else should be used to watch Sra Montes. Elvira said he had his own ideas on that point.

The outer office of the Homicide squad was empty. Ramírez was standing at the window.

'Where's Cristina gone?' asked Falcón.

'She's found a Narcotics guy who thinks he knows how to locate Salvador Ortega,' he said. 'Are you going to tell me about that?'

'What about the postboxes?'

'Just the Emilio Cruz one. None for Montes or Vega,' said Ramírez. 'I've been calling the banks, trying to find a safe-deposit box to fit this key. There's one in the name of Emilio Cruz at the Banco Banesto.'

'That's good,' said Falcón. 'Any news on Montes's lawyer?'

'I spoke to him. He hadn't heard from Alberto Montes in three years. The last time they spoke was to make an adjustment to the will,' said Ramírez, and held up his hand. 'Now you've got to tell me about Salvador Ortega. I know who he is, just tell me why we want to talk to him.'

'Because Pablo used to see him and he might know what the problem was between the brothers,' said Falcón.

'Is that going to help us find Vega's killer?' said Ramírez.

'Think for a moment about how Vega was killed.'

'It was nasty . . . vindictive. They wanted him to suffer. Mafiosi are like that. They do it to set an example to others who might be thinking of cheating them.'

'That's right, which is why we need to work on clarifying their motive because at the moment all I can see is that Vega was important to their plans,' said Falcón. 'Now, listen to these names and let me tell you that they all knew each other: Raúl Jiménez, Ramón Salgado, Eduardo Carvajal, Rafael Vega, Pablo and Ignacio Ortega.'

'You think there's a paedophile connection,' said Ramírez. 'How do you know the Ortegas knew Carvajal?'

'They were in a shot together on Raúl Jiménez's study wall,' said Falcón. 'And all those names were in Vega's –' Falcón stopped. 'I've just had a thought. I'll have to check it. Tell me what adjustment Montes made to his will.'

'He added a property to his assets,' said Ramírez. 'A small finca, worth less than three million pesetas.'

'I bet that made your heart leap for a moment.'

'I don't think I would have got the information so easily if it had been a 200-million-peseta villa in Marbella.'

'Did he say where it was?'

'He couldn't remember. He's going to look it up in the copy of the will and call me back.'

'Was there a mortgage on it?'

'He didn't know. He wasn't involved in the purchase of it.'

'When you've got an address for it, check out the deed and see if he ever talked about it to the people in his squad.'

The phone rang in the outer office. Ramírez took it, hunched over and scribbled furiously for a few minutes. He slammed the phone down, triumphant.

'We've got a result on Rafael Vega's ID trace,' he said. 'The first Rafael Vega died back in 1983 at the age of thirty-nine in a shipping accident in the port of La Coruña; the second one died from drinking acid last week.'

'How did he manage that?'

'The first time he died was just at the point when they were changing records from manual to computer. According to the computer records he was still alive. Only by going back to the old paper records did they find the death certificate.'

'He was the right age.'

'He was the right age, physically similar and he had no family. The original Rafael Vega was an orphan who became a merchant seaman. He never married.'

'So, not only was our Rafael Vega trained, but he was well connected in the clandestine world as well,' said Falcón. 'Finally we get the break, José Luis, but...'

'Yes, I know,' said Ramírez. 'He isn't who he says he is ... but who the fuck is he?'

'There's an American connection. Krugman was sure he'd lived there and now we know he was getting mail sent to him from there,' said Falcón. 'And there's possibly a Mexican one.'

'The Mexican wife might just be another fake,' said Ramírez. 'It would be more plausible for a man of that age to have been married before.'

'He's looking to me as if he's Central or South American origin now.'

'If you were originally Argentinean, would you use a fake passport from your country of origin?'

'Maybe not, but that still leaves the rest of the subcontinent,' said Falcón. 'Perhaps we need to have a meeting with Juez Calderón. We're due one early this week. I think this classifies as a development.'

He put a call through to Calderón's secretary. The judge was just finishing a meeting. She would talk to him and see if there was a chance before lunch. After lunch was out of the question. Falcón hung up and sat back in his chair.

'What sort of people need the level of secrecy at which Rafael Vega was operating?' he asked.

'Someone who was a covert intelligence operative for a government or a terrorist organization,' said Ramírez. 'Someone involved in the drugs trade.'

'What about an arms dealer?' said Falcón. 'The Russian connection. Where's the easiest place to get military hardware?'

'Russia, via the mafia,' said Ramírez. 'And the money is coming from the building projects. Those land deals were done directly between the original owners and the Russians. No money trail to Vega.'

'Plausible, but that just gives us more questions. Who is he supplying and, before we let our imagination run completely wild,' said Falcón, 'why kill him?'

'A terrorist organization that doesn't want a lead to their door,' said Ramírez.

Calderón's secretary called back and said that he could see them in half an hour. They drove to the Edificio de los Juzgados and went straight up to Calderón's office. He was facing away from his desk, looking through the slats of the blinds, smoking. He heard them come in. He told them to sit.

'Case or no case?' he asked, without turning around.

'Complications,' said Falcón, and talked him through the secret life of Rafael Vega.

As Falcón spoke, Calderón turned in his chair. If the last time Falcón had seen him he'd looked as though he'd come back to the city after being lost in the mountains, now he looked as stricken as a man who'd had to eat his comrades in order to survive. He was haggard, the smudges beneath his eyes were now grape-dark and his forehead was stepped with furrows. He seemed to have lost weight. His neck did not fill his collar. Falcón finished. Calderón nodded, he seemed pensive but distracted. The new information did not galvanize his ambition.

'Well, you've got a bit more background information on Vega now,' he said, 'but you still haven't given me any real development in the case – no witness, no motive. What exactly do you want?'

'We could start with a search warrant for the safe-deposit box in the Banco Banesto,' said Ramírez, cutting in, exchanging a look with Falcón.

'Whose box is it?' asked Calderón.

'It's Vega's, of course,' said Ramírez, puzzled by the judge's lack of comprehension, 'but in the name of Emilio Cruz.'

'I'll work on it,' said Calderón. 'What else?'

'We have theories. We want more time,' said Falcón, and gave him the examples of the Russian mafia connection to military hardware, and the names of the men who all appeared to know each other from Vega's address book and Raúl Jiménez's photographs.

'That's all conjecture,' said Calderón. 'Where's the evidence? Vega has been running a successful construction business in Seville for nearly twenty years. He's built it more or less from scratch. So, he happens to run his business in a certain way and . . .'

'You seem to be forgetting that he's a man with perfect fake Spanish documents and an Argentinean alias with Moroccan visas for a quick getaway,' said Ramírez. 'I hardly think that level of secrecy would classify him as, say, a married man embarking on illicit affairs.'

Calderón shot him a look that whistled past his ear.

'I can see that,' said the judge. 'Obviously the man had a past. He's escaped from something and rebuilt his life. Maybe his past has caught up with him in some way, but that doesn't help you determine which direction you're going to take. You're talking about arms dealing, drug running, people-trafficking and terrorism, but you haven't shown me a lead that would indicate a direction. You've just got theories. The Russian land deals look odd, agreed. Their connection to Vega is unhealthy, to say the least. But we have no access to the original owner of the plots. You can look up the sale price on the deed, but that won't tell you much because everybody puts a low value on land sales for tax purposes. There has to be a chain of logic that the Juez Decano can see if public money is to be spent chasing these . . . notions.'

'You don't see any connection between Sr Vega's death and the suicide of his neighbour?' said Ramírez.

'You haven't told me of one, apart from names in an address book and people appearing together in photographs,' said Calderón, stifling a yawn. 'Juez Romero said he couldn't see any either. The two deaths seem to be a coincidence, with the difference that there's no doubt in one case and some uncertainty in the other. An uncertainty which is in our minds and not in any evidence you've brought before me.'

'What about the note referring to a famous terrorist act?' said Ramírez.

'That is a slice of information as relevant to the court as his files on war crimes tribunals, or the fact that he kept a battered old car in a garage, or that he wasn't who he says he was. It's all informa-tion, but like the anonymous threats it's not connected to anything,' said Calderón. He turned to Falcón. 'You're not saying anything, Inspector Jefe.'

'Are we wasting our time with this?' said Falcón, weary of it all now that Calderón's listlessness had seeped into his own blood-stream. 'We might find more bits of fascinating information which supply neither witness nor motive. We're down to three people because of the holidays. We have a serious situation in the Jefatura . . .'

'I heard about that,' said Calderón, staring into his desk, hands clasped between his knees.

'Our chances of finding the only witness, Sergei, grow slimmer by the day. Do we finish with it or carry on? If we carry on, which direction should we take?'

'OK, you're annoyed. I can see you've done good work and found interesting information,' said Calderón, catching Falcón's tone and trying to get some enthusiasm into his voice. 'At the moment, in my mind, given the psychological profile of the victim – of which we have *clear* evidence from a doctor and Maddy Krugman's photographs – and even taking your new findings into consideration, I am still more inclined to believe that Vega killed his wife and then himself. If you can accept that, I will return a verdict of suicide. If you're still curious enough to carry on, I'll give you forty-eight hours.'

'To go in which direction?' asked Ramírez.

'Whichever you like,' said Calderón. 'Do you have any chance of talking to the Russians face to face?'

'They're in Portugal,' said Falcón. 'It's possible they'll come over to look at their investments.'

'Who would they contact?'

'Probably Carlos Vázquez.'

'There's a man with something to hide,' said Ramírez.

'What about finding out who Vega really is?' said Falcón.

'How?' asked Calderón, half turning back to the window.

'The American connection,' said Falcón. 'Let's say he *was* living there twenty years ago, and that he had escaped from something and rebuilt his life. I've just remembered that detail in the autopsy report about the old plastic surgery. It seems a likely scenario. Maybe he had a criminal record or was known in some way to the FBI.'

'Do you have contact with the FBI?' asked Calderón.

'Of course.'

'So you're going to take my offer of forty-eight hours?'

On the way down from Calderón's office Falcón took a call from Elvira, who had just spoken to his boss, Comisario Lobo, and between them they'd decided that Falcón should run the investigation into

Montes's suicide. Falcón asked Elvira if he could supply a good and responsive FBI contact who would help with the identification of Rafael Vega, and reminded him about the prison director.

In the car he called Carlos Vázquez and after being kept waiting for some minutes was told that he was out. The lawyer's offices were just up the road from the Edificio de los Juzgados. They decided to make an unscheduled visit.

'What's up with Juez Calderón?' asked Ramírez as they got into the car. 'We're not going to see a search warrant with his mind in that state.'

'I think he might have met his match,' said Falcón.

'La Americana's fucked his brains out?' said Ramírez.

'It might a bit more serious than that.'

'She's done that to him?' said Ramírez incredulous. 'I thought Juez Calderón was more experienced than that.'

'Than what?'

'To fall down on rule number one,' said Ramírez 'and to fall down on it before he's even got married.'

'What's rule number one?'

'Don't get involved,' said Ramírez. 'That's the way to fuck up your entire life.'

'Well, he's involved and all we can do is . . .'

'Sit and watch,' said Ramírez, clapping his hands as if he was about to watch his favourite soap opera.

'Montes told me there were plenty of people who wanted to see Juez Calderón fall from grace.'

'Who?' said Ramírez, face bland with innocence, fingers to his chest. 'Me?'

They went up in the lift, Ramírez staring at the numbers of the floors as they lit up. His shoulders were humped up like the neck muscles of a wild bull.

'This time, Javier, I lead, you follow,' he said, and they stormed out of the lift straight past the receptionist, who held up a single purple talon in an attempt to stop them.

They did the same to Vázquez's secretary, who followed them

into her boss's office. Vázquez was drinking water from a plastic cup and standing by the dispenser looking out of the window.

'In a murder investigation,' said Ramírez, in a voice full of pent-up rage. 'You never refuse to talk to the Inspector Jefe unless you want all kinds of shit to come down on your head.'

Vázquez looked pugnacious enough to square off against Ramírez, but even he could see that the Inspector was up for anything, including violence. He waved the secretary out.

'What do you want?'

'First question,' said Ramírez. 'Look into my eyes and tell me what you know about Emilio Cruz.'

Vázquez looked blank. The name meant nothing to him. They sat down.

'What provision did Sr Vega make for the running of his company in the event of his death?' asked Falcón.

'As you know, each project had Sr Vega, a company representative and an investor on the board. In the event of his death the projects would be managed by the remaining company representative, with the proviso that all financial and legal decisions be referred to a temporary board in the holding company, consisting of myself, Sr Dourado and Sr Nieves, who is the senior architect.'

'How long would this temporary state of affairs last?'

'Until a suitable director for the company was found.'

'Whose job is it to find such a person?'

'The temporary board.'

'Who do the clients refer to?'

'The temporary board.'

'And who would get the initial phone call?'

'Me.'

'So when did the Russians contact you?' asked Ramírez.

'They haven't.'

'Look, Sr Vázquez, it's been nearly a week since Sr Vega died,' said Ramírez, conspiratorial, friendly. 'There's a lot of money in those Russian projects, which are unmanaged. Do you really expect us to believe –'

'They're not unmanaged. They've still got the company representative looking after them.'

'Who is?'

'Sr Krugman, the architect.'

'That's a good choice,' said Falcón. 'The outsider.'

'Who does Sr Krugman get his instructions from?'

'He hasn't received any from me because I haven't heard from the client. He is just carrying on with the project.'

'So, after Sr Vega's death who told the illegal labour not to show?' asked Ramírez.

'What illegal labour?'

'We can physically wring this stuff out of you, if you'd prefer,' said Ramírez. 'Or you could talk to us like a normal, law-abiding human being.'

'Are you scared, Sr Vázquez?' asked Falcón.

'Scared?' said Vázquez, asking himself, hands clasped, knuckles blanching, especially around the gold signet ring on his third finger. 'Why should I be scared?'

'Have you been told not to talk to us on pain of something nasty happening to you or your family?'

'No.'

'All right, we'll go to the town hall and file a report on these two projects,' said Ramírez. 'The fact that illegal labour has been used should be enough.'

'There's no illegal labour.'

'That sounds as if you're in touch with these projects.'

'I am,' said Vázquez. 'You told me about illegal labour being used last week. I made my inquiries. There is no illegal labour being used.'

'And the two sets of books for each project that we saw in Vega Construcciones offices last week?'

'There's only one set of books.'

'Not according to Sr Dourado,' said Ramírez.

'That's not what he told me,' said Vázquez.

'The Russians *have* been busy.'

On the way back to the Jefatura they stopped off in Vega Construcciones offices and asked Sr Dourado about the two sets of books. He had no recollection of the discovery of an alternative set of books in Vega's computer system. Even when Ramírez threatened him with a warrant his smile didn't waver. He welcomed the search.

Falcón and Ramírez drifted down the office corridors in silence, all purpose gone from this aspect of their investigation.

'We played this very badly,' said Falcón. 'We trusted these people too much.'

'Dourado was going to help us. I know it. I was there. I saw the printouts. He talked me through them. I should have taken a fucking copy.'

'He didn't look scared to me,' said Falcón. 'Vázquez seemed scared, but Dourado looked cheerful.'

'They know what they're doing, these Russians,' said Ramírez. 'Vázquez thinks he's in charge, so they get him by the balls and squeeze hard. With Golden Boy, they need his knowledge of the computer system, so they tickle his.'

Falcón tried not to allow these images to infect his imagination. He said he'd go and talk to Krugman while Ramírez went back to the Jefatura and pushed Elvira to make FBI contact.

Krugman was standing at his office window, looking out through a pair of binoculars. Falcón knocked. Krugman beckoned him in. The man seemed strangely energized, his eyes were bright, pupils dilated and sparkling.

'You're still running your Russian projects,' said Falcón.

'That's right.'

'Have they contacted you by any chance?'

'Of course they have. They've got a twenty million euro investment there, you don't let that sort of money run around on its own.'

'That's interesting,' said Falcón. 'Were you aware of any financial irregularities . . ?'

'That's business. I'm an architect.'

'Were you aware of illegal labour on the sites?'

'Yes. There's illegal labour on all building sites.'

'Are you prepared to sign –?'

'Don't be a crazy fool, Inspector Jefe. I'm trying to help.'

'When did you speak to the Russians?'

'Yesterday.'

'What did you discuss?'

'They told me to carry on running the projects, but said that I shouldn't talk to the police. I told them that I would have to speak to the police because they were coming to my house and office all the time. They said that I shouldn't talk about the projects.'

'What language were you speaking?'

'English. They don't speak Spanish.'

'Do you know who you're dealing with, Sr Krugman?'

'Not personally, but I used to work in New York City and I've come across the Russian mafia before in my own back yard. They're powerful people who, with a few exceptions, are quite reasonable as long as you see things their way. You could try taking them on if you thought it would serve a very important purpose. But in the end you're looking for Sr Vega's murderer, or the reason he committed suicide, and I doubt they're going to be able to help you, because I'm pretty sure that the very last thing they wanted was for Sr Vega to die.'

Falcón nodded. Krugman sat back in his chair.

'What were you looking at with the binoculars?'

'Just keeping an eye on things, Inspector Jefe,' he said, very seriously, then he laughed. 'Only kidding. I bought them today. I'm just seeing what I can see.'

Falcón stood up to leave. He was disturbed by Krugman's evangelical look.

'Have you seen my wife recently?' asked Marty, as Falcón held out his hand.

'I saw her in the street on Saturday,' said Falcón.

'Where was that?'

'In a tile shop in Calle Bailén, near my house.'

'You know she's really very fascinated by you, Inspector Jefe.'

'Only because she has some rather strange specialist interests,' said Falcón. 'Personally, I don't like her intrusions.'

'I thought it was just a few snaps of you on the bridge,' said Krugman. 'Or was it more than that?'

'That was enough,' said Falcón, 'to make me feel as if she was trying to take something from me.'

'Well, that's Maddy's unique problem,' said Krugman. 'As your friend, the judge, will find out.'

Krugman turned to the window and put the binoculars to his face.

22

Monday, 29th July 2002

Back at the Jefatura Ramírez sat smoking in the outer office. He
said that Cristina Ferrera was on her way back with Salvador Ortega,
who'd been found in a 'shooting gallery' in the Polígono San Pablo.
He also informed him that Virgilio Guzmán, the crime editor for
the *Diario de Sevilla*, was being patient in his office. This was
unnerving because Virgilio Guzmán did not do stories any more.

Virgilio Guzmán was a few years younger than Falcón but his life
and work had aged him considerably. Before coming down to Seville
he had been in Bilbao and Madrid, covering ETA terrorist activity.
His ambition and tenacity had cost him his marriage, the constant
tension had left him with high blood pressure and heart arrhythmia
and, he believed, not seeing his six-year-old son had given him colon
cancer, from which he'd made a full recovery at the cost of a length
of his guts. He'd had to leave the fear of his work to live in fear of
his anatomy.

It had changed him. His wife had left him before the cancer diag-
nosis because he was too hard a man. Now he had softened, not to
mush just to flesh and blood but it had not dulled any of his journalistic sharpness. He had the vital journalist's tool: an infallible nose
for when things were not right. And he knew that the first suicide
by a senior officer in the Jefatura meant that something, somewhere,
was rotten. He was polite. He asked if he could put the dictaphone
on the desk between them. He clicked it on and sat back with his
notebook.

Falcón did not say a word. He made an instant decision about
Guzmán – this was a man he could trust and not just by reputation
alone. He also thought, and he sniffed at his own naïvety on this
matter, that with only forty-eight hours left to make a case for Vega's

murder, Guzmán, with his extensive experience, might be able to bring different information to the game which could develop into different leads and directions. All this might cost him something from the Montes inquiry, but then the exposure of corruption, and its cutting out, should be a good thing – shouldn't it?

'So, Inspector Jefe, I understand that you are conducting the investigation into the death of your colleague, Inspector Jefe Alberto Montes?'

Falcón said nothing for two long minutes during which Guzmán looked up, blinking like a subterranean animal.

'I'm sorry, Inspector Jefe,' he said, shrugging into the flak jacket of his journalistic hardness, 'but that's the easiest opening question I can think of.'

Falcón leaned over and turned off the dictaphone.

'You know with that machine on I can only tell you the facts of the case.'

'Well, that's a start,' said Guzmán, 'and then it will be up to me to extract the rest. That's how it goes where I come from.'

'You know the facts already,' said Falcón. 'They are the newsworthy event of a police officer's fall to his death. It's the why that contains the human story.'

'And what makes you think I'm looking for a human story and not, say, "a catalogue of corruption that reaches to the heart of regional government" story?'

'It's possible that you'll end up with that sort of story, but you have to start with the human story to get there. You have to understand the thoughts that led a respected officer, who'd never shown any suicidal tendency, to take such drastic action.'

'Do I?' said Guzmán. 'Normally we journalists, or rather journalists of my reputation, deal in facts. We report facts, we build on facts, we create a greater fact from the smaller facts we discover.'

'Then turn on your machine and I will give you the fully corroborated facts of the death of a fellow officer who was much admired by his squad and superiors.'

Guzmán laid down his notebook and pen on the desk and sat back assessing Falcón. He sensed that there were possibilities for him here if he could find the right words, and that the possibilities might not be only work related. He had arrived in Seville alone, admired and, he thought, respected by his fellow journalists, but alone. He could use a friend, and that was the possibility he saw on the other side of the desk.

'I've always worked alone,' he said, after a minute's thought. 'I've had to, because working with somebody and their unpredictability in threatening situations was too dangerous. I only ever wanted to be responsible for my own thoughts and actions and not the victim of others'. I've spent too long in the company of men of violence to be thoughtless.'

'In a human story such as this, there's always tragedy,' said Falcón. 'People feel hurt and betrayed, while others suffer loss and grief.'

'If you remember, Inspector Jefe, I worked on the story of the Guardia Civil death squads sent out by the government to remove ETA terrorist cells. I understand the tragedy of a betrayal of values on the large and the human scale. The repercussions were felt everywhere.'

'Conjecture is something that police officers have to indulge in to find a direction for their investigation, but it is not something that's allowable in court,' said Falcón.

'I told you about my belief in facts,' said Guzmán, 'but you didn't seem to like it so much then.'

'Information is a two-way street,' said Falcón, smiling for the first time.

'Agreed.'

'If you discover something inflammatory you will always tell me before it appears in your newspaper.'

'I'll tell you, but I won't change it.'

'The facts: I didn't know Montes until I went to see him last week. I was and still am investigating the death of Rafael Vega.'

'The suspicious suicide out at Santa Clara,' said Guzmán, picking up his notebook and pointing the pen at Falcón. 'Pablo Ortega's neighbour. Crisis in the Garden City – that's not a headline, by the way.'

'I came across a couple of names in an address book, one of whom was Eduardo Carvajal,' said Falcón.

'The paedophile ring leader who died in a car crash,' said Guzmán. 'I always remember things that stink. Is your inquiry going to crack open that cesspit as well?'

Falcón held up a hand, already nervous that he'd made some pact with the devil.

'I knew the name from a previous investigation so I went to see Montes and asked him about Carvajal. He was the investigating officer on the Carvajal paedophile ring.'

'Right. I get it. Very interesting,' said Guzmán, terrifying Falcón with the rapacity of his brain.

Falcón tried to slow his own brain down as he detailed his conversation with Montes about Carvajal procuring from the Russian mafia, the people-trafficking business and its influence on the sex industry. He told him about the two projects owned by Ivanov and Zelenov and managed by Vega Construcciones, and how he'd twice spoken to Montes about the Russians, once when Montes had been very drunk, to see if the names meant anything to him.

'I was due to talk to him this morning,' said Falcón, 'but I didn't make it in time.'

'Do you think he'd been corrupted?' asked Guzmán.

'I have no evidence for it, apart from his sense of timing and his suicide note, which, in my opinion, has some ugly subtext,' said Falcón, handing him the letter. 'For your eyes only.'

Guzmán read the letter, tilting his head from side to side as if his factual brain wasn't inclined to agree with Falcón's more creative interpretation. He gave it back.

'What was the other name in Vega's address book that caught your attention?' asked Guzmán.

'The late Ramón Salgado,' said Falcón. 'It could be completely innocent because Salgado had supplied a painting for Vega's office building. But after Salgado's murder last year we found some very distressing child pornography on his computer.'

'There are some big gaps to fill here,' said Guzmán. 'What are your theories?'

Falcón stayed him with his hand again. There were complications, he said, and gave him the secret life of Rafael Vega.

'We're hoping that he has a record with the FBI and that they might be able to help us identify him,' said Falcón.

'So you think he might have had a past that's caught up with him?' said Guzmán. 'Which would be a separate theory to some kind of link to the Carvajal paedophile ring?'

'The situation has been complicated with each new development in Vega's secret life,' said Falcón. 'My original theory came when those names jumped out at me from his address book. After I'd talked to Montes the first time, and then found a connection between Vega and the Russians, I began to think that Vega had possibly replaced Carvajal as the procurer for the paedophile rings. But the major problem with that theory is that I have no proof of Vega's interest in paedophilia, only his connection to people who were, and the extremely advantageous nature of the deals he was giving the Russians.'

'What made the Vega suicide look suspicious to you?' asked Guzmán.

'The method, the cleanliness of the crime scene and, although there was a note, it was not what I would call a suicide note. First of all, it was in English. Secondly, it was only a partial sentence. And later we found that he had traced over the indentations of his own handwriting, as if he was trying to find out what he himself had written.'

'What were the words?'

'". . . in the thin air you breathe from 9/11 until . . ."'

'9/11?' said Guzmán.

'We're assuming that he'd taken up the American way of writing the date.'

'When you were talking me through his secret life you mentioned the American connection, which made you think that he was probably of Central or South American origin. Well, you know, most people forget this since the events of last year in New York, but there were two 9/11s. Where do you think I come from, Inspector Jefe?'

'You've got a Madrid accent.'

'I've lived in Madrid nearly all my life,' he said, 'so most people forget that I'm actually Chilean. The first 9/11, the one that nobody now will ever remember, was 11th September 1973. That was the day that they bombed the Moneda Palace, killed Salvador Allende and General Augusto Pinochet took power.'

Falcón held on to the arms of his chair, looked into Guzmán's eyes and knew, as his organs seemed to realign out of their planetary chaos, that he was right.

'I was fifteen years old,' said Guzmán, whose face for a moment looked like that of a drowning man with his life flashing before him. 'It was also the last day that I saw my parents. I heard later that they were last seen in the football stadium, if you know what that means.'

Falcón nodded. He'd read about the horrors of the Santiago football stadium.

'A week later I'd been taken out of Santiago and was living in Madrid with my aunt. I only found out later what happened in the football stadium,' he said. 'So people say 9/11 to me and I never think of the twin towers and New York City, I think of the day a bunch of US-sponsored, CIA-backed terrorists murdered democracy in my own country.'

'Wait one moment,' said Falcón.

He went next door. Ramírez was hunched over the keyboard.

'Has Elvira come back with the FBI contact?'

'I'm just pasting Vega's photograph into the e-mail,' said Ramírez.

'You can now add that we believe him to have been a Chilean national.'

Falcón went back into his office and apologized to Guzmán, who was standing at the window, hands behind his back.

'I'm getting old, Inspector Jefe,' he said. 'Since I arrived in Seville my brain seems to have changed. I can't seem to remember anything of my day to day life. I see movies which I can't tell you anything about. I read books by writers I can't recall. And yet those days in Santiago before I left are pin-sharp in my mind. And they come at me like a film in the dark. I don't know why. Maybe it's because I'm at the end of my career and all that stuff. You know, it was the whole reason I became the kind of journalist I was.'

'And you still are,' said Falcón. 'Although I was surprised to see you here. I didn't think you did stories any more. I thought you were the editor.'

'When the news came through about Montes I could have sent anybody down here,' said Guzmán, 'but then I heard that you were going to run the inquiry and for no good reason I decided it was time to meet Javier Falcón.'

'Well, you've given me a break, so I'm glad.'

'It's a strange line that that – in Vega's note. It seems almost poetic. There's emotion in there. It's like a spirit threatening,' said Guzmán. 'Why do you think I'm so right about it?'

'Apart from the South American connection,' said Falcón, 'we've also heard about discussions Vega had with his American neighbour, Marty Krugman, and a few things he'd mentioned to Pablo Ortega. Between them they built a picture of a man with very right-wing views, anti-communist, pro-capitalism and largely pro-American in terms of the spirit of enterprise. But he also held some negative views about the way in which US governments interfered with other countries, how they were your friends until you were no longer useful to them . . . that kind of thing. I also found files in his study on international courts of justice and the work of Baltasar Garzón. Look at all that in the context of his secretive nature, the fact that he seems to have been a trained, connected Hispanic with a knowledge of American society, and this guy begins to look like a politically motivated, disappointed man who died with what he considered to be an important date in his hand.'

'And why do you think he did that?'

'Personally, I think it was because he was being murdered, that he wanted to make sure that his death was investigated as murder and that whatever secrets he held would be discovered and told to the world.'

'So now where is your theory about Carvajal, the Russians and Montes?'

'What do you mean?'

'You seem to think that Montes was responding to pressure that you were unconsciously applying. The mention of Carvajal and the Russians – Ivanov and Zelenov. Would that have been enough to push him over the edge? Or was he looking at those names in the context of the Vega investigation, and it was *that* which made him certain that you were on to something?'

'Let's wait until we get a response from the FBI. If he did have a criminal record, that might be indicative of something that's relevant here.'

'If he's Chilean he sounds like a disaffected pro-Pinochet man to me,' said Guzmán. 'And there were plenty of them about in the ranks of Patria y Libertad – the extreme right-wing organization who were bent on destabilizing Allende from the moment he won the election. A lot of their members did some very nasty things before, during and after the coup – the kidnappings and assassinations abroad within Operation Condor, the killings and torture at home, the Washington car bomb – and they thought they deserved better. They'd stopped the rampage of communism up to America's back door and they felt they should be properly rewarded for it. But you said he was keeping these files on the justice systems and Garzón. That sounds as if he was heading for the confessional.'

'I think he was looking for something a bit bigger than the confessional,' said Falcón. 'More like the witness stand in a major court. Something seems to have happened to him at the end of last year. Something personal, which might have changed him. He was suffering from anxiety attacks . . .'

'Well, maybe that clouded his judgement. People who were involved always think they're more important than they actually were,' said Guzmán. 'Colonel Manuel Contreras, the ex-chief of DINA – the secret police – is now in jail, beautifully betrayed by Pinochet, and what's happened? Documents were released by the Clinton administration in 1999, and what's happened? More material was released by the CIA themselves in 2000, and what's happened? Have we had any justice? Have the perpetrators been punished? No. Nothing has happened. It's the way of the world.'

'But what could have happened? Who's left? Who's accountable?'

'There are some CIA men who should still be sweating in the dark and there's my old friend, the Prince of Darkness – Dr K himself. He was Nixon's National Security Adviser and Secretary of State over that whole period. Nothing happened in Chile without him knowing about it. If anybody should be held to account, he should.'

'Well, if you could finger him, you'd go down in history,' said Falcón. 'And if Vega was about to do that there must be plenty of people who'd want to kill him?'

'In my experience, if the CIA had decided he was dangerous for their public relations profile, they'd want to make it look like suicide – and then make a complete mess of it,' said Guzmán. 'These American neighbours of his, what's their background?'

'He's an architect working for Vega, she's a photographer. It was her photographs of him that gave us an insight into his personal crisis. That's her speciality.'

'Well, that's pretty good cover if you wanted information on somebody,' said Guzmán.

'They've both got totally genuine backgrounds,' said Falcón. 'They were even suspects in a murder inquiry into the death of the woman's lover back in the USA. No charges were brought.'

'They don't smell so sweet, even if they are real enough,' said

Guzmán. 'But then that's the nature of perfect cover, I suppose. We all have something ugly hidden away.'

Falcón got to his feet and started pacing the room. The complications were building by the hour and he had no time, never any time.

'If this *is* some sort of intelligence operation,' he said, 'and the Krugmans have been pressurized into service, then there must be collusion between the CIA and the FBI. And we're now asking the FBI for information on Rafael Vega.'

'For a start, you can't do anything else,' said Guzmán. 'And anyway, these are not perfect organizations. I imagine very few people will know about this. They've got their hands full with the War on Terror. This is a side game, a small issue. Possibly private.'

Falcón went to the phone and started dialling.

'I'm going to talk to Marty Krugman again,' he said. 'I'll come at him from a different angle.'

'But you don't know anything yet.'

'I realize that, but I have no time. I have to start now.'

Falcón was saved by the fact that Krugman was not in his office or at home and his mobile was turned off. He slammed the phone down.

'Krugman has a weakness,' said Falcón. 'His wife is a beautiful woman who is much younger than him.'

'And he's a jealous man?'

'It's his weak point,' said Falcón, 'a way to lever him open.'

'All this will go up in smoke if you don't get a positive ID from the FBI,' said Guzmán. 'So don't do anything until then. In the meantime, if you think it will help, I'll put that line he was holding in his hand out into the Chilean expatriate communities here and in England, see what they make of it. And if you do get a positive ID and he was Chilean and military, or DINA, I am in contact with people who could help build a profile.

'I'll also write an article about Montes and the first suicide of a senior officer at the Jefatura. It will be a kind of obituary with the big moments of his career, including the Carvajal scandal, pointed up. I'll emphasize your in-depth investigation into Montes's career.'

'And what will we get out of that?'

'You'll see. It'll smoke people out. There'll be plenty of anxiety around, especially from the ones who turned a blind eye to Carvajal's "accident",' said Guzmán. 'It'll be interesting to see the pressure that comes down on you from upstairs. If Comisario Lobo doesn't call you into his office first thing in the morning after the *Diario de Sevilla* has hit the streets, I'll buy you lunch.'

'Only the facts,' said Falcón, a wave of anxiety ripping through him.

'That's the beauty of it. Everything I'll write about Montes will already be in the public domain. There won't be any need for conjecture. It's just the way in which I put it all together that will frighten people to death.'

23

Monday, 29th July 2002

It was past three o'clock. Falcón was hungry. Ramírez left for lunch, telling him that Ferrera was in interrogation room number 4 with Salvador Ortega, and that Elvira had called to say that he'd cleared Alicia Aguado with the prison director to give Sebastián Ortega a full psychological assessment.

'I called Juez Calderón, too,' he said. 'I thought we should remind him about the search warrant for the safe-deposit box. He's gone, nowhere to be seen, not expected back and he's done fuck all about the warrant. *Buen provecho.*'

On the way down to the interrogation rooms he called the prison director to arrange a liaison person and a time. His secretary told him they could begin straight away and that the best time was between 18.00 and 21.00 p.m.. He called Alicia Aguado, while looking through the door's glass panel at Salvador Ortega's shattered face. They agreed on 18.30 and he called the prison to confirm a 19.00 appointment. This was going to be a long day. Cristina Ferrera came out and told him that while the narcotics agent had been looking for Salvador she'd done some questioning around Nadia's apartment building. Nobody had seen a thing. Even the people who had seen her taken away now couldn't remember anything about it. He went to get three coffees from the machine.

Salvador Ortega smoked while looking at the backs of his yellow fingers. He made darting eye contact with Cristina Ferrera, who was sitting next to him and partially succeeding in engaging him. His hair was explosive and he had a wispy beard and moustache which disguised his good looks. His T-shirt was so faded that only the vaguest colours and the word 'Megadeath' were discernible. He wore long shorts and his lower legs were scabbed with sores.

He smoked intensely while they sipped their coffees.

'When was the last time you spoke to your father?' asked Falcón.

'I don't speak to my father,' he said. 'He doesn't speak to me.'

'Have you seen a newspaper recently?'

'News has no importance for me in my circumstances.'

'Did you have any relationship with your Uncle Pablo?'

'He was always very entertaining when I was a child,' said Salvador. 'Which was a relief.'

'A relief from what?'

Salvador smoked hard and exhaled to the ceiling.

'Uncle Pablo was fun,' he said. 'I only spent any time with him as a child.'

'You were still at home when he brought Sebastián round to stay while he went on theatre tours and film shoots. How old were you at the time?'

Salvador's mouth operated but no words came out. He seemed to be biting off air in small chunks. Ferrera patted him on the shoulder.

'This is not a test, Salvador,' she said. 'I told you on the way here that there will be no repercussions. You are not a suspect. We just want to talk to you to see if we can help your cousin.'

'I was sixteen,' he said. 'And nobody can help my cousin.'

'Did you follow what happened to Sebastián?'

Salvador's cigarette hand trembled. He nodded and breathed down whatever was rising in him.

'You're a heroin user?' said Falcón, to move on to more certain ground.

'Yes, I am.'

'For how long?'

'Since I was fifteen.'

'And before that?'

'I smoked hashish from about the age of ten until . . . it didn't work any more. Then I moved on to the stuff that does work.'

'How does it work?'

'It takes me away from myself . . . to a place where my mind and body feel at home.'

'And where's that?'

He blinked and flashed a look at Falcón, unprepared for these sorts of questions.

'Where I feel free,' he said, 'which is nowhere.'

'You were already using heroin when Sebastián first came to stay with you?'

'Yes, I remember it was . . . all right.'

'What do you remember of Sebastián?'

'He was a sweet kid.'

'Is that all?' said Falcón. 'Didn't you talk to him or play with him? I mean, his mother had left him and his father had gone away. He must have thought of you as an elder brother.'

'It takes time to get the money together if you're a sixteen-year-old heroin user,' said Salvador. 'I was too busy stealing handbags from tourists and running from the police.'

'Why did you start smoking hashish so young?'

'Everybody smoked it. You could buy it in the bars with a Coca Cola in those days.'

'Ten years old is still very young.'

'I was probably unhappy,' he said, smiling with no conviction.

'Was that because of problems at home?'

'My father was very strict,' said Salvador. 'He beat us.'

'Who do you mean by "us"? You and your sister?'

'Not my sister . . . He wasn't interested in her.'

'He wasn't *interested* in her?' said Falcón.

Salvador crushed out the cigarette and jammed his hands between his thighs.

'Look,' he said, 'I don't like . . . to be hassled.'

'I just want to be clear about what you're saying, that's all,' said Falcón.

'*She* could do what she liked, is what I meant.'

'So who is "us", when you say he beat *us*?'

'My friends,' said Salvador, shrugging with a jerk. 'That's how it was in those days.'

'What did your friends' parents say about their children being beaten by your father?'

'He always said he wouldn't tell how naughty they'd been, so they didn't talk to their parents.'

Falcón glanced at Ferrera, who shrugged her eyebrows and looked at Salvador. Sweat stood out on his forehead, even in the high air conditioning.

'When did you have your last fix?' asked Falcón.

'I'm OK,' he said.

'I have some distressing news for you,' said Falcón.

'I'm already distressed,' said Salvador. 'You can't distress me any further.'

'Your Uncle Pablo died on Saturday morning. He took his own life.'

Cristina Ferrera lit a cigarette and offered it to him. Salvador hunched over and rested his forehead on the edge of the table. His back shook. After a minute he sat back. Tears streamed silently down his face. He wiped them away. Ferrera gave him the cigarette. He puffed on it, took the smoke down.

'I'm going to ask you again: did you have a good relationship with your Uncle Pablo?'

This time Salvador nodded.

'How often did you see him?'

'A few times a month. We had a deal. He would give me money for heroin if I controlled my habit. He didn't want me to steal and end up in jail again.'

'How long had that being going on?'

'The last three years since I got out and before they put me away.'

'You were done for dealing, weren't you?'

'I was, but I wasn't dealing. I was just caught with too much on me. That was why I only got four years.'

'Was Pablo disappointed in you?'

'The only time he got angry with me was when I stole something from his collection,' said Salvador. 'It was a just a drawing, some smudges on paper. I sold it for twenty thousand pesetas' worth of gear. Pablo said it was worth three hundred thousand.'

'He wasn't angry?'

'He was furious. But, you know, he never hit me, and by my father's standards he was well within his rights to flay me alive.'

'And after that you did the deal?'

'Once he'd calmed down and got the drawing back.'

'How much did you see of Sebastián in that time?'

'A fair amount when Sebastián started at the Bellas Artes. Then I didn't see him for a bit until I heard Pablo had bought him a small apartment on Jesus del Gran Poder. I used to go there to get off the street to shoot up. When Pablo found out, he built another clause into our deal. I had to promise not to see Sebastián until I was clean. Pablo said he was in a fragile state and he didn't want to add drugs to the problem.'

'Did you keep to that?'

'Sebastián was never interested in drugs. He had other strategies for blocking out the world.'

'Like what?'

'He called it "a retreat into beauty and innocence". He had a room in his apartment which he'd soundproofed and blocked out the light. I used to shoot up in there. He painted luminous points on the ceiling. It was like being wrapped in a velvet night. He used to lie in there and listen to his music and the tapes he'd made of himself reading poetry.'

'When did he make this room?'

'As soon as Pablo bought the apartment . . . five or six years ago.'

'Why did he buy him the apartment?'

'They were finding it difficult to live together. They used to fight . . . verbally. Then they stopped talking to each other.'

'Did Pablo ever beat Sebastián?'

'Not that I saw or heard about.'

'What about your father?'

Silence.

'I mean when he was living with your family,' said Falcón.

Salvador seemed to be having trouble with his breathing. He began to hyperventilate. Ferrera got behind him and calmed him down with her hands on his shoulders.

'Would you like to help Sebastián?' asked Falcón.

Salvador nodded.

'There's nothing to be ashamed of in here,' said Falcón. 'Anything you say will only be used to help Sebastián.'

'But there *is* something to be ashamed of in *here* –' he said, suddenly livid, thumping himself in the chest.

'We're not here to judge you. This isn't a trial of morality,' said Ferrera. 'Things happen to us when we're young and we have no way of –'

'What happened to *you?*' said Salvador viciously, pulling himself away from her touch. 'What the fuck has ever happened to you? You're a fucking policewoman. *Nothing* has happened to you. You don't know anything that happens out there. You come from the safe world. I can smell it on you – your soap. You leave the safe world and just ruffle the surface of things where we live, catching people doing their little wrongs. You have no idea what it's like on the other side.'

She moved back from him. Falcón thought she was shocked at first, but she was just asserting her presence. She was telling Salvador something with her silence and he couldn't look at her. The atmosphere in the interrogation room was more dramatic than if she'd stripped naked.

'You think because of the way I look and the job I do that nothing has ever happened to me?'

'Go on then,' said Salvador, goading her, 'tell me what's happened to you, little policewoman.'

Silence, as Ferrera weighed things in her mind.

'I don't have to tell you this,' she said, 'and it's not something I particularly want my superior officer to know about me. But I am going to tell you because you need to know that shameful things happen to others, even little policewomen, and they can be talked about and people will not judge. Are you listening to me, Salvador?'

They made eye contact and he nodded.

'Before I became a policewoman I was training to be a nun. The Inspector Jefe knows that much about me. He also knows I met a man and that I became pregnant. It meant that I stopped my training and got married. But there's something else he doesn't know, which I am very ashamed of and it will cost me a lot to say it in front of him.'

Salvador didn't respond. The silence was ringing in the room. Ferrera breathed in. Falcón wasn't sure he wanted to hear this, but it was too late. She was determined.

'I come from Cádiz. It's a port town with some rough people. I was staying with my mother, who did not know that I'd met this man. I'd reached the point where I was going to have to tell the nuns what had happened in my life, and I decided I would go and see the man I loved and talk to him first. I was still a virgin because I believed in the sanctity of marriage and that I should come whole to it. On the way to my lover's apartment that night I was attacked by two men who raped me. It was very quick. I didn't resist. I was pathetically small and weak in their hands. In a matter of ten minutes they did what they wanted with me and left me totally defiled. I staggered back to my mother's apartment. She was already asleep. I showered and got into bed shaking and shattered. I woke up hoping it had been a bad dream, but I was aching all over and full of shame. A week later, when the bruising had died down I went to bed with my lover. The day after that I told the nuns I was leaving. I am still not completely sure who is the father of my first child.'

She eased her leg back until she felt the seat of the chair and dropped down into it so that it rocked. She seemed exhausted. Salvador's eyes fell away from hers to the cigarette in his hand, which trembled.

'The reason I don't see my father any more is that I hate him,' he said. 'I hate him with a hate so massive that if I saw him I'd commit an act of serious violence. I hate him because he is a betrayer of trust, and not just any trust. He is the betrayer of the greatest trust available to human beings – the trust between parent and child. He beat me to keep me scared. To stop me from even thinking about telling anyone what he was doing to me. He beat me because he knew the legend of his beatings would be passed around the neighbourhood and all the kids would be scared of him, too. And when they came to the house he was so sweet to them they let him do whatever he wanted, but they never dared talk. Those men ruined you. My own father ruined me until I was twelve years old. Then it stopped. I thought I could deal with it. I thought I could smoke it away. Smoke away my childhood and get clear of him and start my own life. It might have been possible. But then Uncle Pablo brought Sebastián to the house. And that is my shame. That is why I am like this. Because I said nothing while my father did to Sebastián what he'd done to me. I should . . . I should have protected him. I should, as you say, have been his elder brother. But I wasn't. I was a coward. And I saw him ruined.'

After some minutes real life creaked back into the room. One of the lights buzzed. The tape machine tickered.

'When did you last see your Uncle Pablo?' asked Falcón.

'I saw him on Friday morning, just for half an hour. He gave me some money. We talked. He asked me whether I knew why Sebastián had done the things that he'd done. I knew what he was getting at, what he wanted from me. But I couldn't tell him what I've just told you. I couldn't admit how I'd failed to Sebastián's father, my uncle, who had helped me so much. I think he'd already worked it out or he'd known it all along and hadn't been able to believe it of his own brother. He was looking to me for the final corroboration of the facts. I should have been able to tell him, but I didn't. At the end of our talk he hugged me and kissed my head. He hadn't done that since I was a small boy. I cried into his shirt. We walked to the door of the apartment and he patted the side of my face with one of his massive hands and he said: "Don't judge your father too harshly. He had a hard life. He took all the beatings for us when we were children. All of them. He was a tough little bastard. He took it all in silence."'

'Do you know why Sebastián did what he did?' asked Falcón.

'I hadn't seen him for some time before that. The agreement, remember? I didn't want to break that part of it. Once you've found trust, you try not to blow it.'

'Were you surprised by Sebastián's crime?'

'I couldn't believe it. I couldn't think what could possibly have happened in his mind in the years I hadn't seen him. It went against everything I knew about him.'

'Two more questions,' said Falcón, turning the tape machine off, 'and then that's it. I've asked a clinical psychologist to talk to Sebastián to see if we can unblock his mind. It would help if I could play this tape of what you've just told me. She'll be the only one to hear it and she might want to talk to you or get you to help Sebastián in some way.'

'No problem,' he said.

'The next question is more difficult,' said Falcón. 'Your father has done some very bad things . . .'

'No,' said Salvador, his face hardening to wood, 'you can't make me do that.'

On the way back to the Polígono San Pablo Falcón sat in the back with Salvador and worked out a way to contact him in case Alicia needed his help. He also mentioned that Pablo had left him something in his will and told him to get in touch with Ranz Costa.

They dropped him on the outskirts of the barrio. Ferrera kissed him on both cheeks. Falcón sat up front. They watched Salvador's jittery walk, an undone shoelace from his busted trainers lashing his thin scabby calves.

'You didn't have to do that,' said Falcón, as Ferrera turned the car round.

'Kiss him?' she said. 'That was the least he deserved.'

'I meant you didn't have to tell your story to make him tell his,' he said. 'Becoming a nun, answering that vocation is, I imagine, a process – revealing and cleansing yourself before God. Police work is a vocation, too, but there's no God that you have to reveal yourself to.'

'Inspector jefes are quite high up,' she said, smiling. 'And, anyway, it was a practice run for the real thing. I still have to tell my husband.'

24

❦❦❦

Falcón woke up from his siesta and slapped the alarm dead. He lay in the darkened room arms flung out, panting as if he'd surfaced, lungs bursting, from a deep lake. Something had hardened in his mind. What before had been a vague dislike of Ignacio Ortega had taken shape and become a determined mass that was going to put the child molester away for as long as possible. He was enjoying the anger just as Ferrera had when she'd first become a policewoman, roaming the streets of Cádiz, hoping to find those two brutes who'd raped her.

He showered, thinking about Ignacio Ortega. There was cunning in him. All those easy lies he'd told in their first meeting. The learned presentation of half-truths. He wondered if this had all started from envy – 'I was just an electrician and he was a famous actor.' Two men coming from the same brutal childhood, one becomes a famous actor who escapes into roles, while the other, anonymous and filled with hate, desecrates the innocence of children. Was there some strange balancing out going on in Ignacio's head?

As he dressed he remembered the point that had occurred to him whilst talking to Ramírez about the names in Vega's address book. There had been only one Ortega in it and no initial. He drove to the Jefatura, brought the address book up from the evidence room. He was right, no initial and the number, which was for a mobile, belonged to Ignacio. Another thought. He called Carlos Vázquez.

'Who does Vega Construcciones use to install the air-conditioning systems in their buildings?'

'It's put out to tender,' said Vázquez. 'There are four or five companies who compete with each other for the business.'

'Does any one company win more tenders than the others?'

'I'd say that seventy per cent of the work is done by AAC, Aire Acondicionado Central de Sevilla. It's run by a man called Ignacio Ortega, who only ever overprices himself if he can't do the work.'

He called Vega Construcciones and asked for Marty Krugman; still not there. Krugman answered his mobile. He seemed to be in heavy traffic from the noise. The signal was bad.

'I'm not supposed to be talking to you, Inspector Jefe, remember?' he said cheerfully. 'I haven't spoken to our cold, eastern friends yet.'

'Just one question about the Russian projects: who did you get to tender for the air-conditioning systems?'

'I didn't,' said Krugman. 'Rafael told me to use a company called AAC.'

'You didn't get a competitive quote?'

'He said the client had already authorized it.'

'How do you understand that?'

'It normally means that AAC is owed a favour, probably because they've done another job very cheaply for them.'

'Do you know Ignacio Ortega of AAC?'

'Sure, I've met him. He does a lot of work for the company. He's hard-nosed,' said Krugman. 'Is he related to Pablo?'

'They're brothers.'

'They don't look it.'

'What can you tell me about Ignacio and Sr Vega – their relationship?'

'Nothing.'

'Were they close?'

'I told you, Inspector Jefe . . .' said Krugman, and Falcón missed the end of the sentence as the signal started to break up.

'Can we talk face to face about this?' asked Falcón, thinking now more about what Guzmán had been saying.

'It won't make any difference,' said Krugman. 'And anyway, I'm busy now.'

'Where are you? I'll come to you. We'll have a beer before dinner.'

'Now you love me, Inspector Jefe. What have I done?'

'I just want to talk,' said Falcón, shouting through the fracturing signal.

'I told you the Russians haven't contacted me yet.'

'This isn't about the Russians.'

'What *is* it about then?'

'I can't say . . . I mean, it's more about the Americans.'

'I'm getting nostalgic for those Cold War days,' said Krugman. 'You know, it's an interesting thing . . . the Russians are a much more effective force as the Mob than they ever were as communists.'

The signal collapsed. Falcón redialled. Not available. Ramírez put his head in the office. Falcón briefed him on Salvador and Ignacio Ortega while he sat listening with his face all pushed up by his hand, mouth open, intelligent-looking. Before he could ask any questions Falcón briefed him about the conversation with Guzmán, which left him with his eyelids at half mast.

'Joder,' he said, after some time, the Sevillano not particularly impressed by the developments. 'Have you talked to Krugman about this?'

'I've just lost the signal to his mobile, and anyway I need to sit in front of him if I'm going to talk to him about extra-curricular activity for the CIA.'

'I don't believe it,' said Ramírez. 'I think Virgilio Guzmán lives in a fantasy world of conspiracy theories. We're in Seville here, not Bilbao. He's had his head turned by all that spying on ETA and the Guardia Civil.'

'Come on, José Luis, he's a respected professional.'

'So was Alberto Montes,' said Ramírez. 'What do you think Guzmán's doing down here?'

'Something with less pressure than when he was in Madrid,' said Falcón.

'In my opinion,' said Ramírez, winding his finger around his temple, 'the guy's lost it.'

'Is this based on any empirical research, or just your gut feeling?' asked Falcón. 'What about Guzmán's theory on the piece of paper in Vega's hand? Is that bullshit as well?'

'No, that sounds right. I like that. It doesn't help us, but I like it,' said Ramírez.

'It does help us; it narrows the search down for the FBI,' said Falcón. 'Have you heard from them yet?'

Ramírez shook his head.

'I want to find Krugman,' said Falcón.

'You're beginning to think that *he* killed Vega.'

'I have an open mind. He had the opportunity, given that Vega would have let him into his house at that time in the morning. And now we've got a possible motive, even if you do think it's Guzmán's fantasy,' said Falcón. 'I'm also worried about Krugman. When I went to see him after we'd been to talk to Dourado, he seemed unstable. He was looking out of the window using a pair of binoculars.'

'Probably trying to see if his wife is fucking Juez Calderón, which is why we're not getting our search warrant.'

'So you *do* think that Vega was "operating" in some way,' said Falcón. 'And you *do* think that what he has in his safe-deposit box is going to be important for us. You just don't think that Krugman –'

'Well, *I* wouldn't use Krugman for fucking anything, let alone an "operation",' said Ramírez. 'He's too unpredictable. There's too much going on in his brain. But if you let me have his mobile number I'll get the boys in the telephone centre to keep trying it, and if he answers we'll track it.'

'Is anything happening with the Montes inquiry?'

'We're still waiting for Elvira to give us another pair of hands.'

'Did the lawyer come back on the property he added to the list of assets in Montes's will?'

'Yes, I'm getting the Aracena town hall to check out if there was a building project on the property.'

'It's up in the sierra, is it?'

The phone rang. Ramírez picked it up, listened, said that Falcón was on his way and put it down.

'Alicia Aguado,' he said.

'I'd like you to check where exactly Ignacio Ortega was on the night that Rafael Vega was murdered.'

'I thought he was at the beach.'

'He didn't come into the frame until his brother died. I contacted him via his mobile. We've never checked him out properly.'

He drove to Calle Vidrio and sat at traffic lights with his hands pattering nervously on the steering wheel. A sense of doom stacked up inside him, while outside the relentless heat bore down on the straining city.

He played the tape of Salvador Ortega's interview to Alicia Aguado as they drove out to the prison. It took the whole journey. They sat in the car park listening to the end and some silence until the tape clicked off.

'I asked him if he'd testify against his father,' said Falcón. 'He refused.'

'People like Ignacio Ortega retain tremendous power over their victims, and the victims never lose their fear of the molester,' said Aguado as they got out of the car.

They walked up to the prison. She held his arm.

'I spoke to a friend of mine who works at the prison,' she said. 'He assesses disturbed prisoners, but he wasn't on Sebastian's case when he applied for solitary confinement, although he did hear about it. There was no sign of any disturbing behaviour. Sebastián was intelligent, friendly and completely benign – which I realize doesn't necessarily mean anything. But he did say something interesting. They all thought that Sebastián was not only happy to be where he was, he was also relieved.'

'To be away from the other inmates?'

'He couldn't say. He just said he was relieved,' she said. 'And, by the way, I'd like to talk to Sebastián alone. But if there's a room where you could observe from the outside, I'd be interested in you seeing the session.'

The director met them and arranged for the interview to be held in one of the 'safe' cells, where prisoners who were considered a possible danger to themselves were put for observation. There was CCTV and audio tape available. Two chairs were brought into the cell and placed side by side in opposite directions, to resemble the S-shaped chair in Alicia Aguado's consulting room. She sat facing the door. Sebastián was brought in and sat facing the wall. The door was shut, but it had a large reinforced observation panel. Falcón sat outside.

Alicia Aguado started off by explaining her method. Sebastián looked into the side of her face, valuing her words with the intensity of a lover. He bared his wrist to her and she laid her fingers on his pulse. He stroked her two fingernails with the tip of his finger.

'I'm glad you came back,' he said, 'but I'm not sure what you're doing here.'

'It's not unusual for prisoners who've suffered distressing news to be given a psychological assessment.'

'I didn't think I'd given them any cause to be concerned. I *was* upset, that's true. But now I'm calm.'

'It was a very strong reaction and you are a prisoner in solitary confinement. The authorities are concerned about the effects of distress, reactions to it and the possible reverberations in the prisoner's mind.'

'How did you go blind?' he asked. 'I don't think you've always been blind, have you?'

'No. I have a condition called retinitis pigmentosa.'

'I knew a girl at the Bellas Artes who had that,' he said. 'She was painting, painting, painting like mad . . . to get all the colours down before she went blind, because afterwards she'd have to stick to monochrome. I like that idea, cramming all the colour into the early years, before simplifying it in later life.'

'You're still interested in art?'

'Not to do it. I like to look at it.'

'I heard you were very good.'

'Who from?'

'Your uncle,' she said, and frowned, adjusted her fingers on his wrist.

'My uncle knows nothing about art. He has zero aesthetic sense. If he thought my work had been good, I would be worried. He's the sort of person who has concrete lions mounted on his gate posts. He hangs lurid tinted landscapes on his walls. He likes to spend his money on very expensive sound systems, but he has no taste in music. He thinks that Julio Iglesias should be sanctified and that Placido Domingo should learn some decent songs. He has an ear so finely tuned that it can perceive the slightest defect in his hifi speaker's output, but he can't hear a single note,' said Sebastián, who hadn't stopped looking at Alicia Aguado for a moment. 'I'd like to know your first name, Dra Aguado.'

'Alicia,' she said.

'What's it like being in the dark *all* the time, Alicia?' he said. 'I like being in the dark. I had a room where I could shut out all light and noise, and I used to lie on the bed with a sleeping mask on. It was velvet on the inside. It sat over my eyes, soft and warm as a cat. But what's it like having no choice, being in the dark but with no escape into the light? I think I should like it.'

'Why?' asked Alicia. 'It makes life very difficult.'

'No, no, Alicia, I disagree. It simplifies things. We are bombarded by too many images and ideas and words and thoughts and tastes and textures. Take away one of the major senses and think how much time that frees up. You can concentrate on sound. Touch will be so exciting because your fingers will never be bored by what the mind is telling them to expect. Taste will be an adventure. The only give-away is smell, the delicious smell of your food. I envy you, because you will rediscover life in all its richness.'

'How can you envy me that,' she said, 'after what you have done to yourself?'

'What have I done to myself?'

'You've closed yourself off from the world. You've decided that you want nothing of life in all its richness.'

'Are they really concerned for me after my father's death?' he asked.

'*I'm* worried about you.'

'Yes, you are. I can tell,' he said. 'And that's the thing, if I was blind I would know your beauty, and the ability to see you would only interfere with the purity of that.'

'You were very upset by your father's death and yet you ignored the letter he'd written to you.'

'It's not that unusual to hold two conflicting emotions in your mind at the same time. I loved him and I hated him.'

'Why did you love him?'

'Because he needed it. He had plenty of adoration, but almost no love. He was addicted to the adoration, which he mistook for love. When there was no adoration he felt unloved. So I loved him because he needed to be loved.'

'And why did you hate him?'

'Because he couldn't love me back. He hugged and kissed me, and then put me to one side, like a doll, to go and find what he thought was the real love. He did it because it was less complicated. That's why he had the dogs, Pavarotti and Callas: he liked that uncomplicated giving and receiving of love.'

'We talked to your cousin, Salvador.'

'Salvador,' he said. 'The saviour who cannot be saved.'

'Or the saviour who was unable to save?'

'I don't know what you mean by that.'

'Do you ever think about your mother?'

'Every day.'

'And what do you think about her?'

'I think about how she was misunderstood.'

'But you don't think of maternal love?'

'I do think of that, yes, but in remembering it I always find that the next thought was how she was misunderstood. It sticks in a son's mind to hear his mother referred to as a whore. She wasn't a whore. She loved my father and admired him. He never reciprocated. He went off to claim his fame in Spain and around the world. And she found other people to love.'

'You didn't think that she'd abandoned you?'

'Yes, I did. I was only eight years old. But I found out later that she couldn't stay with my father and she couldn't take me with her because *he* would not consent to it. Her life was on the move. Her boyfriend was a film director. I didn't hear *that* from my family. From them I heard she was a whore.'

'How did you fit in with your new family after she'd gone?'

'My new family?'

'Your uncle and aunt. You spent a lot of time with them.'

'I spent more time with my father than I did with them.'

'But what was it like living with them?'

Falcón's mobile vibrated on his thigh. He went up the corridor to take the call from Ramírez.

'The FBI have come back with a perfect match on Vega,' he said. 'Size, age, eye colour, blood group all fit and he's a Chilean national. They sent a picture back of him with more hair and a full beard. The shot was taken in 1980 when he was thirty-six years old. He's ex-Chilean military, ex-DINA and he was last seen in September 1982 when he absconded from a witness protection programme.'

'Why was he being protected?'

'It says that he testified in a drug-trafficking case, that's all.'

'Do they give a name?'

'His original name, that is prior to the witness protection programme, was Miguel Velasco.'

'Send those details to Virgilio Guzmán at the *Diario de Sevilla*. He said he'd got contacts who can give a profile on any Chilean military or DINA personnel,' said Falcón. 'Any news on Krugman?'

'Nothing yet,' said Ramírez. 'Expect a call from Elvira, he's looking for you.'

Falcón didn't make it back to the session before Elvira called. He told him that after a discussion with Comisario Lobo they had decided that nobody from within the Jefatura was going to be used to monitor Sra Montes's movements. An agent from Internal Affairs was being sent down from Madrid and he would report directly to Elvira on the matter. Falcón was relieved.

Alicia Aguado hadn't managed to draw the interview back to Ignacio since he'd taken Ramírez's call. They were talking about Sebastián's mother's death and its effect on him, and the lack of effect on his father. It had resulted in him leaving home and moving into an apartment his father had bought nearby.

'Were you still seeing your uncle at that stage?' asked Aguado. 'Wasn't he someone . . ?'

'I would never have spoken to *him* about my mother. He was *not* sympathetic to her. He would have derived satisfaction from hearing of her death.'

'You don't think very much of your uncle.'

'We have different sensibilities.'

'What was your uncle like as a father?'

'Ask Salvador.'

'He was a surrogate father to you.'

'I was scared of him. He believed in discipline and total obedience from any child that came into his orbit. He could get angry like you would not believe. The veins stood out on the side of his neck. He had a lump that would come up on his forehead. That's when we knew to hide.'

'Did you talk to your father about your uncle's violent behaviour?'

'Yes. He said he'd had a hard childhood and that it had marked him.'

'Was your uncle ever violent with you?'

'No.'

Alicia Aguado finished the session at that point. Sebastián was reluctant to let her go. Falcón called the guard and picked up the audio tape of the session. They went back to the car in silence. She said she would sleep on the way back. She didn't wake up until they arrived at Calle Vidrio. They went upstairs. She was groggy.

'He tired you out,' said Falcón.

'Sometimes it's like that. The psychologist feels under more pressure than the patient.'

'You seemed perplexed by his pulse at the beginning.'

'To start with he didn't react when I was certain he should have been hitting emotional blips. He seemed to be able to divorce the mental from the physical. I thought he was drugged at first. It'll get better. I'm sure I can open him up. He likes me enough to want to do it.'

He gave her the tape and went back down to the car. As he was about to move off, Inés called him. She was jittery.

'I know I shouldn't be calling you about this,' she said, 'but I know you saw Esteban today.'

'We had a meeting on the Rafael Vega case this morning.'

'Did he seem all right to you?' she asked. 'It's none of my business, I know, but . . .'

'He looked tired and seemed distracted.'

'Did you talk about anything else apart from the case?'

'I was with Inspector Ramírez,' said Falcón. 'Is something wrong?'

'I haven't seen him since early Saturday morning. He hasn't been back to the apartment. He's turned his mobile off.'

'I know Juez Romero spoke to him on Saturday morning from the crime scene at Pablo Ortega's house,' said Falcón.

'What did he say?' she said urgently. 'Where was he?'

'I don't know.'

'We were supposed to be having Sunday lunch with my parents, but he cancelled. Too much work.'

'You know how it is if he's got a busy Monday morning,' said Falcón.

'His secretary says he hasn't been back to his office since lunchtime.'

'That's not so strange.'

'It is for him.'

'I don't know what I can say, Inés. I'm sure he's OK.'

'It's probably nothing,' she said. 'You're right.'

She hung up. He drove back to Calle Bailén and showered and changed. Consuelo asked him over for supper. He left in the dark, listening to the news. The winds had dropped in the Sierra de Aracena and the fire around Almonaster la Real had been brought under control. Three thousand hectares had been burnt and four isolated homes destroyed. Arson was suspected. A shepherd had been arrested. There was to be a full inquiry starting tomorrow.

He parked outside Consuelo's house. The Krugmans' house was in darkness. On the way to the front door his mobile rang. Ramírez.

'I don't know if this is relevant, but I've just had a call from the Jefatura. They know we're looking for Sr Krugman. A woman has called in from an apartment building in Tabladilla. As she came into her building she noticed a tall foreigner in the foyer. He was sweating and nervous and looking at his watch. He followed her upstairs and stopped on the second floor while she continued to the top floor. He was standing outside an apartment, which she knew was empty because the woman was away on holiday. Twenty minutes later she heard a gun shot from the apartment below hers, which was the same one the foreigner was looking at. They've sent a patrol car round there.'

'Do we know the name of the owner of the apartment where the shot came from?'

'Wait a second . . .'

Falcón sweated standing in the street.

'I think this *is* relevant,' said Ramírez. 'The apartment belongs to one Rosario Calderón.'

25

Monday, 29th July 2002

Falcón explained the problem to Consuelo. She listened to him as if he was diagnosing a disease – comprehending without taking it in. He asked if she'd heard from her sister and the children. She said a police officer had turned up to look after them late morning. He kissed her and got back in the car. She closed her front door before he pulled away.

The Jefatura informed him that three more cars had been sent to the incident, which was in an apartment block on Calle Tabladilla at the intersection with Calle del Cardenal Ilundain. 'I don't want any cars parked in view of the incident, and no crowds,' said Falcón. 'All exits should be manned, including the underground garage, if there is one. No member of the public should be allowed into the building. Put two men on the roof and two in the stairwell above and below the incident. Evacuate everybody in the apartments above, below and opposite. All the occupants of the other apartments should be told to stay put. And get someone with binoculars into an apartment in the block opposite with a clear view of the incident.'

They confirmed his orders back to him and told him that the apartment did belong to Juez Calderón's sister and that she was currently away on holiday in Ibiza.

The advertising on Avenida de Kansas City flashed past as he headed back into the city. He had to get right across to the other side of town, but there was little traffic and in twenty minutes he'd been allowed through a police cordon and was parked on Calle Tabladilla, opposite a government building about fifty metres down from the incident. The street was empty apart from patrolmen sticking close to the shops underneath the long stretch of the development. One of the men told him that it was all quiet. He radioed through to his partner in the apartment block opposite looking for a view point. He was in apartment 403 overlooking Calle Tabladilla.

It was an oppressive night and the sweat gathered in Falcón's hair as he crossed the street to the grey, stone-clad apartment block with its chrome balconies. It was the kind of place where a young, well-off professional would buy. He took the lift up to the fourth floor and was let in by a young guy in a pair of shorts who had no interest in what was going on. A movie was showing on the television. He sat on the sofa with his girlfriend, drinking beer.

The patrolman was out on the balcony, his binoculars trained across the street. He handed them to Falcón. There was a lot of greenery overhanging the balconies of the apartments opposite, most of which were shuttered. The incident was easy enough to find. It was in the only apartment with any lighting. There were no internal blinds or curtains drawn. There was about 1.50 metres of wall between a large window and the sliding doors out on to the balcony. Calderón and Maddy Krugman were sitting side by side on the sofa. The judge held himself rigid, feet and knees together, arms folded tightly across his chest. Maddy Krugman was almost lying down on the sofa in an absurdly relaxed fashion. They were both dressed as if they were about to go out to dinner. Judging by the direction they were looking, Marty Krugman was standing in front of them with his back to the wall separating the window from the balcony. He came into view for a second. He had no jacket, there was a dark strip of sweat down the back of his creased shirt and he had a gun in his left hand.

The movie on the television finished and was replaced by ads. The young guy came to the doors out on to the balcony.

'What's going on over there?'

'Just a domestic situation that's got out of control,' said Falcón.

'We heard the gunshot – I thought it was on the movie.'

'What time?'

'Just after ten.'

It was now 10.40 p.m. Falcón surveyed the interior walls of the apartment. He found the bullet hole in the wall above Maddy Krugman's head. She obviously hadn't taken her husband seriously enough and had been reminded that this was neither a game nor a replica gun. He called Comisario Elvira and gave his report.

'What's Krugman's mental state been like in the interviews you've conducted?'

'He's an intellectual with an obsessive streak, prone to ranting but controllable. He listens. He's normally civilized and sophisticated, but he's become more disturbed over the past few days, probably as a result of his wife's liaison with Juez Calderón. If he's psychotic it's uncontrollable jealousy that's tipped him over the edge,' said Falcón. 'We've been getting on fine. There's mutual respect. I'd like to go in there and try to talk him down.'

'All right. Call him on the fixed line first. Tell him you're going to knock on the door. No surprises. García, from the Antiterrorism squad, is coming down there and he's bringing a marksman with him. Wait until they arrive.'

'Krugman's not a terrorist.'

'I know that now, but I didn't know that then. I alerted García when the information was imperfect. Anyway, he's got experience in these situations.'

García made contact a few minutes later. Falcón sent the patrolman to bring him up. He came out on to the balcony with the marksman, who seemed satisfied with the angle and went back inside to assemble his gun.

'You're going in?' asked García.

'I know the gunman.'

'There'll be three of you and him on his own. He'll have to keep an eye on you, which will give me possibilities out here.'

'I think I can talk this man down. He's not crazy or on drugs.'

'That's good, but if he does lose control there's not much opportunity for a marksman from out here without endangering the lives of the hostages.'

'What are you saying?'

'It would be better to storm the apartment.'

'I don't think it'll come to that.'

They worked out some emergency signals for Falcón and he made the call to the apartment. Maddy answered the phone before Marty could exert his control over the development. Falcón asked to speak to her husband.

'It's for you,' she said ironically, and held out the phone to Marty.

'I still haven't spoken to the Russians,' said Krugman, chuckling. 'I'm busy.'

'I'm outside, Marty,' said Falcón, leaving the apartment and heading downstairs.

'I thought the shot might attract some attention,' he said. 'This was supposed to be a private thing, but Maddy can be headstrong and I just had to show her I wasn't playing games. Anyway, what can I do for you, Inspector Jefe?'

Falcón crossed the street and started going up the stairs to Calderón's sister's apartment.

'I want to come in and speak to you. I'm right outside the apartment door. Will you let me in?'

'I suppose you've got some kind of SWAT team out there with you?'

'No, it's just me.'

'The street is very quiet.'

'It's been cleared for everyone's safety, that's all,' said Falcón. 'We don't want anybody getting hurt, Marty.'

'People have already been hurt,' he said.

'I realize that –'

'No, I mean really hurt. . . physically,' said Marty. 'This isn't what you think it is.'

'Then what is it?'

'It's private. We're beyond any mediation.'

'I'm not here to mediate.'

'Then you must have come to bear witness to the destruction of people's lives.'

'No, I certainly haven't come for that,' said Falcón. 'I've just come to hear you out.'

'I told Maddy they don't make cops like you back home,' said Marty. 'They like people with square heads that fit neatly into vices. It's easier to narrow their minds that way. They don't see colour or any gradations, just black and white.'

'We only come into people's lives at the crisis points,' said Falcón. 'Sometimes we have to simplify, cut out the grey. I try not to do it, that's all. I'm going to ring the doorbell now and I'd like you to let me in.'

'OK, Inspector Jefe, you can come in. I need a fair man to listen to me. But you have to know something first,' he said. 'By coming in you only endanger yourself. You will not affect the outcome. That is already written. Fate dictated it some time ago.'

'I understand,' said Falcón, and rang the bell to keep the pressure on.

Calderón opened the door. He was sweating heavily and shivering in the chill of the apartment. He had the sunken, pleading eyes of a street beggar. Maddy Krugman stood behind him looking fierce and behind her Marty held the gun to the back of Calderón's head.

'In you come, Inspector Jefe. Close the door, double lock it and put the chain on.'

Krugman was calm. While Falcón dealt with the door, he got the other two to lie down in the hall, hands behind their heads. Krugman frisked Falcón's upper body and thighs and asked to see his ankles. They all went into the sitting room. Calderón and Maddy resumed their seats. She was quite languid in her movements, as if none of this was her concern and it was just a tiresome family reunion she'd been forced to attend.

'I'll sit here,' said Falcón, choosing an armchair near the sliding doors so that García had a clear view of him.

'Why not join us in the front row?' said Maddy.

'You're fine there,' said Marty.

'How did you get in to the apartment, Marty?' asked Falcón.

'Lovers like to go out to dinner.'

'We're *not* lovers,' said Maddy, irritated.

'I was waiting outside for them.'

'He thinks we're lovers,' said Maddy, trying to explain the absurdity of the notion to Falcón.

'If you're not, then what the fuck are you?' said Marty in English. 'What the fuck are you doing in this apartment, dressed like that, going out to fucking dinner – if you're not lovers?'

'Your wife is going to answer your questions, Marty,' said Falcón, 'but people get nervous when you wave a gun in their faces. They get defensive, angry –'

'Or totally fucking silent,' said Marty, twitching the barrel of the gun in Calderón's direction.

'You're accusing him of being your wife's lover. Maybe he thinks it's best to keep his mouth shut.'

'I can smell his fear.'

'That's a loaded gun.'

'If you're doing what he's doing, you have to be prepared for that.'

'I don't know what your problem is, Marty. You knew from day one when Esteban came round to our house that, like all the other guys, he wanted to get me into bed. You also knew that I wasn't interested. He's not my type.'

'I know you, Maddy. I know how your mind works – remember that. In here your public relations don't make any difference, because these two guys are not going to be able to help you . . . even if they do believe what you're saying.'

'What happened to you, Marty?' she asked, her face suddenly a mask of profound concern.

'I met you,' he said, his eyes wide and fierce.

'Now you see my problem,' she said, turning to Falcón. 'How is anybody supposed to live with this? I live with it all the time and I need some relief from it. It's too intense. So I go out with Esteban. He's charming. He flatters me . . .'

'Flatters you,' said Marty. 'Flattery! You're telling me you're doing this for a bit of flattery? Are you fucking crazy?'

'Keep calm, Marty,' said Falcón.

'Now the bitch wants a bit of flattery,' said Marty. 'She'll chuck nearly twelve years of marriage out of the window for a bit of flattery. I can do flattery. Flattery is a piece of cake. You make Man Ray look like a fucking amateur, honey. How's that? Your name will be spoken in the same breath as Lee fucking Miller. Any better?'

'Marty,' said Falcón, and Krugman's head whipped round. 'You deserve answers, and you'll get them, but this is a domestic situation. It does not merit the use of a gun. Give me the gun and let's . . .'

'Where I come from, everything merits the use of a gun. That's how we're brought up. It's in our constitution.'

'Leave it out, Marty,' said Maddy, bored stupid.

'You don't understand what this is about, Inspector Jefe,' said Marty, adjusting his grip on the gun. 'You don't know what I've done for *her*.'

'What, Marty? What?' said Maddy. 'What have *you* done for *me*?'

Marty faltered. All the logic seemed to break down in him. All his wiring, so carefully laid down, short-circuited. Part of him knew why he was there; there was a great breaking wave of certainty inside him. But there was another part of him which found it all a complete mystery. It was the usual thing. He wanted out but couldn't leave. He didn't want to be with her but could not resist her orbit.

'I'm here because of what I did for you,' he said. 'We are eternally joined by that act.'

'What did you do for her, Marty?' asked Falcón.

'It's a long story.'

'We've got time.'

'Be careful,' said Maddy. 'You've got no idea how much talk this guy has in him. You give him licence and this could be the State of the Union address to the power of ten.'

'Let him speak,' said Calderón, through tight, white lips.

Silence. Marty blinked at the sweat in his eyes. Seconds passed, feeling like minutes.

'We were living in Connecticut,' he said, as if this was history. 'I was working in Manhattan. Maddy worked part time in the city. I worked long hours. I'd get home at the weekend and feel as if I'd been away on a trip, I'd seen so little of the house in daylight. One morning at work I fainted and hit my head on the desk. They sent me home. Maddy was supposed to be there, but when I arrived she was out. I went to bed, slept. I woke up and thought about how I'd allowed my life to get out of control. I decided it was time for a change. I'd take some time off. We'd go away, live in Europe. I was standing at the bedroom window, full of these possibilities, when I saw her coming back to the house. She was walking in a way that I'd never seen her walk before. It was more like skipping . . . like a girl skipping. And I realized that I was looking at a very happy person.

'I went down to meet her. As she came through the door, I was standing there and I saw her face fall. All her happiness and gaiety disappeared. The lead went back into her feet. She smiled at me as if I was a mentally ill relation. And I realized that somebody else was making her happy.

'I didn't tell her of my plans, I just told her about my accident. And I started watching her and I noticed all the things I hadn't seen before. There's nothing like suspicion to refresh your sight and tune up your hearing. I started delegating my work to juniors. I found time wherever I could. I spied on her and I discovered Reza Sangari.'

Marty used his gun arm to wipe his forehead. Just saying that name cost him something. He licked his lips.

'I'm a good spy, you know,' he said. 'Not such a good spy that the woman I was living with wouldn't ever find out, but good enough to pin Reza Sangari to the board. I got to know about the other women he was seeing pretty fast. He had them all operating to a timetable. Françoise on these days, Maddy on those, Helena on the others and a whole lot more in between. It was easy.'

'What was easy?' asked Maddy, no longer affecting boredom.

'To call you into the city on a day that was not supposed to be yours. We had lunch, remember? And in the afternoon I knew you wouldn't be able to resist. It was a Tuesday, which was Helena's turn. I was there when she came out of the door and you took it like a slap in the face. You were standing in a doorway across the street. I could have offered you a cigarette and a light and you wouldn't have seen me, you were looking at his door so hard. I was there when you crossed the street to go up and scratch his eyes out and you ran into another one. I didn't know her name. She wasn't one of the regulars –'

'You were *there*?' said Maddy.

'I went back with you on the train. I saw you crawl into the house. I was with you all the way.'

'You're a sick fuck, Marty Krugman,' she said.

'You got your own back,' said Marty. 'I kept watching her, you see, Inspector Jefe. I got addicted to it. I found myself doing what she did in her photographs. Watching her in her unconscious moments. Hearing her when she thought she was alone.

'The crying. You've never heard anybody cry like that. She cried like a sick dog vomiting. She cried with her face to the bathroom floor, gagging against her lungs in her throat. Anybody ever cry for you like that, Inspector Jefe?'

Falcón shook his head.

'Have you ever seen someone you love cry for someone else like that? Cry themselves senseless, until their organs seized up?'

Falcón shook his head again.

'She didn't go back to him,' said Marty. 'You can't measure the pride that sits in that woman. It's fatter than a Buddah. And that's what she drew on next. Her pride turned to fury. She used to go up into the attic and scream. Scream until her larynx shredded.'

'Did you ever talk about any of this?' asked Falcón.

Marty shook his head.

'Then the writing started – and Maddy doesn't write,' said Marty. 'She's never kept a diary in her life. Her photographs are her diary. But a few weeks after she realized what sort of a man she'd fallen in love with, she started writing. And why do you think she started writing, Inspector Jefe?'

Falcón shrugged.

'Because she knew I was watching. She knew I'd be burning to see it. And I was. I had to see it. I had to know it. I'd put money into her pain and I wanted my dividend.

'She locked the notebooks away, but I got in there. I know you're interested in psychology, Inspector Jefe. And I'm sorry that those papers don't exist any more, because I doubt you've ever seen anything quite as horrific as the scribblings of Maddy Krugman. She didn't just want him dead, Inspector Jefe. She wanted him to die under prolonged, medically assisted torture. You know, I'm sure sex and torture are connected somewhere in the human brain. Maddy thought so – didn't you, honey?'

'I don't know what you're talking about, Marty,' she said. 'This is definitely your trip and it's a solo one.'

'You don't remember "the lover's tongue like an electrode on the nipple"? The touch of his penis "like a cattle prod in the vagina"? You wrote those things.'

'What did you do about it, Marty?' asked Falcón.

'I did what she wanted me to do. I planned it all out for a Saturday afternoon. It was autumn, the light was failing early and, at the weekend, Reza Sangari's part of town was almost silent. I went to see him. I introduced myself. He let me into his apartment and I listened to his apologies. He had a soft voice. It was as seductive as a torturer who doesn't need to find out anything but just wants to cause you pain. I stood amongst the expensive silk carpets where he'd fucked my wife and I was filled with rage by the ease with which he made his excuses. It was surprisingly easy to beat him to death. Did you hear that, Inspector Jefe? I, Marty Krugman, sophisticate, intellectual, aesthete, the man who finds the whole idea of a bull-fight loathsome, I found it surprisingly easy to bludgeon a man to death. Something else I learnt: the violence that flowed through my veins at that moment – I haven't felt power like that, ever.

'I came home in the dark, the caveman with his club, and she was there to meet me in her apron. She cooked a special dinner and we ate it by candlelight. It was another of our wordless dinners, except that this one was different because at the end she took off her clothes and asked me to fuck her. And I, with this new blood in my veins, obliged. Now that, Inspector Jefe, was a fuck to remember. I'd finally found the thing that thrilled Maddy Krugman.'

'Don't flatter yourself, Marty,' she said, full of contempt.

'Anyway, the madness ceased in the house. We started living like human beings again. A few days later the news carried the story of Reza Sangari's murder and she was totally impassive. We smoked pot, ate marvellous food and drank expensive wine, and we had a lot of very violent sex.

'The FBI came during the next week sometime. They asked to speak to Maddy in private. I left them to talk. Then they wanted to interview me. She asked if she could talk to me first. We slipped into our roles without a word. She came into the kitchen and told me straight about Reza Sangari for the first time. My performance was flawless. I behaved as if I was stunned by the news, when, in fact, I was just stunned by the brilliance of our act.

'The cops went away, but they kept coming back. I had no alibi. I had a motive. I'd been seen going into the city on the Saturday, although I was pretty sure I hadn't been seen coming back. They came to see me at work. They built up the pressure on me.'

'And the only time you and Maddy spoke about Reza Sangari was when the FBI agents were in the house that first time?' asked Falcón.

'And we never spoke about it again,' said Marty. 'The murder inquiry was suddenly terminated. They found Sangari was heavily in debt due to a cocaine habit. They put it down to a drug killing. We came to Europe. My blood slowed down.'

Maddy Krugman was grunting with incredulity.

'This is all in your head, Marty,' she said. 'Pure fantasy.'

'And now she's doing the same again with our friend the judge,' said Marty, swivelling the gun towards Calderón. 'She wants me to kill you, Sr Calderón. Do you know why?'

Calderón's head wobbled on his shaky neck.

'Because she hates you. She hates what you represent – the roving, predatory male who sows his seed wherever he can. I know her now, like I've never known anybody in my life. That's how deep it goes when you do someone's killing for them. I'm telling you, Juez Calderón, she gets a sexual thrill from the idea of you dead. You lying there with your unseeing eyes open and a hole in your stony heart. It will make her feel brilliant.'

'Shut up, Marty!' she roared. 'Just shut the fuck up.'

'I discovered that unexpected bonus. It lasted for quite a while.

It bound us together. It exhilarated our . . . sex life,' he said, as if puzzled by how little that meant now.

'Until . . ?' said Maddy, breathing heavily from her outburst.

'Until what?' said Marty.

'Until you started *thinking* again, you dumb fuck. Until you disappeared inside your fucking head. I was in love with Reza Sangari. He fooled around with other women. I stopped seeing him. And then you killed him – or did you, Marty? Maybe all that is in your head, too. Your weird little fantasy. I didn't set you up to *murder* him. If you did kill him, you did that all on your own. And once he was dead I needed you and you were there for me, and that's why we were drawn together. This shit you're talking about Esteban, I don't know where you –'

'There's something missing in this story,' said Falcón. 'There's a big gap between the FBI applying pressure and you appearing in Seville as a next-door neighbour to Rafael Vega.'

Three faces turned on Marty. He changed the gun to the other hand, wiped his palm on his trousers, changed it back to his left hand.

'What happened there, Marty?' asked Falcón. 'Homicide cops don't normally let people with an opportunity, no alibi and a strong motive off the hook. The FBI are no different. After years in the job we all have an instinct for murderers and we squeeze them until they crack. Why don't you tell us why they let you off the hook?'

Marty Krugman shrugged. What the hell.

'I met someone on a train,' he said.

Maddy sat up and frowned to herself.

'People don't talk much on commuter trains and they don't normally ask you how you feel about your country, but this guy for some reason wanted to know all the famous theories of Marty Krugman. He wanted to know how good an American I was. He wanted to know how strong my fear was, how ravenous my greed. I think, looking back on it, I qualified on the grounds of fear. I told him that I wanted America to remain the most powerful nation of earth because I know where I stand with them at the helm. We met again some days later and went for a walk in Bryant Park behind the New York Public Library. It was freezing cold. There's a good place to eat lunch there – the Bryant Grill. And it was there that this man revealed that he understood the nature of my problem and that he could solve it.'

'What was this man's name?' asked Falcón, looking at Maddy.

'Foley Macnamara,' said Marty, without missing a beat.

Maddy blinked, mouth open a crack.

'We became regulars at the Bryant Grill. Foley told me how important presentation was in the maintenance of control. How the ends justify the means, and how the means necessarily have to be outrageous and quite ruthlessly executed in order to remind those with delusions of power who they're up against. He said that this was a big part of the Agency's job: to maintain image, to hold loyalty to the brand.'

'The *Agency*?' said Maddy, incredulous. 'What agency, Marty?'

'That was when I asked him whether he was with the CIA, and he said he was not.'

'Oh, shit, Marty. . .no,' said Maddy. 'You've finally fucking flipped. The Agency. Jesus Christ.'

'He said he was a consultant and that he provided information for certain departments. He said that he only worked in the business and political arenas, never military.

'He liked my profile: I'd never worked for the government, I had a well-documented career as an architect, I already spoke near-perfect Spanish. All they wanted me to do was go to Seville, make contact with an estate agency and they would put us next to Rafael Vega.'

'For a start, Marty, we did not intend to go to Seville. If you remember, we took a small house in Provence. That was where we were going to spend a year, to try and live the life of that stupid fucking book – *if* you remember.'

'But we went to Barcelona to see my old pal Gaudí and we ended up in Seville, Maddy,' he said. 'All I had to do was to keep up the flow of information about Vega, his situation, what he was thinking and any plans he might have. In return, the thrust of the Reza Sangari investigation would be redirected. We would be free to leave the country and restart our lives. No admission of guilt was implied.'

'This is crazy,' said Maddy, burying her face in her hands. 'You can't tell these people this stuff.'

'Did you know who you were spying on?' asked Falcón.

'I only found that out as things started to develop in Rafael Vega's life. The theory being that, the less I knew, the more convincing I could be.'

'Who was your contact here in Seville?'

'His code name was "Romany". I used to meet him down by the river, between the bridges.'

'Did he give you Rafael Vega's real identity?'

'Don't tell me you believe this stuff, Inspector Jefe?' said Maddy. 'Because I can tell you . . . I mean, this proves that we are dealing with an insane person here.'

'I learnt everything about him myself,' said Marty, ignoring her. 'Which meant I learnt nothing for months. We discussed all sorts of things, but he never talked about himself. He was completely watertight until the end of last year when for the first time he got really drunk in my company and started to talk about his "other life". I didn't learn everything in one go. I had to piece it together from a series of discussions, but what was causing his distress was that he'd been married before, to a woman who'd died some years ago in Cartagena in Columbia. They'd had a daughter, who had subsequently married and had children herself. He'd kept in touch with his daughter and the news he'd received at the end of last year was that she, her husband and the children had been killed when a truck had forced their car off the road. It was a devastating blow and, of course, he had no one to talk to except me.'

'Did he believe it was a genuine accident?' asked Falcón.

'In his confused and stricken state the real paranoia of the man came out,' said Marty. 'He didn't know whether it was his enemies coming back at him or just divine retribution.'

'So he told you what he'd been doing in his "other life"?' asked Falcón. 'Why he'd had to cut himself off from his wife and daughter?'

'Not exactly,' said Marty. 'He told me he'd started seeing faces from his past.'

Maddy spread her hands as if this was proof of the man's complete delusion.

'In dreams?' asked Falcón.

'I think they started as dreams and then dream and reality began to merge and that's what was frightening him. While they were dream faces he found himself intrigued by why his mind had marked them out. Once he started to see these same faces on living people, he thought he was going mad. He wouldn't go and see anybody about it. He said that he'd started taking something for his anxiety. But the faces kept coming at him in parks, shops, cafés, and still he couldn't work out who they were.

'It came out that he'd been in the military,' said Marty. 'And using some very simple powers of deduction I reasoned that he'd been involved in the Chilean military take-over of 1973. I put it to him that some very unpleasant things happened in the process of the Pinochet revolution and that perhaps these faces were from people who'd suffered at the hands of the new régime. And as I was saying this I knew I'd hit home. He retreated into his head and spoke to himself and I heard him say: "They were the ones who didn't ask for their mothers." I think that they were people he'd tortured.'

'Was that why you killed him, Marty?' asked Falcón.

'I understand your need to tidy things up, Inspector Jefe,' said Marty. 'So pin the killing on me if you must. But this was a man who was going to do the job himself.'

'What about the *Agency*?' said Maddy, more provocatively this time.

'They didn't want him dead,' said Marty. 'They still hadn't found out what they wanted to know.'

'And what was that?' asked Falcón.

'They didn't know. They were just sure he had something that could be damaging to them or their interests.'

'Do you think these people are going to believe that bullshit?' said Maddy, hitting high, screechy notes. 'My husband is a CIA undercover agent? You're pathetic, Marty Krugman. You are fucking pathetic and always have been.'

'And now, gentlemen,' said Marty. 'This is over.'

The bullet entered her chest to the right of her left breast. Marty slid to the floor with his back against the wall. He put the barrel of the gun into his mouth. Falcón threw himself at Marty, trying to knock the gun away, but everything had been calculated. Marty pulled the trigger and the white wall spattered red behind him.

26

Not much strength is required to throw off a cotton sheet, but Falcón couldn't find it. His arms had been weakened by last night's failures. He was glad he'd already written his report; his fingers felt like squid. Comisario Elvira had insisted on him faxing the report through, after he'd delivered his verbal account while driving Calderón back to his apartment.

Snapshots of last night's events flipped through his mind. The close-up of the light going out in Marty Krugman's eyes. Calderón paralysed on the sofa, his face full of horror at the blood spreading out into Maddy Krugman's silk top. The young patrolman surveying the carnage in the room and gagging into his hand. García pushing past them to shake his head at the human mess. The three of them going downstairs, Calderón holding on to the bannister. The police marksman, unused, sitting in the front of García's car with his case on his knees. The drive back with Calderón on the mobile, giving Inés a monosyllabic account. Inés in strappy, pointy, high-heeled shoes, standing in the glare of the headlights in the street outside the apartment building. Calderón, with his hands weighing thirty kilos apiece by his sides, as Inés engulfed him in her arms. Their faces as he moved off – hers with lower lip trembling, eyes sparkling with tears, and his lifeless apart from one shift of the eyes to the corners, which said: 'You've seen me, Javier Falcón, now go, get away, let me be.'

The distance that seven hours of deep, anaesthetic sleep had put between him and these events had made them seem like a journalist's account of a crime committed in the 1950s. He felt different, as if a surgeon had mistakenly removed something that had never troubled him, and the result was going to change his life.

His conversation with Consuelo came back to him. He'd called her lying in bed, just moments before he blacked out. The last exchange:

'Marty Krugman was clearly insane,' she said.

'Was he?'

He drove to the Jefatura, black and sick in his stomach, as if he'd drunk coffee on a bad hangover. He gripped the steering wheel tightly. As he came into the empty outer office he saw Ramírez standing at the window, leaning forward, supporting himself on his hands.

'I heard about last night's disaster,' said Ramírez. 'Are you all right?'

Falcón nodded, more or less.

'Elvira's already been on the phone, asking to see you as soon as you come in.'

The Comisario was standing at his window, hands behind his back, looking across Calle Blas Infante to the Parque de los Príncipes. His predecessor, Lobo, used to do the same thing – drawing the illusion of power from surveying a domain.

'Take a seat, Inspector Jefe,' he said, nipping behind his desk, swift and agile, giving his moustache a finger and thumb wipe. 'I've read your report and Juez Calderón's, which arrived first thing this morning. I've already been in touch with the American Consul and he's asked for copies. They should come back to us this morning on the CIA nonsense. They won't want to let that notion build up any authority in our ranks.'

'So you don't give it any credibility, sir?'

'Sounds like the ravings of a deranged mind to me,' said Elvira. 'But then again, when I heard that our government had sent death squads to wipe out ETA terrorist cells I didn't believe that either . . . I couldn't believe it. So, officially, I would call myself sceptical, whilst privately thinking the whole story completely fantastical.'

'He was deranged,' said Falcón. 'There's no doubt about that. But you can't totally write him off. I'm sure the FBI don't let people off the hook that easily and what he told me about Reza Sangari matches what I found out myself. I see no reason why he should lie about killing the man – unless that, too, was some fantasy which, in his confused mind, he hoped would draw his very strange wife back to him. The stuff he spouted about the Agency . . . Who knows. I'm sure his wife didn't believe a word of it. It'll be interesting to see what Virgilio Guzmán comes back with on the profile of Miguel Velasco.'

'What's Guzmán got to do with it?'

'He's a Chilean. He has expatriate contacts who can help with that sort of material,' said Falcón. 'One thing I do know about these dream faces he mentioned is that Pablo Ortega saw Vega badly spooked in the Corte Inglés one day and I imagine that he'd been seeing one of his visions.'

'You've got to be careful with Virgilio Guzmán,' said Elvira. 'There are people who say that he can't seem to take anything at face value any more. He's sees a conspiracy theory in everything.'

'He clarified the 9/11 element of the "suicide note" and that helped with the identification of Rafael Vega.'

'I thought he came to see you about Montes's suicide?'

'He did. The inclusion of Eduardo Carvajal's name in Vega's address book was why I'd gone to see Montes in the first place,' said Falcón. 'Montes mentioned Russian mafia involvement in the sex trade, and the next thing I find is a Russian connection to Vega. I ask Montes about these Russians and very soon after that he killed himself.'

'And you talked to Guzmán about this?'

'I gave it to him as context, but we had an agreement that he would not write about anything circumstantial, only the provable facts. And, as yet, we have nothing that links Montes to the Russians.'

'You're making me very nervous, Inspector Jefe. The Montes suicide is an internal matter at the moment. If there is corruption within the force we have to be extremely careful about how it is handled.'

'A journalist was sent to talk to me in my position as the investigating officer. I was not briefed on what could, or could not, be discussed with him. I believe, with someone of the reputation of Virgilio Guzmán, that transparency is the best policy. Have you read the *Diario de Sevilla* today?'

'Yes. There was a very extensive report on the career of Inspector Jefe Montes.'

Falcón nodded, waited, but nothing more was said.

'I think you should search the Krugmans' house before the Americans come back to us,' said Elvira. 'I've already arranged a warrant.'

Falcón headed for the door. Elvira spoke to the back of his head.

'If Virgilio Guzmán approaches you on the events of last night I'd like you to be very oblique about why Juez Calderón was in the apartment. I don't want a scandal about the Juez de Instrucción having had an affair with the deceased.'

'Has he admitted to that?'

'I asked for a separate statement on that subject. He seems to have been obsessed by her,' said Elvira, who added without looking up from his papers: 'I'm surprised that you didn't mention in your statement his action of bravery at the end.'

'His bravery?' asked Falcón.

'"As Krugman raised his gun to fire,"' said Elvira, reading from Calderón's statement, '"I threw myself towards him in the hope of distracting his aim. The bullet hit Sra Krugman in the chest. Inspector Jefe Falcón was unable to prevent Sr Krugman from putting the gun into his mouth and killing himself."'

'I'll search the Krugmans' house,' said Falcón, leaving the office.

'García didn't see it either,' said Elvira, as the door closed.

Back in the office Falcón sent Cristina Ferrera off to the lab to pick up the Krugmans' house keys from Felipe and Jorge, who had removed them from the crime scene back in Tabladilla. Ramírez was still slumped at his desk.

'CIA?' he said, incredulous.

Falcón threw up his hands.

'Or not CIA, but some shadowy consultancy connected to the CIA,' he said.

'Fantasy,' said Ramírez.

'Let's say that Guzmán's conspiracy theory is correct. If you were part of the American administration responsible for some very ugly things happening in South America during the seventies, and you were worried that Rafael Vega had something that could prove personal involvement by senior members of the US administration . . . what would you do?'

'Kill him anyway.'

'That's because you're a ruthless bastard, José Luis,' said Falcón. 'The fact is, you wouldn't use the CIA, would you? You wouldn't have the power to use it. But there must be ex-CIA men with contacts and influence who have "debts". You see what I mean about Crazy Krugman . . . you can't just dismiss him as a madman.'

'I can,' said Ramírez. 'He's too unstable for that kind of work.'

'What if he's your only option?' said Falcón. 'And what do you make of his final admission, that the Agency didn't want Vega dead because they hadn't found out what they wanted to find out? That's a bit of an anticlimax, isn't it?'

'You mean he was doing all these vital, secret tasks but none of the information he came up with was crucial enough that Vega had to be killed?' said Ramírez. 'Maybe what they were looking for is locked up in Vega's safe-deposit box, for which we *still* don't have a search warrant.'

'You're beginning to believe, José Luis. You'd better remind Juez Calderón, if he comes in for work today."

The phone rang in the outer office. Ramírez went to answer it while Falcón thought about Krugman. 'They', if they existed, couldn't have been expecting Marty to find papers or a video tape. That would have been too much. What they were looking for were reports on Vega's state of mind. Was this a man about to go to Baltasar Garzón or the Belgian justice system and offer his services, for instance?

'That was the town hall in Aracena,' said Ramírez, leaning against the door jamb. 'They passed a restoration project on Montes's ruined finca valued at twenty million pesetas. A total rebuild, complete remodernization, three-phase electricity – the works.'

Falcón passed the news on to Comisario Elvira, who reacted as if he'd been expecting it all along. He told them to proceed with the Krugman house search. Ferrera came back with the house keys and they drove out to Santa Clara.

The house was cold and silent and looked undisturbed as the three of them snapped on their latex gloves.

'I'll go upstairs,' said Falcón. 'Join me when you've finished down here.'

'What are we looking for?' asked Ferrera.

'A little note from Dr Kissinger saying, "Keep up the good work,"' said Ramírez. 'That should do it.'

Falcón went upstairs. The door to Maddy Krugman's exhibition room was open. All the photographs had been removed from the walls and only one exhibit was left on a plinth in the centre of the room. It consisted of a cut-out of a blown-up version of Vega standing barefoot in his garden. The cut-out was encased in Perspex and suspended within the transparent block, like the skeletons of autumn leaves, were the ghostly prints of human hands. They all seemed to be pressing in on the lonely figure, who stood imprisoned, as if by his own history, like an insect in amber. There was a printed card attached to the piece written in Spanish: *Las Manos Desaparecidas* – The Vanished Hands.

He went across to her work room. Ferrera was going to have to spend a day going through all the prints, transparencies and negatives, checking every one. Up against the wall were the framed shots which had been hanging in the other room. He flipped through them, looking for the shot she'd taken of him. He found the empty frame. He checked the paper shredder and saw his image hanging in ribbons.

Marty Krugman had converted one of the other bedrooms into his office. There was a desk, a laptop and a drawing board. Rolls of plans stood in the corners. Falcón went through the desk drawers. He found a school exercise book with what appeared to be a collection of Krugman's odd thoughts jotted down.

Boredom is the enemy of humanity. It is why we get up and kill.

The torturer learns his skills from the agonies of his own mind, transformed by power.

Guilt defines us as human but in consuming the mind destroys all that made us human. Only by public admission is our humanity restored. That is the measure of our mutual dependence.

Falcón flipped through to the last entry.

I know what you're doing. I'm going to chain you up, refuse you food and water, watch you wither and crack, fade and split, and roll a rich red wine over my tongue while you die.

That was the problem with Krugman. He was like an unreliable witness taking the stand. The purity of his intellect was always getting infected by the bacteria of emotion.

Ramírez appeared at the door.

'Did you see the exhibit?' said Falcón. '*The Vanished Hands.*'

'I came up here to ask Cristina's question in private,' said Ramírez. 'What the fuck are we looking for?'

'That exhibit – do you think it's Sra Krugman's artistic interpretation of what was going on in Vega's mind, or did she know more?' said Falcón. 'This is a book of Krugman's thoughts – he talks about the mind of a torturer.'

'These are hints, not clues,' said Ramírez. 'They are not usable.'

'We're here because Elvira is covering his back. He's sceptical, but he wants to make sure there's no obvious connection between Krugman and – what shall we call him? – a mysterious American,' said Falcón. 'That means we're going to have to go through all of Sra Krugman's shots and –'

'But she photographed strangers all the time.'

'But not ones talking to her husband down by the river.'

'And if we find a shot?'

'You've gone back to being a non-believer again, José Luis,' said Falcón. 'If I'd told you fifteen years ago that Russian mafia gangs would control seventy per cent of prostitution in Europe, you'd have laughed in my face. But anything, and everything, is possible now. People have started to see aeroplanes as bombs. You can buy a new identity on the streets of any European city in forty-eight hours for a few thousand euros. An AK-47 can be yours in minutes. There are al-Qaeda cells in almost every country of the world. Why shouldn't the CIA be running a small operation in Seville, when the whole of Europe has become a civilization simmering with anarchy and decadence?'

'Remind me to live in fear, Javier,' said Ramírez. 'My point is: so what if we find a shot of Krugman with a mysterious American? The consulate denies everything. Krugman was a madman who shot his wife and then himself. Where are we?'

'Six people have died in less than a week. Five of them lived next door to each other. Even if I wasn't a cop, I would find that extraordinary,' said Falcón. 'We might be witnesses to some sort of collective unconscious implosion, where each death or suicide applies mental pressure to the next victim, or . . . we might simply be unable to see the connections, because we don't quite know enough.'

The mobile in his pocket vibrated. Elvira ordered him back to the Jefatura. The American Consulate was sending someone over. Falcón left them at the search and drove back to Calle Blas Infante.

The man from the American Consulate was a communications officer called Mark Flowers. He was about fifty years old, good-looking, tanned with black hair that must have been dyed. He spoke flawless Castilian Spanish and was well prepared for what he had to do.

'I've read these two statements from Inspector Jefe Falcón and Juez Calderón. I was told that they were written separately. The impressive detail seems to match and, in the absence of any serious contradictions, I informed the Consul that I believed them to be accurate and true. Both statements were therefore sent to the CIA in Langley for their comments. They categorically deny any knowledge, not only of Marty Krugman, but also this so-called consultant, Foley Macnamara. Comisario Elvira also asked if the CIA had any record of one Miguel Velasco, aka Rafael Vega, who was ex-Chilean military, receiving any CIA training. They've informed me that they did a file search of all personnel as far back as the creation of the CIA after the Second World War, and found that nobody of that name had received any training. They also offered the opinion that at no point last night did Marty Krugman refer to Rafael Vega as Miguel Velasco, and that the information he gave seemed to be his interpretation of Sr Vega's mental problems. Krugman himself deduced that Vega had been in the Chilean military and that he had been involved in torture. They describe Sr Krugman as a classic fantasist, with access to an imagination infected by psychosis who, given his personal experience of South American politics of that era, would have no trouble –'

'What personal experience of South American politics?' asked Falcón.

'Immigration ran a search on Marty Krugman's travels outside the USA and found that he was attracted enough, through his own liberal and left-leaning politics, to make four trips to Chile between March 1971 and July 1973. As you know, during the Allende administration, the American government was very concerned at the development of their Marxist policies and, as a consequence, US citizens visiting that country were closely monitored.'

'What about Vega's late wife and his daughter's family?' asked Falcón.

'That, as you can imagine, is rather more difficult for them to verify. All they can say is that neither Miguel Velasco nor Rafael Vega was married on US soil,' said Flowers.

'I meant Krugman's assertion that Vega's anxiety stemmed from his paranoia that they might have been killed by his enemies.'

'Who are these enemies?'

'The people who provided him with a witness protection programme from which he thought it best to escape.'

'You might be interested to know that the CIA's research on Chilean military personnel revealed Miguel Velasco to be quite a notorious member of the Pinochet régime, known for his extremely unconventional and distasteful interrogation techniques. The opposition revolutionary movement, the MIR, knew him by the nickname *El Salido* – the Pervert.'

'But what did the CIA have to say about the FBI input on the matter?' asked Falcón. 'Surely absconding from an FBI protection programme, after acting as a witness in a drug-trafficking trial, should be something the CIA would be interested in?'

'The CIA were only examining these documents in the light of Sr Krugman's behaviour and claims. I know they have a file on Miguel Velasco because of his actions in the Pinochet administration. If there's anything else it would, of course, be classified.'

'Your response has been very rapid and thorough,' said Falcón.

'They pride themselves on it,' said Flowers. 'Since 9/11 there have been changes in the Service, especially on reaction time to all inquiries in which there is a reference to that date, even if it did refer to 1973.'

'I added a summary of the Vega case to the statements,' said Elvira. 'For the purposes of clarification.'

'It was very helpful, Comisario,' said Flowers.

'What would be the reaction from the CIA if we could provide photographic proof that meetings had occurred between Sr Krugman and . . . US government officials?' asked Falcón, who was finding Mark Flowers to be rather too amicable and gracious.

'Extreme surprise, I would imagine,' said Flowers, whose face remained completely impassive.

'As you know, Sr Krugman's wife was a well-known and active photographer who particularly enjoyed taking shots of people down by the river, which was where her husband said he had meetings with code name "Romany".'

Flowers blinked once but said nothing. He handed Elvira his card and left.

'Do you have photographic evidence?' asked Elvira.

'No, Comisario,' said Falcón. 'It's just a way of terminating a line of inquiry. If Sr Krugman was a fantasist, we'll never hear from Mark

Flowers again. But if he was supplying information there will be some anxious people in the consulate. I'd be interested to hear if you receive communication from a higher authority.'

Elvira's phone rang. Falcón got up to leave. Elvira stayed him with his hand. The Comisario listened, made notes and hung up.

'That was a senior officer from Aracena,' he said. 'He's just been informed by the fire department that the forest fire raging around Almonaster la Real in the past few days was an arson attack, and that they have now traced the start of the fire to an isolated finca which belonged to Inspector Jefe Alberto Montes. The contents of the house have been almost completely destroyed, but they have found a rudimentary timer, which they believed was attached to an incendiary device that ignited a large quantity of petrol.'

27

Tuesday, 30th July 2002

It was still brutally hot outside the city, which crouched in a haze behind Falcón like a beast in its own fetor, but the openness of the rolling plain ahead of him, the swaying brown grasses, the distant hills, made him feel free of the discomfort of his own body. The temperature dropped as he drove through the sierra and, although it never reached below blood heat, the sense of release from the city's feverish concrete into the high greenery of the chestnut trees induced a mild delirium. Or was it Elton John singing 'Benny and the Jets' on the radio?

It was impossible to think that anything terrible could happen out here. Whereas the city drew the poor, the lost, the corrupted and the depraved to the mangled teat of its bristly underbelly, this country seemed untouched. The jostling leaves of the trees filtered the sunlight to the pure, dappled memory of less confused times. Until Falcón turned off the main road to Almonaster la Real.

The charcoal stink of torched forest reached him before the sight of blackened stumps and scorched, defoliated trees with their bark-flayed arms stretched out in the distress of serious burn victims. The forest floor of black-and-grey coals still smouldered, as if panting from the devastating consumption. The white sky provided a piti-less backdrop, as if to emphasize to those doubters who passed through this monochromatic horror that what had happened here was as wrong as war.

The police and firemen he met in the local bar in Almonaster were grim and the townspeople shocked and in despair, as if they were the survivors of some wartime atrocity. They knew things that Falcón, as yet, didn't.

He was led down to the finca, which was several kilometres outside the town and isolated in the forest. There was a kilometre of rough dirt track up to the house, whose windowless, roofless, blackened shell looked like a giant, stoved-in human skull.

Everything wooden in the house had been consumed. The first floor no longer existed. It had burnt or collapsed under the weight of the falling roof on to the concrete below. The ground floor was piled with black terracotta roof tiles, charred beams and furniture, smoking mattresses, screenless televisions and pools of molten, but now hardened, plastic.

They took him down through the concrete floor into the basement, which was badly scorched but intact. It didn't look like any basement he'd ever seen. There were four metal doors, two on either side of a short corridor. The doors had bolts on the outside, which could also be padlocked. None of the rooms had windows. All had burnt wooden pallets and mattresses. They were cells in which people had been kept.

In one of the cells, whose walls were unplastered, revealing the original stone, there was some writing scratched on to a rock in the corner by the bed. It was in Cyrillic script. An enamelled metal plate lay upside down on the floor.

They led him back upstairs and out on to the land whose grass had been burnt off, leaving a bald stretch of black and brown beaten earth, which now looked like the hide of a diseased dog. At the edge of the land, inside what would have been the tree line, were two piles of earth.

'With the forest burnt down we could see these two humps,' said the officer. 'We dug down about a metre and found these –'

Falcón looked down on the skeletal remains of two people nestled in the dark earth.

'We didn't want to dig further until we had proper forensics here, but the local doctor measured them and thinks that they are a boy and a girl of around twelve or thirteen years of age. He thought that they'd been buried for between eight months and a year, given that there is no tissue left.'

'What do you know about how this house was being used?' asked Falcón, needing to get something out, because his rage was reaching uncontainable levels.

'Weekends only and not every weekend. Friday and Saturday nights, mostly.'

'Did you ever meet the owner?'

'Inspector Jefe Montes? Of course. He came and said hello to us. He said he'd bought the house and that some friends were going to do it up and use it as a hunting lodge.'

They walked back to the house and Falcón could see that there were air-conditioning units for the lower and upper floors.

'So they came in the summer as well?' said Falcón, pointing at the blackened boxes.

'Not to hunt, obviously,' said the officer. 'In the end, they didn't do much hunting at all . . . We didn't think much about it at the time. And, because Inspector Jefe Montes was the owner, we didn't think anything . . .'

The officer's voice trailed off. 'Illegal' seemed an ineffective word to describe what had gone on in this house of horror.

'Whoever started this fire had to bring a great deal of petrol up to the house,' said Falcón. 'They probably used plastic jerry cans and they'd have needed a pick-up. Can you contact every petrol station in this area and . . . well, you know what to do.'

Falcón called Elvira and gave him a report. He asked for Felipe and Jorge to be sent out with a change of clothes, because they were certainly going to have to spend the night. He also asked for some manpower to phone around the petrol stations in the Seville area, looking for a pick-up with probably two people who'd filled possibly ten plastic jerry cans with petrol, late Saturday night or very early on Sunday morning. He hung up and told the officer that the area was to be cordoned off and kept under guard. Nobody was to touch anything on the property until the forensics arrived. He checked the air-conditioning boxes on the ground floor but didn't find what he was looking for. He asked for a set of ladders. A car was dispatched to town. Falcón stood in the blackened landscape and drew fury from the destruction.

The car returned with a set of ladders. Falcón leaned them up against the house and found himself mentally praying. He took out an evidence bag and a pair of tweezers and climbed up to the air-conditioning units, one by one. On the third unit he found what he wanted – scorched, but not destroyed, was the peeling sticker of the company that had installed the units: Aire Condicionado Central de Sevilla. Ignacio Ortega's company.

He took out another evidence bag and walked down the rough

track and scooped up some dust. He expected it to match the dust found on Vega's old Peugeot.

Ortega. Vega. Montes, he thought. And only one left alive.

Ramírez was bored as he took Falcón's call on his mobile. There were thousands of Maddy Krugman's prints on paper and on hard disk, and the task did not inspire him. His boredom evaporated as Falcón briefed him on Montes's finca near Almonaster la Real.

'Did you check Ignacio Ortega's alibi?' asked Falcón.

'Yes, but that was for the night that Rafael Vega died.'

'Where was he?'

'He was in bed with his wife on the coast.'

'I told him about Pablo's death late on Saturday night and he didn't come back to Seville until Sunday morning.'

'I can ask him for proof of his whereabouts for that week if you want?'

'I don't want to spook him.'

'Well, if he organized that arson attack you already have,' said Ramírez. 'How many people know what happened at Montes's finca?'

'By now the whole of Almonaster la Real. I mean, not in detail, but they know it's nasty. They'll probably know about the bodies.'

'So that's all going to be on the news this evening.'

'We haven't got enough on him to link him to what was actually happening at Montes's finca. We'll have to find the arsonists first and they might give us the link,' said Falcón. 'Leave Cristina at the Krugmans' house and go back to the Jefatura and make it all happen, José Luis.'

Falcón went back down into the basement of the house and, with a pen torch in his mouth, copied down the Cyrillic script written on the wall. As he looked around the four cells he realized that the mattresses had all been doused with petrol and set alight, but that there hadn't been enough oxygen to keep them going.

More people were dispatched to town to bring large plastic sheets, which they laid out on the scorched earth. The mattresses and pallets were numbered off and lifted out of the basement and laid on the plastic. Falcón conducted a minute search of the walls of the empty cells.

In the second cell he noticed a dark stain on the floor, coming from the back wall out into the centre of the room. He chipped out a piece of concrete and bagged it. In the fourth cell he found a one-euro coin behind a loose piece of mortar. He bagged that.

Outside they started work on the mattresses, peeling back the outer fabric and working through the stuffing. The mattress from cell two had a shard of curved glass in it, a section of a broken wine goblet. The mattress from cell three had the real treasure: a used Gillette II razor blade, still with some bristles attached.

At 3 p.m. they broke for lunch. Felipe and Jorge had arrived in Almonaster la Real and, over pork chops, chips and salad, Falcón told them to concentrate on the interior of the house before they moved on to exhuming the bodies.

'Square metre by square metre. Photographs all the way. Dust everything for prints, even if they look completely burnt out – all televisions, video recorders, remotes. There's a lot of congealed plastic in there, which might be from videos; see if there's one centimetre of tape available. We're also looking for personal items – money, jewellery, clothing. People come to a place like this, they lose things. I want a finger search of all the land around the house. Be meticulous, do everything by the book. Nobody, and I mean nobody, who has been to this house and been involved with what's been going on here should have the slightest chance of being able to get away with it on a technicality.'

A grim determination settled over the lunch table. Calls were made to the neighbouring towns of Cortegana and Aracena for more people to help with the finger search of the land. By the time they returned to the finca there were thirty people. Falcón put twenty-six on to the finger search and four to help Felipe and Jorge lifting things out of the house.

All findings were photographed in situ, logged in a school exercise book with the photograph number and bagged. Any large items with discernible prints were wrapped in plastic. Falcón asked Elvira to have two lab technicians standing by to receive the material and process the evidence.

By 7 p.m. they had completed the finger search of the land and about two-thirds of the house interior. Ramírez called.

'I've found your arsonists,' he said. 'I'm putting a squad together to go and pick them up now. They live out in Tres Mil Vivendas and I don't want them getting away from us in that little hell hole.'

'That was quick work, José Luis.'

'I got lucky,' he said. 'I reckoned they'd be doing this at night, so I started with all the late-night garages on the road out to Aracena. I thought they might not be stupid but, in this heat, they could easily be lazy. I reckoned they wouldn't fill all the jerry cans up at one petrol station and draw attention to themselves, but they might want to do it on the way. Two of the garages remembered a pick-up with two guys filling plastic jerry cans, but neither of them had close-circuit television. I worked back from there until I found a petrol station with CCTV, and this was where I got lucky. The guys came back twice to fill up. I went out there to view the tapes. Both guys were wearing hats, so they knew they were vulnerable to CCTV, and I didn't get a sight of them or the vehicle because it was parked on the other side of the pumps. But the second time there was a truck parked where they wanted to be, so they had to come into the light between the shop and the pumps. The CCTV cameras were pointed so that they picked up the activity on that part of the forecourt. Their registration number just slid beautifully into view.'

'Have you got names?'

'Yes, and they've both got police records for petty theft and burglary, and one of them picked up an assault conviction too, but neither of them has been done for arson.'

'I'm on my way back with the first vanload of evidence.'

He closed down the mobile, which rang again instantly. Alicia Aguado told him she could find a friend to take her out to the prison for her next session with Sebastián Ortega.

One of the Aracena police officers with a relative in Seville volunteered to accompany the vanload of evidence. Falcón headed back to the city alone at speed, as if he was rushing towards a brilliant conclusion. He had to pull over to take three calls on the way back.

The first was from Cristina Ferrera, saying that she'd been through Maddy Krugman's prints and hard disk and come across two shots of Marty Krugman sitting with a different stranger in each. In one he was animated and talking, in the other he seemed to be waiting. In both shots he was either in the background or off to one side. The one in which he appeared in the background had been taken from the hard disk and she'd had to blow up that section of the shot to confirm it was him.

The second call was from Ramírez, confirming that they'd arrested the two arsonists and he was conducting a search of their apartment.

The third call came from Elvira just as he was about to hit the main road into Seville. The Comisario wanted to see him as soon as he arrived back in the Jefatura.

Falcón went straight up to Elvira's office. His secretary had already left. The Comisario's door was open. Elvira sat at his desk, staring into it as if contemplating a terrible loss.

'Something's going on,' said Elvira, pointing him into a chair.

'Whatever it is it doesn't look good.'

'There's political pressure coming from . . . unseen powers,' said Elvira. 'That article published in the *Diario de Sevilla* this morning. . .'

'You didn't seem too concerned by that earlier today.'

'The extensive obituary alongside it was a very carefully angled piece of writing. There were no reasons given for Montes's suicide, and the piece didn't make any claims, but people who "know" were in no doubt when they came away from that article that there were implications – serious ones. There has been a reaction to those implications from senior people at the town hall and important members of the Andalucían parliament. They want to know the state of our . . . house.'

Falcón started to say something and Elvira held up his hand.

'I've just heard two other reports, which could be interpreted as unfortunate holiday accidents or sinister coincidences. Dr Alfonso Martinez, a member of the Andalucían parliament, is now in intensive care after his car left the road on the motorway from Jerez de la Frontera to Cádiz and crashed into a bridge. And the wife of Enrique Altozano found her husband's clothes in a pile on a beach between Pedro de Alcántara and Estepona and alerted the authorities. They are currently searching the coast, but he has not been found. He was the man in the planning department of the Seville town hall who was responsible for awarding licences to new building projects.'

This time Falcón didn't try to say anything.

'Powerful people are like jackals on the prairie. They put their noses to the air for the smell of scandal, and the faintest whiff carries to them from kilometres away,' said Elvira. 'The job of the politician is to always maintain power. He does not necessarily want to deny that something disgraceful has occurred, but he does want to contain it, so that institutions don't completely disintegrate.'

'You're preparing me for something, Comisario,' said Falcón. 'I hope it's not going to be a disappointment in those institutions, or the people that run them.'

'I am telling you how it is, so that we can develop this case in a way that maximizes the number of convictions and minimizes the serious political damage,' said Elvira. 'If we show that we are only interested in taking down everybody involved, we will be prevented from doing that. We have the example of our own government. That, if you remember, was how Felipe González survived the death squad scandal.'

'Are you concerned that I might be a fanatical zealot?'

'It would be understandable, given what we know so far of the unpleasantness of this case.'

'Let me get this straight,' said Falcón. 'Two powerful people have either been killed or attempted suicide. This has alerted other powerful people, who have hinted to the Jefatura that, should we want to press this case to its logical conclusion, we will suffer an in-depth examination of the state of our own force. In other words, if we show their corruption to the world, they will show ours.'

'Comisario Lobo said you would understand perfectly.'

'Our problem is that the crucial conviction in this case is the one that will bring down the whole house of cards,' said Falcón. 'I'll tell you what I think has happened, Comisario. Ignacio Ortega took over the procuring work for the paedophile rings from Eduardo Carvajal as he had a connection to the Russians. That connection is strong enough that they were able to award him contracts without consulting Rafael Vega. Montes was already corrupted at the time of the death of Eduardo Carvajal. He was forced into further incrimination by the purchase of this finca near Almonaster la Real, which Ignacio Ortega helped to restore. As a result of Montes's involvement in the finca, the authorities never bothered to investigate how the house was being used. I'm nearly sure that Rafael Vega was a client. We'll do a few tests which might confirm that to us. Mark Flowers gave us an indication of Vega's tastes when he told us his nickname at the time of the Chilean coup. These two latest casualties you've just told me about could mean that Martinez and Altozano may have been clients, too. To completely stamp this out we should, ideally, take out the Russians, but I don't know how we can get to them. The next rung down is Ignacio Ortega. The problem is that he is not a character who will go down quietly. He will demand from his friends that he be saved, or he will bring down the individuals in these highly valued institutions of ours.'

'Don't allow any of that bitterness to creep into your words,' said Elvira. 'I understand why you should feel like that, but outside people will dismiss you as "difficult" and you will never get what you want. What have you got on Ortega?'

'Very little,' said Falcón. 'He came under suspicion because of his behaviour around the death of his brother. I interviewed his son, who is a heroin addict, and he reluctantly told me about the systematic sexual abuse that he and his cousin had suffered, as well as a number of his friends, when they were children. Favours were being done in the building trade between Ignacio Ortega, Vega and the Russians. The minimum Ortega did was to install the air-conditioning units in Montes's finca. Inspector Ramírez has caught the arsonists who set fire to the finca. We're hoping they will provide a more concrete link to Ignacio Ortega. That will give us the minimum option of holding Ortega on "conspiracy to arson" charges. The next step might be more difficult.'

'The sexual abuse charges against his son don't have much hope, given his drug problems. I know it's wrong, but that's the perception.'

'He said he wouldn't testify against his father, anyway.'

'And Sebastián Ortega has been convicted of a serious crime.'

'Which we are hoping we can prove that he did not commit, but that won't help us with Ortega. We need more time.'

'All right,' said Elvira, sitting back, tired and exasperated. 'See if there's a link between Ignacio Ortega and the arsonists. If there is, we have to plan our next move. And, I don't need to tell you, but you can't talk to Virgilio Guzmán about any of this.'

28

Tuesday, 30th July 2002

In the outer office Cristina Ferrera was sitting at a desk, feet hooked round the chair legs, looking at the two paper printouts of the shots of Marty Krugman down by the river. She turned the two A4 sheets round on the desk for Falcón to look at.

The first shot showed Marty off to the left of the frame, sitting on a bench by the river. He was not the focus of the shot. The man sitting next to him was a stranger to both Marty and Falcón.

'The second shot is a blow-up of the background of a larger shot,' said Ferrera.

In this shot Marty Krugman was turned sideways on the bench and was talking to a man Falcón immediately recognized as Mark Flowers.

'And these are off the hard disk?' said Falcón. 'No film negatives?'

She handed over a CD in its box.

'She used two cameras. If she saw something she thought she liked she used 35 mm film. If she was just snapping people generally she used a digital camera. The only record of these two shots are on this CD and in her laptop.'

'I can see this took a lot of hard, boring work.'

'I know it would have been better to have had negatives,' she said.

'This is good enough,' said Falcón. 'None of this is going to end up in court. Where's Inspector Ramírez?'

'He's downstairs, setting up the interrogation rooms,' said Ferrera. 'He's very excited. He found something good in the arsonist's apartment.'

'I want you to take this to the lab,' said Falcón, handing her the used razor blade he'd found in the finca. 'There are bristles on the blades. It's a long shot, but I want them to run a DNA test on it and make a comparison with Rafael Vega.'

'By the way, Sra Krugman's laptop is in the evidence room,' said Ferrera, 'but I left everything else at the house.'

'What about the keys?'

She pushed them across the desk at him.

'One other thing,' said Falcón, giving her the paper with the Cyrillic script. 'You remember the Russian translator we used with Nadia Kouzmikheva? Ask her to translate that for us. Tomorrow will do.'

Ramírez was sitting in interrogation room 4, with his elbows on his knees and his head hanging down. Smoke rose from the fingers of his right hand. He didn't move when Falcón entered the room. He didn't move until Falcón touched him on the shoulder. He sat back slowly, as if in pain.

'What's the problem, José Luis?'

'I've been checking a tape.'

'What tape?'

'I've revised my opinion of the arsonists. They were bloody idiots, *tontos perdidos*. They went in there with the minds of petty thieves and before they torched the finca they stole a TV and video recorder. And inside the video recorder . . .'

'. . . was a tape,' said Falcón, galvanized by the development.

'And it was what I thought it would be – child pornography. But what I didn't expect was to recognize one of the participants.'

'Not Montes?'

'No, no – thank God. That would have been too terrible. This was a guy from the barrio. You remember I told you about the one who'd done very well for himself, but it was never enough? He had to come back and tell us all how rich and important he had become . . . ram it down our throats. He was the cabrón on the tape.'

'So this tape is a recording of events filmed in the finca?'

'I presume so, but I didn't get beyond the first minute. I started feeling sick.'

'Elvira's going to have to know about this,' said Falcón. 'But is there any way we can make a copy of it before we send it upstairs?'

Ramírez gave him a long hard look.

'Don't tell me what I think you're going to tell me,' he said.

'Elvira is on our side.'

'Sure he is,' said Ramírez. 'Until someone starts treading on his balls.'

'That's why we make the copy – because they're already treading,' said Falcón. 'But they're in ballet shoes at the moment.'

'You wait,' said Ramírez. 'When they hear about this tape, especially if there's someone important on it, they'll be down here in their cuban heels.'

Ramírez drummed the floor of the interrogation room with his feet.

'Who knows you've got the tape?'

'Nobody. The TV and video recorder were dumped inside the arsonists' front door. It was only when I got them back here that I thought to look and see if the video was loaded.'

'Good. Then we copy the tape, hand over the original, and see what happens.'

'Do you know how to copy tapes?'

'I know you need two VCRs.'

'And we can't do it here,' said Ramírez. 'And we can't ask anybody to explain how it's done in small, easy to understand words, or the whole Jefatura will know.'

'You've got a machine at home and so have I,' said Falcón. 'Get one of your kids to explain to you how to copy a tape and bring your machine over to my place where it's quiet.'

Falcón set up the video ready to show the interviewees what they'd stolen. Ramírez gave him the vehicle details, the record of its sightings in the garages, a copy of the CCTV tape and the hat worn by one of the arsonists, who was called Carlos Delgado.

'Have we got a photo of Ignacio Ortega to show them?' asked Ramírez.

'Not a clear one,' said Falcón. 'But they'll know his name and they'll be very scared to say it, I'm sure. Knock on the door when you need to use the tape.'

'First one to get a confession. Loser buys the beer,' said Ramírez.

The two arsonists were brought down. Ramírez took Pedro Gómez. Falcón sat down with Carlos Delgado and made the necessary introductions to the tape recorder.

'What were you doing on Saturday night and early Sunday morning, Carlos?'

'Sleeping.'

'Were you with your friend Pedro?'

'We live in the same apartment.'

'And he was with you that night?'

'He's in the next room, why don't you ask him?'

'Was anybody else there?'

Carlos shook his head. Falcón showed him a shot of the pick-up.

'Is this yours?'

Carlos looked down, nodded.

'Were you using this vehicle on Saturday night or Sunday morning?'

'We went to see Pedro's aunt in Castillo . . . about eleven o'clock on Sunday morning.'

'Do you know who was using your vehicle on Saturday night, Sunday morning?'

'No.'

'Is this your hat?'

'Yes,' said Carlos. Then, after a few beats: 'Who are you guys with? You ask about my car . . . my hat. What the fuck's all this about?'

'We're investigating a very serious sex crime.'

'A sex crime? We haven't committed any sex crime.'

Falcón asked him to come over to the TV screen while he played the CCTV tape from the garage. The screen revealed the grey images of the pick-up arriving, Carlos getting out, filling up the jerry cans and going to pay in the shop. Javier froze the frame.

'That pick-up has the same registration as the one on the table, which you said is yours.'

'We didn't commit any sex crime.'

'But that is your pick-up?'

'Yes.'

'And this person is you, paying for the petrol?'

'That's me, but I didn't –'

'That's OK. That's all I need to know.'

'What's this sex crime?' asked Carlos. 'Somebody rape the girl in the shop?'

'What did you do with the jerry cans, once you'd filled them up?'

'We went home.'

'Straight away?'

'Yes. We bought the petrol for Pedro's aunt.'

'But you'd been to this garage before, and a couple of other ones where you filled two jerry cans in each. And you filled up others at petrol stations on the way out to the turn-off to Aracena. What were you doing out there?'

Silence.

'Why did you drive all the way up to Almonaster la Real with all that petrol in your pick-up?'

'We didn't.'

'You didn't,' said Falcón. 'You know, Carlos, arson is a serious offence, but that's not the only thing we're interested in at the moment. What we want to do is put you away for a very long time for a sex crime as well.'

'I haven't committed any –'

'When you were picked up in your apartment, Inspector Ramírez searched it and found a television and a video recorder in your possession.'

'They're not ours.'

'What are they doing in your apartment with your fingerprints on them?'

'That stuff isn't ours.'

'Come with me.'

'I don't want to come with you.'

'We're just going to the television.'

'No.'

Falcón pushed the television closer. He removed the CCTV tape and put in the other tape. He turned up the volume and pressed play. The scream from the television even made him jump. Carlos Delgado kicked his chair back, waved his hands at the screen and then gripped his thick, curly hair, as if for support.

'No, no, no. Stop it. That's nothing to do with us,' he shouted.

'It was in your possession.'

'Turn it off. Just turn it off.'

Falcón stopped the tape. Carlos was shaken. They sat.

'Child abuse is a very serious offence,' said Falcón. 'People convicted of such crimes go to prison for a long time and have miserable lives there. Most choose to go into solitary confinement for the seven to ten years of their sentence.'

'We stole the television and the video recorder,' said Carlos.

'Where from?'

Carlos told the story. They'd been paid 1,500 euros to buy petrol and been given directions and a key to the finca. They'd set fire to the place, as they'd been asked to do, and they stole the stuff on the way out. That was all. They had no idea what was in it. They just wanted a bit of extra cash for the equipment. Falcón nodded, encouraging more exonerating detail.

'Who paid you the fifteen hundred euros to do this?' he asked.

'I don't know his name.'

'How do you know him? How does he know you?' asked Falcón. 'You don't ask just anybody to burn a house down. That's a serious thing, isn't it? There has to be some trust. You only trust people you know.'

Silence from Carlos as he swallowed hard.

'Are you afraid of this man?' asked Falcón.

Carlos shook his head.

'How old are you?'

'Thirty-three.'

'You're a Sevillano. You've never lived anywhere else?'

'That's right.'

'Still got friends from your childhood?'

'Pedro. Pedro's the only one.'

'You're the same age?'

He nodded, unable to think where this was going.

'When was the last time you saw your old childhood friend Salvador Ortega?'

Carlos was stunned. He sat there blinking, uncomprehending.

'I don't know anybody called Salvador Ortega,' he said.

Falcón felt something cold developing in his stomach.

'Was the name of the man who gave you fifteen hundred euros to burn down the finca Ignacio Ortega?'

Carlos shook his head. Falcón looked into his eyes and knew that he'd never heard that name before, that it inspired no fear, no dread and no horrific memories.

'Tell me the name of the man who paid you to burn down the finca. Speak clearly, please.'

'Alberto Montes.'

Falcón left the room and knocked on Ramírez's door. He leaned against the wall in the corridor feeling sick.

'You got him already?' asked Ramírez, closing the door.

'I didn't get the right result, though,' said Falcón. 'I should have thought this out properly. I've been believing in my own stupid instinct too much. He's just named Alberto Montes.'

307

'Joder,' said Ramírez, thumping the wall.

'And now it's all fallen into place,' said Falcón. 'This is precisely what Montes would have done. He'd panic, or his self-disgust would finally get the better of him, or both, and he'd just want to get rid of the problem. Burn the place down. Except . . . the whole sierra caught fire, thousands of hectares were destroyed. And he'd blown it again. That's why he jumped.

'The day I saw Ignacio Ortega I knew he was a cunning little bastard and I didn't think. He's on a different level. The reason why we're getting the pressure is that he's told those people to put pressure on us. He would never do anything as stupid and unsubtle as arson. He's gone straight to the top of his client list and told them to stop us dead, or face the consequences.'

Carlos and Pedro were sent back down to the cells without writing their statements. Falcón took the audio tape of Carlos's confession and kept it with him. He picked up Maddy Krugman's laptop from the evidence room. Ramírez went home. They reconvened at Falcón's house and copied the tape. It was grim viewing, but they realized it was the product of a secret camera hidden in the wall of one particular room. It featured only four clients. The businessman from Ramírez's barrio, a well-known defence lawyer, a TV presenter and an unknown.

'This is how the Russians get things done,' said Ramírez, as they packed everything away. 'I don't know why they do it. I'm not a clever lawyer or businessman and I can't think of any sexual excitement that would induce me to expose myself to such risk.'

'This isn't about sex,' said Falcón. 'This is about damage. Having had damage done to you, or doing damage to others. Sex is a long way from what's going on on that tape.'

'Whatever,' said Ramírez, pouring out another two beers. 'We've done this. We've made the copy of the tape. And now what? We're fucked, aren't we? This isn't going anywhere. As soon as it comes out that Montes paid the arsonists, we're dead in the water. We have to keep our mouths shut or they go through us with a hobnail enema.'

'Elvira gave me a lecture about not being too zealous in the pursuit of justice in this case,' said Falcón. 'Institutions are protected by powerful people who want to hold on to power and they will ensure that I never get what I want. But when you see something like this, and that finca out in the sierra, and you begin to understand the level of corruption that made it possible, I start thinking that maybe we should clear the whole lot out and start again. I've realized that I'm very naïve when it comes to these elevated heights of operation.'

'Well, you know who that will include, if you want to clear out the old,' said Ramírez, tapping his chest. 'My past is not so sweet. I think that priest I confessed to aged a decade when he heard me out.'

'What are we talking about, José Luis? A few favours from hookers?'

'It's not good,' he said, shrugging. 'In this sort of atmosphere, nobody gets let off.'

'You're not in the same league as these people.'

'And you know what it is about these people?' said Ramírez, the beer hitting his empty stomach. 'That cabrón from the barrio – he's successful, wealthy, has a couple of houses here, some more on the coast, a yacht, a speedboat, more cars than trousers, and yet he still wants more. You see, there's only so much lobster you can eat, only so much champagne you can drink, only so many pretty girls you can fuck for money . . . and then what?'

'The excitement of the forbidden fruit,' said Falcón. 'So, maybe I was wrong, before. Maybe it isn't about damage, at this level. Maybe it's about power. The power to do these things with impunity.'

'I'd better go. I can see where this evening is heading,' said Ramírez. 'But I tell you, once they get hold of the Montes shit, they're going to make sure we live in fear.'

'Did you see the printouts Cristina found of Marty Krugman?'

'I didn't recognize the guy he was talking to.'

'He's called Mark Flowers,' said Falcón. 'He's the communications officer at the American Consulate.'

'Hah! Not so crazy Krugman.'

'There's probably a very reasonable explanation for it.'

'They were lovers,' said Ramírez. 'Good night.'

Desperate for some good news, Falcón called Alicia Aguado and was glad to find her still elated after her session with Sebastián Ortega.

The first big step had been taken. He'd revealed the extent of the sexual abuse he'd suffered at the hands of Ignacio Ortega. Despite the horror of what the boy had been through, the breakthrough had made her happy – the healing process had started. Falcón longed for that sort of job satisfaction. Instead, on nights like these, with the arrowroot stalks of fortune up in the air, he could only see his work as a desperate shoring-up of the breakdowns, a sticky plaster applied to the gourd-sized stinking abscess in the body of society. He wished her well and hung up.

He hid the video behind two locked doors in Francisco's old studio. Back in the study, he checked he had Krugman's house keys, the laptop, the printout of Mark Flowers, and his loaded revolver. He drove out to Santa Clara and parked his car in Consuelo's driveway. He went in to explain his night's work to her and she insisted on feeding him. She was not herself. She was listless, quiet, distracted, even depressed. She said she was missing her children, that she was worried about them even with the police protection, but there seemed to be something else as well. At 10.30 p.m. he walked across to the Krugmans' house, let himself in and went upstairs and put Maddy Krugman's laptop back in her work room. He went to the bedroom, switched off his mobile, lay down and dozed fitfully.

At two o'clock in the morning his eyes opened to a sharp click from downstairs. He waited and listened to the complete silence of a good thief at work. There was no sound for several minutes. Then a flashlight came on in the corridor outside the bedroom. He was a first-rate, methodical thief, not a cheap, rowdy one, prone to defecating on the floor. He went into Maddy Krugman's work room. There was a sound like a nylon zip opening as the thief booted up the laptop.

Even breathing sounds loud when a good thief is at work. But while he was waiting for the laptop to boot up he was using the time to go through the physical prints. Falcón used that noise to get off the bed, wait for the feeling to come back into his right hand, take out his revolver and walk down the corridor towards the light bouncing in the room.

'Are you looking for this?' he asked, holding out his gun.

The thief looked up from the laptop, whose screen lit his irritation. He sat back on Maddy's work stool and put his hands on his close-cropped head and looked bored.

'I'm not interested in you,' said Falcón. 'I'm interested in what you do when you've found what he wants.'

'I call him and we meet down by the river.'

'Call him and tell him you got lucky,' said Falcón. 'Slow movements.'

The thief made the call, which took seconds because he said only one word: 'Romany'. They went down to Falcón's car and the thief drove them back into the city. They parked on Cristobal Colón and went down the steps to the walkway by the river. They waited in the dark. After some minutes footsteps came down on to the walkway. A man stood looking around. Falcón came at him from the shadows.

'Is this what you're looking for, Mr Flowers?' asked Falcón, holding out the printout lit by his pen torch.

Flowers nodded, studying the shot.

'I think we should take a seat,' he said.

The thief ran off up the steps. Flowers handed back the printout. He took out a handkerchief.

'Sorry for underestimating you, Inspector Jefe,' said Flowers, wiping his brow and face. 'I came down here from Madrid ten months ago. The Madrileños have a rather jaded view of the Sevillano mentality. I should have been less crude in my methods.'

'Ten months ago?'

'We're taking a more active interest in our North African friends and the way they come into Europe since last September.'

'Of course you are,' said Falcón. 'And how did Marty Krugman fit into all that?'

'He didn't,' said Flowers. 'The Vega business was a side issue, although we got a fright when we heard about his "suicide note", until we found out where that came from.'

'Which was?'

'It had been scratched on to the wall of one of the cells in the Villa Grimaldi torture centre in Santiago de Chile by an American called Todd Kravitz, who was held there for a month in 1974 before being "disappeared",' said Flowers. 'The full inscription reads: *We will be in the thin air you breathe from 9/11 until the end of time.* Poetic enough to stick in his mind and come back nearly thirty years later to haunt him.'

'He mentioned to his doctor that he was having sleepwalking problems,' said Falcón, 'but not the unconscious writing.'

'The pressures on a mind that didn't know it was guilty,' said Flowers.

'Let's talk about Marty Krugman,' said Falcón. 'Why don't we start with what he was doing, and who was he doing it for?'

'That's a little more awkward for us to discuss.'

'This isn't America, Mr Flowers. I'm not wearing a wire. My only interest as the Inspector Jefe del Grupo de Homicidios is who murdered Rafael Vega and why.'

'I have to take precautions,' said Flowers.

Falcón stood. Flowers frisked him expertly, found the gun immediately. They sat back down.

'The Vega business was not strictly a government operation,' said Flowers. 'It was more of an Agency issue – Company business. The tying up of loose ends.'

'But there was co-operation between the FBI and the Agency, which extended to allowing Krugman to walk away from the Reza Sangari killing.'

'They couldn't make a case without Marty cracking up and confessing the whole thing to them, and I told you about his trips to Chile in the seventies. What I didn't tell you was that the Chilean authorities did eventually catch up with him and he spent three weeks in the London Clinic, which was another torture centre, on Calle Almirante Barroso. In three weeks of punishment he didn't give anybody up. The only reason he didn't suffer the same fate as Todd Kravitz was because it was later on in the game and the human rights people were being more assiduous by then. This was not a guy who was going to crack under some FBI questioning.'

'So you thought it was fitting that he should be reporting back to you on someone who had been a notorious member of that régime?' said Falcón.

'Most Europeans think that Americans have no sense of irony, Inspector Jefe.'

'Was that why you didn't give him any information on Rafael Vega's real identity?'

'One of the reasons,' said Flowers. 'But if you're supposed to be reporting back on the state of mind of a person, it's better not to have your insight distorted by history.'

'What was so important about Vega's state of mind?'

'This was a guy we lost track of in 1982 when he absconded from a witness protection programme.'

'So that was true about him testifying in a drug-trafficking trial?'

'That was the surface truth. He held some damaging information about US Army officers and Agency personnel who were involved in running drugs for arms back in the late seventies and early eighties, so we cut a deal. He would act as a witness in a show trial and we would give him a new identity and fifty thousand dollars. He took both and disappeared. We couldn't find him anywhere.'

'But you knew about the wife and daughter?'

'That's all we could do, keep an eye on them and hope that he resurfaced. He was careful. He didn't come back for his daughter's wedding, which we were all expecting, and we assumed he was dead. We stopped watching, but we did send someone down to his wife's funeral.'

'When was that?'

'Not that long ago, something like three years – I can't remember exactly. But the funeral was when we found him again. He'd finally thought he was safe,' said Flowers. 'We researched his life, found that he was a successful businessman and thought that we had nothing to worry about, until the Russian mafia connection came to light about eighteen months ago.'

'Did you think he was in the arms dealing business again?'

'We just thought we'd better take a closer look at Rafael Vega,' said Flowers. 'But, I lied to you earlier, we did train him. He knew our ways. He knew our type of people. So we looked for other candidates and that was where the FBI came in. Marty Krugman was our perfect candidate – apart from some instability in his marriage.'

'Do you know what I'm feeling now, Sr Flowers?' said Falcón. 'That you're giving me just enough information to satisfy my curiosity.'

'The full story would take a long time.'

'One moment you're talking about tying up loose ends and the next you're talking about reporting on his state of mind.'

'It was both.'

'What "loose ends" were you really nervous about?'

'We had begun to think that he might be operating again in some way,' said Flowers. 'It's an addictive profession, Inspector Jefe. We found out that he'd bought a passport in the name of Emilio Cruz and that he'd taken Moroccan visas.'

'I assumed that was his escape route.'

'What did he need to escape from?'

'Maybe it was from you, Sr Flowers,' said Falcón.

'He had the Emilio Cruz passport before we put Marty Krugman next to him, before we discovered his Russian mafia connection.'

'Why did he run from the witness protection programme in the first place?'

'They're living deaths, those things,' said Flowers. 'I'd have done the same.'

'Did he have good reason to believe that his daughter's family was not killed in an accident?'

'That was twenty years after he'd absconded,' said Flowers. 'It's one of the unfortunate side effects of an addiction to this profession – you can never take things at face value. People die in road accidents all the time, Inspector Jefe.'

'And did you discover what the Russian mafia connection was all about?'

'He allowed them to launder money through his projects and they indulged his paedophilia. I understand he liked to watch. El Salido, remember?'

'So what was Marty's job – if you already knew all that?'

Silence from Sr Flowers. A big, bored sigh.

'When did you tell him that Rafael Vega was Miguel Velasco?' asked Falcón.

'No, no, you're wrong there, Inspector Jefe. I'm not lying to you about that,' said Flowers. 'You're thinking we told him, and because of his past involvement in Chilean politics that was enough to incite him to murder.'

'Forcing a man to drink acid . . .' said Falcón.

'It's a nasty way to die,' said Flowers. 'It *sounds* like a revenge killing. But I want to be clear on that. We did not give away Vega's real identity. We did not want Vega dead. You have to believe Marty when he told you –'

'So what did you want to know?'

'We're not sure.'

'This doesn't sound very convincing, Sr Flowers,' said Falcón.

'Probably because it's the truth, and we've developed this magnificent myth about American infallibility.'

'How about this for a theory. . .' said Falcón. 'You wanted to know his state of mind because you were worried that he had information that would further compromise more important members of the US administration of that era. The Secretary of State, for instance.'

'We were worried that if he did have something he might look for ways of using it against us, but we didn't know what it could be.'

'Who is "us"?' asked Falcón.

'That is all I'm saying on the matter,' said Flowers. 'You told me that your concern was whether Krugman killed him, and I can tell you that he didn't. Be satisfied.'

'How can I be sure of that?'

'Because Marty Krugman was with me on the night that Rafael Vega died, from between two and five o'clock in the morning,' said Flowers. 'I have a timed and dated recording of that meeting because it took place in the American Consulate.'

29

Wednesday, 31st July 2002

On the way to the Jefatura Falcón stopped for a café solo on the Avenida de Argentina. He felt bleary and down like everybody else in the bar. The heat had wrung all the natural *alegría* out of the Sevillanos, leaving some introverted version of themselves to wander the streets and populate the bars.

There was no sign of Ramírez or Ferrera in the office. He took the audio tapes of the interviews with the arsonists and the original videotape stolen from the Montes finca and went up to Elvira's office. He met Ramírez coming down.

'I spoke to the arsonists again and asked them how they knew Montes,' said Ramírez. 'Twenty years ago Montes used to run a youth football side for disadvantaged kids. They were on his team. I've just checked it with the inspector from GRUME and I've had a proper look at their files. Montes was involved in helping them with all their brushes with the law.'

'Did they know Montes had killed himself?'

Ramírez shook his head, wished him good luck with Elvira.

He was not allowed in to see the Comisario, not even into the secretary's office. She put him in the corridor with the single-word explanation: Lobo.

Ten minutes later he was called in. Lobo stood by the window, arms folded across his chest – tense, angry. Elvira sat at his desk, his face drawn, as if he'd been there all night.

'What have you got for us?' asked Lobo, leaping the chain of command in his fury.

'Two audio recordings of the arsonists –'

'Did they name Ignacio Ortega?'

'No, they named Alberto Montes.'

Lobo pounded Elvira's table with three devastating blows that jumped his pencils into disarray.

'What else?' said Lobo.

'One video tape with footage from a hidden camera in the finca, showing four men participating in sexual acts with minors.'

'Are any of them known to us?'

'There's a defence lawyer and a TV presenter.'

'Joder,' said Lobo.

'Ramírez can identify one of the other men – a businessman who comes from his barrio. The fourth is unknown.'

'Who knows about this tape?'

'Ramírez and myself.'

'Keep it that way,' said Lobo, still brutal with rage.

'What about the arsonists?' asked Elvira.

'I don't think they knew what they'd stolen.'

'So, the only link between Ignacio Ortega and Montes's finca is that he installed the air-conditioning units,' said Elvira. 'You have no proof that he was procuring children from the Russians for use at the finca. And you have no proof that he brought clients to the finca to participate in sexual acts with minors.'

'That is correct,' said Falcón, knowing this had all gone wrong before he'd even started. 'The only way I could establish that he was taking clients to the finca is by speaking to the men on the tape.'

'Is there anything on the video that proves the footage comes from the Montes finca?' asked Lobo.

'That's difficult to say now that the building has been completely gutted by fire.'

'Have you had a report back from Felipe and Jorge about their findings?'

'Not yet. They probably stayed up in the sierra last night. They were still working at seven o'clock in the evening when I left. The lab technicians here will be working their way through the first batch of evidence. Hopefully there will be some surviving fingerprints on –'

'I tried to call you last night,' said Lobo.

'I had my mobile switched off,' said Falcón. 'I was working on my other case – Rafael Vega.'

'What progress there?'

Falcón gave his report on his meeting with Mark Flowers.

'I think I should have a meeting with the American Consul about that,' said Lobo.

'How does that leave you with your investigation?' asked Elvira.

'Juez Calderón gave me forty-eight hours. My time is up. I'm finished. I have no suspects and, unless Sergei the gardener turns up, I have no possible witnesses or leads,' said Falcón.

'What about this safe-deposit box key you found in Vega's house?' asked Elvira.

'It belongs to a box kept in the name of Emilio Cruz at the Banco Banesto. Juez Calderón has not had time to supply a search warrant yet.'

'You'll keep us informed when he does,' said Elvira.

'You might have to content yourself with the fact that Rafael Vega was a bad man who either punished himself or got what he deserved,' said Lobo.

'I expect Juez Calderón to terminate the case when I see him later this morning,' said Falcón. 'In terms of connecting Ignacio Ortega to the finca, we have one final possibility with the two bodies buried on the property.'

'Any thoughts about what happened there?'

'In the corner of one cell by the bed I found an inscription scratched into the wall in Cyrillic script. I'm having it translated. I suspect that it has something to do with the large stain in the middle of the floor, which I did not see until all contents were removed. The stain is likely to be blood. A sample of the concrete is being tested. In the mattress of the same room I found a piece of glass. I assume there was another piece which was used by the occupants of the cell to slash their wrists. I suspect that these two bodies were suicides.

'A local Juez de Instrucción was being used at the crime scene at the finca. I would suggest that a Juez de Instrucción is appointed to oversee the case here, as this is where all the evidence will be processed and will be where we hope to convict Ignacio Ortega.'

'That is being discussed with the Juez Decano de Sevilla at the moment,' said Elvira. 'What do you intend to do now, Inspector Jefe?'

'The obvious move is to establish a link to Ignacio Ortega by questioning one or more of the men on the video tape. Once he's confirmed as the central figure in this paedophile network we can bring him in and proceed in the direction of the Russian mafiosi –

Vladimir Ivanov and Mikhail Zelenov,' said Falcón. 'I realize that the last element in that very ugly equation might be the most difficult to satisfy.'

Elvira's drawn features eased away from the intensity of Falcón's glare. They both ended up looking at the darkening cumin complexion of Lobo's furious face.

'For the moment, Inspector Jefe,' he said, 'in the light of what you've just told us about one of our senior officer's involvement in this case, I am going to ask you to do nothing and say nothing.'

In the silence that followed that request, which included a weighty admission, the questions started stacking up in Falcón's mind. He couldn't ask a single one. He said good morning and went to the desk to pick up the tapes.

'Best to leave those,' said Lobo.

Falcón's hand withdrew as if the wolf had snapped.

Down in the outer office Ramírez was sitting with his feet up, smoking. He put a finger to his lips, nodded next door and mouthed the words Virgilio Guzmán.

'I can't talk to you now, Virgilio,' said Falcón, walking behind Guzmán and into his chair.

'About what?'

'Anything.'

'What about Alfonso Martinez and Enrique Altozano?'

'One is in intensive care, the other has disappeared.'

'Enrique Altozano miraculously *reappeared* this morning,' said Guzmán. 'Doesn't that sound like someone who's been told the coast is clear?'

'It can sound like anything to speculative minds.'

'All right,' said Guzmán. 'Shall I tell you about Miguel Velasco?'

'I already know about him.'

'What do you know?'

'That he was in the Chilean military . . .'

'That's a bit vague.'

'Is it going to help me to know any more than that?'

'I'll give you the short history and then you tell me,' said Guzmán. 'He was born in 1944, the son of a Santiago butcher. He was an alumnus of the Catholic University and a member of Patria y Libertad. His mother died in 1967 from a heart attack. He joined the Chilean military in 1969. After the coup he was transferred to the force that was eventually to become the DINA in June 1974. His father, who did not like Allende's politics but also did not agree with the Pinochet coup, disappeared in October 1973 and was never seen again. During his service with the DINA he became one of the chief interrogators at the Villa Grimaldi and a close personal friend of the Head of the DINA – Colonel Manuel Contreras.'

'That note he held in his hand when he died, I heard that it was an inscription on a cell wall in the Villa Grimaldi,' said Falcón. 'I was also told he was known by the MIR as El Salido.'

'Perhaps you didn't hear about his work at the Venda Sexy,' said Guzmán. 'That was the name of a torture centre at 3037 Calle Irán, in the Quílú quarter of Santiago de Chile. It was also known as La Discoteca because loud music was heard coming from it day and night. Before Miguel Velasco was moved to the Villa Grimaldi he devised the techniques practised there. He forced family members to watch and participate in taboo sexual acts such as incest and paedophilia. Sometimes he would encourage his fellow torturers to join in.'

'That helps explain things . . . or rather, not explain but . . .'

'Tell me.'

'Finish the biography, Virgilio.'

'He was an outstanding interrogator, and from the Villa Grimaldi he was moved to one of the active cells in Operation Condor, specializing in kidnappings, interrogations and assassinations abroad. In 1978 he was moved to the Chilean Embassy in Stockholm, where he headed covert operations against the Chilean expatriate community. He transferred back into the military in late 1979 and it's believed that he received some CIA training prior to developing a lucrative "drugs for arms" business. That trade was exposed in 1981 and there followed a trial in which he acted as a witness for the prosecution. In 1982 he was put into a witness protection programme, from which he disappeared almost immediately.'

'Stockholm?' asked Falcón.

'The Swedish Prime Minister, Olaf Palme, was vociferous in his disgust at the Pinochet régime. In the days after September 11th, the Swedish Ambassador in Santiago, Harald Edelstam, ran around the capital extending asylum to anyone who was resisting the coup and so Stockholm, naturally, became a centre for a European anti-Pinochet movement. A DINA/CNI cell was set up there to run drug-smuggling operations in Europe and to spy on Chilean expatriates.'

'Interesting . . . but none of it helps me any more,' said Falcón. 'That case is about to be closed.'

'I can sense some disappointment in you, Javier.'

'You can sense what you like, Virgilio, I've got nothing to talk to you about.'

'People think I'm a bore, because a lot of my sentences start with the phrase "When I was working the death squads story . . ."' said Guzmán.

Ramírez grunted his agreement from the outer office.

'You must have learned a lot . . .'

'During that investigation I always managed to turn up in people's offices at crucial times,' said Guzmán. 'Call it zeitgeist or tapping into the collective unconscious. Do you believe in all that crap, Javier?'

'Yes.'

'You've become monosyllabic, Javier. It's one of the first signs.'

'Of what?'

'That I haven't lost my sense of timing,' said Guzmán. 'What do you think the collective unconscious is?'

'I'm not in the mood, Virgilio.'

'Where have I heard that before?'

'In your own bed,' Ramírez shouted from the outer office.

'Have a go, Javier.'

'You're not going to talk your way in here,' said Falcón, pushing over a note with his home address and *10 p.m.* written on it.

'Do you know why I left Madrid?' said Guzmán, ignoring the note. 'I was pushed. If you ask people why, they'll tell you that I'd started to live in a hall of mirrors. I didn't know what was real any more. I was paranoid. But the reality was that I was pushed because I'd become a zealot. I got that way because the stories I would run with always had something that made me writhe with rage. I couldn't control it. I'd become the worst thing possible – the emotional journalist.'

'We don't allow that in the police force, either . . . or we all start cracking up.'

'It's an incurable disease,' said Guzmán. 'I know that now, because when I read what Velasco used to get up to in the Venda Sexy I hit that same white-hot vein of rage. That's what he used to do to human beings. Not just torture them, but fill them with his own appalling corruption. And the next thing I know I'm back to thinking *that* was Pinochet. *That's* what Pinochet thought of human beings. And why was he there? Because Nixon and Kissinger wanted him there. They would rather have someone who promoted the electrocution of genitals, the raping of women, the abuse of children than . . . than what? Than a tubby, bespectacled little Marxist who was going to make life difficult for the rich. Now you see my problem, Javier. I have become what my bosses used to call me – my own worst enemy. You're not allowed to feel, you're only allowed to report the facts. But, you see, it's in that feeling that my instinct lies and it hasn't failed me, because I know that the rage I felt when I found out about Miguel Velasco's speciality guided me here this morning. And it's guided me here because it wants my nose to be in the door of the cover-up as it slams shut.'

Guzmán snatched up the note, kicked back his chair and stormed out.

Ramírez loomed large in the doorway, looking back at the vapour trail left by Guzmán in the outer office.

'He's going to do himself some harm if he carries on like that,' said Ramírez. 'Is he right?'

'Did you see me come back with anything?' asked Falcón, opening his hands to show no tapes.

'Lobo's a good man,' said Ramírez, pointing a big finger at him. 'He won't let us down.'

'Lobo's a good man in a different position,' said Falcón. 'You don't get to be Jefe Superior de la Policía de Sevilla unless people want you to be. He has political pressure on his shoulders and he has a big mess in his own house, left by Alberto Montes.'

'What about the bodies of those two kids up in the Sierra de Aracena? They've been seen. Everybody knows about them. No one can hide that sort of thing.'

'If they were local kids, then of course not. But who are they?' said Falcón. 'They've been dead a year. The only piece of really usable evidence we've got from the house is the video tape and, as Lobo pointed out, we can't even prove that what they were doing took place in Montes's finca. Our only chance is if we're *allowed* to interview those people on the tape.'

Ramírez walked over to the window and put his hands up against the glass.

'First of all we had to listen to Nadia Kouzmikheva's story and do nothing. Now we're going to watch these cabrones walk away, too?'

'Nothing is certain.'

'We have the tape,' said Ramírez.

'After what Montes has done we have to be very careful about the tape,' said Falcón. '*That* is not something to proceed with lightly. Now I'm going out.'

'Where to?'

'To do something that I hope will make me feel better about myself.'

On the way out of the office he bumped into Cristina Ferrera, who had been to see the Russian translator about the inscription on the wall of the finca.

'Leave it on my desk,' said Falcón. 'I can't bear to look at it.'

Falcón drove across the river and along Avenida del Torneo. As the road swung away from the river towards La Macarena he turned right and into La Alameda. He parked and walked along Calle Jesus del Gran Poder. This was Pablo Ortega's old barrio. He was looking for a house on Calle Lumbreras, which belonged to the parents of the boy, Manolo López, who had been the victim in Sebastián Ortega's case. He had not called ahead because he didn't think the parents would welcome this new intrusion, especially given what he'd heard about the father's health problems.

He walked through the cooking smells of olive oil and garlic and up to the house where the boy's parents lived. It was a small apartment building in need of repair and paint. He rang the doorbell. Sra López answered it and stared hard at his police ID. She didn't want him to come in, but couldn't find the confidence to ask him to leave them alone. The apartment was small, airless and very hot. Sra López sat him down at a table with a lace cover and a bowl of plastic flowers and went to bring her husband. The room was full of Mariolatry. Virgins hung on walls, found themselves cornered on bookshelves and blessed stacks of magazines. A candle burned in a niche.

Sra López steered her husband into the room as if he was a lame cow in need of milking. He looked to be in his late forties but was very unsteady on his feet, which made him seem older. She got him into a chair. One arm seemed to be dead, hanging useless at his side. He picked up Falcón's ID card with a shaky hand.

'Homicidios?' he said.

'Not on this occasion,' said Falcón. 'I wanted to talk to you about your son's kidnapping.'

'I can't talk about that,' he said, and immediately started to get to his feet.

His wife helped him out of the room. Falcón watched the complicated process in a state of increasing desolation.

'He can't talk about it,' she said, coming back to the table. 'He hasn't been the same since . . . since . . .'

'Since Manolo disappeared?'

'No, no . . . it was afterwards. It was after the trial that he lost his job. His legs started to behave strangely, they felt as if they had ants crawling all over them. He became unsteady. One hand started shaking, the other arm seemed to give up. Now he does nothing all day. He moves from here to the bedroom and back . . . that's it.'

'But Manolo is all right, isn't he?'

'He's fine. It's as if it never happened. He's on holiday . . . camping with his nephews and cousins.'

'So, you have much older children as well?'

'I had a boy and a girl when I was eighteen and nineteen, and then twenty years later Manolo came along.'

'Did Manolo have any reaction to what had happened to him?'

'Not exactly to what happened to *him*,' said Sra López. 'He's always been a happy boy in himself. He was more disturbed by what happened to Sebastián Ortega. He finds it difficult to imagine him in prison.'

'So, what's been bothering your husband?' said Falcón. 'He seems to be the one who has reacted badly.'

'He can't talk about it,' she said. 'It's something to do with what happened with Manolo, but I can't get him to say what it is.'

'Is he ashamed? That's not an unusual reaction.'

'For Manolo? He says not.'

'Would you mind if I talk to him on his own?'

'You won't get anywhere.'

'I have some new information which might help him,' he said.

'The last door to the left at the end of the corridor,' she said.

Sr López was lying on the dark wooden bed under a crucifix. A ceiling fan barely disturbed the thick stale air. He had his eyes closed. One hand twitched where it lay across his stomach. The other lay dead by his side. Falcón touched him on the shoulder. His eyes stared out from a frightened mind.

'All you have to do is listen to me,' said Falcón. 'I am no man's judge. I've come here to try to put things right, that's all.'

Sr López blinked once, as if this was a devised sign language.

'Investigations are strange things,' said Falcón. 'We set off on a journey to find out what happened, only to find that more things happen on the way. Investigations have a life of their own. We think we are running them, but sometimes they run us. When I heard what Sebastián Ortega had done, it had nothing to do with the investigation I was working on, but I was fascinated by it. I was fascinated because in those cases it's very rare for the victim to be allowed to leave and for him to bring the police to where the perpetrator is waiting to be arrested. Do you understand what I'm saying, Sr López?'

He blinked once again. Falcón told him about the Jefatura and how stories circulate and how he'd heard about what had really happened in Manolo's case. The demand for a stronger statement to help the prosecution's case was not an unusual occurrence. That Sebastián would not defend himself against the stronger statement was unforeseen and resulted in a much harsher sentence than the actual crime merited.

'I have no idea what is playing on your mind, Sr López. All I know is – through no fault of your own, and perhaps because of Sebastián's own mental problems – an unnecessarily severe justice has been done. I am here to tell you that, if you so wish, you can help balance the scales. All you have to do is call me. If I do not hear from you, you will never see me again.'

Falcón left his card on the bedside table. Sr López lay on the bed, staring up at the slow fan. On the way out Falcón said goodbye to Sra López, who took him to the door.

'Pablo Ortega told me that he had to leave this barrio because nobody would talk to him any more, or serve him in shops and bars,' said Falcón as he stood on the landing. 'Why was that, Sra López?'

She looked flustered and embarrassed; her hands shifted about, straightening her clothes. She eased herself behind the door and shut it without answering his question.

In the flinching brightness of the street Falcón took a call from Juez Calderón, who wanted to see him about the Vega case. Before he got back into his car he went into a bar on the Alameda and ordered a café solo. He showed his police ID and asked the same question of the barman as he had of Sra López. He was an older guy, who looked as if he'd seen a few things in his time as a bar owner at the seedier end of the Alameda.

'We all knew Sebastián,' he said, 'and we liked him. He was a good boy until . . . he did wrong. When he did what he did, people started to talk about how abusers start out as the abused. Conclusions were drawn and it wasn't helped by the fact that nobody much liked Pablo Ortega. He was an arrogant prick who thought the whole world loved him.'

The sweat cooled quickly on Falcón's body as he sat in Calderón's office, waiting for him to come back from another meeting. As Calderón took his seat it was clear that whatever had been troubling him over the past days had gone. He was his usual solid self. The certainty had returned.

Falcón told him he was finished with the Vega case, that he'd found out everything there was to know about him, except who'd killed him. He gave Calderón a compilation report on what he'd learnt from Mark Flowers and Virgilio Guzmán.

'Have you checked this "recording" of Marty Krugman in the American Consulate from the night of Sr Vega's death?'

'Comisario Lobo is going to talk the whole issue through with the Consul,' said Falcón. 'I don't expect to hear whether that recording existed or not.'

'So you think Marty Krugman killed Rafael Vega?'

'I do,' said Falcón. 'And despite his wife's denial on Monday night, I think she drove him to kill Reza Sangari.'

'If he hadn't killed Reza Sangari you don't think he'd have been able to kill Rafael Vega?'

'I don't think he was developing a taste for it, but there's no doubt that he'd been excited by the power he felt from his first experience,' said Falcón. 'And when he found out who Vega really was,

326

whether by his own deduction or being told by Mark Flowers, he felt he had the power to do it again. I think he killed Sangari passionately and Vega intellectually.'

'And Sra Vega?'

'That was the problem. Krugman knew Mario was staying at Sra Jiménez's house so he didn't have to worry about the boy. He also knew that Lucía Vega was a heavy sleeper. He and Rafael had long discussions sometimes in Vega's house and they never disturbed her, but he didn't know that she took *two* sleeping tablets a night to knock herself out – the second one at around three in the morning. So when Rafael Vega went into his death agonies she probably came downstairs, saw the horror and ran back up to the bedroom with Krugman in pursuit. That's why her jaw was broken. She was screaming and he hit her. Then he had to kill her, too, which would explain why Krugman was so unstable from the outset.'

'And all these threats from the Russians?'

'Perhaps they were just trying to discourage us from investigating too hard and finding out about their money-laundering arrangements.'

'Is that all?' asked Calderón. 'That's a bit heavy-handed, don't you think?'

'They're heavy-handed people,' said Falcón.

'You're depressed, Javier.'

And you're not, thought Falcón, but he said: 'I failed in the Vega case. I failed to prevent the Krugmans from dying before my very eyes and . . . yes, well, my psychologist tells me it's bad to use the word "fail" with the first person singular, so I'll shut up.'

'I've heard rumblings,' said Calderón.

'It's lunchtime.'

'Tectonic rumblings coming from the Jefatura,' said Calderón. 'Heads will roll. Jobs will be lost. Pensions terminated.'

'Because Montes jumped out of his office window?'

'That was the start of it,' said Calderón, back to enjoying himself in the intrigue of the moment. 'What about Martinez and Altozano?'

Falcón shrugged. Calderón could find out for himself why the Russians were really threatening.

'You know something, Javier, don't you?'

'So do you,' he said, oddly irritated by the familiarity.

'I know the Juez Decano and the Fiscal Jefe had a meeting behind closed doors for one hour this morning, and you don't often get them in the same building in the same room.'

'Those rumblings you heard are the sound of the powers that control us closing ranks,' said Falcón.

'Tell me,' said Calderón.

'We're the blind, the deaf and the dumb today, Esteban,' he said, and got to his feet. 'I'd still like that search warrant for Vega's safe-deposit box. We might as well satisfy our curiosity.'

'I'll have that ready for you this afternoon,' said Calderón, checking his watch, joining him at the door. 'I'll walk down with you. Inés and I have got some shopping to do.'

They went downstairs and through the bear pit of justice, where people bowed and scraped to the young judge. He was back in his element. The horrors were off the horizon. They went through security. Inés was on the other side. Falcón kissed her hello. She put an arm around Calderón's back and he pulled her to his chest, kissed her on the head. Inés gave Falcón a tinkling wave before she turned with a little back kick of her high heels and a big, happy smile thrown over her shoulder. Her hair swung across her back like the girls' in the shampoo ads.

Falcón watched them go and tried to imagine what could have possibly passed between them since that fatal Monday night. And with that thought came the answer: absolutely nothing. They had clung to each other in the terror of their possible loneliness, wished it all away and thrown their arms open to what life had been before. Was that the man that Isabel Cano had said was on the hunt for difference? Was that the woman whose stamp of approval Falcón had thought he so desperately needed? He watched them heading towards the city and a life of small, hurtful destructions.

Consuelo called, asking to meet for lunch. She sounded as she had done last night – distant and preoccupied. They agreed to meet at his home on Calle Bailén and he would do the cooking. Falcón bought food in the Corte Inglés on his way home. He emptied his mind in the kitchen. He sliced onions, fried them slowly in olive oil until caramelized. He boiled up potatoes and poured oloroso sherry over the onions and reduced it to a syrup. He cleaned and seasoned the tuna, made a salad. He arranged the prawns with wedges of lemon and mayonnaise. He drank chilled manzanilla and sat in the shade on the patio to wait for Consuelo.

She arrived at two o'clock. As soon as he let her into the house he knew that something was wrong. She was closed off, shut in. He'd had this feeling from women before, a sense that everything will be withheld until the air is cleared. Her mouth did not respond to his kiss. Her body kept its distance. He felt the quickening plummet in his stomach of the lover who is about to be told something very kindly. He led her to the kitchen as if they were condemned and this was their last meal.

They ate the prawns and drank manzanilla while he told her that the Vega case was officially closed. He got up to fry the tuna steaks. He reheated the oloroso syrup and poured it over the fish. He sat down with the pan between them unable to bear it any longer.

'You've got tired of me already,' he said, serving her a steak.

'Quite the opposite,' she said.

'Or is it my profession?' he said. 'I know you've come here to tell me something, because I've been told this sort of thing before.'

'You're right, but it's not because I'm tired of you,' she said.

'Is it because of what happened on Sunday? I can understand that. I know how important your children are to you. I'd have been –'

'I've learnt to recognize what I want, Javier,' she said, shaking her head. 'It's taken me a lifetime but I *have* learned that valuable lesson.'

'Not many people do,' said Falcón, serving himself a tuna steak, which now looked banal on his plate.

'I used to be a romantic. You're talking to a woman who once fell in love with a duke, remember? Even when I came down here, I still entertained those romantic illusions. Once I had my children I realized I didn't need to fool myself any more. They gave me all the love, the real unconditional kind, that I needed and I returned it doubled. I had an affair to satisfy my physical needs. You met him – that idiot Basilio Lucena – and you understood the relationship that we had. It wasn't love. It was much less complicated and manageable than that.'

'You don't have to let me down lightly,' said Falcón. 'You can just say: "I don't want to do this any more."'

'This is me being honest with a man for the first time in my life,' she said, looking him straight in the eye.

'I thought that what we had going between us was a good thing. It felt right,' said Falcón, the emotion rising in his throat. 'For the first time in my life, it felt absolutely right.'

'It *is* a good thing, but it is not what I want now.'

'You want to devote yourself to your children?'

'That's part of it,' she said. 'The rest is me. We have a good thing going now, but it will change. And I don't want the intensity, the complications, the responsibility . . . But most of all, and this is *my* failing, I do not want the daily confrontation with my weakness.'

'Your weakness?'

'I have weaknesses. Nobody sees them but they are there,' she said. 'This is my big weakness. You know everything about me, every terrible thing because our relationship started in the terrible arena of a murder investigation. But you don't know this: I am hopeless in love and I cannot bear it.'

'How do you know, if you've only had the illusion of it before?'

'Because it's already started,' she said.

She stood up, the tuna untouched, the sauce congealing on the plate. She came round to his side of the table. He tried to say things. He wanted to talk her out of it. She put her fingers on his lips. She held his face, ran her hand over his hair and kissed him. He felt the wetness of her tears. She pulled back, squeezed his shoulder once and left.

The door slammed. He looked at his plate. There was nothing that could get past what he had growing in his throat. He scraped the tuna into the bin, looked at the brown smear left on the plate and then he hurled it against the wall.

30

Wednesday, 31st July 2002

Strange siesta sleep left Falcón feeling oddly rested but with his brain sitting awkwardly in his head, like a breach birth. The morning's events drifted in his mind slow as river mist. It had been so disastrous that a hysterical positivism staged a small rampage in his head. He sat on the edge of the bed, shaking his head, dredging for laughs, and an idea came to him, which propelled him into the shower where it grew, clearing his mind.

He drove to San Bernardo, hitting the steering wheel at odd intervals, thinking that it wasn't finished between him and Consuelo. She wasn't going to drift away from him that easily. There was still some talking to be done, some persuading. He went up to see Carlos Vázquez and caught sight of himself in the lift mirror: there was a mad determination in him.

'I'd like to speak to the Russians,' said Falcón, walking into Vázquez's office. 'Do you think you could arrange that for me?'

'I doubt it.'

'Why not?'

'They wouldn't have anything to say to you . . . Inspector Jefe del Grupo de Homicidios.'

'You could invite them over – you know, something to do with their projects – and I could join you for the meeting.'

'That would not be possible.'

'Charm them, Sr Vázquez.'

'Vega Construcciones are no longer actively involved in their projects. They have no reason to come and see me,' said Vázquez. 'They sold the buildings.'

'They *sold* them?'

'They were theirs to sell.'

'Don't you think, Sr Vázquez, given their intricate involvement with your late client, that it would have been judicious to have informed us?'

'I was told not to inform anybody except the third party in the sale.'

'But you didn't think that we deserved some notification?'

'Under normal circumstances I would have told you,' said Vázquez, hands clasped, knuckles white.

'And what was so abnormal about these circumstances?'

Vázquez opened his desk drawer and took out an envelope.

'I bought my children a dog last Christmas. A puppy. They took it down to the coast with them for the holidays,' said Vázquez. They called me at the end of last week to say the dog had disappeared. They were all in tears. On Monday morning I received a package sent from Marbella which contained a dog's paw and this envelope.'

Falcón shook out the contents: a single photo of Vázquez's family sitting on the beach looking happy. On the reverse side was a note – 'They're next.'

'What do you think of that for psychology, Inspector Jefe?'

Falcón drove to the Jefatura. It occurred to him that since Sunday there had been no more threats from the Russians and now he knew why. They'd accomplished what they set out to do. They'd extricated themselves from the Vega projects and his investigation was now officially over. And their most criminal action had been the slaying of a children's pet.

Ramírez and Ferrera sat in the office, wordless.

'What's going on?' asked Falcón. 'Shouldn't you be down in the lab with Felipe and Jorge?'

'They've been told to work behind closed doors and to only discuss their findings with Comisario Elvira,' said Ramírez.

'What about the razor blade I sent down there?'

'They're not allowed to talk to us about anything.'

'And the arsonists?'

'They're still with us,' said Ramírez. 'We don't know for how much longer. In your absence I called Elvira to ask if we should get them to write their statements. He told me to do nothing. And I'm an expert at that. So, here we are, doing fuck all.'

'Any calls?'

'Lobo wants to see you, and Alicia Aguado wants to know if you're going to be able to take her to the prison this evening.'

'It's not over yet, José Luis,' said Falcón.

He took the lift up to Lobo's office on the top floor. He called Alicia Aguado and arranged to pick her up. He wasn't kept waiting by Lobo, who was now calm. They sat and looked at each other as if there was some disastrous battle plan laid out between them, which had resulted in the deaths of thousands.

'The detective work by you and your squad has been excellent,' said Lobo, which flattery Falcón took to be a bad sign.

'You think so?' said Falcón. 'To me it's been a remarkable catalogue of failures. I have no killer for Vega and a landscape littered with dead bodies.'

'You've cracked a major paedophile network.'

'I don't think I *cracked* it, exactly. Ignacio Ortega has been ahead of me all the way, as is proven by the fact that I have nothing on him, other than his installation of the air-conditioning units in the finca, and the late Alberto Montes has been tripping me up with his every action,' said Falcón. 'Now Ortega is laughing in my face and the Russians are still out there, free as birds, to continue their trafficking of adults and children for sexual purposes.'

'Ignacio Ortega is finished. He's a marked man. Nobody will go anywhere near him.'

'Applause,' said Falcón. 'He's still living in his comfortable house, running his successful business. He'll keep his head down for a few years and then, because of the nature of his particular obsession, he'll be back. That sort of person has a compulsion to desecrate innocence and it's no less strong than the serial killer's compulsion to feel fresh bodies struggling for life in his hands. And, I don't need to tell you, Comisario, that Ignacio Ortega is just one little link that we've managed to temporarily cut. The big monster, the Russian mafia, is still out there, spreading its tentacles over the whole of

Europe. Despite what the public relations section of your mind is telling you, this is one of our most significant failures. And it's a failure that is being perpetrated by the very administration who are supposed to be supporting us.'

'I might as well tell you that Montes's wife was caught retrieving a box from a storage warehouse which contained one hundred and eighty thousand euros,' said Lobo. 'But we're satisfied from the interviews we've conducted so far that he was acting alone.'

'More applause,' said Falcón. 'What are we going to say to the stunned population of Almonaster la Real about the two bodies, the boy and the girl, found dead at the finca? What's going to happen to the four men on the tape? What's going to happen to the other children –'

'Felipe and Jorge will make a full report of their findings,' said Lobo methodically, 'and that will form a part, as will every aspect of your investigation, of a file which Comisario Elvira will present to me. We are already conducting an internal investigation within the Jefatura. We've named the fourth man on the tape. Everything has been documented.'

'And there'll be a reading of it in the Andalucían parliament?'

Silence.

'And all these people will appear in court?'

'The reason why we have an organized society and not chaotic anarchy is that people believe in our institutions,' said Lobo. 'When Franco died in 1975, what happened to all his institutions? What happened to the Guardia Civil? You can't tear them apart and throw them all out, for the simple reason that they are the only people who know how to run things. So what do you do? You curb their powers, you control their recruitment, you *change* the institution, from the inside out. That's why people believe in us now. That's why they no longer fear us. That's why the Guardia Civil no longer operates as a secret police force.'

'Talk to Virgilio Guzmán about that,' said Falcón. 'The point is that nobody from this case is going to face justice, not because they don't deserve to, but because our institution has dirty linen and the administration that controls us is using that, because theirs is even dirtier.'

'They're all marked men,' said Lobo. 'You'll see – people will lose their power, have contracts taken away from them, lose their status. . . they will suffer.'

'They might not realize their ambitions, which will be their little tragedy,' said Falcón, 'but they'll remain at liberty, which will be ours.'

'So you believe that we should expose everybody, reveal the corruption within –'

'Yes,' said Falcón. 'And start again.'

'All those years as a cop and you've learnt nothing about human nature,' said Lobo. 'How long will it be before the Russian mafia starts working on the next generation?'

'I'm having my say, Comisario, that's all,' said Falcón, feeling that weakness coming back into his arms.

'You know, Javier, this is not something peculiar to Spain,' said Lobo. 'It's happening all over the world. We've just had the CIA on our doorstep, and what were they doing? Preserving their institutions. Maintaining the dignity of office of the President of the United States and the Secretary of State.'

'Is that what the Consul told you?'

'In so many words,' said Lobo.

'So you didn't see the "recording" that Flowers said proved Krugman's innocence?'

'The Consul confirmed that it existed.'

'Such trust between institutional powers!' said Falcón. 'You didn't see that recording because there isn't one. Flowers gave Krugman an alibi because it was probably his decision to end the uncertainty about what secrets Vega was holding – the man had become too unstable to predict. I think Krugman killed him when Flowers gave him the man's real identity and – let's have a moment's silence for the forgotten Lucía – he also had to kill his completely innocent wife.'

'I cannot call the integrity of the US Consul into question to his face, Javier,' said Lobo, annoyed now.

'I know these things, Comisario. I'm naïve in the workings of power but not totally inexperienced. But every time something like this happens – and let's remember the financial impropriety of your predecessor, which put you in the exalted office you hold now. Every time something like this happens, a little of that dirt rubs off on me. I scrub and I scrub, but there's always that understain showing through. I start thinking I'll have to get back into my suits, just to give myself the illusion that good can still prevail.'

'We need men like you and Inspector Ramírez, Javier,' said Lobo. 'Don't be in any doubt about that.'

'Do you? I'm not so sure. The tools of the good are so pathetic and predictable when compared to those of the bad,' said Falcón. 'If we're these dirty people with a deep understanding of ingrained dirt from our years working in these corrupted institutions, maybe we should learn something from that. All this first-hand knowledge of the forces of darkness should not go to waste.'

'Well, that *is* a dangerous path to tread,' said Lobo.

Back in the office Ramírez and Ferrera looked up for the chink of hope. Falcón stood before them and opened his hands to show the emptiness within. He went into his office. There was a small piece of paper in the middle of his desk on which he knew was written the translation of the inscription found at the finca. He put his hands on either side of it and braced himself to read it.

I'm sorry, Mummy, but we cannot do this any more.

He left the office without a word and went to pick up Alicia Aguado. He was glad to be with her. She was happy and looking forward to her next session with Sebastián. She was pleased by his progress. Pablo's death had released him from his past and he was revealing things in days that would normally have taken months to extract.

When they arrived in the observation cell it was obvious that Sebastián was glad to see her. He sat and bared his wrist, impatient. Falcón could hardly concentrate on their discussion. His conversation with Lobo was still spiralling through his mind and forming a triple helix with Ignacio Ortega and the Russians. Every avenue of contact to the Russians had been cut – Vega, Montes and Krugman were all dead and Vázquez paralysed with fear. The only way left was the darkest path of all, through Ignacio Ortega, and that was where the three strands of his triple helix met – Lobo's last words to him.

Some intensity from the observation cell broke through to him and he concentrated on the dialogue for a moment.

'How old were you?' asked Aguado.

'I was fifteen. It wasn't an easy time for me. School was difficult. My home life was constantly disrupted. I was unhappy.'

'Tell me how it came out.'

'We were driving to Huelva. He was appearing in a play there and we were going to carry on to Tavira in Portugal and spend the weekend on the beach.'

'Why did you choose that moment?'

'I didn't choose it. I got angry with him. I got angry with him telling me what a wonderful guy his brother was. How considerate he was. How helpful. My father was useless at running his finances and Ignacio was constantly helping him out. He also sent electricians and plumbers around to the house to do repairs. He even rewired the house free of charge. It was nothing to Ignacio. It didn't cost him anything. He put it all through his company. But my father thought he was a great guy for doing all this. He didn't see what Ignacio was up to. He didn't see how much his brother loathed him, how much he despised him for his talent and his fame. So in one of these moments, when Pablo was polishing away at his brother's gilded image, I told him.'

'Can you remember your exact words?'

'I remember everything as if it just happened,' said Sebastián. 'I said: "You know, when you used to go away on tour and you left me with your brother . . ." and my father turned to me and smiled and his face was full of love for what he was about to hear – another wonderful thing about Ignacio. It was so pathetic I nearly couldn't bring myself to say it, but my anger got the better of me and I rammed it home. I said: ". . . he used to sexually abuse me every night." He lost control of the car. It came off the road and we ended up in a ditch. He started hitting me, slapping me around the head and face, so I opened the window and clambered out into the ditch. He came after me, heaving open his own door like a man coming out of a tank.

'The thing about my father was that you never knew when he was acting. He could do anger and turn around and do love. But that afternoon there was no mistaking his rage. He caught up with me in the field by the road. He grabbed me by the hair and swung me around. He slapped me about the face and head, with the front

337

and back of his massive hands, until I was a ragdoll. He pulled my face up to his and I saw his sweat and his teeth and his lips stretched white and the smell of his breath as he forced me to take back my words. He made me say to him that I had lied. He made me beg for his forgiveness. And when I did, he gave it to me and said that we would never speak about this day ever again.

'And we didn't. We never really spoke to each other again after that day.'

'Do you think he talked to Ignacio about it?'

'I'm sure he didn't. I would have known about it. Ignacio would have come after me to frighten me back into silence.'

They sat quietly for a moment. Alicia weighed the enormity of that day in her mind. Falcón sat outside remembering the dream Pablo had told him and his subsequent collapse on the lawn. He could see the thoughts in Alicia's twitching unseeing eyes. Was this the right time? What should my next question be? What question will unlock the reasoning behind Sebastián's extreme action?

'Have you been thinking over the past few days why your father killed himself?' she asked.

'Yes, I have. I've thought very hard about his note to me,' said Sebastián. 'My father loved words. He loved to talk and write. He liked his own voice. He liked to be verbose. But in that letter he reduced himself to one line.'

Silence. Sebastián's head trembled on his neck.

'And what did that line mean to you?'

'It meant that he believed me.'

'And why do you think he'd come to that conclusion?'

'Before I was convicted, my father had reached a point in his life when he never questioned himself. Whether it was to do with his belief in his own brilliance, or the sycophants around him, I don't know. But he never thought that he might be wrong, or have made a mistake. . . Until I was arrested. Once they put me in here I refused to see him, so I can't be sure, but I think that was when doubt started to creep into his mind.'

'He had to leave the barrio,' said Alicia. 'He was ostracized.'

'They didn't much like him in the barrio. He thought they all loved him in the same way that all his audiences loved him, but he never bothered with any of them as individual people. They were just there for the further glorification of Pablo Ortega.'

'That must have given him reason to doubt.'

'That, and the fact that his work was drying up gave him reason to start living in his own head more. And, as I know, if you do that you come across all sorts of doubts and fears, and they grow large in your loneliness. He probably spoke to Salvador, too. He wasn't a bad man, my father. He took pity on Salvador and helped him with money for his drugs. I doubt Salvador would have told him straight, because of the force of my father's personality and his own fear of Ignacio, but once there was doubt in his mind he might have started to pick up on things. And when they were added to his doubts he might have found the answer to that horrible equation in his head, which was the sum of all his fears. It must have been devastating for him.'

'But don't you think that this was an incredibly drastic action on your part – to put yourself in here?'

'You don't think I did this just to get my father's attention, do you?'

'I don't know why you did this, Sebastián.'

He took his wrist away from her and covered his head with his arms. He rocked to and fro on his chair for several minutes.

'Perhaps we've had enough for today,' she said, finding his shoulder.

He calmed down, disentangled himself. Held out his wrist again.

'I was scared of what I had growing in my own mind,' he said.

'Let's take this up tomorrow,' said Alicia Aguado.

'No, I'd like to try and get this out,' he said, putting her fingers to his wrist. 'I'd read somewhere . . . I couldn't help reading this sort of thing. The newspapers are full of stories of child abuse and my eyes used to close in on *every* story because I knew they were relevant to me. I extracted things from these stories which created doubt in me, and I began to find a corner of myself that I could no longer trust. It grew from there, until it became a certainty in my head. Only a matter of time before . . . before . . .'

'I think this is too much for you today, Sebastián,' she said. 'You're driving your mind too hard.'

'Please let me get this out,' he said. 'Just this one thing.'

'What did you extract from these stories?' said Alicia Aguado. 'Just tell me that.'

'Yes, yes, that was the beginning of it,' he said. 'What I saw in these stories that was relevant to me was that . . . the abused become abusers themselves. When I first read that I didn't think it could be possible . . . that I could end up with the same sly little look that Uncle Ignacio had when he sat on my bed at night. But when you're lonely, doubt creates more doubt, and I really began to think that it could be something that might happen to me. That I wouldn't be able to control it. Already, I found that kids liked me and I liked them. I loved to share in their innocence. I loved to be with them in their unconscious world. No past horrors, no future worries, just the glorious unravelling present. And the thought grew that eventually I might do something unspeakable, and I lived in constant fear of it. And then one day I couldn't bear it any longer and I thought that I would just do it. When the moment came, though . . . I couldn't, but it didn't matter any more because the fear inside me was already so great. I let him go, Manolo, and while I waited for the police to come I found myself praying for them to put me in a cell and throw away the key.'

'But you couldn't do it, Sebastián,' she said. 'You didn't do it.'

'My fear was not telling me that. My fear was telling me that eventually it would happen.'

'But what did you feel when you faced the reality of your intention?'

'I felt nothing but revulsion. I felt that this would be a very wrong, unnatural and cruel thing to do.'

Falcón dropped Alicia back in Calle Vidrio and continued home. He went to his study with a bottle, and a glass full of ice. The whisky tasted good after the day he'd had. He sat in his study with his feet up on the desk, thinking about the man he'd been only twelve hours ago. He wasn't depressed, which surprised him. He felt oddly solid, connected and determined, and he realized that anger was holding him together. He wanted to get Consuelo back and he wanted to bury Ignacio Ortega.

Virgilio Guzmán arrived punctually at 10 p.m. Falcón poured him a whisky and they sat in the study. After the morning's outburst, he'd expected Guzmán to come in hard about the cover-up he'd smelt in the Jefatura, but he seemed more interested in talking about his holiday in Mallorca, which was coming up in a week's time.

'What's happened to the crusading journalist who stormed out of my office this morning?' asked Falcón.

'Drugs,' said Guzmán. 'The whole reason I left Madrid was to come down here and lead a more relaxed lifestyle. I get a whiff of that story and I go mad. My blood pressure went through the roof. Now I'm on tranquillizers and, you know, life's really quite nice when it comes to you filtered.'

'Does that mean you're dropping the story?'

'Doctor's orders.'

They sat in silence while Falcón tested that for veracity.

'Did someone talk to you, Virgilio?'

'It's a very close-knit community down here,' said Guzmán. 'The paper's not going to run with it unless somebody else cracks it open first. And you know something, Javier? I don't give a shit. That's drugs for you.'

'How about giving me some advice, as an impartial observer?'

'Don't make me drink too much whisky,' he said. 'It doesn't mix with the drugs.'

Falcón told him everything about the cover-up: the Montes finca, the dead bodies up in the sierra, the arsonists, the tape – both the original and the copy upstairs. Guzmán listened and nodded throughout as if this was stuff that came to his ears every day.

'What do you want from all this?' said Guzmán. 'What's your minimum requirement?'

'To put Ignacio Ortega away for a very long time.'

'That's understandable. He sounds like a very nasty piece of work.'

'Do you think I'm being too narrow-minded?' said Falcón. 'Should I be gunning for our hallowed institutions?'

'That's the whisky talking,' said Guzmán. 'You haven't got a chance. Concentrate on Ortega.'

'He seems to be well protected by his connections.'

'So, how do you weaken that protection to get at him?'

'I don't know.'

'Well, that's your training. You're trained to think within the limits of the law,' said Guzmán, putting down his empty whisky glass. 'I'm going now before it's too late.'

'And you're not going to tell me?'

'It wouldn't be right for me to tell you. I don't want that responsibility,' said Guzmán. 'The answer's in front of you, but I don't want to be the one to infect your mind.'

31

Thursday, 1st August 2002

'Bad night?' asked Ramírez, looking out over the Jefatura car park.

'Bad dreams. Bad night,' said Falcón. 'I lay awake fantasizing about nailing the Russians.'

'Tell me.'

'I thought I'd go to Ignacio Ortega and ask to be put on the Russian payroll. Tell him I liked the look of the hundred and eighty thousand euros Sra Montes was caught with.'

'Was it that much?'

'That's what Lobo told me,' said Falcón. 'I could spin Ortega some line – that I could be the guy running the Grupo de Menores while they find a suitable replacement for Montes . . .'

'That would never happen for a start,' said Ramírez.

'Then I'd persuade him to set up a meeting with the Russians.'

'And he'd believe you?'

'Well no, but he'd do it anyway and then I'd find out where the meeting was to take place and secretly let you know.'

'I'm not even sure that this fantasy is B-movie quality.'

'The meeting would take place in a garage in the middle of nowhere. I'd be with Ortega. We'd be sitting around an oil drum waiting for the Russians. We'd hear a car coming from some way off. Then Ivanov and Zelenov would arrive. They'd give me a very ugly interview in which it was clear they didn't believe a word I was saying. And just when they'd got to the point of laughing at me, the garage door would crack open and you'd come in and blow them all away.'

'My kids could think of something better than that.'

'Maybe instead of you coming in blasting away we could think of something more subtle. The garage door would still crack open. It always does that. But you'd only cover them with your gun. I'd disarm them. Then the shutter to the main entrance of the garage would roll up and there would be police cars, with flashing lights – that's another thing that always happens. One of the police cars would reverse in. The Russians would be cuffed and, as they were being put into the car, they would turn to see us slapping Ortega on the back, shaking his hand, and they'd think that they'd been served up. By the time they reached the Jefatura the defence lawyer would already be there. The same one from the tape in Montes's finca. They'd be out in four hours. Then cut to Ortega's house. Ignacio sitting at his desk, listening to Julio Iglesias on his perfect sound system, eyes closed until an alien sound opens them and . . . the horror. Two silenced shots. Blood flowers on his white shirt and his face is ruined.'

'The audience would be drinking beers before the credits rolled,' said Ramírez.

Ferrera put her head round the door to say good morning.

'Let's have a talk,' said Falcón.

Ferrera backed into the outer office. Ramírez went to close the door.

'You too, Policía Ferrera,' said Falcón, and Ramírez narrowed his eyes at him. 'Close the door behind you.'

They sat around the desk.

'We're the voices of experience here,' said Falcón. 'And you, Policía Ferrera, are the voice of morality.'

'Is that in my role as ex-nun?'

'You're in,' said Ramírez. 'That's all that matters. So shut up and listen.'

'I think you've realized by now that there's a cover-up going on,' said Falcón. 'The crimes committed at the Montes finca are being covered up from both ends. Because of Montes's involvement, the Jefatura is vulnerable to attack from the politicians. There is fear amongst our masters that a major scandal, involving a number of figures from public life, may cause a collapse of faith, and they are determined to maintain the dignity and integrity of their institutions. The three of us know that what went on in the Montes finca was wrong and that the perpetrators should face justice and public shaming. Comisario Lobo has told me that everything that has happened at the finca will be documented. He has been unable to

343

guarantee that any of it will be heard. He has only been able to assuage my sense of outrage by assuring me that no one involved in what went on in that finca will get away scot free. They will suffer loss of position, status and wealth.'

'I'm crying for them already,' said Ramírez. 'What about the media?'

'Virgilio Guzmán said they wouldn't touch it unless somebody else broke the story first,' said Falcón. 'He's ill and has had to go on medication.'

'What did I tell you about that guy?' said Ramírez.

'The Russians are untouchable. They've pulled their money out of the Vega projects. They've threatened Vázquez's family. Our only access to them is through Ignacio Ortega, and he isn't about to pass on our card. We have no physical evidence, even of their money-laundering operations, which is presentable in court. We couldn't justify arresting them even if we *could* get to them.'

'What chance have we got of taking Ortega down?' asked Ramírez.

'He is protected. That's how he survives. As we've seen from his secret filming in the finca, he has the dirt on everybody. That's why we've been cut off from all forensic information and everything has to be directed through Comisario Elvira. All we have now is the tape.'

'What tape?' asked Ferrera.

'The arsonists stole a television and video from the finca before they torched it. The video recorder was loaded with a tape which shows four men having sex with minors,' said Falcón. 'The original is with Elvira. We have retained a copy.'

'What about the Madrid newspapers?' asked Ramírez.

'That's a possibility, but we would have to give them the whole story and it would all have to be backed up with information we don't have access to. There would be no question of anonymity. We would be seen as having broken ranks with the Jefatura and we'd be out on our own, probably facing the end of our careers. There's also a lot that's unpredictable in using the media, even our own here. You put people with their backs to the wall and they will fight dirty. We could all end up getting hurt – your families too – and we still might not get the result we're looking for.'

'Let's send a copy each to their wives and get on with our lives,' said Ramírez.

'But we still wouldn't take Ortega down,' said Falcón.

Silence for some time, broken only by the metronome of Ramírez's huge finger thumping up and down on the edge of the desk.

'Something that would give me a lot of pleasure,' said Ramírez, looking up at the ceiling as if for divine inspiration, 'would be to give my old friend from the barrio a private showing of his part of the tape. That would mean I'd get to see his face, and then I would tell him that there was nothing I could do about it, but that he could have words with Ignacio Ortega.'

'Words?' asked Falcón.

'He'd kill him,' said Ramírez. 'I know that guy. He would not let anybody live with that kind of hold over him.'

Silence again. Cristina Ferrera looked up to find both men's eyes fixed on her.

'You're not serious, are you?' she said.

'And then I could arrest him for murder,' said Ramírez.

'I can't believe you're even asking me to contemplate thinking about such a thing,' said Ferrera. 'If you *are* serious, you don't need a moral guide, you need a full transplant.'

Falcón laughed. Ramírez joined in with a loud guffaw. Relief spread across Ferrera's face from the small nose outwards.

'Well, nobody can say we didn't consider every possibility,' said Falcón.

'I'm going back to the computer,' she said and left, closing the door behind her.

'Were you being serious?' asked Ramírez, leaning over the desk.

Falcón didn't move a muscle in his face.

'*Joder*,' said Ramírez. 'That would have been something.'

The phone rang very loudly, startling both men. Falcón snatched it to his ear. He listened carefully while Ramírez rolled an unlit cigarette in his fingers.

'You've made a very courageous decision, Sr López,' said Falcón, and put the phone down.

'Some good news at last?' said Ramírez, putting the cigarette into his mouth.

'That was the father of the boy who was supposedly abused by Sebastián Ortega. The boy, Manolo, is on his way back to Seville now. He's going to come straight to the Jefatura and give a revised and completely true account of what happened.'

'That's not going to be much of a wedding present for Juez Calderón.'

'But you know what that means, don't you, José Luis?'

The unlit cigarette dropped into Ramírez's lap.

The phone rang again. This time it was Juez Calderón, confirming that he now had a signed search warrant for Vega's safe-deposit box, held in the name of Emilio Cruz at the Banco Banesto. Falcón picked up the box key and the two men left for the Edificio de los Juzgados. On the way out he told Ferrera that Manolo López was going to arrive with his mother to make a revised video statement and that he wanted her to read the Ortega file, prepare the questions, and interview him.

They drove to the Edificio de los Juzgados. Calderón's secretary gave Ramírez the search warrant. They continued to the Banco Banesto and asked to see the manager. They showed their IDs and the warrant and were taken down into the vault. Falcón signed himself in and the manager accompanied them to the boxes. She inserted her key, turned it once and left them to it. Falcón used his key and they pulled out the stainless steel-covered box, which they put on a table in the middle of the room.

On top of the papers in the box was an old Spanish passport and some travel tickets. The passport was issued in 1984 and the photograph was of Rafael Vega, but it was in the name of Oscar Marcos. The tickets were held together by a paper clip and they were in date order. The first trip was from Seville to Madrid on 15th January 1986 and then back to Seville on 19th January. The next trip took place on 15th February 1986 and was by train from Seville to Madrid to Barcelona and finally Paris. On 17th February there was a train ticket from Paris to Frankfurt and on to Hamburg. On 19th February he went from there to Copenhagen and on 24th February he crossed into Sweden and went up to Stockholm. The return trip started on 1st March and was from Oslo to London by air. Three days were spent in London and then he flew to Madrid and took the train to Seville.

'This stuff,' said Ramírez, who was going through the papers underneath, 'must be in code, because they read like a child's letters to his father.'

Falcón called Virgilio Guzmán and asked him if he could come to his house on Calle Bailén immediately. They emptied the safe-deposit box and put the contents into a large evidence bag. Falcón told the manager the box was now empty, gave her a receipt and returned the key. They drove to Calle Bailén and Falcón read the letters while they waited for Virgilio Guzmán. Each letter had its envelope clipped to it. They were all posted from America to the postbox address in the name of Emilio Cruz. The letters made sense individually but not as a whole.

Guzmán arrived. He sat at the desk with the papers. He looked through the passport and then checked through the travel tickets.

'End of February 1986, Stockholm, Sweden,' he said. 'Do you know what happened then?'

'No idea.'

'On 28th February 1986 the Prime Minister, Olaf Palme, was shot as he came out of the cinema with his wife,' said Guzmán. 'The assassin was never found.'

'What about all those letters?' asked Ramírez.

'I've got somebody who can help me with decoding them, but I imagine they were his instructions for one last operation for his old friend Manuel Contreras,' said Guzmán. 'He had the perfect cover. He was fully trained. It was the kind of thing they did in Operation Condor all the time. No possible trail back to the Pinochet régime, and one painful thorn is finally removed from the President's hide. It's perfect.'

'So why would he keep all this stuff?'

'I don't know, except that killing the Prime Minister of a European country is no small thing and perhaps he might have felt the need for a bit of security in case things changed later on.'

'Like now?' said Falcón. 'The Pinochet régime is finished . . .'

'Manuel Contreras is in jail, having been betrayed by his old friend the General,' said Guzmán.

'And Vega thinks it's time to even the score. Show what the Pinochet régime was capable of?' said Falcón. 'It's the strategy of no return. You might put Pinochet away, but you finish yourself as well.'

'And that's what he did,' said Guzmán. 'He died with that note in his hand. You did what he wanted you to do. By investigating the crime you found his safe-deposit box key and now his secret will be revealed to the world.'

They photocopied all the letters from the safe-deposit box and Guzmán took them off to his code-breaking friend who, he revealed, was an ex-DINA man now living in Madrid.

'Know thine enemy,' said Guzmán, explaining the relationship. 'I'll scan these into the computer, e-mail them up to him and he'll read them like a book. I'll have an answer for you by this afternoon.'

Falcón and Ramírez returned to the Jefatura in time to meet Sra López and Manolo, who was already at work on his video interview and enjoying Cristina Ferrera's company. By one o'clock the boy had finished and Falcón called Alicia Aguado. He played the statement to her over the phone and she agreed to put it to Sebastián Ortega.

Ferrera took a patrol car to the Polígono San Pablo to find Salvador Ortega, while Falcón drove Alicia Aguado to the prison. They showed Sebastián Manolo's video interview and he broke down. He then wrote his own fifteen-page statement detailing five years of abuse at the hands of Ignacio Ortega. Ferrera called to say that Salvador was now at the Jefatura. Falcón faxed Sebastián's statement through for Salvador to read. Salvador asked for a meeting with Sebastián.

Ferrera drove him out to the prison and he and Sebastián talked for over two hours, after which Salvador agreed to write his own statement. He also gave Falcón a list of seven names of other children, now adults, who'd suffered at his father's hands.

At five o'clock Falcón was eating a chorizo bocadillo and drinking a non-alcoholic beer when Virgilio Guzmán called, saying that he'd had the letters decoded and he wanted to e-mail him the translations. They proved to be a series of instructions to Vega. Where and when to go and pick up his passport in Madrid. The route he should take to Stockholm. Intelligence on the movements and non-existent security of Olaf Palme. Where to go in Stockholm to pick up the weapon. Where to dispose of the weapon after the hit, and finally his return route to Seville.

'I'm running with this story in tomorrow's paper,' said Guzmán.

'I didn't expect you to do anything else, Virgilio,' said Falcón. 'It's only going to hurt people who deserve to be hurt.'

By six o'clock in the evening Falcón had a dossier with the revised video statement from Manolo López and the two from Sebastián and Salvador.

'And what happens if they block you on this?' said Ramírez, as he left the office.

'Then you'll be the new Inspector Jefe del Grupo de Homicidios, José Luis.'

'Not me,' said Ramírez. 'Tell them they'll have to look to Sub-Inspector Pérez, when he gets back from holiday.'

As well as the three statements he took the contents of Vega's safe-deposit box and printed out the decodes of the letters from Guzmán's e-mail. He went up to see Comisario Elvira, who was again in a meeting with Comisario Lobo. They didn't keep him waiting.

Falcón talked them through the contents of the safe-deposit box and read out the pertinent decodes which contained the assassination instructions and the target. The two men sat in stunned silence.

'And who would have known about this, apart from the obvious people in the régime?' asked Lobo. 'I mean, do you think the Americans knew anything about it?'

'They knew something about Vega,' said Falcón. 'Whether they knew any or part of this detail, I have no idea, but I doubt it. I now believe Flowers when he said that they didn't know what they were looking for. They were just hoping that it was nothing that would reflect badly on them or the administration of the time.'

'Do you think the Americans could have been involved in killing Vega, or are you satisfied that he was either murdered by Marty Krugman or committed suicide?'

'Mark Flowers has given me an enormous amount of information. The only problem is that I don't know what's true and what isn't,' said Falcón. 'There's a part of me that believes that they weren't involved in his murder because this is what they wanted to find out – the contents of the safe-deposit box, which they never found. But I also think that Flowers might have decided to stop the uncertainty and been a party to taking Vega out.'

'Case closed?' said Elvira.

Falcón shrugged.

'What else?' said Lobo, eyeing the dossier on Falcón's lap.

He handed it over. As Lobo read each page he handed it to Elvira. Both men glanced up nervously as they worked through the catalogue of abuse. When they finished, Lobo was looking out across the park, as he used to do when he occupied this office. He talked to the glass.

'I can guess,' he said, 'but I'd like you to tell me what you want.'

'My minimum requirement from all the crimes that were committed in the Montes finca was that Ignacio Ortega should go down,' said Falcón. 'That was not possible. I don't agree with it, but I understand why. This is a separate case. Nothing that happened in the Montes finca will surface in this family abuse case. I want a Juez de Instrucción to be appointed – not Juez Calderón, of course. I want to arrest Ignacio Ortega and I want him to face these charges and any others we might be able to bring after talking to those on the list of names supplied by Salvador Ortega.'

'We're going to have to discuss this and get back to you,' said Lobo.

'I don't want to put any undue pressure on your discussion, but I do want to remind you what you said to me in your office yesterday.'

'Remind me.'

'You said: "We need men like you and Inspector Ramírez, Javier. Don't be in any doubt about that."'

'I see.'

'Inspector Ramírez and I would like to make the arrest tonight,' said Falcón, and left.

He sat alone in his office, aware of Ramírez and Ferrera waiting for news. The phone rang, he heard them jump. It was Isabel Cano, asking if she could have a response to the letter she'd drafted to send to Manuela about the house on Calle Bailén. He said he hadn't read it, but it didn't matter because he'd decided that if Manuela wanted to live in the house she was going to have to pay the market value, less the agency commission, and there would be no discussion on the matter.

'What's happened to *you*?' she asked.

'I've hardened inside, Isabel. The blood now rifles down my cold, steel veins,' said Falcón. 'Did you ever hear about the Sebastián Ortega case?'

'He's Pablo Ortega's son, isn't he? The one who kidnapped the boy?'

'That's right,' said Falcón. 'How would you like to handle his appeal?'

'Any strong new evidence?'

'Yes,' said Falcón, 'but I should warn you that it might not make Esteban Calderón look very good.'

'It's about time he learnt a bit of humility,' she said. 'I'll take a look.'

Falcón hung up and sank back into the silence.

'You're confident,' said Ramírez, from the outer office.

'We are men of value, José Luis.'

The phone went in the outer office this time. Ramírez snatched it to his ear. Silence.

'Thank you,' said Ramírez.

He hung up. Falcón waited.

'José Luis?' he said.

There was no sound. He went to the door.

Ramírez looked up, his face was wet with tears, his mouth drawn back, tight across his teeth as he fought the emotion. He waved his hand at Falcón, he couldn't speak.

'His daughter,' said Ferrera.

The Sevillano nodded, thumbed the huge tears out of his eyes.

'She's all right,' he said, under his breath. 'They've done every test in the book and they can't find anything wrong with her. They think it's some kind of virus.'

He slumped in his chair, still squeezing fat tears out of his eyes.

'You know what?' said Falcón. 'I think it's time to go and have a beer.'

The three of them drove down to the bar La Jota and stood in the cavernous cool and drank beers and ate strips of salt cod. Other police officers came along and tried to strike up conversation but didn't get very far. They were too tense. The time clipped round to 8.30 p.m. and Falcón's mobile started vibrating against his thigh. He put it to his ear.

'You're all clear to arrest Ignacio Ortega on those charges,' said Elvira. 'Juan Romero has been appointed the Juez de Instrucción. Good luck.'

They went back to the Jefatura because Falcón wanted to make the arrest in a patrol car with flashing lights, to let Ortega's neighbourhood know. Ferrera drove and they parked outside a large house in El Porvenir which, as Sebastián had described, had gate posts topped with concrete lions.

Ferrera stayed in the car. Ramírez rang the bell, which had the same electronic cathedral chime as Vega's. Ortega came to the door. They showed him their police IDs. He looked over their shoulders at the parked patrol car, lights flashing.

'We'd like to come in for a moment,' said Ramírez. 'Unless you'd rather do this in the street?'

They stepped into the house, which did not have the usual headache chill of fierce air conditioning but was completely comfortable.

'This air conditioning . . .' started Ramírez.

'This isn't air conditioning, Inspector,' said Ortega. 'You are now in a state-of-the-art climate-control system.'

'Then it should be raining in your study, Sr Ortega.'

'Can I offer you a drink, Inspector?' asked Ortega, mystified.

'I don't think so,' said Ramírez, 'we won't be staying long.'

'You, Inspector Jefe? A single malt? I even have Laphroaig.'

Falcón blinked at that. It was a whisky that Francisco Falcón had favoured. There was still a lot of it in his house, undrunk. His own tastes were not so eclectic. He shook his head.

'Do you mind if I drink alone?' asked Ortega.

'It's your house,' said Ramírez. 'You don't have to be polite for our sakes.'

Ortega poured himself a cheap whisky over ice. He raised his glass to the policemen. It was good to see him nervous. He picked up a fat remote with which he controlled his climate and started to explain the intricacies of the system to Ramírez, who butted in.

'We're bad losers, Sr Ortega,' he said.

'I'm sorry?' said Ortega.

'We're very bad losers,' said Ramírez. 'We don't like it when we see all our good work go to waste.'

'I can understand that,' said Ortega, covering his nervousness at Ramírez's looming, aggressive presence.

'What do you understand, Sr Ortega?' asked Falcón.

'Your work must be very frustrating at times.'

'Why would *you* think that?' asked Falcón.

Now that he'd caught their tone and found it unpleasant, Ortega turned ugly himself. He looked at them as if they were pathetic specimens of humanity – people to be pitied.

'The justice system is not in *my* hands,' he said. 'It's not up to *me* to decide which cases go to court and which don't.'

Ramírez snatched the remote from Ortega's hands, looked at the myriad buttons and tossed it on to the sofa.

'What about those two kids that we found buried up at the finca near Almonaster la Real?' said Ramírez. 'What about *them*?'

Falcón was appalled to see a little smile creep into Ortega's face. Now he knew what this was about. Now he knew that he was safe. Now he was going to enjoy himself.

'What about them?' asked Ortega mildly.

'How did they die, Sr Ortega?' said Ramírez. 'We know we can't touch you for any of that stuff, but, as I said, we're bad losers and we'd like you to tell us that one thing.'

'I don't know what you're talking about, Inspector.'

'We can guess what happened,' said Falcón. 'But we'd like to have it confirmed how and when they died and who buried them.'

'There are no traps,' said Ramírez, holding his hands open. 'You're well clear of any traps, aren't you, Sr Ortega?'

'I'd like you to leave now, thank you very much,' he said, and turned his back on them.

'We're going just as soon as you've told us what we want to hear.'

'You've got absolutely no right to barge your way –'

'You invited us in, Sr Ortega,' said Falcón.

'Go and complain to your friends in high places when we've gone,' said Ramírez. 'You could probably have us demoted, suspended without pay, thrown off the force . . . with all the contacts you've got.'

'Leave,' said Ortega, turning on them, snarling.

'Tell us how and when they died,' said Falcón.

'We're not going until you do,' said Ramírez, cheerfully.

'They committed suicide,' said Ortega.

'How?'

'The boy strangled the girl and then slashed his wrists with a piece of broken glass.'

'When?'

'Eight months ago.'

'Which was about the time that Inspector Jefe Montes started to drink even more than he was already,' said Ramírez.

'Who buried them?'

'Somebody was sent over to do that.'

'I imagine they're good at digging holes,' said Ramírez, 'Russian peasants. When was the last time you dug a hole?'

Ramírez had gone up close to Ortega now. He grabbed his hand. It was soft. He looked into his face.

'I thought not. No conscience at all . . . but maybe that will change in time,' he said.

'I told you what you wanted to know,' said Ortega. 'Now it's time for you to leave.'

'We're going now,' said Falcón.

Ramírez took a pair of handcuffs out of his pocket. He cuffed the wrist of the hand he was still holding. Falcón removed the whisky glass from the other. Ramírez joined them behind Ortega's back and clapped him on the shoulders.

'You're both finished,' said Ortega. 'You know that.'

'We're placing you under arrest,' said Falcón, 'for the repeated sexual abuse of your son, Salvador Ortega, and your nephew, Sebastián Ortega –'

Ortega's smiling face stopped Falcón mid sentence.

'You seriously think a heroin addict and someone who's been convicted of kidnapping and abusing a young boy have any chance of putting *me* away?' said Ortega.

'Things have changed,' said Falcón, as Ramírez put a huge hand on top of Ortega's head. 'The reason we wanted the boy and girl up at the finca to be prominent in your mind was so that you'd know that you've just been touched by vanished hands.'

CODA

Falcón sat outside La Bodega de la Albariza on Calle Betis with a beer and a tapa of fried fresh anchovies. It was cooler today. There were a lot of people down by the river. He'd given up on his usual spot in the centre of the Puente de Isabel II. It reminded him too much of bad times and intrusive photographers. The river was no longer some Stygian limbo of hand-wringing strangers but, as it always had been, the life force of the city. Now he sat with people at tables eating and drinking, watching couples of all ages kissing as they strolled in the sunshine, at joggers and cyclists as they pushed themselves along the tow path on the opposite bank. The waiter stopped by and asked him if he wanted anything else. He ordered another beer and a plate of chipirones, baby squid.

There were two things from that last torrid week in July that just wouldn't leave him alone. The first was Rafael Vega and his son Mario and his answer to Calderón's question – what couldn't you bear your son knowing about you? He remembered the pity he'd felt for Mario as he was swept away into his new family and he wanted the boy to know, not now but eventually, just one thing about his monstrous father. He wanted him to know that Rafael Vega had been returned to humanity by love and loss. He'd faced his conscience and been tormented by it. He'd died wanting some good to come out of his appalling life. How would Mario ever know that?

The second thing that he could not shake off and didn't want to was what had happened between him and Consuelo. She'd left him and gone away to the coast to be with her children. He'd tried to find out where she was from the restaurant managers, but they were under strict instructions to inform nobody. Her mobile was never switched on. He heard nothing back from the messages he left on her answering machine. He dreamed about her, saw her in the street and ran across squares to grab the arms of shocked strangers. He lived with her in his head, longed for the smell of her, the touch of her cheek on his, the sight of his empty chair opposite hers in a restaurant.

The waiter brought the chipirones and the beer. He squeezed the lemon over the squid and reached for his beading glass. The coldness of the beer brought tears to his eyes. He nodded to a girl who asked if she could take one of his chairs. He sat back and let the high palms of the Seville skyline blur in his vision. Tomorrow was the first day of September. He was going to Morocco in a few days' time. Marrakesh. He was happy. His mobile vibrated on his thigh. He nearly couldn't be bothered to answer it in the languor of the afternoon.